Olav Audunssøn

Olav Audunssøn

OLAV AUDUNSSØN

I. VOWS

SIGRID UNDSET

Translated by TIINA NUNNALLY

UNIVERSITY OF MINNESOTA PRESS
MINNEAPOLIS ◆ LONDON

This translation is for Nathan and Kirsti—with gratitude. T.N.

The University of Minnesota Press gratefully acknowledges the generous assistance provided for the publication of this book by the Margaret S. Harding Memorial Endowment, honoring the first director of the University of Minnesota Press.

The translator would like to thank Nan Bentzen Skille and Anita Eger Gervin for their help.

Map on page xii by Rhys Davies

This volume of *Olav Audunssøn* was originally published in Norwegian as Part I of *Olav Audunssøn i Hestviken* (Oslo: H. Aschehoug and Company, 1925).

English translation copyright 2020 by Tiina Nunnally

Published by the University of Minnesota Press
111 Third Avenue South, Suite 290
Minneapolis, MN 55401-2520
http://www.upress.umn.edu

Printed in the United States of America on acid-free paper

The University of Minnesota is an equal-opportunity educator and employer.

25 24 23 22 21   10 9 8 7 6 5 4 3 2

Library of Congress Cataloging-in-Publication Data
Undset, Sigrid, 1882–1949, author. | Nunnally, Tiina, translator.
Olav Audunssøn / Sigrid Undset ; translated by Tiina Nunnally.
Minneapolis : University of Minnesota Press, [2020]
Identifiers: LCCN 2020020436 (print) | ISBN 978-1-5179-1048-8 (pb)
Subjects: LCSH: Norway—History—1030–1397—Fiction. | GSAFD: Historical fiction.
Classification: LCC PT8950.U5 O613 2020 (print) | DDC 839.823/72—dc23
LC record available at https://lccn.loc.gov/2020020436

Contents

Translator's Note

In 1905, at age twenty-three, Sigrid Undset gathered up the pages of her first completed book, *Aage Nielssøn til Ulvholm*, a lengthy historical novel set in thirteenth-century Denmark, and traveled from Oslo to Copenhagen. There she presented her manuscript to Peter Nansen, head of the prestigious Danish publishing house Gyldendal Forlag, with the hope that he would accept it for publication. Undset had spent several years writing and rewriting this book, after discarding an earlier attempt at a medieval novel.

From her father, the distinguished archaeologist Ingvald Undset (who died when Sigrid was only eleven), she had inherited an intense fascination with the Middle Ages. From her mother, Charlotte Gyth Undset, an intellectual woman who often illustrated her husband's work, Sigrid had inherited both an artistic aptitude and a fierce sense of determination. Both parents cultivated in their three daughters a great love of books, and Sigrid longed to create art and become a writer. In a letter from 1901 to her Swedish pen pal, she wrote: "Someone can have so much love for art and such understanding of what art is that in the morning she burns what she feverishly wrote the night before because she hasn't been able to blow the breath of life into the people who haunt her heart." By the time Sigrid traveled to Copenhagen to seek a publisher for her novel, she was envisioning for herself a full-time career as a writer. And she was hoping that her writing would provide her with sufficient income so she could finally quit her job as a secretary for a German-owned electrical company in Oslo.

A rejection letter arrived a few weeks later. Contrary to how Sigrid Undset would later famously—and bitterly—describe this first rebuff of her work, Nansen's comments were not all negative. We know this because in 2007 Undset's great-nephew made a startling discovery. Inside a book, he found a long-forgotten letter that Undset had written to her sister Signe (dated July 31, 1905), in which she described the actual course of events. In the letter, Undset reported that Nansen did not consider her novel good enough for publication, but he did say it possessed significant talent, with sections of "great finesse and power." He ended his generally positive letter by stating that he would like to see her write a "modern" story and advising her against "disguise"—which Undset took to mean that she should not cloak the work in historical trappings. Though disappointed, she was by no means defeated. In the letter to her sister, Undset said she would keep writing, even though she now recognized "how difficult it will be."

Yet she couldn't resist replying to Nansen's criticism. On August 8, 1905, she boldly sent the publisher a brief letter explaining that she had not intended her story to be a saga, per se, in the Icelandic tradition. And the "violent" events were meant to be seen from a thirteenth-century, not a modern-day, perspective. Thirty years later, in a conversation with her niece, Undset said that she had recently taken another look at *Aage Nielssøn til Ulvholm*, and "it wasn't half-bad." She also referred to this early novel as "my first draft of *Olav Audunssøn*."

◆ ◆ ◆

Although I've spent many years translating Sigrid Undset's work, including her medieval trilogy *Kristin Lavransdatter*, her modern novels *Marta Oulie* and *Jenny*, and a selection of her letters and short stories, it wasn't until 2016 that I first read *Olav Audunssøn*. I knew that when Undset was awarded the Nobel Prize in Literature in 1928, it was largely for her "powerful pictures of Northern life in medieval times"—and that included her four-volume story about Olav Audunssøn, his betrothed Ingunn Steinfinnsdatter, and their families. I'd heard great praise for Undset's second medieval masterpiece, even though it is not as well known as *Kristin Lavransdatter* among readers of English. I had always meant to read it. Finally, when I found myself with a break in my work schedule, I opened the first volume of my Norwegian edition and began to read this epic tale set in the late thirteenth and early fourteenth centuries, a generation before Kristin's story.

Once again I found myself completely drawn in to the customs and concerns of the people living on large noble estates in medieval Norway. I read all four volumes straight through, hardly pausing for breath in between. The vivid descriptions of the Norwegian countryside and the careful attention to historical detail carried me back in time, just as Undset had hoped when she wrote in 1902:

> The whole time, you see, the reader should know where he is, how the land looked, as well as the houses and the people and the animals and the clothing and the weapons and saddlery, and you should quite naturally and easily enter into the life, see and understand why these people *are* this way, how they feel and why they behave as they do; and all of this without pedantic lectures about the era and the spirit of the times and all that muck that can make a story so inartistic because it's historical. No grand gestures, fancy words, or "romantic" events. It should be written in such a way that whatever might seem romantic to us—murder, violent scenes, etc.— becomes ordinary and alive.

Sigrid Undset is a master at weaving her vast knowledge of the Middle Ages into stories of great psychological insight and emotional depth. It is her keen understanding of the human heart that makes her stories so compelling. We see Olav Audunssøn's fateful life unfold against a backdrop of tremendous upheaval in Norway. Barons and kings vie with the church for power and wealth, heathen practices are still prevalent in the mountain villages, and the defense of kinship and honor often leads to revenge, murder, and banishment. But always at the forefront is Undset's compassionate portrayal of two young people who are bound together by an early promise, only to be ruthlessly manipulated by conniving family members and subjected to confusing laws, both secular and religious.

◆ ◆ ◆

The first two volumes of *Olav Audunssøn* were originally published in Norwegian in 1925 under the title *Olav Audunssøn i Hestviken*, with the third and fourth volumes appearing together in 1927 as *Olav Audunssøn og hans børn*. An English translation by Arthur G. Chater was published in four volumes by Knopf in 1928–30 under the collective title *The Master of Hestviken*, with the individual volumes titled *The Axe*, *The Snake Pit*, *In the Wilderness*, and *The Son Avenger*. This new translation reverts to the original Norwegian series title, with different titles for the separate four volumes: *Vows*, *Providence*, *Crossroads*, and *Winter*. From the time of its original publication, the English translation of *Olav Audunssøn* has never been out of print, although it seems to have been neglected by readers in recent years. Chater's translation is better than other (sometimes egregious) contemporary translations of Undset's works, but it does not do full justice to the author's natural, fluid style. I found the overall tone of that translation to be somewhat dusty and dull, with awkward phrasing that gives the story a stumbling rhythm. The dialogue is particularly troublesome. The strange syntax and wording are meant to imitate archaic speech patterns, but they do not ring true. Undset was concerned about this when she confided to her pen pal in 1901 that she feared her characters would "turn out pompous, declaiming instead of talking." It is the translator's responsibility to pay as much attention to conveying the music of the original text as to making accurate word choices. In Norwegian, Undset writes in a straightforward, almost plain style, yet she can be quite lyrical, especially in her descriptions of nature. The beauty of the mountainous Norwegian terrain is lovingly revealed in her lucid prose.

Throughout my translation I have retained the original spelling of Norwegian names. Readers should note that Norwegian surnames were derived from the father's given name, followed by either "-datter" or "-søn," depending on the gender of the child. For example, Olav's surname comes from his father, Audun Ingolfssøn. In some instances I chose to keep the Norwegian titles of *Fru* for women and *Herr* for men.

Back in 1902, when Sigrid Undset was struggling to write the novel that she later called the "first draft" of *Olav Audunssøn*, she explained in a letter to her pen pal that she wanted the historical details to create an authentic setting for "the simple story of a man and the people who intervene in his life." After Peter Nansen rejected her novel, she went on to write numerous "modern" stories that built her reputation as one of Norway's foremost authors of the day. Eventually she returned to her passion for the Middle Ages with her magnificent chronicle about an impulsive and headstrong girl named Kristin Lavransdatter. Yet, despite the fame and accolades the trilogy brought her, Undset was not content to stop there. The turbulent life story of an introspective, loyal, and complicated boy named Olav had stayed with her for decades. And we have to be thankful that Sigrid Undset finally set down on paper her powerful and deeply moving account of Olav Audunssøn and all the individuals—friends, strangers, and foes—who "intervened" to shape his destiny.

Tiina Nunnally
Albuquerque, New Mexico
January 2020

References

Bayerschmidt, Carl F. *Sigrid Undset.* New York: Twayne Publishers, Inc., 1970.

Bliksrud, Liv. *Sigrid Undset.* Oslo: Gyldendal Norsk Forlag, 1997.

Blindheim, Charlotte. *Moster Sigrid, et familieportrett av Sigrid Undset.* Oslo: H. Aschehoug and Company, 1982.

Page, Tim, ed. *The Unknown Sigrid Undset.* South Royalton, Vt.: Steerforth Press, 2001. This book includes my translation of selected letters from Sigrid Undset to her pen pal, Andrea (Dea) Hedberg.

Skille, Nan Bentzen. *Inside the Gate: Sigrid Undset's Life at Bjerkebæk.* Minneapolis: University of Minnesota Press, 2018.

Slapgard, Sigrun. *Sigrid Undset, Dikterdronningen.* Oslo: Gyldendal Norsk Forlag, 2007.

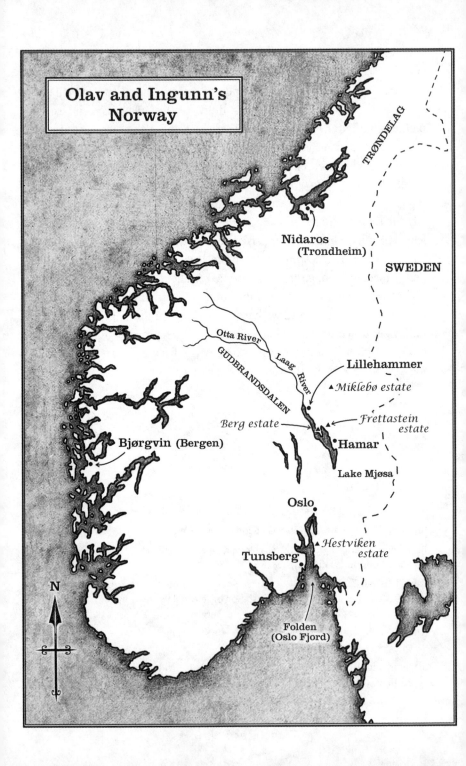

Olav and Ingunn's Norway

Genealogy and Kinship

Olav Audunssøn's Family

Audun Ingolfssøn of Hestviken—father
Cecilia Bjørnsdatter—mother
Ingolf Olavssøn—paternal grandfather
Olav Olavssøn—paternal great-grandfather
Torgils "Dirt Beard" Olavssøn—paternal great-uncle
Olav Half-Priest—elderly kinsman
Helge of Tveit—distant kinsman
Jon Helgessøn—distant kinsman
Sir Barnim Erikssøn—maternal uncle in Denmark
Fru Margrete—maternal grandmother
Erik Erikssøn—maternal grandmother's first husband
Bjørn Anderssøn—maternal grandmother's second husband
Steinfinn Toressøn—foster father
Ingebjørg Jonsdatter—foster mother
Ingunn Steinfinnsdatter—foster sister

Ingunn Steinfinnsdatter's Family

Steinfinn Toressøn of Frettastein—father
Ingebjørg Jonsdatter—mother
Tora Steinfinnsdatter—sister

Hallvard Steinfinnssøn—brother
Jon Steinfinnssøn—brother
Tore Toressøn the Younger of Hov—paternal grandfather
Arnvid Finnssøn—cousin
Fru Hillebjørg—Arnvid's mother
Magnhild Toresdatter—paternal aunt
Ivar Toressøn—paternal uncle
Aasa Magnusdatter—paternal grandmother
Kolbein Borghildssøn—uncle (father's illegitimate half-brother)
Haftor Kolbeinssøn—cousin
Einar Kolbeinssøn—cousin
Hallvard Erlingssøn—cousin of the Toressøns

Other Key Figures

Brother Vegard—Dominican monk in Hamar
Lord Torfinn—Bishop of Hamar
Fat Asbjørn—Dominican monk in Hamar
Alf Erlingssøn of Tornberg—influential earl and favorite of Queen
    Ingebjørg
Teit Hallssøn—scribe from Iceland

Part I

Olav Audunssøn Marries

I

Steinfinnssøn was the name given to a lineage that flourished in rural districts around Lake Mjøsa during the time when the sons of King Harald Gille reigned in Norway. Back then, kinsmen of this family were firmly ensconced on large estates in every parish surrounding the lake.

In the years of strife that later befell the country, the Steinfinnssøn kinsmen thought most about ensuring that their own properties were not divided up, and their estates were not burned down. They were so powerful that most often they were able to do so, whether it was defending themselves from the Birch Legs or any of the other numerous adversaries rife in the county of Oppland.[1] They did not seem to care much about who would eventually become king of Norway, although some of the men in the family had served King Magnus Erlingssøn and then Sigurd Markusfostre both faithfully and well. None of them supported Sverre and his kinsmen more than they deemed necessary. The elder Tore Steinfinnssøn of Hov and his sons championed King Skule, but when peace once again came to the land, they reconciled with King Haakon.

Yet from that time onward the renown of the lineage began to decline. Life was calmer in the villages, and law and order were considered of greater importance among the people. The men who gained the most power were those appointed the king's representatives, or those who had served as royal retainers and had won the king's trust. But the Steinfinnssøns stayed home on their estates and made do with managing their own properties.

Even so, it was a lineage of wealthy men. The Steinfinnssøns had been the last of the noble lords to own thralls in Oppland, and they continued to take on the offspring of their freed thralls as servants and leaseholders on their estates. Folks in the villages whispered that the Steinfinnssøns were a power-hungry family, yet they'd had sense enough to choose their underlings wisely so they would be easy to manage. The men of this lineage were not among the cleverest, yet neither could they be called stupid, since they had shown such shrewdness when it came to securing their own properties. Nor were they unkind masters toward those of lesser standing, as long as no one ventured to contradict them.

But two years before King Haakon the Old died, Tore Toressøn the Younger of Hov sent his youngest son, Steinfinn, to become a royal retainer. He was then eighteen years old, a robust and handsome man. Yet the same held true for him as for his kinsmen: folks recognized them by virtue of the horses they rode, the clothing and adornments they wore, and the weapons they carried. If young Steinfinn had appeared in a coarse peasant's tunic, many men would have had trouble recognizing this person who, the night before over the ale bowls, had called himself their companion and dear friend. The Steinfinnssøns were most often handsome men, though they were said to look much like everyone else in the parish. The peers of this Steinfinn said that his intelligence was not the worst, though it was far outweighed by his arrogance.

Steinfinn went to Bjørgvin,[2] and there he met a maiden named Ingebjørg Jonsdatter, who was living at the royal palace as an attendant to Queen Ingebjørg. The maiden and Steinfinn became fond of each other, and he sought her hand in marriage from her father, Jon Paalssøn. He replied, however, that his daughter was already betrothed to Mattias Haraldssøn, a retainer and close friend of the young King Magnus. Yet Steinfinn refused to accept that his proposal had been denied. He asked again and again, arranging for wealthy men and even Queen Ingebjørg herself to speak on his behalf. None of this did any good, for Jon Paalssøn would not break his word to Mattias.

Steinfinn then accompanied King Haakon on his last campaign west across the sea. At the battle of Largs, he won for himself a commendable reputation for valor. When the king lay ill in Kirkevaag,

Steinfinn often kept vigil over him at night, and, at least in his own opinion, it was then that King Haakon had shown him great favor.

The following summer Steinfinn was again in Bjørgvin. On a beautiful morning right after Saint Jon's Day,[3] some of the queen's attendants had just come from Nonneseter Abbey and were heading toward the royal palace when they saw Steinfinn and his manservant approach, riding along the narrow lane. The two men had with them a handsome horse. Steinfinn said he had bought the steed that very morning, just as they saw it, outfitted with a woman's saddle and bridle. He greeted the maidens with great courtesy and gentle teasing, inviting them to try out this horse of his. Then they all went over to a meadow, where they amused themselves for a time. But when Ingebjørg Jonsdatter sat in the saddle, Steinfinn said that she should borrow the horse and ride back to the royal palace. He would accompany her.

The next word anyone had of these two was that they had traveled by way of Vors up into the mountains. Finally they reached Hov. At first Tore was angry about his son's misdeed, but later he gave him the estate Frettastein, which stood in an out-of-the way spot in a forested area. There Steinfinn lived with Ingebjørg Jonsdatter as if they were lawfully wedded husband and wife, and when she gave birth to his daughter the following spring, he celebrated by hosting an ale feast with the most splendid of guests.

No one sought to punish him—not for abducting a woman or for deserting from the king's retinue—and folks said he could thank Queen Ingebjørg for that. Eventually the queen arranged a reconciliation between the two young people and Jon Paalssøn, who granted Steinfinn his daughter's hand in marriage and celebrated their wedding at the royal palace in Oslo, where he was serving as a royal official.

At that time Ingebjørg was expecting their third child, yet neither she nor Steinfinn showed the proper humility toward Jon, nor did they thank him as they ought to have done for his fatherly beneficence. Steinfinn gave his wife's father and kinsmen costly gifts, but otherwise both he and his wife behaved with great arrogance. They pretended they had already been living honorably and had enjoyed such respect before, as if there had never been any need to supplicate themselves in order to rectify their situation. They brought their elder daughter, Ingunn, to the wedding, and Steinfinn held her in his arms as he danced, showing her to all the guests. She was three years old, and her parents were proud beyond measure of this lovely child.

Their first son, who was born right after the wedding, died; and later Ingebjørg had twin boys who were stillborn. After that the couple went to Jon Paalssøn on bended knee and begged his forgiveness with all their heart. Then Ingebjørg had two sons who lived. She grew more beautiful with every year that passed. She and Steinfinn lived together in a loving marriage and managed a household befitting a nobleman. They were both happy and merry.

There was one man no one cared to think about: Mattias Haraldssøn, Ingebjørg's rightful bridegroom whom she had spurned. He went abroad at the time of Steinfinn's marriage, and there he stayed for many years. Mattias was a short and ugly man, but he was brave, defiant, and enormously wealthy.

Steinfinn and Ingebjørg had been married for seven years, and their daughters Ingunn and Tora were ten and eight winters old, respectively, but their sons were still quite small when Mattias Haraldssøn came to Frettastein one night with a company of men. It was haying season, and many of the servants were away from home, working in the outlying fields. Those at the estate were overpowered as they slept. Steinfinn did not awaken until he was hauled out of bed as he lay next to his wife. That year it was a hot summer, so everyone slept naked. Steinfinn, as bare as when his mother brought him into the world, was now tied up and held by three men as he stood at the head of his own table.

His wife, Ingebjørg, fought like a wild animal, using her fingernails and teeth, as Mattias wrapped her in a coverlet, lifted her out of bed, and set her on his lap.

Mattias said to Steinfinn, "Now I might take the revenge that the two of you deserve. And you, Steinfinn, would have to stand there, a bound man unable to defend your wife, if I wanted to take the one who was always intended for me and not for you. But I am more afraid of breaching God's law and have greater respect for decency and honor than you ever had. So this is how I will punish you, Steinfinn. I will mercifully give you back your wife unharmed. And you, my Ingebjørg, may stay with your husband. May you both live happily and well! After tonight, I think you might remember to thank me every time you take each other in your arms with gladness and joy," he said and laughed loudly.

He kissed Ingebjørg and placed her back in bed. He told his men to prepare to leave, and then he turned to Steinfinn.

Steinfinn had not uttered a word. When he discovered he could not escape his bonds, he stood motionless, but his face was flushed a dark red, and he did not take his eyes off Mattias, who now stepped very close to him.

"Do you not have enough grace, man—or enough sense—to thank me for the mercy I've shown you tonight?" said Mattias, laughing.

"Be assured that I will thank you," said Steinfinn, "if God allows me to live."

Mattias wore a cotehardie with long, slit sleeves and tassels on the end of each sleeve. Now he held the tip of one sleeve in his hand and slapped the tassel across Steinfinn's face as he laughed even more. Then he abruptly punched his fist into the bound man's visage, causing blood to run from Steinfinn's mouth and nose.

After that he went outside to join his men.

Olav Audunssøn, an eleven-year-old boy who was Steinfinn's foster son, rushed over to cut his foster father's bonds. Several men had dragged the boy as well as Steinfinn's children and their foster mothers into the antechamber and held them there while Mattias spoke to his unfaithful betrothed and her husband in the main hall of the estate.

Steinfinn grabbed a spear, and, naked though he was, he ran after Mattias and his men as they rode down the steep slope and straight across the fields, laughing and jeering. Steinfinn threw his spear but struck no one. In the meantime, the boy named Olav ran to the hired men's lodgings and to the barn to let out the servants who had been locked inside. Steinfinn went back to the house, put on his clothes, and picked up his weapons.

Yet it was futile to set off after Mattias, for at Frettastein only three horses were still there, and they had been let out to graze in the pasture. Nevertheless, Steinfinn was determined to ride away at once. He wanted to seek out his father and brothers. While he was dressing, he had spoken alone to his wife, and she had followed him outside when he was ready to leave. There Steinfinn announced to his servants that he would not sleep with his wife again until he had avenged the shame, so that no man might say he possessed her only at the mercy of Mattias Haraldssøn. Then he rode off. His wife went into the loft room above an old storehouse and shut herself inside.

The household servants, both men and women, now dashed into the hall to find out what had happened. They questioned Olav, who sat half-dressed on the edge of the bed where Steinfinn's weeping daughters had crept. They tried to question the two small maidens and the foster mother of Steinfinn's youngest son. When none of them could offer any explanations, the servants grew weary of asking and went back outside.

The boy sat there in the dark room and listened to Ingunn sobbing. Then he climbed onto the bed and lay down beside her.

"Never fear, your father will win his revenge. You can trust that he will. And I plan to go with him, to show that Steinfinn at least has a son-in-law, though his sons are not yet able to wield weapons!"

This was the first time that Olav had dared speak openly of the promise that had once been made by his father and Ingunn's when the children were both very small. When Olav first came to Frettastein, the servants had talked about it and teased the children, saying they were now betrothed. That had always infuriated Ingunn. One day she ran to her father to complain, and he was so incensed that he forbade the servants to talk in such a manner. He grew so angry that some of them even thought that perhaps Steinfinn regretted the pledge he had made to Olav's father.

On this night Ingunn reacted to Olav's reminder of the decision that had been made for them by moving close to the boy and weeping in his arms until Olav's sleeves were completely soaked.

◆ ◆ ◆

From that night on, life at Frettastein was much different than before. Steinfinn's father and brothers advised him to raise an official case against Mattias Haraldssøn, but Steinfinn said that he would decide for himself what his honor was worth.

Mattias had gone straight back to the estate where he lived in Borgesyssel. The following spring he went abroad on a pilgrimage. When folks heard this, and when it became known that Steinfinn Toressøn was so outraged that he had practically become a recluse and that he refused to live with his wife anymore, then one thing and another was hinted about the revenge that Mattias must have exacted from his unfaithful betrothed. Even though Mattias and his men never said anything different about their actions than what was reported from Frettastein, the farther the rumors flew across the land, the worse became the price that folks believed Mattias must have demanded from Steinfinn. And a ballad was composed, describing the events according to what folks thought had occurred.

One evening when Steinfinn was drinking with his men—this was three years later—he asked if anyone present could sing the ballad about him. At first, all the hired men pretended not to know of such a ballad. But when Steinfinn promised a large reward to anyone who could sing the verses, it turned out that all the servants knew the song. Steinfinn listened until the very end, occasionally baring his teeth in an odd smile. Immediately afterward he retired to bed along with his half-brother Kolbein Toressøn, and they could be heard talking in the enclosed bed until almost midnight.[4]

This Kolbein was the son of Tore of Hov and a paramour he'd had before he married. Tore had always felt more affection for the children this woman had given him than for any of his lawfully born offspring. He'd arranged a good marriage for Kolbein and presented him with a large estate farther north near Lake Mjøsa. But things did not go well for Kolbein. He was overbearing and impetuous, and had little respect for the law. He was constantly bringing cases against others, both those of lesser standing and his peers. As a result, he was not an agreeable man. There had been little warmth between him and his lawfully born half-brothers until Steinfinn, after his misfortune, had turned to Kolbein for support. Ever since then, the two brothers had been constant companions. Kolbein looked after Steinfinn and managed all his affairs, but he did so in the same way that he handled his own dealings and subsequently caused much ill will, especially since he was supposed to be acting on his brother's behalf.

It was clearly not Kolbein's intention to harm his younger brother. In his own way he was fond of Steinfinn, who, feeling irresolute as he did, had put himself fully in the hands of his half-brother. In his prosperous days Steinfinn had been both neglectful and indolent, caring more about living a grand life than looking after his own welfare. For a long time after the night of the attack he became quite reclusive. Then, in accordance with Kolbein's advice, he took into his household an entire company of men—young men skilled in weaponry, and preferably those who had previously served as royal retainers elsewhere. Steinfinn slept in the main hall with his men, who accompanied their master everywhere, but they neither could nor wished to contribute much to the estate. These men cost him dearly and offered little in return.

Yet the farmwork at Frettastein was more or less tended to, for Grim, the old farm manager, and his sister Dalla were the children of a thrall who had belonged to Steinfinn's paternal grandmother. Their sole concern was the welfare of their young master. Now, when Steinfinn could have used the income from property that he owned out in the countryside, he had no desire to see to his pastures or speak to his overseers. And Kolbein, who managed everything in his stead, brought endless discord.

Ingebjørg Jonsdatter had been a capable mistress, and in the past this had made up for much of her husband's extravagant and careless conduct. But now she kept to the old loft room above the storehouse with her maids, and the rest of the servants rarely saw her. She brooded and fretted, never inquiring about how the household or estate were being run. Instead, she seemed to grow angry if anyone disturbed her pondering. She said little even to her own children, who lived in the old loft room with their mother; she paid scant attention to their well-being or what they did. Yet in the past, during the good times, she had been a tender mother, and Steinfinn Toressøn had been a happy and loving father, proud of his beautiful and healthy children.

As long as her sons, Hallvard and Jon, were small, Ingebjørg would often hold them on her lap, rocking them as she rested her chin on their flaxen hair, but she was often sullen, sorrowful, and preoccupied. It didn't take long before the boys tired of being in the loft room with their morose mother and all the women.

Tora, the younger daughter, was a good and lovely child. She understood full well that her parents had suffered a great injustice and were now mired in distress and sorrow. She tried to please them, in her kind and loving way. She became her parents' favorite. Steinfinn's face would brighten a bit whenever he looked at this daughter. Tora Steinfinnsdatter was plump in figure, elegant in limb; she matured early, becoming womanly in appearance. She had a long, full face with a fair complexion and blue eyes. She wore her straight, flaxen hair in long braids that hung down in front. Her father would stroke her cheeks and tell her, "What a good child you are, my Tora. May God bless you. Go to your mother, Tora. Sit with her and comfort her."

Tora would sit with her sorrowful mother, taking along her spinning or mending. And she felt more than rewarded if Ingebjørg would say at last, "How good you are, my Tora. May God protect you from all harm, my child." Then tears would roll down Tora's cheeks. She thought about her parents' heavy fate, and, filled with righteous anger, she would look at her sister, Ingunn, who never had the discipline to sit still with their mother. The girl couldn't come into the loft room without making Ingebjørg impatient with her constant restlessness, and finally she would be asked to leave. Without regret or sadness Ingunn would dash out the door and run off to romp and play with the other children on the estate, including Olav and some of the other boys who belonged to the servants at Frettastein.

Ingunn was the eldest child of Steinfinn and Ingebjørg. When she was small, she had been so lovely that she was a delight to behold. But now folks said she was not half as beautiful as her sister. Nor was she particularly clever or quick-witted. In truth, she was not any more obedient or mischievous than most other children. And yet, in a certain way, folks were as fond of her as they were of the younger, quieter, and prettier sister. Steinfinn's men regarded Tora with some degree of awe, but they were happier to have Ingunn keeping them company in the main hall.

There were no young maidens who were Ingunn's age either at Frettastein or on any of the nearby estates or manors. For that reason she ended up playing with the boys. She took part in all their games and all their adventures, joining in whatever sports they undertook. She threw spears and stones, used a bow for target practice, threw balls, set traps in the forest, and fished in the mountain tarn. But she was clumsy at everything, showing neither skill nor courage. She was weak and tended to give up and weep whenever their endeavors turned violent or she was harshly treated during a game. Even so, the boys allowed her to accompany them everywhere. The first reason for this was that she was Steinfinn's daughter; the other was that Olav Audunssøn insisted she should come along. And Olav was always the one in charge of their games.

Everyone on the estate, both old and young, was very fond of Olav Audunssøn, yet none of them would have called him an amiable child. It was as if no one could ever get close to the boy, although he was never unfriendly to a living soul. Instead, he might be described as good-humored and obliging in that taciturn and preoccupied way of his.

He was certainly handsome, even though he was so fair of complexion and flaxen-haired that he was almost like an albino, but he didn't have the albino's light-sensitive eyes or bowed head. Olav's blue-green eyes were pale in color, but they stared straight ahead at the world, and he carried his head erect on his strong, milky-white neck. It was as if the sun and weather had little effect on his skin, which seemed strangely firm and smooth and white. Only in the summertime did a few tiny freckles appear on the bridge of his nose, which was low and wide. Throughout his childhood, this healthy pallor made Olav's face seem somewhat cold and immobile. His features were also rather short and wide, though well-formed. His eyes were set quite far apart, but they were big and beautifully open. His brows and lashes were so fair that they appeared to be only golden shadows in the sunlight. His nose was wide and straight but a bit too short. Nor was his mouth very big, but his lips curved in such a lovely and firm manner that he had to be deemed fair of mouth, if only his lips had not been so pale in that colorless face. But his hair was incomparably fair—so light that it gleamed like silver more than gold, thick and soft and slightly curly. He wore his hair trimmed in a circle so that it covered his wide, white forehead, yet in the hollow at the nape of his neck two strong sinews could be seen.

Olav was not tall for his age, but he gave the impression of more height than he possessed. He was superbly formed, stocky, and muscular, with small hands and feet that seemed quite strong because his wrists and ankles were so sturdy and powerful. And he was both very strong and agile, proficient in all types of sports and weaponry, though no one had ever taught him to develop these skills in the proper manner. As matters stood at Frettastein during his childhood, Olav was forced to look out for himself. When Steinfinn took in the boy, he had promised to serve in his father's stead, but he did nothing to provide the child with the sort of training that would befit a young man of good birth, the heir to a small fortune, and someone who was meant to be the husband of Ingunn Steinfinnsdatter.

This is how Steinfinn Toressøn came to be Olav's foster father.

One summer when Steinfinn was still happy and flourishing, he had business at the Eidsiva ting, the assembly where he and fellow noblemen met to discuss regional matters.[5] He set off, accompanied by friends and kinsmen and taking along his wife and daughter, Ingunn, who was then six years old. The parents were so proud of their lovely child that they insisted on taking her everywhere.

At the ting, Steinfinn met a man named Audun Ingolfssøn of Hestviken. Audun and Steinfinn had been bedfellows while serving as royal retainers. They became good friends even though Audun was older, and the two men were very unlike in temperament. Back then, Steinfinn was merry and garrulous, preferring to talk mostly about himself. Audun was reserved and almost never discussed his own concerns.

In the springtime, during the year when King Haakon embarked on a campaign to Scotland, Audun married. His bride was a Danish woman named Cecilia Bjørnsdatter, who had been Queen Ingebjørg's childhood playmate and had gone with her to Ring Abbey.[6] When the bishop of Oslo abducted young King Magnus's bride Ingebjørg and brought her to Norway because the Danish king had scorned the agreements and refused to send his kinswoman north, Cecilia came along. At first the young queen insisted on keeping the maiden always at her side. Yet by the following year Queen Ingebjørg had changed her mind and was eager to marry off Cecilia. Some people said this was because King Magnus enjoyed talking to the Danish maiden more than his wife deemed proper. Others claimed that it was the young Alf Erlingssøn of Tornberg who had grown fond of Cecilia, but his father, Baron Erling Alfssøn, did not want his son to marry a foreign woman who neither owned land nor had any powerful kinsmen in Norway. Young Alf had a fierce disposition and was accustomed to having his way in all matters, and he loved Cecilia passionately. The queen then made the decision to marry off the maiden, so that no misfortune might befall her.

Whatever the reason, the maiden was both lovely and of good morals. At first, Audun had been rather unwilling, but after he'd had the occasion to speak with Cecilia two or three times, he was eager to marry her. Their wedding was celebrated at the royal palace in Bjørgvin. Old King Haakon provided the bride's dowry. Then Audun took his wife home to Hestviken. There she was well hidden away, no matter whether it was from King Magnus or from Alf Erlingssøn.

During the summer Audun sailed his ship to join the king in Herdluvaag and then accompanied him on the North Sea campaign. When the king died before Christmas out on the Orkney Islands— this was in the winter of 1263—Audun captained the ship that brought the news of his death back to Norway. Then he continued east, going home to his estate. In the summer he returned to King Magnus's retinue. By then his wife had died in childbed, giving birth to a son who survived. Audun had become even more taciturn than before, though now he did mention one thing or another about his affairs to Steinfinn. Living on his Hestviken estate was his paternal grandfather, who was old and rather stubborn. He did not approve of his grandson marrying a foreign woman without kinsmen. Also living on the estate was Audun's old uncle, his father's brother, who was a lunatic. During most of the time that Cecilia lived in Hestviken, she was there alone with these two old men.

"I fear she did not thrive over there in the east," said Audun. To honor her son's paternal great-grandfather, Cecilia had named the child after him—such was the Danish custom—but Olav Olavssøn was enraged by this. He said that in Norway a boy was not named for someone still living, unless it was done to take that man's life. And so Audun became the sole heir to these two old men, though he let it be known that he would not immediately return home to Hestviken. He intended to stay in Bjørgvin to serve King Magnus.

It was shortly after this that Steinfinn abducted Ingebjørg Jonsdatter, and since then he had not heard from or inquired about Audun Ingolfssøn, until he now met the man at the ting. A seven-year-old boy accompanied Audun as he went about trying to find several men from Soleyar, whom he was supposed to meet. He looked exceedingly ill. Audun was a tall man, and he had always been very lean and slender, with a narrow face, a thin, sharp nose, a pallid complexion, and fair hair. Now he had grown stooped and looked as gaunt as a skeleton; his face was sallow and his lips were blue. But the boy was a handsome and sturdy child, broad shouldered and well-built. He was as fair as his father, but otherwise there was little resemblance.

Steinfinn embraced his friend with boisterous joy, but he grew greatly distressed when he saw how ill Audun looked. Steinfinn refused to hear of anything else but that Audun must go with him to the estate where he and his entourage were staying during the ting.

On the way there, Audun explained that the men he was supposed to meet were the sons of his paternal grandfather's nephew.

"They are the closest kinsmen I have. When I die, they will be the ones to assume guardianship for Olav, my son here."

The two old men at Hestviken were still alive, but they were quite infirm, while Audun had a sickness inside his stomach that meant he could enjoy neither food nor drink; he did not have many more weeks to live. He had served King Magnus during all these years, up until just before Christmas. Then he went home to Hestviken because he was so ill. He had visited his estate only once after his wife's death, and it was not until this past winter that he'd spent much time with his son. But now the child's future weighed heavily on his mind. These kinsmen from Soleyar had not arrived, and he did not have the strength to ride to them—he suffered so much pain when he rode—and this was the next-to-last day of the ting.

"No doubt the fathers at Hovedø monastery will take in my son.[7] If the boy has a mind to stay there when he grows up and become a monk, then our lineage will end with him."

When Ingebjørg saw the fair child who would soon be both motherless and fatherless, she wanted to kiss the boy. But Olav tore away from her and sought his father while staring at the lady with his big blue eyes, looking truculent and surprised.

"Won't you kiss my wife, Olav?" asked Steinfinn, laughing heartily.

"No," replied the boy. "For Aslaug kisses Koll."

Audun smiled with some embarrassment. He explained that they were two old people who were servants at Hestviken. Then all the grown-ups laughed long and hard, but Olav turned red and lowered his eyes. His father admonished the boy and told him to greet Ingebjørg in a courteous and proper manner. Then Olav had to step forward and allow the woman to kiss him. When little Ingunn appeared and said that she too wanted to kiss the boy, Olav obediently went over to her and bent his head down so the maiden could reach his lips. But his face had turned bright red, and his eyes brimmed with tears, which made the men laugh, jesting that Olav seemed not to favor the friendly attentions of beautiful women.

Yet later that evening, after everyone had eaten their fill and was sitting over their ale, Olav seemed to thaw a bit. Ingunn was running along the benches, and wherever she found an empty place she would climb up to sit there for a moment, swinging her legs. Then she'd slip down again and run over to the next place, to sit there too. The grown-ups laughed at this, shouting to her and trying to grab her. The maiden grew more and more excited and wild. Then Olav seemed to come to an important decision. He got up from where he was sitting next to his father, adjusted his new knife belt, and walked across the room to sit beside Ingunn. When she slipped down and ran to another place, the boy, a little hesitantly, followed the girl and once again sat next to her. The two children continued this game along the benches, Ingunn laughing and squealing, while Olav persistently and solemnly followed, though every once in a while he would cast a glance at his father and then an uncertain smile would appear on the handsome boy's sullen face.

The children were dozing in a corner when Steinfinn and Audun came to get them, leading them across the floor to stand in front of the hearth in the middle of the room. The guests, who were all quite drunk, formed a circle around them. Steinfinn was also unsteady on his feet as he took his daughter's hand and placed it in Olav's. Then with a handshake Steinfinn and Audun sealed the pact that betrothed the children. Audun gave Olav a gold ring and helped him to place it on Ingunn's tiny finger. Then he held up the child's hand so all could see the too-big ring dangling on her finger. Ingebjørg Jonsdatter and the other women both laughed and wept, for no one had ever seen a fairer sight than this small bridal couple.

Then she handed her daughter a drinking horn and told her to drink to her betrothed. The children both drank, spilling some of the ale on themselves. Steinfinn stood there with his arm around his friend's neck, and in a tearful and loud voice he solemnly swore that Audun need not grieve nor lament over the child he would soon leave behind. He would foster the boy and serve in his father's stead until Olav became a man and could lead his bride home. This was what Steinfinn said. Then he kissed Audun on both cheeks while Ingebjørg took the children onto her lap for a moment and promised to be a mother to Olav, for the sake of Cecilia Bjørnsdatter, whom she had loved like her own sister.

Then they told Olav to kiss his betrothed. The boy stepped forward, quite boldly, and wrapped his arms around Ingunn's neck and kissed her as fervently as he could while the witnesses laughed and drank a toast to the betrothed couple.

But Olav now seemed to have taken a liking to this game. He suddenly lunged at his young bride, again put his arms around her neck, and gave her three or four resounding kisses. Then everyone roared with laughter. They shouted to him, telling him to keep kissing her.

Whether it was the laughter that made Ingunn ashamed or it was some whim on the part of the little maiden, she tried to wriggle out of the boy's embrace. When he merely pulled her even closer, she bit him on the cheek with all her might.

For a moment Olav stood still, staring in bewilderment. Then he rubbed his cheek, where drops of blood had begun trickling out. He glanced at his bloody fingertips and was just about to throw himself forward to strike Ingunn, but his father lifted him up and carried him over to the bed where they were to sleep. Then the betrothed, both the boy and the maiden, were undressed and put to bed, and they soon left all the revelry behind as they fell sound asleep.

The next day, when Steinfinn was once again sober, he would have preferred to back out of this awkward situation. He hinted that it had been done in jest. If they were to make any arrangements on behalf of their children, they would first need to discuss it further. But Audun, whose illness had prevented him from drinking anything at all, protested. He reminded Steinfinn that he had given his word to a dying man, and God would certainly exact revenge if he now broke his promise to a fatherless and forsaken child.

Then Steinfinn reconsidered. Audun Ingolfssøn was from an old and respected lineage, though there were now few members left and they wielded little power. But Olav was an only child, and although he could not expect much of an inheritance other than the family estate at Hestviken, it was nevertheless a large property. And Steinfinn might have many more children with Ingebjørg. If so, Olav might be an equal match for Ingunn, who would receive only a sister's half inheritance when her father died.[8] Now sober, Steinfinn again repeated the pledge he'd made while drunk, agreeing to foster Olav and give his daughter to the boy in marriage when the two children reached a proper and sensible age. And when he left the ting to head north for home, he took Olav Audunssøn with him.

That autumn, word was sent to Frettastein that Olav's father had died a short time after both his paternal grandfather and the lunatic uncle had perished. The messengers brought with them some of the child's inheritance from his father, as well as goods left to him by his mother—clothing, weapons, and a small chest containing jewelry. The estate at Hestviken was to be managed by one of the boy's old kinsmen, a man called Olav Half-Priest.

Steinfinn put away his foster son's belongings, and twice he made an effort to send word with folks going to Oslo in order to arrange a meeting with this Olav Half-Priest. But nothing came of it, and after that Steinfinn made no further attempts. Yet he was not any more enterprising when it came to his own affairs. Both he and Ingebjørg were kind to Olav, and the boy was treated as one of their children until the misfortune struck them. After that, they neglected their foster son in the same way they did their own offspring.

In certain respects, Olav had quickly settled in at Frettastein. He was fond of Steinfinn and Ingebjørg, but he was a quiet and rather reserved child, so he remained somewhat distant from them. He never developed a sense that he truly belonged, although he thrived better here than where he'd come from. He did his best not to think about his first home, at Hestviken, yet now and then memories would appear from that time. An oppressive despondency would come over him whenever he happened to think of all the old folks there. The servants had been ancient, and Olav's great-grandfather was constantly chasing after his old lunatic of a son, whom folks called Dirt Beard, because he had to be fed like a child and kept away from fire and water and sharp objects. For the most part Olav had been left to fend for himself. But he'd never known that things might be any different, and for as long as he could remember, the filth and bad smell that clung to Dirt Beard had merely been part of life on the estate. Olav had also become so accustomed to the lunatic's fits of wailing and shrieking that he wasn't especially frightened when they occurred. But these were memories that he now shunned.

Several times in those last years, Olav's great-grandfather had taken him to church. There he'd seen strangers, men and women and children too, but he'd never thought that he might spend time with them or speak to them. They were simply part of the church service. And for many years after he came to Frettastein, Olav would suddenly feel very alone—as if life here, among all these people, was not quite real or was something out of the ordinary, like a Sunday spent in church, and he was merely waiting to leave and go back to the life from which he'd come. This was never more than a fleeting notion that would vanish at once, but he never felt entirely rooted at Frettastein, even though he had no other home for which he longed.

Yet occasionally memories of a different sort appeared that went straight to his heart and produced a stab of yearning. As if from a past dream, he would recall rocks arching up in the middle of the courtyard at Hestviken.[9] There were cracks in the hot stones, and he had lain there, digging out moss with a splinter of bone. Hovering before him were images of places where he'd walked alone, keeping to himself. Other memories appeared as well, leaving an aftertaste of inexpressible sweetness. Behind the livestock sheds on the estate rose a steep wall of shiny dark stone with water trickling down its face. And tall, green thickets grew in the deep hollow between the cliff and the walls of the outbuildings, an area that was always dark and shaded. Someplace there was also a low-tide shore where he had ambled across seaweed and clattering stones as he picked up snail shells and slimy green pieces of decaying wood, polished smooth by the water. Beyond stretched the glittering sea. Koll, the old house servant, would open mussel shells for bait and give him some to eat. Olav's mouth watered whenever he happened to remember that splendid taste of seawater and the oily reddish-yellow meat that he slurped up from the opened blue mussel shells.

When such glimpses of memory arose, he would fall silent and seem terribly preoccupied if Ingunn spoke to him. But it never occurred to him to walk away from her. He could no more think of parting ways with her whenever she approached and wanted to be with him than he could part ways with himself. That was how things stood for Olav Audunssøn, that was his fate; he would be with Ingunn forever. That was the only certainty in his life. He and Ingunn were inextricably bound to one another. He seldom thought of that evening when he and Ingunn were promised to each other, and it had been many years since anyone had mentioned the betrothal of the two children. Yet underlying everything he felt and thought, it was there like solid ground beneath his feet: the fact that he would always live with Ingunn. The boy had no kinsmen he might turn to. No doubt he knew that Hestviken was now his property, but with every passing year his images of the estate became less and less clear. They were like bits and pieces of a dream he recalled. If he imagined that one day he would return to live there, he found it comforting and right that he would take Ingunn with him. The two of them would face the unknown future together.

He didn't think about whether she was pretty. It seemed to him that Tora was lovely, but perhaps that was because he'd heard others so often say as much. Ingunn was simply Ingunn, familiar and ordinary and always at his side. He never thought about what she was like, just as he didn't think much about the weather—it was merely something to be accepted. He would get angry and scold her whenever she behaved stubbornly or proved bothersome to have along. He'd also had occasion to hit her when they were younger. When they were playing and she acted in a kind and pleasant way toward him and the other boys, Olav was as happy as he was in fair weather. And usually they were good friends, like siblings who got along well. Sometimes they might become annoyed with each other and argue, but neither of them ever thought the other could be any different than he or she was.

Among the Frettastein children, who were paid so little mind, these two, who were the eldest, grew close because there was at least one thing they knew: they would be together. That was the only certainty, and it was good to be certain about something. Unknowingly the boy, who was alone in the family home of a stranger, had set down roots in this young girl to whom he'd been promised. And as he grew, so did his love for the only one he felt was truly his possession and his destiny, though he barely noticed this himself. His affection for her was a matter of habit, long before his love acquired enough radiance and color that he became aware of how it had filled him.

That was how things stood until the summer after Olav Audunssøn had turned sixteen in the spring. Ingunn was then fifteen winters old.

II

Olav had inherited from his father a large battle axe. It was a horned axe with steel welded to the edge and inlaid gold paint on the blade.[10] The haft was wrapped with bands of gilded copper. The axe had a name; it was called Ættarfylgja, or Guardian of Kin.

It was a splendid weapon, and the boy who owned it thought, as was only reasonable, that the likes of such a costly object was not to be found in all of Norway. Yet he'd never spoken of this to anyone but Ingunn, and she believed him and was just as proud of the axe as he was. The axe always hung above Olav's bed in the main hall.

But one day in the spring, Olav noticed a nick in the blade. When he took down the axe, he saw that the steel edge had come loose from the iron blade and was clattering around in the weld. Olav realized it would be useless for him to try to find out who had used and damaged his axe. For that reason he didn't mention it to anyone except Ingunn. They discussed what he ought to do and then agreed that the next time Steinfinn was away from home, Olav should ride to Hamar. That was where a well-known weapons-smith lived, and if he couldn't repair the axe, then no one could. One morning during the week before Saint Jon's Day, Ingunn came to Olav to tell him that on that day her father was intending to ride north to visit Kolbein. So the next day might be a good time for them to head to town.

Olav hadn't planned to take her with him. It was many years since any of the children had gone in to town, and Olav didn't know exactly how far away it was, though he thought he would be able to return home by evening if he set off early in the morning. But Ingunn didn't have her own horse, and there was none at the estate that he might borrow for her. If they were to take turns riding his horse Elgen, they wouldn't reach home until late at night, so it meant she would have to ride while he walked the whole way. He was used to that, after all the times they had accompanied each other to mass in the main church in the big valley below. And Steinfinn and Ingebjørg were bound to be furious when they found out he had taken Ingunn to Hamar. But Olav merely told the maiden that they would have to walk down to the shore and row to the market town. And they would need to leave very early.

It was well before sunrise the next morning when he crept out of the main hall, yet it was already a bright day, chilly and quiet. The air was cold with dew and felt as good as a bath after the heavy stench of men and dogs inside. The boy inhaled the morning air as he stood on the doorstep and looked out at the weather.

Between the fields below, the bird cherry shrubs were pale green with lush blossoms. It was still spring up here in the heights. Far below was Lake Mjøsa, glinting a dull gray with dark rippling currents that boded rain showers later in the day. The sky was rather sallow, with several low-hovering tangles of dark clouds; showers had passed through in the night. When Olav set his feet in the grass of the courtyard, his tall yellow boots made of undyed leather turned dark with moisture; little reddish-brown specks colored the shafts. So he sat down on the doorstep and pulled off his boots. He knotted the laces together and slung the boots over his shoulder to carry them in that fashion, along with his folded cloak and the axe.

Barefoot, he walked across the damp courtyard toward the loft building where Ingunn had chosen to sleep with two of the maidservants so she could slip away from the estate without anyone noticing. For this expedition to town, Olav had dressed in his finest: a long cotehardie of light blue English cloth and hose of the same material. But the garments were now a bit too small for him. The cotehardie was too snug across his chest and too short in the sleeves, while the hem barely reached to mid-calf. The hose was also very tight, and in the autumn Ingebjørg had already cut off the feet, so now the hose came only to his ankles. But the cotehardie was fastened at the neck opening with a beautiful brooch made of gold, and around his waist Olav wore a belt set with silver rosettes and an image of Saint Olav on the buckle. Both the haft and sheath of his dagger had gilded mountings.

Olav went up to the outside gallery of the loft and quietly tapped three times on the door. Then he waited.

A bird began singing, chirping and whistling. The song poured like a gushing spring over the tiny, sleepy bubbling sounds coming from the surrounding shrubbery. Olav saw the bird as a dot in the sky. It sat at the very top of a spruce and was outlined against the yellowish sky to the north. He could see the way the bird gathered its body in and then let it out, like a tiny beating heart. The cloud clusters high overhead began turning red; a crimson light rose above the mountain ridge facing him and was mirrored red in the water. Olav knocked on the door again, much harder this time. The sound echoed in the morning stillness, causing the boy to hold his breath and listen for anyone stirring in the other buildings.

A moment later the door opened a crack and out slipped the maiden, cloaked in her long hair that was tousled and matte, amber brown and very wavy. She wore only a shift of bleached white linen, embroidered with green and blue flowers, although the hem was trimmed with coarse, gray cloth. The garment was too big for her, billowing around her narrow, pale pink feet. She carried her clothes over one arm and held in her hand a provisions sack. This she gave to Olav. Then she dropped her bundle of clothes so she could pull her hair back from her face, which was still flushed with sleep, one cheek redder than the other. She picked up a belt and wrapped it around her shift.

She was tall and thin, with slender limbs, a long slim neck, and a small head. Her face was triangular, with a low, wide forehead, but it was snowy white and curved beautifully at her temples beneath the profusion of shadows from her hair. Her cheeks were too thin, narrowing to the lower part of her face, which made her chin seem too long and sharp. Her small, straight nose was low and short. Nevertheless, there was a uniquely unsettling loveliness about her small face. Her eyes were very big and dark gray, yet the whites were as dazzling as a little child's. Her eyes, deeply shadowed beneath the even, dark lines of her brows, had full, fair lashes. Her mouth was narrow, yet her lips were as red as berries. And with her glowing white and rosy pink complexion, Ingunn Steinfinnsdatter was beautiful at this moment of her youth.

"You must hurry," said Olav. She had sat down on the stairs to bind her linen hose tightly to her legs, and she was taking her time about it. "It would be better to carry your hose and shoes until the grass dries."

"I won't walk barefoot on the wet ground in this cold," said the maiden, shivering a little.

"I'm sure you'll be warmer once you've managed to put on your clothes. You can't keep dawdling like this; look how the sky is already turning red."

Ingunn didn't reply. She pulled loose the lacings and began wrapping them tight again. Olav draped her clothes over the railing.

"You need to take along your cloak. As you can see, the weather might well change today."

"I left my cloak with my mother. I forgot to take it with me last night. It looks to me as if we'll have mostly fine weather, but if there's a shower, I'm sure we can find someplace to seek shelter."

"But if it starts raining while we're in the boat . . . And besides, you can't go in to town without a cloak. But you can borrow mine, just as you always have."

Ingunn turned her head to peer up at him over her shoulder.

"Why are you so annoyed, Olav?" She went back to fussing with her footwear.

Olav was about to reply, but as she leaned down over her shoes, the shift slipped off her shoulder and bared her bosom, armpit, and upper arms. And in an instant a wave of new sensations washed over the boy. Shy and confused, he stood there, unable to take his eyes off that glimpse of her naked body. It was as if he'd never seen it before. What was previously so familiar now appeared in a new light. A landslide occurred inside him, and his feelings for his foster sister took on a new form. What he felt most strongly was a great tenderness that held both sympathy and a slight arrogance. Her shoulders, so fragile and sloping, fitted into the delicate rounding of the shoulder joint; her thin, pale upper arms looked so soft, as if she possessed no muscles beneath the silky-smooth skin. A memory appeared in the boy's mind of grain that holds only milk before it has ripened fully. He had an urge to reach down to caress and console her; he was suddenly aware of the difference between her fragile softness and his own sturdy, muscular body. He had seen her unclothed before, of course, in the bathhouse. He had looked at himself too, at the hard and firm arc of his chest, the flat and tight muscles plaited across his abdomen, the muscles that bulged and knotted whenever he bent his arms. With childish glee he had rejoiced at being a boy.

Now his smug joy at being strong and well-built became strangely suffused with tenderness because she was so weak, and he pledged to protect her. He would have liked to wrap one arm around her narrow back and hide her small girlish breasts under his hand. He happened to remember that day in the springtime when he'd fallen forward onto a post sticking up—it was over at Gunleik's newly constructed house—and he ripped open both his clothes and the skin on his chest. With a shudder that held both horror and sweetness, he vowed that Ingunn would never again be allowed to climb on the roof with them when they went north to Gunleik's place.

He blushed when she looked up at him.

"Why are you staring? Mother won't notice that I've borrowed this shift of hers. It's one she never wears."

"Aren't you cold?" he asked. And Ingunn was even more surprised because he spoke in that low and gentle tone of voice that he occasionally used whenever something happened in their games so that she ended up hurt.

"Oh, I don't think my fingers are at risk of frostbite," she said with a laugh.

"No, but you should hurry and get dressed," he said with concern. "You have goosebumps on your arms."

"I just have to fasten my shift." The edges along the slit in the neckline were stiff with embroidery. No matter how she tried, she couldn't get the fabric through the ring of her little filigree brooch.

Olav put down all the things he had just gathered up to carry.

"You can borrow my brooch. It has a bigger ring than yours." He took off the gold brooch from his chest and handed it to her. Ingunn looked at him in amazement. Several times before she had pestered him to lend her this very brooch, but for him to offer to let her borrow it was something new. It was a costly piece, made of solid gold and quite big. Along the outer edge were etched the first words of the Angel's greeting and *Amor vincit omnia.* Her kinsman Arnvid Finnssøn had said that in Norwegian this meant "Love conquers all," for the Virgin Mary, through her loving intercession, will conquer over all the evil of the Devil.

Ingunn had now donned her Sunday crimson gown and wrapped the silk belt around her waist. She ran her fingers through her tangled hair.

"I think you'll have to lend me your comb, Olav."

Even though he'd once again gathered up all the things he was taking along, Olav put everything down, dug a comb out of his pouch, and handed it to her with no sign of impatience.

As they trudged along the path between the rail fences through open countryside, the sense of dizzying elation slowly left Olav. It was a fine day with blazing hot sunshine, and what he was carrying soon became a burden: the provisions sack, the axe, his cloak, and his boots. It was true that Ingunn had offered once to carry something, but that was when they were walking through the dense forest, where it was cool beneath the tree boughs, with a delightful scent of evergreen sprigs and haircap moss and new leaves. The sun barely gilded the treetops, and the birds were singing in full voice. At that moment the boy was still aware of the newly surfaced emotions inside him. Ingunn asked him to stop. She needed to rebraid her hair, for she'd forgotten her hair ribbon. It was so like her to forget. But the amber mane of her hair tumbled beautifully over her temples when she loosened her braids, making shadowed hollows underneath where tiny tendrils of hair curled along her hairline. Olav felt a sweet tenderness at the sight. When she said she could carry something, he merely shook his head, and she hadn't offered again.

Down at the fjord, summer was in full glory. The children clambered over a rail fence and took the footpath through a pasture. The sloping meadow was an avalanche of blossoms, pale pink clouds of caraway and golden globeflowers. Wherever a scrap of soil surrounded the rocks, blue violets grew as close as a carpet, and in the shade of the alder thickets fiery red campion sprouted in the lush greenery. All of a sudden Ingunn stopped to pick flowers as Olav grew more and more impatient, for he longed to reach the boat and put down everything he carried. He was also hungry; neither of them had eaten yet. But when she said they might as well sit down and eat here in the shade near the stream, he replied curtly that they would keep to his plan. When he'd found a boat for them, they would have some food before they began rowing, but not until then.

"You're always the one who decides," said Ingunn a bit plaintively.

"If I let you decide, we wouldn't get to town until tomorrow morning. But if you listen to me, we may be back home at Frettastein by then."

She laughed, tossed away the flowers she'd gathered, and ran after him.

All the way down the slope the children had been accompanied off and on by the stream that ran north of the buildings at Frettastein. Out in the valley the water swelled to a small river; at the flat area, before it flowed into the fjord, the stream widened and ran deep over a bed of big, smooth-polished stones. This was where Lake Mjøsa formed a large semicircular inlet; the shoreline around the bay was strewn with sharp gray stones from the mountain. Big old alders grew solely along the river, a line of trees stretching all the way out to the lake.

At the high-water mark, where the shore and green turf met, the path led past a pile of stones marking a cairn. The boy and girl stopped and quickly said the *Paternoster* and *Ave Maria*. Each then tossed a stone on the cairn as a sign that they had done their Christian duty toward the deceased. The grave supposedly belonged to someone who had killed himself, but it happened so long ago that neither Olav nor Ingunn had ever heard who the poor soul was.

They had to cross the river to reach the spit of land where Olav was planning to borrow a boat. Barefoot as he was, it was easy enough for him to do, but Ingunn had taken only a few steps when she began to whimper. The rounded stones were slippery under her feet, the water was so cold, and she was ruining her best shoes.

"Stop right where you are and I'll come get you," said Olav, wading back to where she stood.

But when he picked her up, he couldn't see where he set his feet, and in the middle of the river, he fell, taking her down with him.

The icy cold water took his breath away for a moment, and the whole world seemed to capsize. For as long as he lived, he would remember that image as if it had been scorched into his memory—everything he saw as he lay there in the river, holding Ingunn in his arms. Beneath the alder leaves, patches of light and shadow dripped onto the rushing water; beyond, in the sunlight, curved the long gray shoreline, and the lake was a glittery blue.

Then he got to his feet, soaking wet and ashamed, oddly ashamed that his arms were now empty, and they waded ashore. Ingunn complained bitterly as she brushed the water from her sleeves and wrung out first her braids, then the hem of her dress. And she grumbled that she had hurt herself on the stones.

"Oh, hush," Olav quietly begged her, feeling miserable. "Do you always have to whine about everything, no matter how big or small?"

The sky was now blue and cloudless, and the fjord was almost perfectly smooth, with only a few glints of pale sunlight scattered across the surface. Mirrored in the motionless water was the land on the opposite shore, with bright leaves curling in the midst of the dark spruce forest, with farms and fields on the mountain slopes. It had grown quite hot; the sweet, strong fragrance of the summer day swirled around the two children. As wet as they were, it felt cold when they entered the airy shade beneath the birches out on the promontory.

The hovel belonging to the fisherman's widow was no more than a sod hut with a door in the plank that made up one end. The only other building on the property was a cowshed made of stone and turf, with an open lean-to outside for storing hay and bundles of leaves, keeping them out of the winter weather. Tossed outside the hovel were piles of rotting fish guts. There was a terrible stink, and swarms of bluebottle flies rose up when the children approached. Maggots wriggled and crawled through these heaps of waste. As soon as Olav had stated his business and the widow told him that he could certainly borrow the boat, he picked up the provisions sack and went across to a grove of trees. Ever since he was a little boy, Olav had suffered from a peculiar and thoroughly unreasonable sense of loathing whenever he saw maggots living inside of anything.

But Ingunn had brought along a piece of cured pork for the widow, whose name was Aud. She was descended from the thralls who had once belonged to the Steinfinnssøns, and now she wanted to hear news of the estate, so Ingunn was detained for a while.

The boy had found a dry, sunlit patch of ground down by the water; there they could sit and dry off while they ate. A short time later Ingunn appeared, carrying a bowl of fresh milk. With the prospect of having some food, and now that the matter of the boat had been settled, Olav suddenly felt lighthearted. It was a joy, after all, to be out here on an errand of his own and headed for Hamar. And he was actually pleased to have Ingunn along. He was used to her constant company, and if she sometimes was a bit bothersome, well, he was used to that too.

Olav felt a little sleepy after eating. The hired men in the Frettastein household were not accustomed to rising early. He stretched out on the ground, resting his head on his arms and letting the sun bake the back of his wet clothes. He was no longer insisting that they had to hurry. All of a sudden Ingunn asked whether they should bathe in the fjord.

Olav roused himself and sat up.

"The water's too cold," he said, and then his face flushed, turning brighter and brighter red. He looked away and stared at the ground.

"I'm freezing in these wet clothes," said Ingunn. "We'll feel so nice and warm afterward." She wrapped her braids around her head, jumped up, and loosened her belt.

"I'd rather not," whispered Olav uncertainly. Heat prickled his cheeks and forehead. Abruptly he sprang to his feet, and, without a word to her, he turned around and strode across the promontory and into the spruce grove.

For a moment Ingunn stared after him, though she was used to him acting annoyed whenever she refused to do what he said. Then he would sulk for a while until his good humor returned all on its own. Unperturbed, she calmly took off her clothes and teetered across the gray stones that were sharp under her bare feet until she reached a small sandbar.

Olav walked quickly across the woolly fringe-moss that crunched under his feet. These knolls that stuck up from the lake were already bone-dry, and the spruce trees were sweating out the scent of resin. It was hardly more than the distance of an arrow shot from one side of the promontory to the other.

A big, bare rock was sticking out of the water. Olav hopped up on it and lay down, burying his face in his hands.

She wasn't going to drown, was she? he thought suddenly. He probably shouldn't have left her there, but he just couldn't make himself go back.

Down in the water a golden net seemed to tremble over the stones and mud; it was the reflection of the sparkling sun on the lake. He felt dizzy staring down at it, almost as if he were sailing. The rock he lay on seemed to be moving forward through the water.

The whole time his only thought was of Ingunn, and that was a torment. It was as if he'd been plunged into guilt and shame, and it made him sad. They used to bathe from his flat-bottom boat up at the mountain tarn, swimming next to each other as the blossoming branches drizzled golden pollen everywhere. But they could no longer be together in the same way.

He was reminded of lying in the river and suddenly seeing his familiar world turned upside down; right now he felt as if he'd stumbled again. Here he was, humiliated and ashamed and dismayed, seeing what he'd seen every day but from a different angle now, because he had fallen and lay on the ground.

Everything used to be so nice and simple when he thought about the fact that he and Ingunn were to marry when they grew up. He had assumed that Steinfinn would be the one to decide when that might happen. At times the boy would feel a pang of longing when Steinfinn's farmhands boasted about lying with womenfolk. But he had been certain that they behaved in that way because they were footloose fellows, while he, who had inherited an allodial estate and would one day become a landowner,[11] had to conduct himself differently. His sense of calm had never been upset by the thought that he and Ingunn would live together and produce children who would in turn be their heirs.

Now he felt as if he'd been the victim of treachery; he was suddenly not the same as he'd been before, nor was Ingunn the same for him. They were growing up, even though no one had warned them of that, and they would soon be adults. Those things that the Frettastein servants and their womenfolk did, well, Olav was tempted by them too, even though Ingunn was his betrothed and he owned an estate and she kept her dowry in her bridal chest.

He pictured her lying on her stomach in the short, dry grass. She had one arm tucked underneath, making her gown stretch tight over the small swellings of her bosom; her long amber braids twined through the heather. When she'd said they should bathe, an ugly thought had occurred to him, along with a futile disquiet, as strong as some sort of mortal fear. It seemed to him they were like two trees, ripped loose by the springtime floods and set adrift in a stream, and he was frightened that the stream would separate them. In this single, heated moment he seemed to understand fully what it would mean to possess her but also to lose her.

Yet there could be no sensible reason to imagine such things when all those who held power and authority over them had determined that they should be tied to each other. Nothing, not a single person, would ever separate them. Nevertheless, with a shiver of alarm he felt his childish faith in life wither and disappear. Gone was the certainty that for him all his days had been forevermore strung together like the beads of a necklace. He couldn't help thinking that if Ingunn was taken from him, he would know nothing of the future. Somewhere in the very depths of his being the voice of temptation was murmuring that he should make her his, the way the crude and simple farmhands secured the rough women on whom they had set their sights. And if anyone reached out for his possession, he would grow as fierce as a male wolf, baring its teeth as it stood over its prey, or a stallion, rearing and snorting with rage to face a bear, whirling and fighting to the death to protect its mares, while they formed a circle around the frightened and trembling foals.

The boy lay motionless, feeling shaky and hot as he stared at the slithering play of light on the water and struggled with all that was new, both what he'd become aware of and what he could only vaguely glimpse beyond. When Ingunn called from right behind him, he leaped up as if jolted awake.

"How stupid you were not to go swimming," she said.

"We need to leave!" Olav jumped down from the rock and dashed ahead of her along the promontory shore. "We've lingered here for far too long."

After he'd been rowing for a while, he grew calmer. It felt good to move his body at a steady pace. The sound of the oars thudding in the oarlocks and the water sloshing under the boat quelled his agitation and fear.

It was roasting hot now; the light from the sky and the lake dazzled and stung his eyes, and the shoreline was awash in a searing haze. After Olav had been rowing for nearly two hours a terrible fatigue came over him. The boat was heavy, and he hadn't thought about the fact that he wasn't used to rowing. This was not the same thing as lolling in a boat, drifting about and splashing in the tarn back home. He was forced to keep a good distance out in the lake because the shore curved inward to form bays and inlets; once in a while he worried that he'd completely lost his way. The town might lie hidden behind one of the promontories, invisible to him from where he sat in the boat; maybe he'd rowed right past it. Olav now realized that he was a complete stranger here. He recognized nothing from the last time he'd come this way.

The sun was baking his back, his hands were aching, and his legs had fallen asleep from sitting so long with his feet braced against the ribs of the boat. Worst of all was the pain at the back of his neck, at the very top of his spine. The lake glittered all around the small boat that was now far from land in every direction. Occasionally he felt as if he were rowing against the current. And there wasn't another vessel in sight on this day, either in the water or on shore. Olav struggled to keep rowing, stifling his misery and fretting that he might never reach Hamar.

Ingunn sat in the stern of the boat, facing the sunlight so that the drapes of her red gown gleamed; her face, shaded by the velvet hood, glowed from the reflected light. She had put on Olav's cloak. She said it was a little chilly out on the water when she was sitting so still, and then she had pulled up the hood to shade her eyes. It was an elegant cloak made of gray-green Flanders linen with a small hood of black velvet. It was one of the things that Olav had inherited from Hestviken. Ingunn was now warmly wrapped in the capacious folds of the garments. She sat there trailing her hand in the water. With a physical sense of envy, Olav realized how good and cool that must feel. The girl looked fresh and not the least bit tired. She sat there enjoying herself.

He began rowing harder. The more his hands and shoulders and the small of his back ached, the harder he rowed. He gritted his teeth, pulling on the oars so fiercely that the water surged around the bow for a while. For him, this rowing expedition seemed a great deed he was carrying out for Ingunn's sake, and he felt both proud and somewhat slighted, because he knew that he would never receive a word of thanks. There she sits, he thought, running her hand over the gunwale, with no idea how hard I'm toiling. The sweat poured off him, and the too-snug cotehardie he wore pinched and tugged more and more at the armholes. He no longer recalled that this whole outing had been his idea. Once again he clamped his lips together, rubbed his arm over his red, sweat-drenched face, and then gave a few more mighty pulls on the oars.

"I can see the towers above the treetops now," said Ingunn a little later.

Olav turned to look over his shoulder. The stab of pain in his stiff neck was shocking. On the other side of a fjord that looked hopelessly wide he saw the light-colored stone towers of the cathedral Christ Church rising above the forest on the promontory. By now he was so tired he would have liked nothing more than to give up.

The boat rounded the headland. There, at the very end, stood the monastery of the Dominican brothers on upward-sloping ground. The monastery was a cluster of dark-brown timbered buildings surrounding a stave church,[12] which had wide, tarred-shingle roofs, one tier on top of the other, with dragon heads at the gables and gilded weather vanes above the ridge tower in which the bronze bell hung.

Olav docked at the monks' wharf. He rinsed off the worst of the sweat before crawling out of the boat, slow and stiff. Ingunn was already standing at the monastery gate, talking to a lay brother who was supervising some workmen. They were carrying bales of goods down to a small cargo vessel. When Olav approached, she told him that Brother Vegard was home; they should ask to speak with him, for he could advise them on how best to proceed.

Olav didn't think they should bother the monk with such a trivial matter. Brother Vegard came to Frettastein twice a year, and he was the children's father confessor. He was a wise and amiable man who always made use of the opportunity to offer the advice and admonitions that the young people on the estate otherwise seldom received. But Olav had never spoken a word to Brother Vegard without being addressed first. He thought it far too bold to ask that the monk should bother to come to the parlatory for their sake. Surely the brother who was the porter could tell them the way to the smithy.

Yet Ingunn refused to give in. As Olav had hinted, it could be foolhardy to hand over such a valuable weapon to a blacksmith they didn't know. Brother Vegard might send a man from the cloister to go with them. It was even possible that he would offer to accompany them himself. Olav didn't think that was likely, but he allowed Ingunn to have her way.

She had another motive for her wish, though she said not a word about it. One time, long ago, she had visited the monastery with her father, and they had been given wine that the monks made from apples and berries picked in their garden. She hadn't tasted such a sweet and delicious drink, either before or since, and she was secretly hoping that Brother Vegard might offer them a glass.

The parlatory was nothing more than an alcove in the guest quarters. This was a poor monastery, but the children had never seen any other, so they thought the room was both lovely and elegant, with a big crucifix hanging above the door. A short time later Brother Vegard came in. He was a large, tall man in middle age, with a weather-beaten face and a graying fringe of hair.

He greeted the children in a friendly manner, though he seemed to be in a hurry. Embarrassed and ill at ease, Olav explained why they were there. Curtly and clearly Brother Vegard told them what route to take: past Christ Church, heading east along Grønnegate, past the Church of the Cross and down to the right along the fence of Karl Kjette's yard, then down to the property where they'd see a pond. The blacksmith's farm was the biggest of the three on the other side of the little marsh. Then the monk bade the children goodbye and was about to leave. "Will you sleep here in the hostel tonight?"

Olav said they had to head home after vespers.

"But you will have some milk, won't you? And you'll come back for the vespers service?"

They had to agree, although Ingunn looked a bit disappointed. She had expected to be offered something other than milk, and she'd been looking forward to attending vespers in the cathedral. It was so lovely when the postulants in the school sang. Yet now they wouldn't dare go anywhere but to the monastery's Saint Olav Church.

The monk was already at the door when he abruptly turned around, as if something had just occurred to him.

"So . . . Steinfinn has sent a message for blacksmith Jon today?

Is it possible that you're summoning a weapons-smith to do work at Frettastein, Olav?" he asked, looking a little apprehensive.

"No, Father. I'm here on an errand of my own," Olav replied truthfully and held up the axe for the monk to see.

The monk took the axe and weighed it in both hands. "That is a handsome weapon, Olav my boy," he said, though in a tone of voice much colder than Olav had ever imagined someone might use to speak of his axe. Brother Vegard looked at the gold paint on the narrow parts of the blade. "It's an old one, it certainly is. They aren't made like this anymore. Is it one that you've inherited?"

"Yes, Father. The axe has come down to me from my father."

"I've heard that a horned axe like this was once used at Dyfrin, back when that was the home of the old baron's lineage. That must be a hundred years ago by now. There were many legends about the axe, and it had a name. It was called Jarnglumra, or the Weapon of Glumra."[13]

"Yes, my lineage comes from there. Olav and Torgils are still kinship names. But this axe is called Ættarfylgja. And I don't know how it came into my father's possession."

"Then it must be a different one. Horned axes like this were often used in the old days," said the monk. He ran his finger lightly along the beautifully curved blade. "And that is a fortunate thing for you, my son. If I remember rightly, the axe I spoke of brought great misfortune."

He repeated the directions he'd given the children, said a friendly goodbye, and left.

Then they set off to find the smithy. Ingunn strode ahead. She looked like a grown maiden, dressed as she was in the ankle-length, flowing garments. Olav trudged after her, worn out and despondent. He had been looking forward to this trip to town, though he hardly knew precisely what he'd expected. On those occasions when he'd come here before, he'd been in the company of adults, and it was always on a market day in town. To his solemn and inquisitive eyes, everything had looked exciting and festive: the purchases the men made, the stalls, the townyards, and the churches they had visited. They had taken something to drink in the alehouses, and the streets had been crowded with horses and people. Today he was merely a half-grown boy walking along with a little maiden, and there was nowhere he might turn. No one knew him, he had no money, and there was no time to venture inside the churches. In a couple of hours they would have to start for home. And he couldn't put into words how much he dreaded the endless rowing, followed by the long walk back up through the valley. God only knew what time of night they would reach home! And no doubt they would be reprimanded for running off.

They found their way to the blacksmith's workshop. The man carefully examined the axe, taking his time and turning it this way and that. Then he said it would be difficult to repair. These types of horned axes were rarely used anymore. It wasn't easy to make the blade hold so that it wouldn't come loose if the axe struck a forceful blow—to a helmet, for example, or merely to someone's hard skull. This was because of the blade's shape, the big half-moon arc with horns at both the top and bottom. The blacksmith said he would do his best, though he warned that the gold paint might suffer damage when he welded and pounded on the blade. Olav hesitated for a moment, but he couldn't think of anything else to do. He gave the axe to the blacksmith, and they agreed on the price for the repair.

But when Olav mentioned where he was from, the blacksmith gave him a searching look.

"Does that mean you want it back in haste? Are they now making the axes ready at Frettastein?"

Olav said he knew nothing about such matters.

"No, I don't suppose you would. If Steinfinn is planning something, he's not likely to tell his young lads."

Olav looked at the blacksmith and seemed about to speak, but changed his mind. Then he said goodbye and left.

They had passed the pond, and Ingunn was about to turn onto the track between the rail fences that led up to Grønnegate. But Olav took her arm and said, "Let's go this way."

The townyards along Grønnegate were built on a slope. Below ran a filthy creek at the edge of the fields behind the townsfolks' privies and vegetable gardens. A well-trod footpath followed the creek.

Ash trees, apple trees, and big rose bushes in the yards shaded the path, making the air cool and damp. Bluebottle flies flitted and flashed through the green semidarkness, where nettles and all manner of tall, coarse weeds grew in abundance. Folks tossed their waste on this side, leaving greasy heaps of rubbish behind the privies. The path was slippery with fluids that had seeped out from the rotting piles, and the air was heavy with odors: the stench of manure, the stink of carrion, the delicate scent from the wild angelica that lined the creek bed with clouds of greenish-white flowers.

But beyond the creek the fields were flooded with afternoon sunlight; the small groves of leafy trees cast long shadows across the grass. The fields reached all the way down to the small buildings on Strandgaten, and beyond them was the lake, blue and glittery gold, with an afternoon haze hovering over the low shoreline of Helge Island.

The children walked in silence, Olav now a few paces ahead. It was very quiet here in the shade behind the yards; they heard only the buzzing of flies. A cowbell clanged from an outlying pasture above the town. A cuckoo cried once, a ghostly clear sound from far away on a wooded ridge.

Then a woman squealed near one of the houses, followed by laughter from both a man and a woman. In the yard a man was clasping a girl from behind. She had dropped a basin full of fish heads and slop, and it now rolled down to the fence, with the two of them running after it, stooping low. When they caught sight of the children on the path, the man let go of the girl. They stopped laughing and whispered to each other as they watched the children pass.

Without thinking, Olav had paused for a moment, and Ingunn came up alongside him. Then he walked between her and the fence. His fair complexion slowly flushed crimson, and he kept his eyes on the path as he led Ingunn past. There were certain houses in town that Steinfinn's hired men had talked about a great deal. For the first time Olav felt hot and troubled thinking about such places, and he wondered whether this might be one of them.

The path turned, and Olav and Ingunn saw a short distance ahead, above the treetops, the immense light gray walls and pale leaden rooftop of Christ Church along with the stone walls of the bishop's palace. Olav stopped and turned to face the maiden.

"Ingunn, did you hear what Brother Vegard said? And the blacksmith?"

"What do you mean?"

"Brother Vegard asked whether Steinfinn was summoning weapons-smiths to Frettastein," said Olav cautiously. "And Jon the blacksmith asked whether we were now making our axes ready."

"What did they mean by that? Olav, you look so strange."

"I'm not sure. Except there might have been news from the *ting*. It must be about time for folks to be leaving the *ting*, the first of them at any rate."

"What are you saying?"

"I don't really know. Except Steinfinn might have made some sort of declaration."

The young girl abruptly raised her hands and placed them on Olav's chest. He lifted his own hands and pressed hers close. As they stood there like that, a feeling again surged inside Olav, even more powerful than before—this new sensation that they had been set adrift. Something that had previously existed was now gone forever; they were heading for something new and unfamiliar. As he stared into Ingunn's dark, anxious eyes, he saw that she was aware of this too. And he felt, in his entire body and soul, that she had turned to him and reached out her hands because the same thing was happening to her as to him. She sensed the change that was about to overwhelm both them and their fate, and so she had involuntarily reached for him because it was as if they had merged, one into the other, having shared a whole childhood of neglect and abandonment. Now the two of them were closer to each other than to anyone else.

And knowing this felt inexpressibly sweet. As they stood there, motionless and looking into each other's eyes, it was as if they became one flesh, simply by pressing their warm hands together. The raw cold from the path that seeped through their wet shoes, the hot sunshine that swirled around them, the mixture of strong odors they breathed in, the faint afternoon sounds—all this they seemed to take in through the senses of one body.

The clang of church bells broke through their mute, silent elation. They heard the mighty bronze tones from the cathedral tower, the small, eager bell from the Church of the Cross, and the distant sound of the bell at the Saint Olav monastery out on the headland. Olav let go of Ingunn's hands.

"We need to hurry."

They both felt as if the ringing bells were proclaiming that a mystery had now been resolved. Without thinking, they reached for each other's hands, as if they were leaving a wedding, and they kept on walking hand in hand until they reached the town street.

The monks were in the chancel and had already begun singing vespers when Olav and Ingunn entered the small, dark church. No candles had been lit. The only light came from the lamp in front of the tabernacle and the tiny oil wicks burning on the lecterns of the monks. Paintings and adornments made of metal could be barely glimpsed through the brown twilight that darkened to night beneath the traversing roof beams. There was a strong smell of tar because the church had recently been retarred, as it was every year. There was also a faint, acrid scent of incense that lingered in the church from the midmorning prayer service.

Still overcome by a strangely poignant mood, Olav and Ingunn knelt side by side just inside the door, bowing their heads much lower than usual as they whispered their prayers with uncommon devotion. Then they stood up and tiptoed away, each to the proper side of the church.

There were few people in the church. On the men's side a few old men sat on the bench while a couple of younger men knelt in the narrow nave between the bench and the pillars. They seemed to be mostly workmen from the monastery. Olav saw no one but Ingunn on the women's side. She was leaning against the pillar closest to the front, trying to make out the images that had been painted on the canopy above the side altar.

Olav sat down on the bench; now he again noticed how terribly stiff his whole body felt. The palms of his hands were covered with blisters.

The boy understood nothing of what the monks sang. He'd learned only the *Miserere* and *De profundis* of the David psalms, and even those he didn't know well. But he recognized the tone, picturing it in his mind as a long, low wave that broke against the shore with a faint, sharp sound and then trickled back across the stones. At first, every time the monks came to the end of a psalm and sang "Gloria Patri, et Filio, et Spiritui Sancto," Olav would whisper the response: "sicut erat in principio, et nunc, et semper, et in saecula saeculorum. Amen." The monk who sang the lead had a beautifully deep and dark voice. Drowsy and content, Olav listened to the soaring of the magnificent solo voice as the choir joined in, verse after verse, through the psalms. After all the shifting emotions of the day, a sense of peace and well-being came over his soul as he sat there in the dark church and looked at the singing, white-clad men and the tiny flickering flames behind the chancel grating. He wanted to do what was right and shun what was not, and no doubt God's power and mercy would help him and safeguard him through all travails.

Images began whirling before his inner eye: the boat; Ingunn's fair face beneath the velvet hood; the sun glinting on the water behind her; the shiny fish scales on the planks in the bottom of the boat; the damp, dark path through the nettles and angelica; the rail fence they had clambered over; the meadow of wildflowers they had run through; the golden net on the lake bottom—all these sights, one after the other, raced past behind his drooping, burning eyelids.

Olav awoke when Ingunn tugged at his shoulder.

"You fell asleep," she said with disapproval.

The church was empty and next to him the south-facing door stood open to the monastery's green courtyard, which was bathed in evening sunlight. He felt a terrible dread about their journey home, and for that reason he spoke to her with somewhat greater sternness than usual.

"It will soon be time for us to leave, Ingunn."

"Yes." She sighed heavily. "If only we could stay here tonight."

"You know we can't do that."

"Then we could have attended mass in Christ Church in the morning. We never see any folks we don't know because we always have to stay at home, and that makes time pass so slowly."

"One day things will be different for us, as you well know."

"But you've even been to Oslo, Olav."

"Yes, but I remember nothing about it."

"When we move to Hestviken, you must promise me that you'll take me to Oslo someday, to the market or the assembly."

"I think that's something I can promise."

Olav was so hungry that his stomach was growling. For that reason the warm porridge and watery milk they were given in the cloister's guest quarters tasted especially good. But the whole time he couldn't help thinking about the homeward rowing. He was also worried about how the repair would go for his axe.

Then they happened to fall into conversation with two fellows who were also eating in the hostel. They were from a small farm on the coast a little farther north of the promontory where Olav and Ingunn were to go ashore. The men asked the children if they might travel with them, but they wanted to stay until after the compline service.

Once again Olav sat in the dark church and listened to the deep male voices singing the lay to the king of kings. Again images from the long, eventful day flickered behind his tired eyelids; he was on the verge of falling asleep.

He was roused when the singing voices shifted into a different tone. Through the small dark church the words of the hymn resounded:

Te lucis ante terminum
Rerum Creator poscimus

Ut pro tua clementia
Sis præsul et custodia.

Procul recedant somnia
Et noctium phantasmata;
Hostemque nostrum comprime,
Ne polluantur corpora.

Præsta, Pater piissime
Patrique compar Unice,
Cum Spiritu Paraclito
Regnans per omne sæculum.[14]

That was a hymn Olav knew. Arnvid Finnssøn had often sung it for them in the evening, and Olav also knew more or less what the Latin words meant in Norwegian. Quietly he slipped from the bench to kneel down, and with his face pressed against his folded hands, he said his evening prayers.

Clouds had moved in by the time they walked down to the boat. High overhead the sky was a furrowed gray, and the fjord was a leaden color with darker streaks farther out. The forest-covered ridges on both sides seemed drenched in darkness.

The two strangers offered to row, so Olav sat down in the stern next to Ingunn. They moved at much greater speed with the farmer's sons taking long, hard strokes of the oars, but Olav didn't feel his boyish pride particularly offended. It was just so good to sit still while someone else did the rowing.

After a while a few drops of rain began to fall. Ingunn raised the heavy, voluminous folds of the cloak she wore and invited Olav underneath.

They sat there together, both of them wrapped in the cloak. He couldn't resist slipping his arm around her waist. She was so lovely and slim, warm and soft in his embrace. The boat flew easily through the water in the blue-gray summer night. Thin veils of mist carried rain showers across the water and toward the mountains, but they were spared any more rain. Gradually the heads of the two young people sagged toward each other until they were sitting cheek to cheek. The farmer's sons laughed and told the children to stretch out on the empty sacks in the bottom of the boat.

Ingunn nestled close to Olav and fell asleep at once, while he leaned back with his head resting against the transom in the stern. Several times he opened his eyes to peer up at the clouds overhead. He was overcome with a weariness that felt both sweet and good. He awoke with a jolt when the boat scraped against the sandy bottom outside Aud's hovel.

The men laughed. Why should they have wakened him earlier? It was not such a great distance to row.

It was midnight. Olav realized that they'd been rowing for less than half the time it had taken him in the morning. He helped the men shove the boat up on shore, and then they bade him good night and left. At first they dwindled to two blurry black specks moving across the dark stony shore of the bay, but soon they disappeared entirely into the dark, overcast summer night.

The back of Olav's clothing was wet because he'd been sitting in the water in the bottom of the boat, and he felt stiff from sleeping in such an awkward position, but Ingunn was so worn out that she began to whimper. She wanted them to rest before they began the climb through the valley. Olav would have preferred to set off at once; he knew that his sore muscles would quickly ease by walking through the fresh cool night, and he was worried what Steinfinn would say if he had returned home by now. But he saw that Ingunn was too tired, and they were both afraid of going past the cairn and then wandering about in the middle of the night.

So they shared the last of their provisions from the sack and then crept inside the hovel.

Right inside the door was a small hearth that still gave off some heat. A narrow channel divided the earthen floor into two raised sections. On one side they heard Aud snoring. They fumbled their way among all the wooden tubs and gear to the resting place they knew they'd find on the other side.

Yet Olav couldn't fall asleep. The air was thick with smoke that reached all the way to the ground, making his chest hurt, and there was an unbearable stink of raw fish and smoked fish and rotten fish. His aching limbs twinged and throbbed.

Ingunn was restless, tossing and turning in the dark.

"There's no place to put my head. I think there's a stone basin right above me."

Olav groped his hand forward in an attempt to shove the basin back. But there were so many things piled up that he worried everything might fall on top of them if he moved anything. Ingunn slid farther down, then curled up and rested her head and arms on his chest. "Am I squashing you?" A moment later she was sound asleep.

After a while Olav slipped out from under her warm body that was heavy with sleep. Then he set his feet in the earthen floor channel, stood up, and crept out.

By now it was already growing light. A faint cold gust, like a shiver, rushed through the long, supple birch boughs, spraying a few icy drops. In the distance an ashen squall blew across the mirrored, steel-gray surface of the lake.

Olav turned to look inland. It was so unbelievably quiet. No one was stirring up in the valley. The farms slept, and the meadows, fields, and groves slept, looking pallid in the dawn light. Up on the scree slope, beyond the closest farmsteads, were a few scattered spruce trees that seemed lifeless, so still and straight did they stand. The sky was almost white, gradually turning yellow to the north above the black treetops. Only high above did some dark wisps remain from the nighttime clouds.

It felt so lonely to be him, standing here, the only one awake, driven outdoors by the new sensations that were ceaselessly chasing him further and further away from the secure self-confidence of his childhood. It was about this time yesterday that he'd gotten up; that now seemed like years ago.

Reticent and heartsick, he stood there listening to the silence.

Now and then he heard the sound of a wooden bell from the widow's cow wandering in the grove. Then the cuckoo's cry, clear and phantomlike, from somewhere far away in the forest's darkness, and a few little songbirds were starting to awake. Each of these faint sounds seemed only to heighten the impression of a vast, muted space.

Olav went over to the cowshed and peered in, then jerked his head back when the sharp stench from inside reached him. But the ground was nice and dry outside beneath the shed roof; the earth was brown and bare, with only a little debris left from the winter's hay and bundles of leaves. He lay down, curled up like an animal, and instantly fell asleep.

He awoke to find Ingunn tugging at his arm. She was kneeling in front of him. "Why are you sleeping here?"

"The smoke was so thick inside the hut." Olav got to his knees and shook the debris and twigs off his clothes.

The sun burst over the mountain ridge; the spruce tops looked like fiery embers as it rose. And now the birds began singing in full voice through the whole forest. Shadows still lay across the valley and stretched over the deep blue of the lake, but at the very top of the slope on the other side of the water, sunlight flooded over the woods and the cluster of farms on the green ridge.

Olav and Ingunn remained on their knees as they turned to look at each other, as if in awe. And without either of them saying a word, they wrapped their arms around one another and leaned close.

They let go at the same time, both of them with a faint, surprised smile. Then Olav raised his hand to touch the girl's temple. He swept back her tousled amber-colored hair. When she didn't pull away, he put his arm around her, drew her close, and gave her a long and passionate kiss at that sweet and tempting little hollow just below her hairline.

Afterward he looked into her eyes and felt a tingling heat pass through him. She liked what he was doing. Then they kissed each other on the lips, and finally he dared kiss the white arch of her throat.

But not a word did they say. When they stood up, he grabbed the empty provisions sack and his cloak and set off. They walked in silence, Olav in front, Ingunn behind, taking the path up through the valley as the morning sun shone farther and farther down the slopes.

At the top of the valley folks were awake in all the farms. By the time the children emerged from the forest, it was broad daylight. But when they reached the section of fence with the guardrail, marking the beginning of Frettastein's closest fields, there was no one in sight. Perhaps they'd be able to avoid punishment for this escapade of theirs, after all.

They paused for a moment behind the leafy shrubs near the fence and looked at each other. A giddy, blissful surprise again appeared in their eyes. Swiftly he touched her hand, then turned back to the fence and lifted away the guardrail.

When they entered the courtyard, the door to the cowshed stood open, but they saw no one. Ingunn headed for the loft building where she'd slept the night before. Suddenly she turned around and came running back to Olav.

"Your brooch." She took it off and held it out to him.

"You can keep it. I want you to have it," he said quickly. He took off the smaller one that was hers, the one he'd been wearing instead, and put it in her hand next to the gold brooch. "You don't have to give me yours in return. I have plenty of brooches."

Blushing, he turned on his heel and fled her touch to race toward the main hall.

He breathed a sigh of relief, very grateful, in spite of everything, to find that all the rooms were empty. One of the dogs got up and came toward him, wagging its tail. Olav patted the animal and said a few quiet words.

He stretched and yawned contentedly after he'd taken off his tight clothing. The shirt had chafed terribly under his arms; he couldn't possibly wear it again unless it was altered. No doubt that was something Ingunn could do.

As he was about to climb into the enclosed bed, he noticed that a man was already lying inside. "So all of you have come back?" said the man, groggy with sleep. Olav recognized the voice of Arnvid Finnssøn.

"No, it's just me. I went to town on an errand," he said matter-of-factly, as if there were nothing unusual about his going off to Hamar on his own. Arnvid grunted something. The next moment both were snoring.

III

When Olav awoke, he saw by the light in the hall that it was afternoon. He propped himself up on his elbows and noticed Ingunn and Arnvid sitting on the bench, looking both worried and pensive.

When Ingunn heard him stir, she stood up and came over to the bed. She was wearing the same bright red gown she'd worn the day before. Now that Olav viewed her differently, he felt a joyous warmth when he saw how beautiful she was.

"I think we may well find out what Brother Vegard meant, and the blacksmith too, when they spoke of axes," she said with great distress. "Arnvid says that Mattias Haraldssøn was at the ting and then headed north to the estate he owns at Birid."

"Oh?" said Olav. He was bending forward to fasten the laces on his shoes. Then he straightened up and held out his hand to Arnvid in greeting.

"I suppose it's a matter of what Steinfinn will do when he hears of this."

"He has already heard," replied Arnvid. "Ingebjørg says that's why he rode north to see Kolbein."

"Go out and fetch me a little food, Ingunn," said Olav. As soon as the maiden had left the hall, he asked Arnvid, "Do you know what Steinfinn is planning to do now?"

"I know what Ingebjørg thinks," replied Arnvid.

"That should not be hard to guess."

Olav had always liked Arnvid Finnssøn best of all the men he knew, though he'd never actually given this much thought. He took pleasure in Arnvid's company, yet it would never have occurred to him to call this man his friend. Arnvid had been a grown man and married for almost as long as Olav had known him; now he'd been widowed for more than two years.

But today the difference in their ages seemed to vanish; that's how it felt to Olav. He considered himself full-grown, and Arnvid was still young; he wasn't settled and set in his ways like the other married men. His marriage had been a yoke that had been forced upon him while he was still a youth, and ever since he'd involuntarily striven to rid himself of its marks. All this Olav sensed, though without knowing how he knew.

In the same way, Arnvid seemed to realize that the two young people had drawn much closer to him in age. He spoke to them as equals. While Olav ate, Arnvid cut from a wind-dried piece of reindeer shoulder some delicate, leaf-thin strips of meat. Ingunn was fond of them.

"The worst of it is that Steinfinn has let this offense last so long," said Arnvid. "It's too late to raise a case against Mattias. Now he will have to take a harsh revenge if he's going to regain his standing in the eyes of others."

"I don't see how Steinfinn could have done anything before," said Olav. "That man Mattias set off on a pilgrimage, dashing out of the country with his tail between his legs. But now that we've won two spineless youths as kings,[15] a man might take matters into his own hands and not consent to have the landowners' *ting* pass judgment when it's a question of his honor. That's what I've heard Steinfinn and Kolbein discussing."

"Yes, I suppose one man or another might be preparing to do as he pleases, without heeding either the law of the land or the laws of God," said Arnvid. "No doubt there are those here in Norway who are planning to flex their muscle now."

"What about you?" asked Olav. "Will you join Steinfinn and Kolbein if they decide to seek out Mattias at his home and . . . punish him?"

Arnvid didn't reply. He sat there, a big man with hunched shoulders, one slender, finely shaped hand shading his forehead so that his small, ugly face was hidden in shadow.

Arnvid Finnssøn was very tall and lean with a handsome physique;

his hands and feet were especially well-formed. But his shoulders were too broad and hunched, his head was quite small, and his neck was short; this detracted almost entirely from the otherwise appealing look of his body. His face was also odd and unsightly, as if it had been squeezed, with a low, wide brow and a short, wide jaw. His curly black hair looked like the curling locks on the forehead of an ox. Even so, for the first time Olav saw a resemblance between Arnvid and Ingunn. Arnvid also had a small nose that looked somehow unfinished, although on the man it seemed to have been pressed up under his forehead. Arnvid had big, dark blue eyes as well, but his were deep set just beneath his brow.

Arnvid did not belong to the Steinfinn lineage, but Tore of Hov had been married to his father's sister. And there was no mistaking a certain similarity between his heavy, ugly appearance and Ingunn's unsettling loveliness.

"It seems you have little wish to join your kinsmen in what they're now planning. Am I right?" asked Olav a bit scornfully.

"You must know that I don't intend to shirk my duty," said Arnvid.

"What will Bishop Torfinn, your father confessor, say if you join forces with us in what Steinfinn is now about to do?" asked Olav with that little, mocking smile of his.

"He's in Bjørgvin now, so he won't have the chance to say anything until afterward," replied Arnvid curtly. "There is nothing else I can do. I have to side with my cousin and kinsman."

"And you're not one of his priests," said Olav, in the same sardonic tone.

"No, that I'm not," said Arnvid. "If only I were. The worst thing about this matter between Steinfinn and Mattias is that it has gone on for so long. Steinfinn has to do something now, so that he can reclaim his honor. But you know full well that all the old talk will be revived, and that will cause an ugly stench. I don't think I'm more fearful than any other man, yet I wish I could stay out of this matter."

Olav remained silent. They were again broaching a topic that Olav understood as little as did the kinsmen of the Steinfinnssøn lineage. As a child, Arnvid had been sent away to become a priest. Then both of his older brothers had died, so his parents brought him back home and married him off to the wealthy bride who had been promised to one of his brothers. Yet Arnvid did not consider himself fortunate when he was called to be the head of his lineage and was given the main family estate in Elfardal instead of becoming a priest.

His wife was both beautiful and rich and only five or six years older than Arnvid, but the two young people didn't seem to thrive in their marriage. No doubt this was partly because as long as Arnvid's parents were alive, the young couple had very little to say about matters on the estate. Then Arnvid's father, Finn, died, and soon after his young wife, Tordis Erlingsdatter, died in childbirth. After that, Arnvid's mother took over, and she was said to be quite imposing. Arnvid allowed her to take charge of both the estate and his three young sons, and he complied with all her wishes and demands.

In the past many men of the Steinfinnssøn lineage had been priests, and even though none of them had made much of a name for himself in service to the church, they had nevertheless been good priests. But when it became the custom for priests in Norway, as in other Christian countries, to remain unmarried, the Steinfinnssøn kin had stopped seeking priestly learning. It was through judicious marriages that the lineage had always increased its power; they didn't believe that a man might make his way in the world without the benefit of marriage.

The summer heat had firmly settled in on the day that Olav and Ingunn had run off to Hamar.

Visible from the crag above the outlying barn was the fjord far below, beneath the undulating forests on the slopes and the planted fields in the hollows. On clear mornings the shoreline promontories were reflected in the waters of Lake Mjøsa, rippling with streaks of light that promised good weather. Later in the day flickering rays of warm sunshine hovered over everything; the land on the opposite shore lay under a steamy blue mist, and shining through were strips of green farmland, shimmering and pure in color. Far to the south, snow still glistened on the heights of Skreifjeldet, sparkling like water and clouds, but because of the heat the patches of snow were dwindling from one day to the next. Fair-weather clouds billowed all along the horizon, casting shadows as they sailed across the forests and lake. Occasionally they would merge and spread out, turning the sky a faded white and the lake a matte gray that no longer mirrored the land. But the rain never came. The clouds blew away, and all the trees glittered and glinted with flickering leaves in the sun, as if the land itself were gasping from the heat.

The sod roofs began to turn a seared yellow, and there were withered spots in the fields where the earth had been planted, but weeds had shot up and grown tall above the light-colored seedlings of young grain. The meadow was bursting with flowers, a lush red-blue from lilacs and wolf's bane and Saint Olav's candlestick.

There was little to do on the estate right now, and so nothing was done. The few folks who were at home spent their time waiting.

Olav and Ingunn were strolling between the houses. As if by chance they each decided separately to head toward the stream north of the estate. The water ran deep between its banks, cutting through the turf and rushing over several big, firmly rooted boulders that filled the entire streambed, then falling into pools below with a strangely drowsy and moldering sound.

The two young people sought the shade of a grove of aspen trees with clattering leaves a short way up the slope. Here the ground was dry with a thin layer of downy grass and no flowers.

"Come and lie in my arms and I'll pick the lice off you," said the maiden.

Olav moved over a little and placed his head in her lap. Again and again Ingunn combed her fingers through his fair, silky-fine hair until the boy dozed off, his breathing even and audible. She pulled out the little linen cloth from the neckline of her gown to wipe the sweat from Olav's face. Then she sat there holding the cloth and waving away mosquitoes and flies.

From higher on the slope she heard her mother's sharp and vehement voice. Fru Ingebjørg and Arnvid Finnssøn were walking the path along the edge of the grain field.

Every day Ingebjørg Jonsdatter would go up to sit on the knoll above the estate while she rambled on and on about her long-standing and fierce hatred toward Mattias Haraldssøn and about the old plans for revenge that she and Steinfinn had endlessly discussed. Arnvid was the one who had to accompany her and listen to what she said, always offering the same replies to the mistress's rants.

Olav was asleep with his head in Ingunn's lap. She sat with the back of her head leaning against the trunk of an aspen as she stared into the blue, blithely happy, when Arnvid approached, wading through the high meadow grass.

"I noticed the two of you sitting here."

"It's nice and cool," said Ingunn.

"Looks like it's about time for them to do the haying," said Arnvid. He gazed up at the slope. A gust of wind rippled across the meadow.

Olav awoke and turned over to place his other cheek in Ingunn's lap.

"Yes, we'll start on it this sabbath. I spoke to Grim this morning."

"It seems that Steinfinn relies on you quite a bit when it comes to running the estate, Olav," Arnvid ventured.

"Oh . . ." Olav hesitated before answering. "There's little to be done at the moment, so it doesn't take much to lend a hand. And yet . . . But things are about to change, and then Steinfinn will no doubt have more desire to see to things himself. This is probably the last summer that I'll spend here."

"Will you be leaving Frettastein?" asked Arnvid.

"Sooner or later I need to go home and see to my own properties," replied Olav, sounding older than he was. "When Steinfinn has settled this matter of his, I suppose it will be time for me to move back to Hestviken. Steinfinn will probably be happy to be rid of me and Ingunn."

"It's not certain that Steinfinn will have the peace to deal with such matters anytime soon," said Arnvid, a bit subdued.

Olav shrugged, his expression haughty.

"All the more reason why, for his sake, I should take charge of my own estate. My foster father knows that I will not shirk my duty but offer him my full support."

"The two of you are young to be taking over such a large estate."

"You were no older, Arnvid, when you married."

"No, but we had my parents to help us. Even so, I was the youngest of my siblings. But they were afraid the lineage would come to an end when my brothers died."

"And I am also the last man of my lineage."

"That's true," replied Arnvid. "But Ingunn is terribly young."

It was this decision that Olav had come to after returning from Hamar.

During the day and night they'd spent away he was filled with a sweet giddiness as he tumbled from one confusing feeling to another regarding this girl who had been his childhood playmate, but he grew calm as soon as they were back home at Frettastein. No one had even noticed they'd been gone. And that had a strangely soothing effect on the upheaval he was feeling. There was also the fact that everyone and everything seemed to be warning of impending change and weighty events at the very moment when he felt he had become an adult. That made it seem all the more reasonable that he too should be changed.

He stopped playing with the other boys in the village, but no one seemed surprised. The apprehension that now reigned at Frettastein had spilled over to the entire surrounding area up on the ridge.

And so Olav found it only sensible for him to give serious thought to his marriage. During the time he spent with Ingunn on those long summer days sated with sunlight, he felt a robust satisfaction that he now had a much better view of the future that was intended for him than had been possible when he was a mere child.

Instead of uneasiness and fearful awkwardness, he felt a joyous and inquisitive anticipation. Something was about to happen. Steinfinn would surely seize the opportunity to strike. What the consequences might be if Steinfinn did indeed strike were of little concern to Olav. He had involuntarily adopted the attitude of the Steinfinnssøn lineage toward his own virtues and might; no one could do him or them any harm. And afterward, when he asked for permission to travel home to celebrate his wedding feast with Ingunn, he didn't consider that Steinfinn's response would be anything but an immediate yes. It would probably take place in the autumn or winter. And his newly aroused desire to possess her merged with his newly awakened determination to be his own master. Now, when he took Ingunn in his arms, it was as if he were holding the pledge for his own adult authority. When they went to Hestviken, they would sleep together and oversee everything together, both outside and within the estate, and no one but the two of them would be allowed to decide or take charge. Then, in the eyes of the law, they would have come of age.

Nowadays Olav seldom showered caresses on his betrothed. Although he was no longer shy or afraid, and by no means melancholy as he'd been during the first rush of desire, he was now aware of what was both manly and seemly. Only in the evening, before they went to their separate sleeping quarters, did he seek an opportunity to find Ingunn alone and bid her goodnight in a manner he considered suitable for two friends who would soon be married.

The fact that Ingunn's eyes revealed far too much if they merely happened to look at each other was something that Olav regarded as the good fortune that fate had prepared for him. He noticed that she would steal glances at him, and her expression was so strangely solemn and filled with a pleasing darkness. Then she would meet his eye, and a little spark would flare inside her; she would look away, afraid she might smile. She would surreptitiously touch his hand whenever they met, and she liked to tousle his hair the moment they were alone. She was eager to do small favors, offering to mend his clothing, or bring him food when he arrived for meals a bit later than the other men. And when he said goodnight to her, she would cling to him as if she were both hungry and thirsty for his caresses. Olav assumed this meant she too was longing for their wedding, and he thought it only reasonable. Time must be passing very slowly for her as well, here on the estate; she must be looking forward to becoming her own mistress. It never occurred to him that some young folks might not be fond of each other, even though they were betrothed.

But the trip to Hamar continued to seem like a dream to Olav. He preferred to think about it when he lay in bed at night. That's when he would relive everything and feel that strange, sweet shivering in both body and soul. He remembered how they had knelt at dawn behind the widow's shed, leaning close, chest to chest, and he had dared to kiss her temple, that hollow under her hair that smelled so warm and good. Then such a perplexing sorrow and fear would come over him that he would try instead to think of the future. For them the path led straight to the church door and the high seat and the bridal bed.[16] But his heart seemed to falter and grow forlorn during those nighttime hours, whenever he sought to feel a joyous anticipation about everything awaiting them, as if nothing in what the future promised could, after all, feel as sweet as that morning kiss.

"What is it?" asked Arnvid, annoyed. "Can't you lie still?"

"I'm going outside for a while." Olav got up, put his clothes back on, and wrapped a cloak around his shoulders.

The light was already diminishing at night; the leafy crowns of the trees seemed darker against the distant hazy blue mountain ridges. There were brass-colored streaks in the clouds to the north. A bat whirled past him, black and lightning swift.

Olav went over to the loft storehouse where Ingunn was sleeping. The door had been left ajar because of the heat, yet it was still stifling inside, with a smell of sun-baked timbers and beds and sweating people.

The maidservant who lay next to the wall was asleep, snoring loudly. Olav knelt down and leaned over Ingunn, who lay on the outer edge of the bed. Gently he touched his cheek and lips to her chest. For a moment he remained still, feeling the soft warmth of her bosom as it quietly rose and fell with her breath as she slept. And he listened to the beating of her heart. Then he slid his face upward and she awoke.

"Get dressed," he whispered in her ear. "Come outside for a little while."

He waited outdoors in the gallery.[17] In a few moments Ingunn appeared, ducking through the low doorway, and then stopping, as if surprised by the silence. She took several deep breaths. The night was cool and pleasant. They sat down side by side on the top step.

Now they both found it so strange that they were the only ones awake on the estate. And neither of them was used to being outside at night. They sat there, without moving and hardly daring to whisper more than an occasional word to each other. Olav had thought he would wrap his cloak around Ingunn and put his arm around her waist. Instead he merely placed his hand on her lap and ran his finger along hers. Then Ingunn pulled her hand away, threw her arm around his shoulder and buried her face against his neck.

"The nights seem darker now, don't they?" she said quietly.

"There's a heaviness in the air tonight," he told her.

"Yes, maybe it will rain tomorrow," she said.

A gray-blue mist hovered over the part of the fjord they could glimpse from where they were sitting, and the mountains were hidden on the other side. Olav stared straight ahead, pondering.

"I don't think that's certain. There's an easterly wind. Can't you hear the river up in the gorge? It sounds so loud tonight."

"I suppose it's best for us to go back to bed," he whispered after a while. They kissed, a brief and timid kiss. Then he slipped away down the stairs, and she went back inside.

It was pitch-dark inside the main hall. Olav undressed and got back in bed.

"Did you go out to talk to Ingunn?" asked Arnvid, lying wide awake next to him.

"Yes."

A moment later Arnvid spoke again.

"Do you know what arrangements were made for the two of you regarding your marriage property, Olav?"

"No, I don't. As you know, I was so young when we were betrothed. But Steinfinn and my father must have come to an agreement about what we would both bring to the marriage. Why are you asking about this?" Olav suddenly wondered.

Arnvid didn't reply.

Olav said, "No doubt Steinfinn will make sure that we're given what was agreed."

"He may well be my cousin," said Arnvid a bit reluctantly, "but you will soon be our kinsman, so I expect I can tell you. They say that Steinfinn's circumstances are not as good as they used to be. I've been lying here thinking about what you mentioned, and I think that you're right. It would be wise for you to hurry the marriage along so that Ingunn is given her dowry as quickly as possible."

"And there's no reason for us to wait," said Olav.

Mass was held the following day, and the day after that they began the haying at Frettastein. Arnvid and his servant went along to help bring in the hay. Early in the morning the air had already turned a pallid gray, and by afternoon big black clouds began sailing in from the south, spreading over the hazy, light gray sky. Olav looked up as they paused for a moment to sharpen their scythes, and the first raindrops fell on his face.

"Maybe we'll have rain showers tonight," said one of the old farmhands.

"Tomorrow is Midsummer Day," replied Olav. "If the weather turns on that day, we'll have as many days of rain as we had days of sunshine before. That's what I've always heard. I don't think the haying season will be better this year than it was last year, Torleif."

Arnvid was standing a little farther down in the field. Now he dropped his scythe and quickly made his way up to the others. Then he pointed. Far down the slope a long line of men, dressed as soldiers, was riding through a small clearing in the forest.

"There they are," said Arnvid. "It looks as if they have something else on their minds than haying. And now I wonder what will become of the haying work on the estate this year."

Late that night the rain came pouring down, and steamy clumps of thick white fog drifted over the fields and the nearest forest-covered slopes. Olav, who stood with Ingunn on the gallery to her sleeping loft, was staring angrily at the pelting rain.

Arnvid came running across the soggy courtyard and slipped under the eaves to join them as he shook off the rain.

"So you weren't invited either to take part in the men's council?" asked Olav scornfully.

Olav had wanted to follow the men when they went over to the old storehouse loft where Ingebjørg lived. That's where they wanted to talk so the servants wouldn't hear. But Steinfinn told his foster son to stay in the hall with the farmhands. Olav was offended because in his own mind he now considered himself Steinfinn's son-in-law, yet he'd forgotten that his foster father didn't know their kinship was on the verge of being finalized.

Arnvid leaned against the wall, unhappily staring straight ahead.

"I won't shirk my duty; I'll follow my kinsman as far as he demands, but I refuse to take part in the decisions they make."

Olav turned to look at his friend as his pale and delicately shaped lips formed a somewhat mocking smile.

IV

On the following evening, the men headed down the slope. The rain had stopped during the day, but it was cold, windy, and overcast.

Kolbein rode with five men, while Steinfinn had with him seven hired men and Olav Audunssøn. Arnvid followed with a manservant. Kolbein had made arrangements for boats that were docked in a remote bay farther north on Lake Mjøsa.

Ingunn retired early to her loft room and went to bed. She didn't know how long she had slept when she was awakened by someone patting her chest.

"Is it you?" she whispered, still groggy with sleep. She expected to touch Olav's soft hair, but instead she felt a wimple-covered head. "Mother?" she said with great surprise.

"I can't sleep," said Ingebjørg. "I've been outside walking. Get dressed and come with me."

Ingunn obediently got up and put on her clothes. She was astonished beyond all measure.

When she stepped outside, she saw that it wasn't as late as she'd thought. The weather had cleared. The moon, nearly full, was visible above the ridge to the south and as pale pink as an evening sky, yet it gave no light.

Ingebjørg's grasp was fiery hot when she took her daughter's hand. She pulled the young girl along, meandering here and there beyond the estate buildings but saying hardly a word.

For a moment they leaned over the rail fence enclosing a field. Below they saw a pond surrounded by tall, lush vegetation that was reflected as dark shapes in the water. But in the middle of the smooth surface of the pond shone the moon; it had now risen so high that it had turned a gleaming yellow.

Ingebjørg stared in the direction of Lake Mjøsa and the country-side, which lay under a light, placid mist.

"I wonder whether you have any notion what's at stake for all of us," she said.

Ingunn felt her cheeks turn pale and cold at her mother's words. She had always been aware of what was commonly known about her father and mother; she was also aware that weighty events were about to happen. But it was only now, as she walked along beside her mother and noticed the agitation stirring Ingebjørg to her very core, that she understood what it actually meant. A faint sound, like the squeak of a mouse, escaped from her lips.

What was almost a smile suddenly appeared on Ingebjørg's haggard face.

"Are you afraid to keep vigil with your mother on this night? Tora wouldn't have refused to stay with me, but she's such a child, so pious and gentle. You aren't like that. And you're the oldest, after all," she added fiercely.

Ingunn clasped her slender hands tightly. Again she felt as if she'd climbed a little higher up a mountain and now had a somewhat broader view of the world. She had always realized her parents were not particularly old, but she now saw that they were quite young. It seemed that their love, which had always sounded to her like a saga from the past, could be revived to burn in bright flames, like the fire awakened from the smoldering embers under the ashes. With surprise and reluctance, she saw that her mother and father still loved each other—the way she and Olav loved each other, except much more ardently, the way a river is bigger and flows stronger near its estuary than high up on the slope. And even though Ingunn was embarrassed by the way she now viewed her parents, she also felt proud of their unusual fate.

Timidly she stretched out both hands and said, "I will gladly keep vigil with you all night, Mother. Yes, I will."

Ingebjørg grasped her daughter's hands.

"Surely God cannot refuse to grant Steinfinn his wish that we will now be able to wash off the shame," she said fervently. Then she put her arms around the young girl and kissed her.

Ingunn wrapped her arms around her mother's neck. It had been a long time since Ingebjørg had kissed her. She remembered such affection as belonging to the life that had ended on the night when Mattias came to their estate.

Nor was it something that Ingunn had missed, since she'd never been an especially demonstrative child. What she and Olav shared had seemed like an entirely new discovery. It had suddenly appeared the way spring arrives: one day it miraculously surfaces, yet the next moment it may seem as if summer will last forever. At first, spring appears only at the very edge of the field. As long as the ground is bare with withered grass after the snow has melted from around the rocks, spring is merely a small gray meadow between the strips of field. But then it turns into a forest of tangled and wild vegetation, and it's almost impossible to push your way through.

Now the springtime barrenness of Ingunn's childhood had become an overgrown and lush summer. She pressed her cool, soft cheek against her mother's bony face.

"I will very gladly wait with you, Mother."

The words seemed to sink into her own soul. She had to wait for Olav, after all. She felt as if she hadn't been thinking properly when he rode down the mountain with the others in the evening; she hadn't acknowledged that the men were setting off on a dangerous mission. Fear fluttered inside her, but it caused only a faint trembling in her heartstrings. She couldn't seriously imagine any harm coming to the one who was hers.

Yet she couldn't help asking, "Mother, are you frightened?"

Ingebjørg Jonsdatter shook her head.

"No. God will grant us justice, for that is our right." When she noticed her daughter's expression, she added, with a smile that Ingunn found disturbing because it looked so strange and sly, "You see, my daughter, it was fortunate for us that King Magnus died in the spring. We have kinsmen and friends among the men who will now wield the greatest power. That's what Kolbein says. And many of them hold no affection for Mattias. Do you remember what he looks like? No, I don't suppose you do. Mattias is short in stature, yet many think he ought to be even a head shorter than he is. Queen Ingebjørg never liked him. That's something you must realize. Otherwise he wouldn't be sitting over there at Birid, when all the knights and barons have now gathered in Bjørgvin where the young king will be crowned."

Ingebjørg kept on talking as they walked along the fences. Ingunn had such a deep yearning to tell her mother about Olav Audunssøn, but she could see that Ingebjørg was so immersed in her own thoughts that she wouldn't care to hear about anything else. Yet Ingunn couldn't resist saying, "Wasn't it a shame that Olav didn't have time to fetch his axe before they set off?"

"Oh, your father has no doubt made sure that all the men he took with him are as well armed as they need to be," said Ingebjørg. "Steinfinn didn't want to take the boy, but he begged to go along."

A little later she said to her daughter, "You're freezing. You should put on your cloak."

Ingunn's cloak was still hanging in her mother's loft. Two weeks had passed but she'd neglected to reclaim it. Instead she had used Olav's cloak—the one he kept for special occasions—if she needed an outer garment. Now Ingebjørg followed her daughter inside. She stirred the embers in the hearth and lit a lantern.

"Your father and I used to move into the big loft room in the summertime. If we'd been sleeping there when Mattias arrived, he wouldn't have been able to catch Steinfinn unawares. Now it will be safer for us to sleep over there until Steinfinn has received dispensation from the king."[18]

The big loft room did not have an external staircase because it was used to store the valuables belonging to members of the household. A ladder led up to the loft from the storeroom below. Ingunn had only rarely been inside; even the smell provoked in her a sense of solemnity. Bags containing pungent herbs hung among the hide coverlets and leather sacks. Everything hanging from the ceiling made for a rather eerie sight. Along the walls stood large chests. Ingunn went over to look for Olav's; it was a carved chest made of light-colored linden wood.

Ingebjørg threw open the door to the outside gallery. She removed everything that had been piled up inside the enclosed bed and began rummaging through chests and trunks while Ingunn held the lantern. Then she dropped everything she was holding and went out to the gallery.

The moon had now risen high in the western sky. Its light shone like a golden bridge above the water as it slowly sank toward several towering clusters of blue cloud from which a few wisps had pulled loose and became gilded as they drifted up toward the moon.

Ingebjørg went back inside and returned to rummaging through the chests. She lifted out a voluminous gown made of silk. It was green with a pattern of yellow flowers woven into the fabric. In the light of the lantern, the entire garment took on the color of aspen leaves turning yellow.

"I want you to have this."

Ingunn curtsied and kissed her mother's hand. She had never before owned any silk clothing. From a small box made of walrus tusk, her mother now took out a green velvet ribbon closely embroidered with roses made of gilded silver. She placed the ribbon on her daughter's head, moved it a little more forward, and then tied the ends of the ribbon at the back of the girl's neck underneath her hair.

"That's how it should be worn. You haven't turned out as fair as we thought you would when you were a child, yet this summer you've certainly grown lovelier. You can wear a wreath now; you're a maiden who is ready to marry, my Ingunn."

"Yes, Olav and I have talked of that," said Ingunn, gathering her courage. Without thinking, she did her best to speak in a matter-of-fact and nonchalant tone.

Ingebjørg looked up. They were both squatting in front of a chest.

"This is something you and Olav have discussed?"

"Yes." Ingunn again spoke nonchalantly as she meekly lowered her gaze. "We're both old enough now for you to honor the agreement that was made for us."

"Oh, that agreement was not the kind that can't be broken," said her mother. "If the two of you aren't willing, we would never force you."

"But we are pleased with the arrangement you've made for us," said Ingunn piously. "We both feel that our fathers did well when they reached this agreement on our behalf."

"I see." Ingebjørg pensively stared straight ahead. "I suppose it might be possible. Are you very fond of Olav?" she asked.

"Yes, I am. We've known each other for so long, and he has always been very kind to us and obedient to you and Father."

Her mother nodded thoughtfully.

"Steinfinn and I didn't know whether the two of you actually remembered the agreement or had given it any thought. But I suppose it might be possible, one way or another. As young as you both are, you can't have formed a proper attachment to each other. Olav is a handsome lad, and Audun left him a sizable inheritance."

Ingunn would have liked to say more about Olav, but she could see her mother was again far away in her own thoughts.

"We took out-of-the-way routes, your father and I, when we traveled over the mountains," said Ingebjørg. "From Vors we rode up to the plateau and then continued through remote valleys on the heights. There was still a lot of snow in the mountains. In one place we had to stay in a stone hut for an entire week. It was near a lake, and there was a glacier in the water. At night as we tried to sleep we could hear the ice floes creaking and breaking apart. Steinfinn took a gold ring from his finger and left it as an offering to the first church we came to as we rode down from the heights. They were celebrating mass that day. The poor folks in that mountain hamlet were all eyes as they stared at us. We had left the town wearing our Sunday finery. By then the clothes were quite bedraggled, yet those folks had probably never seen the likes of such garments in that valley.

"But I was a weary bride when Steinfinn brought me home to Hov, and I was already carrying under my heart . . ."

Ingunn stared at her mother with rapt attention. In the faint glow from the lantern that stood on the floor between them, she saw that she was smiling so strangely. Ingebjørg reached out to stroke her daughter's hair and then let the girl's long braids slide through her fingers.

"And now you're all grown up."

Ingebjørg stood up and handed the girl a big embroidered cover-let, telling her to go out to the gallery to shake off the dust.

"Mother!" shouted Ingunn from outside.

Ingebjørg came running.

It was almost daylight, and high overhead the sky was clear and pale, but inland low clouds and fog had drifted down. On the other side of the lake to the northwest a big fire flared, coloring the hazy air red all around. Black smoke billowed out, then gusted away to merge with the fog, making it denser and darker far up the slope. Every once in a while they saw actual flames rise high in the air, but the estate on fire lay hidden beyond a forest-covered promontory.

For a short time the two women stood there, staring. Ingebjørg didn't say a word, and her daughter didn't dare speak. Then the mistress turned to dash back inside the loft. The next moment Ingunn saw her mother running across the courtyard toward the old storeroom loft.

Two maidservants wearing only their shifts came rushing out and headed for the courtyard fence. Then Tora appeared, her fair hair loose and fluttering around her; she was followed by Ingebjørg, who was leading both of her young sons and all the women on the estate. Their shouts and cries reached Ingunn as she stood on the gallery.

But when everyone began crowding into the loft room, she slipped away. With her head bowed and her hands clasped under the cloak she had wrapped tightly around herself—and wishing fervently she could make herself invisible—she crept over to her own loft room and climbed into bed.

Terrible sobs racked her body. She didn't know why she was crying so hard, but she felt overwhelmed by all the emotions that had flooded through her on this night. She couldn't bear to have anyone near, and then the tears spilled out. She was so tired. And by now it was already morning.

When Ingunn awoke, the sun was shining in the doorway. She jumped up and put on her shift. She could hear horses outside in the courtyard.

Four or five of their own steeds, no longer saddled and with a light steam rising off them, were grazing. The dappled gray that belonged to Olav was among them. And a whinnying could be heard from up in the pasture. The maidservants were dashing between the cookhouse and the main hall. All of them were dressed in their best.

Ingunn threw on her cloak and ran for the big loft room on the eastern side of the estate. Briar roses and meadowsweet had been strewn on the floor. It took her breath away. She hadn't seen any sort of celebration on the estate since she was a little girl. On the sabbath there was often drinking in the hall and feasting, but never the sort that prompted anyone to strew the floors with flowers. The silk gown and the golden wreath had been left on top of Olav's chest. Ingunn grabbed them and ran back.

She had no mirror, but she gave it little thought as she stood there in her loft room, dressed in all her finery. She felt the weight of the golden garland on her flowing hair, and she looked down at her body swathed in the yellow-green silk. The gown fell in long folds from her bodice all the way to her feet; the silver belt cinched it in slightly at the waist. The gown was so wide and long that she had to lift the skirts with both hands as she strode across the courtyard's grassy expanse. Filled with joy, she knew she looked like one of the carved images in a church: tall and slim, with a small bosom and slender limbs, glittering with jewelry.

She paused in the doorway to the hall, overwhelmed. The long, narrow hearth had been lit in the middle of the room, and sunlight was flooding in through the hearth-pole vent, making the drifting smoke near the rafters look sky blue. Lit candles stood on the table in front of the high seat. There, next to her father, sat her mother, dressed in red silk. Instead of the ordinary wimple that Ingunn always saw her mother wearing, Ingebjørg now wore one of starched white linen. It rested like a crown on her forehead and was open at the back, so the gleaming gold knot of her hair was visible through its lace net.

No other women were seated at the table. Instead, they were all bustling back and forth, carrying food and drink. So Ingunn picked up a pitcher of ale and held it high in her right hand while she used her left to raise her skirts. Then she made herself look as slender and lithe as she could, thrusting her pelvis forward, letting her shoulders fall back to make her bosom look smaller, and bending her neck as she lowered her head like a flower atop a stalk. Then she stepped forward, treading as lightly as she could.

But the men were already half drunk, and worn out as well after the deeds of the night; none of them paid her any attention. Her father gave a laugh when she poured ale for him. His eyes were shiny, his expression blank, and his face a blazing red beneath his matted amber-colored hair. And now Ingunn noticed that the arm he held to his chest was wrapped in bandages. He had on his best cloak over the tight-fitting leather tunic he'd worn under his coat of mail. Most of the men seemed to have sat down at the table wearing exactly what they'd had on when they dismounted from their horses.

Steinfinn motioned for Ingunn to pour ale for Kolbein and his two sons, Einar and Haftor, who were sitting to his right.

On Steinfinn's left sat Arnvid. His face was flushed, and his dark blue eyes gleamed like metal. Tremors passed over his face when he stared at his young kinswoman. Ingunn saw that at least he found her fair-looking tonight, and she smiled with joy as she leaned across the table to serve him ale.

She went over to where Olav Audunssøn was sitting on the outer bench and squeezed in between him and the man next to him when she poured ale for those on the other side of the table. The boy put his arm around her knees and, hidden by the table, pulled her close, causing her to spill some of the ale.

Ingunn saw at once that Olav was drunk. He was straddling the bench with his legs stretched out, his head propped on one hand, and his elbow resting on the table amid the food. It was so unlike Olav to sit in this manner that she had to laugh. He was often teased because no matter how much he drank he remained as steady and quiet as ever. The others said that God's gifts had no hold on him.

But tonight the ale was having an effect even on Olav's stolid demeanor. When she was about to pour him some ale, he grabbed her hands and put the pitcher to his lips to take a drink, spilling some down his chest and soiling his elk-hide armor.

"Drink some yourself," he said, laughing up at her. His eyes looked so foreign and strange, glittering with a raucous wildness that confused Ingunn, but she filled his tankard and drank. Again he put his arm around her under the table, and she nearly fell onto his lap.

The man sitting next to Olav took the ale pitcher away from them.

"That's enough, you two. Save some for the rest of us."

Ingunn left to refill the pitcher, and that's when she noticed her hands were shaking. With surprise she realized she was shaking all over. This was mostly because she'd been startled by the boy's fervor. But she was also drawn to him in a way that she'd never felt before; it was like a sweetly devouring sense of curiosity. She'd never seen Olav behave like this. Yet it was all so joyous; tonight nothing was the same as usual. As she moved about, serving ale, she kept on sneaking over to press close to Olav so he would have another chance to steal those rough and hidden caresses. She felt as if she were being inexorably pulled toward him.

No one noticed how dark it had grown outside until rain began spraying down through the hearth-pole vent. They had to close the hatch. Then Ingebjørg told the servants to bring in more candles, and the men got up from the table. Some went to their rooms to sleep, but others sat down again to drink and talk with the women, who only now could think about having something to eat.

Arnvid and Einar Kolbeinssøn, who was the son of Steinfinn's half-brother, sat down close to Ingunn. Einar began telling her more about what had happened.

They had traveled by boat along the eastern shore all the way up to the river. There they mounted their horses to ride across to Vingarheim so they would approach Mattias's estate from the north. This turned out to be an unnecessary precaution because Mattias had no guards keeping watch.

"He didn't think Steinfinn was in earnest about any intent to attack," said Einar scornfully. "And it's no wonder, after all the senseless talk and waiting that have gone on. No doubt he thought that if Steinfinn could patiently bear the shame for six years, he could probably bear it for a seventh."

"It seems to me I've heard a rumor about Mattias. He supposedly fled the country because he was afraid of Steinfinn," said Olav Audunssøn, who had come over to join them. Now he squeezed in to sit between Arnvid and Ingunn.

"Yes, and Steinfinn has been lazy, content to sit and wait under the bush until the bird happens to land right above him."

"Do you mean he should have brought a claim against Mattias and argued his case, the way your father did?"

Arnvid intervened to keep the peace between the two men. Then Einar resumed his story.

They had entered the estate unopposed. A few of the men then stood guard near the houses where folks were likely to be sleeping. But Steinfinn and Kolbein's sons went over to the main building along with Arnvid, Olav, and five hired men. Kolbein stayed outside. The men inside were jolted awake when the door was kicked in; some of them were naked, while some wore linen garments, but all of them reached for their weapons. Inside with Mattias were a friend of his, the estate's tenant farmer and his half-grown son, and two manservants. A brief fight ensued, but the men, groggy with sleep, were quickly overpowered. Then it was just Steinfinn and Mattias.

"This is unexpected. Can it really be you, Steinfinn, out at such an early hour?" said Mattias. "I recall how soundly you used to sleep in the past, and what a beautiful wife you had, keeping you in bed."

"She's the one who asked me to come here and bring you her greetings," said Steinfinn. "You made such a strong impression on her the last time you visited that she hasn't been able to forget you. But get dressed," he said. "I've always thought it a cowardly act to challenge a naked man."

Mattias's face turned bright red at these words, but he feigned indifference as he said, "Am I allowed to put on my coat of mail as well, since you seem determined to show how magnanimous you are?"

"No," replied Steinfinn. "For I have no intention of letting you escape this encounter with your life. But I'm willing to fight you without my own coat of mail."

While Steinfinn unfastened his coat of mail, Kolbein, who had now come inside, and another man held on to Mattias, which didn't please him at all. Steinfinn laughed and said, "You seem to be more ticklish than I was, seeing as you can't bear to have anyone touch you!" After that Steinfinn told Mattias to get dressed, and he let him pick up a shield. Then the two men began to fight, one on one.

In his youth Steinfinn had been deemed the most capable of men in terms of wielding a sword, but over the past years he'd fallen out of practice. It quickly became apparent that Mattias, as short and slight as he was, was more than the equal of his opponent. Steinfinn had to retreat, taking one step back after another, and he started gasping for breath. Then, with a powerful thrust, Mattias disabled Steinfinn's right arm so that he had to shift his sword to his left hand. By then both men had long ago dropped their shields. Now Steinfinn's men thought things were looking dire for their master. At a signal from Kolbein, one of the men leaped to Steinfinn's side. That confused Mattias enough that Steinfinn was able to deliver the mortal blow.

"But it was a battle between two stalwart men. That's what all of us saw," said Arnvid.

In the meantime an unfortunate incident had occurred when a few of the men Steinfinn had brought along—hired hands from an outlying valley—began stealing things, while others tried to restrain them. In the ensuing tumult, a heap of birch bark caught fire where it lay in the narrow passageway between the main building and one of the storehouses. The man called Tjostolv, whom nobody liked, was probably the one who had done it. Apparently he'd also brought some of the birch bark inside the living quarters because all of a sudden bright flames engulfed the room, even though the timbers and roof were cold and wet after the rain. The blaze then caught hold inside the main hall. They had to carry Mattias's body outside and let his men go free.

Then folks came running from the neighboring farms, and a group of these farmers launched an attack against Steinfinn and his companions. Men on both sides were wounded, but no one else lost his life.

"We wouldn't have needed to deal with the fire or battle the farmers if Steinfinn hadn't wanted to be seen as the victor who had acted in a chivalrous manner."

Olav had never liked Einar Kolbeinssøn, who was three years older and had always maliciously teased the younger boys. So Olav replied with great contempt, "Well, no one would ever accuse your father or brothers of that. Nobody would think that Kolbein Borghildssøn had urged his half-brother to make an improper show of magnanimous behavior."

"Watch your tongue, you little bastard. Father has always been considered a descendant of Tore of Hov. Our lineage is equal in standing to that of Aasa's descendants. Keep that in mind, Olav. Don't sit there groping at my kinswoman. Take your paw out of her lap right now!"

Olav leaped to his feet, and the two men began brawling. Ingunn and Arnvid rushed forward to try to separate them. That was when Steinfinn rose and demanded silence.

Everyone present—men and women of the estate as well as strangers—pressed closer to the table. Steinfinn leaned on his wife's shoulder as he stood there. His face was no longer red; it was pale, with deep shadows under his eyes. But he stood straight-backed and smiling as he spoke.

"I wish to thank all of you who agreed to accompany me. Above all you, my brother, and your sons, as well as my dear cousin Arnvid Finnssøn, and the rest of you, good kinsmen and loyal men. God willing, we will soon be granted peace and reconciliation regarding what took place last night, for He is a righteous God, and it is His wish that a man should honor his wife and protect her virtue. But I am weary now, good friends, and so I will go to bed, taking my wife with me. And you must pardon me if I say no more. I am tired, and I suffered a small cut as well. But Grim and Dalla will see to your needs, and you must stay and drink for as long as you like. Celebrate and carouse as befits such a joyous occasion. And now you must pardon us as we take our leave of you." By then Steinfinn had begun to stammer and mumble his words. He swayed a bit as he stood there, and Ingebjørg had to support him as they left the hall.

Some of the hired men began to cheer, pounding the table planks with the hafts of their knives and their tankards. But the uproar died out on its own, and folks quietly retreated. They all realized that Steinfinn's wound might be worse than he wanted to acknowledge.

Everyone went outside and stood in silent clusters to watch the tall and handsome couple walking over to the loft room through the rain-soaked summer night. Most noticed when Steinfinn paused and seemed to speak vehemently to his wife. It looked as if she objected and tried to pull his hands away, but he tore off the bandages that held his wounded arm to his chest and impatiently tossed them aside. They heard Steinfinn laughing as he continued on.

Everyone remained silent when they went back inside; Grim and Dalla had more ale brought in and put more wood on the fire. The benches and table were pushed out of the way. But most of the men were tired and seemed to want nothing more than to sleep. Some did go out to the courtyard to dance, but they came back in at once. The rain clouds were right overhead, and the grass was very wet.

Ingunn was again sitting between Arnvid and Olav, and Olav had placed his hand on her lap.

"Silk," he said as he stroked her knee. "Silk is so beautiful," he kept repeating.

"You're talking nonsense," said Arnvid with annoyance. "There you sit, already half asleep. Go to bed!"

But Olav shook his head and laughed quietly to himself. "I'll decide for myself when to leave."

In the meantime some of the men had picked up their swords and lined up to dance. Haftor Kolbeinssøn came over to Arnvid to urge him to sing for them. But Arnvid refused, saying he was too tired. Olav and Ingunn also declined to join in the dancing; they said they didn't know the song. It was the "Lay of Kraka."[19]

Einar stood at the head of the line of dancers, holding his drawn sword in his right hand. Tora held his left hand and had placed her other hand on the shoulder of the man next to her. That's how they were all lined up: alternating a man holding a drawn sword with a woman. The raised blades looked so beautiful as Einar began to sing:

With the sword we struck—

The line of dancers took three steps to the right. Then the men moved to the left, while the women took a step back, allowing the men to stand in a row in front. Then the men crossed their swords two by two and stayed where they were to stomp in time to the song until the women dashed forward underneath the swords and once again completed the chain. Einar sang:

With the sword we struck—
Young I was when east in
Øresund I doled out
food to greedy wolves—

It turned out that none of the dancers were entirely sure of the steps. When the women were supposed to dash under the swords, they barely managed to keep time with the stomping of the men. And there was scant room in the narrow space between the long hearth and the rows of posts that held up the roof and divided the sleeping rooms from the main hall.

The three sitting on the bench at the gable end of the room stood up to get a better view. Now that the dance was already threatening to come to a standstill with the second verse, folks again called for Arnvid to join in. They knew that he could sing the entire song, and he had the most beautiful voice of anyone.

When he picked up his sword, drew the blade, and took his place at the head of the line of dancers, everything at once became more orderly. Olav and Ingunn went over to stand closest to him. Arnvid led the dance with a confidence and grace that no one would have suspected possible from a man whose body looked so hunch-shouldered and stoop-necked. He began singing in a full and clear voice as the women wound their way, in and out, beneath the display of raised swords.

> With the sword we struck—
> Hild's sport we played
> when to Odin's halls
> we sent Helsing's army.
> Bite did the sword
> when we moored in Iva—

Then things went wrong, for there was no woman between Olav and Einar. The dance came to a halt, and Einar demanded that Olav should step away. The two of them argued until one of the older farmhands said that he would willingly leave the dance. Then Arnvid took up the song again:

> With the sword we struck—
> . . . .
> Sharp-weapon in battle
> bit at Sharp-skerry—

But there was constant confusion among the dancers. As the ballad continued, Arnvid was soon the only one who knew the words, though some remembered fragments of different verses. Olav and Einar kept on quarreling the whole time, and far too few were singing the melody. Arnvid was tired, and he said that he'd suffered several flesh wounds that had begun to throb now that he was moving about.

Then the line of dancers broke up. Some left to fling themselves down to sleep, while others stayed where they were, talking and demanding more to drink—or they said they wanted to dance again, but to one of the new ballads that was easier to follow.

Olav stood in the shadow of the posts, still holding Ingunn's hand. He returned his sword to its sheath.

"Come, let's go up to your loft room and talk," he whispered.

◆ ◆ ◆

Hand in hand they ran through the rain across the dark and deserted courtyard. They dashed up the stairs and paused just inside the door, gasping with apprehension, as if they'd been doing something unlawful. Then they threw their arms around each other.

Ingunn pulled the boy's head down toward her chest and sniffed at his hair.

"You smell of smoke," she murmured. "Oh no, oh no," she pleaded fearfully. He was pressing her body against the doorjamb.

"No . . . no . . . I need to leave," he whispered. "I'm leaving now," he kept on saying.

"Yes . . ." But she clung to him, trembling and dizzy, afraid he might do as he said and leave. She realized that they had both lost all control; any sense of what was past and what was present seemed to have been washed away by the flood of wild and unrestrained hours of the last night and day. And the two of them had ended up stranded here in this dark loft room. Why should they part? All they had was each other.

She felt the golden garland slide back from her forehead. Olav was feverishly running his hands through her flowing hair. The wreath fell off, and the silver rosettes clattered as they struck the floor. The boy grabbed fistfuls of her hair and held the tresses to his face as he burrowed his chin against her shoulder.

Then they heard Reidunn, the maidservant who shared Ingunn's sleeping loft. She was below in the courtyard, calling to someone.

They broke away from each other, shivering with guilt. Quick as lightning, Olav reached out to pull the door closed and latched it.

Reidunn came up to the gallery and knocked on the door, calling for Ingunn. The two children stood there in the pitch-dark, shaking, their hearts hammering.

The maidservant continued knocking, then pounded on the door. She must have decided that Ingunn had gone to bed and was sound asleep. They heard the stairs creak under her heavy tread. Out in the courtyard she called to another maid, and they realized she was going over to another building to sleep. Then Olav and Ingunn flew into each other's arms, as if they had escaped the greatest danger.

V

Olav awoke in utter darkness. He instantly remembered what happened and felt himself sink down where he lay. Icy tremors appeared above his eyebrows, and his heart abruptly shrank, the way a defenseless animal makes itself small when a hand reaches out to grab it.

Close to the wall lay Ingunn, breathing like an innocent and happy child as she slept. Terror and shame and sorrow washed over Olav, wave after wave. He lay motionless, as if the very marrow had been blasted out of every bone in his body. He wished so fervently that he could run away; he couldn't bear to hear her lament when she awakened from the blissful forgetfulness of sleep. Yet deep inside, he vaguely sensed that sneaking away was the one thing that could make worse what was already so terrible.

Then it occurred to him that he needed to slip out of the loft before anyone else was awake. He had to find out what time of night it was, but he lay there as if robbed of all strength.

Finally he jolted himself out of his torpor, slipped down from the bed, and went over to crack open the door. The clouds were pale crimson above the rooftops. It was at least an hour before sunrise.

While Olav got dressed, he happened to recall that the last time he'd shared a bed with Ingunn was at Christmas. He'd been furious because he'd had to give up his place in the main hall to a guest, only to be relegated to the bed belonging to Steinfinn's daughters. He had unkindly given Ingunn a shove when he thought she was taking up too much room, and he'd pushed at her when she, in her sleep, had poked him with her sharp elbows and knees. The memory of their innocence back then now weighed on him like the memory of the lost Garden of Eden.

He didn't dare stay here longer; he had to leave. But when he leaned over Ingunn and breathed in the scent of her hair, when he glimpsed her face and limbs, pale and faintly visible in the dark, then in spite of his remorse and shame he felt such a sweetness about this too. He leaned all the way down so his forehead nearly touched her shoulder, and again his heart tightened as he acknowledged the strange mixture of emotions: joy that his young bride was so delicate and lovely, and pain at the thought that she might suffer any harshness or cruelty.

Silently he vowed that never again would he cause her harm. After he'd made this promise, he felt a little braver about seeing her when she awoke. He touched his hand to her face and quietly called her name.

Ingunn abruptly sat up, for a moment dazed with sleep. Then she threw her arms around Olav, making him fall to his knees, with his upper body stretched out next to her in the bed.

She curled around him, pulling him into her slender arms. While he knelt there in that manner, burrowing his face in her marvelously silky soft and supple flesh, he had to clench his teeth so as not to burst into tears. He was both relieved and humbled because she was so gentle and good, neither whimpering nor casting blame. Overwhelmed by a great tenderness for her, yet filled with shame and sorrow and happiness, he didn't know what to do.

Then they heard a howl from down in the courtyard. The long, drawn-out, and eerie howling of a dog.

"That's Erp," whispered Olav. "He was yelping like that last night too. I wonder how he got out again." He crept over to the door.

"Olav, you're not leaving me, are you?" called Ingunn fearfully when she saw that he was already dressed and about to go out.

"I need to take my chances and see if I can slip out unseen," he whispered to her. "That hellish racket will soon wake the whole estate."

"Olav, Olav, don't go." She was now kneeling in the bed. When he ran back to hush her, she threw her arms around him and held on tight. Involuntarily he turned his head away as he removed her arms from around his neck. He drew the coverlet up over her.

"Don't you see that I have to leave?" he whispered. "Things are bad enough already."

Then she began to sob loudly. She flung herself down on the bed and wept and wept. Olav pulled the coverlet up to her chin and stood there helplessly in the dark as he quietly begged her not to cry. Finally he knelt down and slipped his arm under her neck. Then her sobs subsided a bit.

The dog out in the courtyard was barking as if possessed. Olav began rocking the girl. "Don't cry, my Ingunn, please don't cry." But his expression was stern and strained with worry.

Dogs didn't howl like that except at corpses and misfortune. And here he was, kneeling in the cool morning air and cradling the weeping girl in his arms as he became ruthlessly sober and his mind whirled.

He hadn't given much thought to what the price might be for their actions at Mattias Haraldssøn's estate; none of the others had either, as far as he could tell. But it made no difference now. There was nothing else Steinfinn could have done. Yet Olav had a bad feeling about that howling dog in the courtyard. Steinfinn's wounds were not insignificant; that was something Olav knew, for he had held his foster father's arm when Arnvid bandaged it. And he recalled the look on Steinfinn's face, once on the boat when they made their way home, and again when they rode up the mountainside and Kolbein had walked along, leading the horse while he supported his brother. And finally in the evening, when Steinfinn had said goodnight.

Olav suddenly realized how great his affection was for his foster father. He had taken Steinfinn for granted; he had been fond enough of the man, though without acknowledging that he'd also regarded him with some disdain all these years. Steinfinn's disposition was basically indolent, jocular, easygoing, and carefree. Then a bitter burden of sorrow and shame had been thrust upon him, and this lighthearted nobleman had seemed to bear it with such discomfort. Deep inside, Olav had felt some contempt for his foster father, whose character was so unlike his own. But then Steinfinn had taken action and shown what sort of man he was when it counted most, causing Olav to feel in his heart that he was fond of Steinfinn after all, and now he'd done this terrible thing to his foster father. He had brought dishonor upon himself and caused Ingunn the worst possible disgrace. Again his forehead felt icy cold, and his heart seemed to surge upward with a muffled roar. What if the worst misfortune had already occurred?

He pressed his brow against Ingunn's bosom. Why couldn't that dog be quiet out there? A whimper seemed to pass through Olav's soul, homesick as he was for the childhood that was now mercilessly gone. He had a terrifying sense of how young and alone he was. Then he pulled himself together. He would stand straight-backed, determined to suppress any sigh that might cross his lips. Because of his actions, he had assumed the responsibilities of a grown man. It was useless to whine afterward. And surely there must be some way out of this.

At last he heard someone go out to scold the dog and try to bring it indoors. From what he could tell, Erp ran off instead, up to the pasture. Everything was now quiet outside.

Olav wrapped his arms protectively around Ingunn and kissed her forehead at the hairline before letting her go. Then he grabbed his sword and slung the strap over his right shoulder. Feeling the weight of the weapon against his hip seemed to bolster his courage at once. He went over to the door and peered out from the gallery.

"There's nobody in the courtyard right now. I need to slip out."

Ingunn began whimpering.

"No, oh no, don't go. I'm too frightened to stay here alone."

Olav quickly realized it would be useless to try to convince her otherwise.

"Then get up and put on your clothes," he whispered. "If they see us outside together, I don't suppose anyone will suspect anything."

He went out and sat down on the loft stairs to wait. With both hands he gripped the pommel of his sword, resting his chin on his hands and looking at the rose-red glow reflected in the western sky, which faded as the light in the east grew stronger and paler. The grass in the fields was wet with dew and rain.

He was thinking back on all the late nights and early mornings of summer that he'd spent with Ingunn; now the memory of their games and teasing tormented him, filling him with bitter disappointment and resentment. A betrayer—that's what he'd become. Yet it felt as if he too had been betrayed. They had run and played on a flower-covered slope but hadn't had the sense to see or perceive that it would end at a precipice. Before they knew it, they had fallen over the side. And there they now lay. It would do no good to whine about it. That's how he tried to console himself.

After they were married, they would nevertheless receive the customary honor and respect, and then they would no doubt forget about the secret disgrace, which this fall clearly was. But he had been looking forward to their wedding with such anticipation—that day when everyone would pay tribute to their honor, his and Ingunn's, as they took their places as fully acknowledged adults. Now there would be a hidden taste of bitterness when the guests drank to the bridegroom, for neither of them deserved such tributes.

What he had done was considered the most disreputable of conduct. They would be gaining a boy as their kinsman, not a man from whom they could expect loyalty when it was required. A man should pay for a boat or a horse or a bride in the proper manner before he made use of them, unless he was sorely pressed.

For folks of their standing, Olav had thought three months would be the shortest amount of time deemed suitable before they could proceed after the agreements regarding the marriage properties had been announced here at Frettastein. Then he could celebrate their wedding at Hestviken. But now that Steinfinn had the matter of the fire and the murder on his hands, perhaps it would not seem unreasonable if Olav pushed the wedding forward. Then Steinfinn, instead of serving as guardian for two underage wards, would have a wealthy son-in-law from whom he would be entitled to ask for help when having to pay fines and such.

Now Ingunn came outside to join Olav and whispered, without daring to look at him, "If my father knew about what we've done, Olav, he would surely kill us both." But Olav merely gave a brief laugh and reached for her hand.

"That would mean he was a much more stupid man than he is. He has enough on his mind right now, Ingunn. He'll have more use for a kinsman who's alive than one who is dead. But you must know it would be the worst misfortune," he whispered dejectedly, "if he, or anyone else, should find out about this."

It was just before sunrise and icy cold outside. Everything was wet. Olav and Ingunn huddled on the stairs to the loft room, dozing as the yellow-white light from the east spread higher and higher across the sky and the birds sang louder and louder, although most birdsong had faded away for the year.

"There's that dog again!" said Olav, springing to his feet. The dog had come back to the courtyard and taken up position outside the big loft room to howl. Olav and Ingunn ran down the stairs, and Olav began shouting and calling to Erp. The dog had always obeyed him, but this time it refused even to let him near.

Arnvid Finnssøn came out of the main hall and tried, but he couldn't catch the dog either. Each time one of the men came close, the dog would take off and then stop a short distance away to resume howling.

"Are the two of you still wearing the clothes you had on last night?" Arnvid asked, looking from one to the other.

Ingunn's face turned bright red, and she quickly looked away.

Olav said, "Yes. We sat and talked up in the loft room, and then we fell asleep right where we were sitting, until this dog woke us."

Now more folks, both men and women, came out to stare at the dog. Last of all came Kolbein.

Suddenly someone yelled, "Look!"

Up on the loft gallery of the big storeroom they caught a glimpse of Steinfinn Toressøn. His face was so changed as to be almost beyond recognition. He shouted something and then disappeared, as if he'd collapsed.

Kolbein raced over to the loft room, but the storeroom door was latched. Arnvid ran over to join him, and the other men helped Kolbein stand on Arnvid's shoulders so he could hoist himself up onto the gallery. The next moment he leaned over the railing, looking greatly distressed.

"He's bleeding like a slaughtered ox. Send someone up here, but not his maidservants," Kolbein said, and a shudder seemed to pass through him.

A moment later he opened the door below from the inside. Arnvid and some of the hired men went in while Tora and the maidservants ran off to get water and wine, along with linen cloths and ointments.

Arnvid Finnssøn appeared in the storeroom doorway, and all the fear and dread that had gathered in those waiting outside was released in a collective gasp when they saw him. Arnvid stepped forward as if sleepwalking. Then he caught sight of Olav Audunssøn and motioned for him to approach.

"Ingebjørg—" His jaw was trembling so hard that his teeth chattered. "Ingebjørg is dead. May God save us all, poor and sinful souls that we are!

"You have to take Ingunn as well as Tora and the boys over to the main hall. Kolbein wants me to be the one to tell them."

He turned on his heel and led the way.

"What about Steinfinn?" asked Olav urgently. "In God's name . . . Surely it's not . . . Did he kill her?"

"I don't know." Arnvid looked on the verge of fainting. "She was dead, lying in the bed. Steinfinn's wound has reopened and the blood is gushing out of him. That's all I know."

Olav quickly turned toward Ingunn when she came over to them. He held out his hand to stop her as he repeated Arnvid's words.

"May God save us all, poor and sinful souls that we are! Ingunn, Ingunn . . . you must try . . . you must try and let me console you, dear one!"

He took her by the arm and led her away. She had started weeping, quietly and steadily, like a child who refuses to allow terror to take hold.

Later in the day Olav sat in the main hall with the young maidens. Arnvid had told them what Steinfinn was able to recount about his wife's death, and Olav had boldly held his arm around Ingunn's shoulder as they listened, though he wasn't aware he was doing that.

Steinfinn himself knew very little. Before he and Ingebjørg had gone to bed, she had tended to his arm. He'd slept restlessly, delirious with fever during the night, but he seemed to recall that his wife had gotten up several times. She had given him something to drink. He was awakened by the howling dog. By then she was dead, lying between him and the wall.

Ingebjørg had been plagued by fainting spells over the past few years. Arnvid thought that the joy at recovering their honor might have been too much for her. Ingunn lay across Olav's lap and wept as he stroked her back. The fact was that in the first terrifying moments, he, and presumably others as well, had imagined something much worse—although God only knew why Steinfinn would have wished for his wife to die. Yet Arnvid's words released all of them from the rigid strain of apprehension. An underlying thought was trying to surface in Olav's mind, but he tried to fend it off, for it was too shameful, but . . . Steinfinn had said he thought he would follow his wife into death. No matter what happened now, it was possible that Steinfinn and Ingebjørg would never find out that he had betrayed them. Olav couldn't help feeling relieved—both oddly numb yet more confident.

There had been a moment when he'd felt he might fall apart. Right after Ingebjørg had been carried away, he happened to meet some women coming out of the loft room. As was the wont of servant women, they couldn't help pausing to show him the bloody cloths they were holding while they loudly wailed and lamented. One of them had gathered up all the flowers from the floor and piled them on a sheepskin rug. The meadowsweet was drenched in blood, and on top of the flowers lay the strips of linen that Arnvid had cut from both his own shirt and Olav's to bandage Steinfinn's arm. The cloths were soaked with bright and shiny blood. Against Olav's will, everything suddenly came together in a vision of what had happened the night before, when they stood there in the meadow below the burning estate. And he couldn't bear the thought of carrying such horrors within him—the misfortune of his foster parents, and then his own sin against them. It felt as if he'd raped his own sister. The boy's whole world shattered and fell around him in pieces.

His mind couldn't seem to contain everything that had happened, but then the events once again receded. And when Steinfinn's children turned to him, now that no one else on the estate had time to see to them, that in itself seemed to Olav a form of salvation, as he kept watch over them like an older brother.

Tora wept heavily and talked a great deal. She had always been the most sensible and thoughtful of the children. She told Olav that she found it especially heartbreaking that her parents weren't allowed to enjoy some happiness together after all those years of undeserved sorrow and shame. Olav said he thought it would have been much worse if Ingebjørg had died before Steinfinn had exacted his revenge. Tora also knew full well that the redeeming of her parents' honor might prove costly. And she was worried about peace for her mother's soul and the well-being of herself and her siblings if Kolbein should be put in charge. She didn't think much of her uncle's intelligence.

Olav said that Kolbein had at least shown Steinfinn the true loyalty of a kinsman. Mattias had not been killed without cause, and the fire had been started by accident. And it had to be said that Ingebjørg had lived a pious and Christian life during the last few years. She was given an impressive funeral. No one told the children what some folks were saying: that if Bishop Torfinn had been home, it wasn't certain that the mistress would have been laid to rest with such grand honors until it was determined whether the dead woman had played any part in the murder plans.

Olav found the greatest solace from Arnvid Finnssøn. They slept in the same bed, and whenever Arnvid wasn't keeping vigil over his ill kinsman, the two young men would talk far into the night.

It heartened Olav, just as it comforted everyone on the estate, that Steinfinn bore his fate with such manly dignity. He had lost a great deal of blood, yet his wound was not the sort that seemed likely to cause the death of such a strong and robust man. Yet Steinfinn said he knew that he would die, and he appeared to waste away as he drifted toward his imminent demise. Olav thought this was, in a sense, the most seemly end to everything that had taken place at Frettastein. It would have felt much stranger if Steinfinn and Ingebjørg had been able to resume their old, carefree life with all the daily bustle and noise from the past, after everything they had both endured.

And now they would never know about the new shame that had descended upon them through their daughter. He had escaped having to account for that.

It was mostly his concern for Ingunn that tormented Olav. He was plagued by a constant uneasiness. Her grief was mute and still. She sat as silent as a stone while he and Tora talked. Occasionally her eyes would fill with tears and her lips would tremble with quiet pain. A few tears would spill out, but not a sound did she utter. Her despair made her seem so far away and so alone that he couldn't bear to look at her. Why couldn't she mourn and talk and seek solace with the rest of them? Sometimes he felt her glancing at him, but when he turned toward her, he would catch a glimpse of an expression aggrieved and helpless, before she quickly looked away. The words of a song kept ringing in his ears, the refrain from one of the new ballads that he'd heard down at the church during the past winter. He unwillingly re-called the words: "Or are you grieving so for your honor?" He was of-ten on the verge of feeling angry with her because he couldn't banish from his thoughts the nightly darkness that had taken a stranglehold on him when he initially reacted with remorse and sorrow at their fall from grace.

But now Olav was careful to guard his own emotions as he strove to treat her like a good brother. After that first morning he had avoided being alone with Ingunn. And he felt more confident and less guilty because he'd asked Tora to persuade her sister to once again sleep with her in the old loft room. He thought that in Tora's care, Ingunn would be safe—also from him.

VI

One evening Olav came riding down the slope through the forest. He'd gone up to the mountain pasture on an errand for Grim, the farm manager. The evening sun was just about to sink behind the tops of the spruce trees when he came upon the place where the path passed along the lower end of the tarn a little north of the estate. The forest towered around the brown water of the small lake so that darkness fell quickly in that spot. That's when he saw Ingunn, sitting in the heather right next to the path.

He reined in his horse as he came alongside her.

"Why are you sitting here?" he asked with surprise. It would not be safe out here after the sun set.

She looked terribly disheveled. She'd been eating blueberries, so her lips and fingers were colored blue. And she'd been crying, so her face was swollen, and then she had wiped her cheeks with her blueberry hands.

"Has Steinfinn taken a turn for the worse?" asked Olav solemnly.

Ingunn bent forward and began crying even louder.

"He's not dead, is he?" asked the boy in the same tone of voice.

Ingunn managed to stammer that her father was better today.

He gave another tug on the reins because his horse Elgsblakken wanted to continue on. Olav was no longer surprised by Ingunn's spells of weeping, though they annoyed him a bit. It would have been better if she could behave as Tora did. By now Tora had made peace with her grief over her mother and seldom cried. There might soon be plenty of other matters that would provoke tears from all of them.

"What is it?" he asked now, a little impatiently. "What do you want from me?"

Ingunn looked up, her face filthy and tear-stained. When Olav made no move to dismount from his horse, she covered her eyes with her hands and kept on weeping.

"What's wrong with you?" he asked, but she didn't reply. Then he got off his horse and went over to her.

"What is it?" he pleaded fearfully, taking her hands away from her face. For a long while he could get no response from her.

He kept on asking, "What is it? Why are you crying like this?"

"Why shouldn't I cry?" she sobbed, bending low, "when you no longer want to speak to me."

"Why shouldn't I want to speak to you?" he asked in surprise.

"My only sin was to do what you wanted," she lamented. "I asked you to leave, but you refused to let me go. And since then you haven't thought me worthy of even a single word. Soon I'll be both fatherless and motherless, and you're as hard as flint and iron, turning your back and refusing even to look at me. Yet we grew up together as brother and sister. It's only because I was so fond of you that I forgot both proper and seemly behavior on that one occasion."

"This is worse than anything I've ever heard! I think you've lost what little sense you had!"

"And now you've just tossed me aside like this! But you don't know, Olav," she screamed, in a frenzy. "You can't know whether I might be carrying your child!"

"Shush! Don't shout like that," he retorted. "You can't very well know that yourself, not yet," he said angrily. "And I don't know what you mean when you say I won't talk to you. It seems to me that I've done nothing else these past weeks but talk and talk, and I never get even three words out of you in reply, because you keep on crying and crying."

"You spoke to me only because you had to," she gasped between sobs, "whenever Tora and the others were near. But you shun me as if I were tainted with leprosy. Not once have you sought me out so we could talk alone, just the two of us. I have good reason to cry, when I think about this summer and how you used to come to my loft room every evening."

Olav's face turned bright red.

"I think that would be ill-advised right now," he said curtly. He spat on a corner of his cloak and used it to wipe her face, though it did little good. "I've mostly been thinking about what would be best for you," he whispered.

She looked up at him, her expression perplexed and deeply sad. Then he pulled her close. "I only wish you well, Ingunn."

Then they both flinched. Something had moved on the scree on the other side of the lake. There was not a soul in sight, but the lone birch sapling that stood on the scree was shaking as if someone had grabbed hold of the trunk. It was still daylight, but the surrounding forest was bringing darkness to the small lake. Mist was rising from the tarn and the marsh at the east end.

Olav went over to his horse.

"We need to leave this place," he said quietly. "You can sit behind me to ride."

"Won't you come to me in the loft so we can talk?" she pleaded as he slapped the reins. "Come over after the evening meal."

"I will do that if it's want you want," he said after a moment.

She wrapped her arms around him as they rode down toward the estate. Olav felt strangely relieved. If this was how she viewed matters, then he needn't worry about all his good intentions to avoid any further opportunities that might prove tempting. But he also felt humiliated that she had rejected the sacrifice he had been willing to make for her sake.

It suddenly occurred to him that it wasn't true what she'd said about her asking him to leave, and then he'd refused to let her go. Yet he pushed this thought away as a breach of trust. If that's what she said . . . He hadn't been sober enough to swear that he fully remembered everything.

The following evening Olav went over to the loft above the store-house where Steinfinn lay. Arnvid opened the hatch to let him come in. Arnvid was alone with the ill man.

It was dark inside, for Steinfinn suffered so much from the cold that he couldn't bear to have the door open to the gallery. A few rays of sunlight seeped in through the cracks between the timbers, slicing through the dust-sated darkness and casting golden flashes of light on the hide coverlets hanging from the roofbeams. A heavy, oppressive smell filled the loft.

Olav went over to the bed to greet his foster father. He hadn't seen him in many days and only reluctantly had come here now. But Steinfinn was asleep, whimpering quietly as he slept. Olav couldn't see his face as he lay in the dark next to the wall.

There had been no change, either for the worse or for the better, Arnvid told Olav. "Would you stay with him for a while so I can lie down to rest?"

Olav said he would gladly do so. Arnvid tossed some coverlets on the floor and lay down.

Then Olav said, "This isn't easy for me, Arnvid. I don't wish to disturb Steinfinn, as ill as he is, but it seems to me that before he dies, Ingunn and I need to hear his wishes regarding our marriage."

Arnvid was silent.

"I know it's not an opportune time," said Olav vehemently. "But with such grave matters hanging over all of us, I think it's necessary to make clear everything that can be made clear. I don't know whether anyone but Steinfinn is aware of the agreement he made with my father regarding our property."

When Arnvid didn't reply, Olav said, "For me, it's of the greatest importance that I receive Ingunn from her father's hand."

"Yes, I know that," said Arnvid.

A short time later Olav could hear that he had fallen asleep.

The little arrows of sunlight disappeared. Olav sat alone and awake in the dark, feeling the uneasiness inside him like an ache in the middle of his chest.

He had to put right the wrong he had done. This was something he had now learned: that good intentions were useless. It was impossible to turn back from the wrongful path that he and Ingunn had taken. And he sensed that this new knowledge had made his own soul both rougher and rawer. But he couldn't bear to stand at Steinfinn's bier as his unbeknownst son-in-law. He now knew that secret shame was a heavy burden to carry.

Before he died, Steinfinn needed to give Ingunn to Olav. "I know that," Arnvid had said. Olav felt heat flood through his body. What was it that Arnvid knew? When he'd gone back to his sleeping place in the main hall at daybreak, Olav wasn't sure whether Arnvid was actually asleep or merely pretending.

Olav sprang to his feet when the hatch in the floor was raised. The women were bringing candles and food for the ill man. Feeling uncertain, Olav thought about the shadowy visions he'd seen in the daze of sleep: he was walking with Ingunn along the lower end of the tarn; they were following the stream that flowed into the small lake. Then he was with her in the loft room. Memories of fevered caresses in the dark merged with images of the scree up on the mountain cleft. He was lying with Ingunn, holding her in his arms, yet at the same time he seemed to be lifting her over some big fallen trees. Last of all, he'd dreamed that they were walking along the path in the meadow where it opened to the countryside and Lake Mjøsa far below.

He was tempted to believe this was a good portent, signifying that he and Ingunn would soon be leaving the valley together.

Steinfinn asked the women not to bother when they woke him to tend to his wound. He said there was no need and he wanted to be left alone. Dalla refused to listen. She raised up the heavy body of the man and tended to him as if he were an infant. She asked Olav to hold the candle. Arnvid slept soundly, dead tired as he was.

Steinfinn's face was almost unrecognizable; unshaven for weeks, his reddish-brown whiskers had grown all the way up his cheeks. He turned his face to the wall, but Olav saw from the strained cords in his neck that he was struggling not to cry out when Dalla loosened the bandages, which had stuck to the wound.

The secret revulsion that Olav had always felt at the sight and smell of infected wounds now overwhelmed him with nauseating force. Gangrene had set in, and the wound no longer looked like the gash from a knife; pus had appeared, along with spongy gray patches with raw red holes that were bleeding slightly.

Ingunn came over to stand beside Olav. She was pale, staring at her father with big, frightened eyes. Olav had to give her a poke to remind her to give Dalla the new bandage that she was reaching for. Again Olav felt sorrow and shame like a stab to his heart. How could they have forgotten about this ill and suffering man as they'd done? But in that dark loft room, with the two of them alone and lying close together . . . he vaguely sensed how difficult it was then to think with compassion and trust about someone else who wasn't there.

"Stay here," he said to Ingunn when the other women were about to leave. "Tonight we must speak to your father," he added in explanation. He saw that she looked more fearful than happy, and he wasn't pleased.

Steinfinn lay still, exhausted from the pain. Olav asked Ingunn to bring some food for them to eat while they waited.

She had gathered up everything good she could find, Ingunn said when she came back, and with a smile she offered him the food. As Olav sat holding a bowl on his lap to eat, she blew gently on the back of his neck. She now seemed to be bursting with tenderness and ardor. Again Olav felt his heart ache. Here they sat, just out of sight of his ill foster father, and he couldn't decide whether he was pleased by her show of affection or not.

Arnvid stirred. Ingunn jumped up from Olav's lap and began putting together some food for him.

Suddenly Steinfinn asked from where he lay in bed, "Who is that with you, Arnvid and Ingunn?"

"Olav is here, Father," said the girl.

Olav gathered his courage and went over to the bed. He said, "There is a matter I'd like to discuss with you, my foster father. That's why I stayed behind when the women finished tending to you."

"Were you here then? I didn't see you." Steinfinn motioned for the youth to come closer. "Sit here for a while and talk to me, Olav, my foster son. You've been dragged into our troubles, and now we need to talk about what you should do when I die. I think you should go back home to Hestviken and seek the support of your own kinsmen."

"Yes, Foster Father. That's what I wanted to ask you about. I too think it would be best, but I should wed Ingunn before leaving. Then your kinsmen will be spared the long journey to Hestviken, now that all of you are facing great discord ahead."

Steinfinn's gaze wavered, his expression uncertain.

"Let me say this, Olav. I remember well what Audun and I discussed. But even you must realize, my boy, that I can't help it if my position is not the same as it was back then. Now Kolbein and Ivar will be the ones who will marry off my daughters."

Arnvid came over to join them. He said, "Do you recall, kinsman, that I went with you to the *ting* that summer? I was also present when you and Audun promised the children to each other."

"You were only a boy," Steinfinn quickly replied. "You weren't old enough to be a witness."

"That's true," said Arnvid. "But hear me out, Steinfinn. It has happened before, in dire times, when conscripts were being summoned as soldiers for an incursion, or a man was preparing to set off on a long journey. Then, in the presence of witnesses, he would give his daughter to the one to whom she had been promised, but without a wedding. He simply announced the marriage banns before trustworthy witnesses and stated what had been agreed regarding dowry and bridal price. Then he declared that he wished for the betrothal to be considered a binding marriage from that day forth."

Steinfinn turned his head to look at the three young people.

Arnvid eagerly went on. "Brother Vegard arrived today. And I'm here too—your cousin—along with your old servants who know of the agreement that you and Audun made. You could announce the marriage banns, and the monk and I would be the main witnesses. Then these two young people could live in the old loft until it's a suitable time for Olav to travel south with Ingunn. Brother Vegard could bless the wedding ale bowl and their bed, and he could compose the documents regarding their shared properties."

Steinfinn paused to think for a moment.

"No," he then said curtly, and he suddenly seemed very tired. "My daughter shall not go to bed with her betrothed like a crofter's child without having a wedding feast. If that happened it might be later disputed whether or not she was a lawfully wed wife. I don't understand why you would even consider such a thing," he added vehemently, "especially as young as these two children are. Olav may soon have trouble enough, now that he has to meet these kinsmen of his who are strangers to him. I don't want to send him off burdened with an outlawed man's daughter who was smuggled out of the district without the presence of either his or my kinsmen when she was given to him in marriage. If Olav were a full-grown man, we might have considered it, but as things stand, I hardly think it would be a lawful marriage. Child that he is, he cannot enter into a marriage arrangement on his own."

"It seems to me enough that my father agreed to betroth me to the maiden," said Olav. "And you have been my guardian ever since."

"You have no idea what you're saying. You begged to come with us, and that may be ample reason for Mattias's heirs to turn against you. Yet they will win little support if your kinsmen can claim you were an underage boy in my service. But it would be a different matter if you are a married man, of legal age and my son-in-law. No, I owe it to my friend Audun not to allow such foolishness, especially now, when I may soon meet him again."

"Listen to me, Steinfinn," said Olav. "No matter what, after you die I'll be too old to obey others, meaning these kinsmen of mine whom I've never seen or heard from. I would rather marry and be my own master and take the risk."

"You talk like a child," said Steinfinn impatiently. "It will be as I say. But leave me in peace now. I have no more strength tonight."

Before Arnvid and Olav went to bed, Arnvid spoke of the matter with Brother Vegard. But the monk resolutely refused to talk to Steinfinn in an attempt to change his mind. He thought Steinfinn had made a just and wise decision. And as a priest, he was not allowed to be present at a wedding that was arranged without first having the marriage banns read in the parish church on three days when mass was held. It was also doubtful whether Olav, underage as he was, could arrange for the bridal price himself, in order for the marriage to be considered lawful. And besides, Brother Vegard had never approved of folks celebrating a wedding without a wedding mass. He also had no intention of composing documents or the like; he would leave Frettastein at once if they made that sort of arrangement, based on such dubious terms.

Steinfinn grew worse over the following days, and on those occasions when Olav went to see his foster father, he couldn't bear to mention the matter of his marriage again. Nor did he speak any more of it to Arnvid.

Then Ivar Toressøn, who was Steinfinn's full-fledged brother, arrived at Frettastein along with Kolbein and his two sons. They had received word that the ill man was now nearing the end. The day after the arrival of these men, Olav asked Arnvid to go outside with him so the two of them could speak in private.

He hadn't dared to talk to Arnvid before, fearing what he might say. During the past week, Olav had spent several nights with Ingunn in her loft room. She too was disappointed and sad that her father had unexpectedly caused such difficulties regarding their betrothal. But it didn't occur to her that it meant anything other than a slight delay for their wedding at Hestviken. She was grieving terribly over her father's suffering and her mother's death, and overcome with distress, she clung to Olav. She seemed completely done in by sorrow when she wasn't allowed to hide in his embrace. Eventually Olav gave up all thought of holding back; he allowed himself to be drawn deeper and deeper into love's fervor. She was so sweet, after all. But apprehension and guilt were ever-present torments. After she fell asleep, curled up close to his chest, he would lie there in dreadful anguish. It was also disturbing that Ingunn was so trusting in her love; she seemed to harbor neither worry nor fear. When he crept out of the loft room toward morning, he was both exhausted and disheartened.

Olav was afraid that Ingunn would end up in misfortune, but he couldn't bear to mention this to her. He was even less willing to tell her that he feared much greater difficulties. It had never before entered his mind that the validity of their betrothal might be questioned. Yet all of a sudden a new light had been cast upon the position he'd held all these years on Steinfinn's estate. He'd never been treated any differently than Steinfinn's own children, but even though the parents had paid such scant attention to their offspring over the past few years, it was still strange that they had never said a single word about Olav's eventual marriage to Ingunn. Nor had Steinfinn ever tried to find out how the inheritance of his future son-in-law was being managed. The fact that Kolbein had never cared much for Olav had seemed of little concern. Kolbein treated most people with arrogance and hostility. And Olav had never gotten on well with Kolbein's thick-skulled sons. It had never occurred to him there might be any reason for this other than that they considered themselves grown men while they thought him a child. Now it suddenly seemed strange to Olav that all of them would treat him in such a manner if the whole time they had viewed him as someone who would become their kinsman. "In my service," Steinfinn had said. Yet Olav had never been paid wages on the estate, so there was no need to take these words to heart. His foster father had merely intended to provide a way for him to escape the accusation of murder.

Olav headed north across the fields and up to the forest. When he reached the slopes covered only by moss, he stopped. From there he and Arnvid could look down at the buildings on the estate, situated as they were with the steep meadows below and the forest all around.

"We can sit here," said Olav. "In this place we'll be safe from anyone listening to us." Yet he remained standing as Arnvid sat down and looked at the youth.

Olav drew his white eyebrows together as he stood there. The lock of fair hair in front had grown so long that it now nearly hid his entire forehead, making his face seem wider and shorter and more taciturn. His firm, pale lips were pressed tightly together. He looked defiant and unhappy, and he'd grown older in appearance over the past few weeks. The bright and innocent childishness had suited the boy well because he was full-grown and had such a serious demeanor, but it had now vanished like dew into thin air. A different sort of solemnity had come over his angry, tormented face. And his pale and fair complexion no longer appeared as healthy. There were dark shadows under his eyes, and he looked tired.

"You never mentioned to me that you were present when Ingunn and I were promised to each other," said Olav.

"I was only fourteen," replied Arnvid. "My presence was of no importance."

"Who else was there?" asked Olav.

"My father and my brother Magnus, Viking and Magnhild from Berg, Tore Bring of Vik and his wife. The others were strangers to me. The hall was full of people, but I don't remember seeing anyone else that I knew."

"Was there no one accompanying my father?" asked Olav.

"No. Audun Ingolfssøn was alone."

Olav stood in silence for a moment. Then he sat down and said, "That means that of those witnesses, the only ones still alive are Magnhild and Tore of Vik. But maybe they could point out some of the other witnesses."

"I suppose they could."

"If they're willing," said Olav in a low voice. "What about you, Arnvid? Your testimony might have little import, since you were only a child, but what is your opinion? Were we betrothed on that night, Ingunn and I?"

"Yes," said Arnvid firmly. "I have never thought otherwise. Don't you remember that they made you give her a ring as a token of your betrothal?"

Olav nodded.

"Steinfinn must have that ring somewhere," said Arnvid. "Would you be able to recognize it? That seems to me sufficient proof of what took place."

"I remember that ring well. It was my mother's signet ring, engraved with her name and an image of the Mother of God on a green stone. Father had promised it to me. I remember I wasn't pleased that I was supposed to give it to Ingunn." He laughed a bit.

Neither of them spoke for a while.

Then Olav asked quietly, "What did you think of Steinfinn's response when I asked him about the matter?"

"I don't know what to say to that," replied Arnvid.

"I'm not certain I can trust that Steinfinn has spoken to Kolbein," said Olav more hesitantly. "Or whether he realizes it was a binding agreement when Steinfinn and my father promised that I should have Ingunn."

"Kolbein will not be alone in making decisions for the children," said Arnvid.

Olav shrugged, his smile scornful.

"As I told you," Arnvid went on, "I've always considered that a binding betrothal agreement was made on that evening."

"So the men who will now be making the decisions regarding marriage pacts cannot break the agreement?"

"No, they can't. I seem to recall hearing about this when I was in school. A betrothal agreement cannot be broken if it was made by the fathers of both children, unless the children themselves speak to their parish priest when they reach the appropriate age—I believe it is fourteen winters—and request that the betrothal be dissolved. But in that case, both of them must swear to the priest that she is a pure and chaste maiden."

The faces of the two young men had now flushed bright red, and they avoided looking at each other.

"And if they were unable to swear such an oath?" Olav asked at last, his voice barely audible.

Arnvid looked down at his hands.

"Then it would be *consensus matrimonialis*, as it's called in Latin. It means that by their actions they have agreed to their parents' wishes, and if either of them should later wed someone else, either by force or willingly, then it would be considered whoredom."

Olav nodded.

"I wonder if you could help me," he said after a moment. "I need to find out what Steinfinn has done with the ring."

Arnvid mumbled something. Then they both got to their feet and walked down the slope.

"Autumn will come early this year," Olav remarked. Yellow leaves were visible among the green on the birch trees, and in the fields the grain stalks had faded in the midst of tall thistles and ragwort. Drifting white specks filled the clear air, glittering in the sunlight—seeds from the willow trees and withered fireweed.

The evening sun shone directly into Olav's face, making him squint. His eyes gleamed, icy-blue and piercing, from under his white lashes. The line of fair, downy hair on his upper lip looked golden against the boy's milky-white skin. Arnvid felt a painful ache in his chest when he saw how handsome his friend was. He pictured his own appearance—dark and ugly as a troll, with hunched shoulders and a short neck—in comparison to Olav's robust and resplendent youth. It seemed only reasonable that Ingunn would hold such great affection for him.

Whether the two young people were right or wrong, it would fall to others to decide. He would help them as best he could. He had always liked Olav and found him to be steadfast and dependable. And Ingunn, who was so weak . . . That may have been why he'd always held such affection for the little maiden; she looked as if a hand might break her in half.

The air was stifling in the loft room that evening, making it hard for the holy candle, which they lit every night for the dying man, to burn very strongly. It gave off only a lackluster and drowsy light.

Steinfinn lay still, utterly exhausted. His fever was not as great, but he'd spent a long time talking with his brothers, and that had taken a toll on him. Then, while his wound was being tended, he'd felt so drained that tears had poured down into his beard when Dalla had found it necessary to use force to remove some of the pus.

Finally, late at night, Steinfinn seemed to be sleeping more calmly. Arnvid and Olav stayed with him, but they eventually realized the oppressive air was making them so tired that they were having a hard time staying awake.

"Well," Arnvid whispered at last. "Shall we look for the ring?"

"I suppose we should." Olav cringed at the very thought, and he could see that it was weighing on Arnvid as well, but it had to be done. As quietly as two thieves they searched Steinfinn's clothes and pulled his keys from the pouch on his belt. As they did this, it occurred to Olav that once a person stepped off the honest path, he could easily encounter such rough terrain that he might have to take many more leaps aside. But he could think of no other way.

Yet as he knelt in front of Steinfinn's clothing chest with Arnvid, Olav didn't think he'd ever before felt as dreadful as he did now. In unison they both cast a glance at the bed. It was as if they were robbing a corpse.

Arnvid found the small box adorned with decorative bands of wrought iron. That's where Steinfinn kept his most precious jewelry. They had to try one key after another before they found the one that would open the lock.

Crouching down, they rifled through the brooches, chains, and buttons. "Here it is," said Olav, breathing a great sigh of relief.

The two men held the ring up to the candlelight. It was a gold ring set with a big green stone. Arnvid could make out the engraving around the image of the Mother of God holding the child beneath the eaves of a house, with a woman kneeling at her side. *Sigillum Ceciliae Beornis Filiae.*

"Do you want to take it with you?" asked Arnvid.

"No. It will be of no use, as proof of the agreement, unless it's found with Steinfinn's possessions after he dies," said Olav.

Then they relocked the box and cleared everything away.

Arnvid asked, "Will you sleep now, Olav?"

"No, I will gladly wait and let you sleep first. I'm not tired."

Arnvid lay down on the bench. After a moment he said, sounding wide awake, "I wish it had not been necessary for us to do that."

"I wish the same," replied Olav with a quaver in his voice.

Surely it's not a great sin. It can't be, he thought. Yet it was a terrible thing to have done. And he was frightened, for it seemed to him a bad omen for the life that lay ahead of him. Was it right for a man to feel compelled to do so much—and even more—that he found as abhorrent and unspeakable as what he'd just done?

They took turns keeping vigil until morning. It made Olav happy every time he was able to do some small service for his foster father, offering him something to drink or straightening the bedclothes.

Finally, early in the day, Steinfinn awoke and asked, "Are the two of you still here?" His voice was weak, but clear and alert. "Come over here, Olav," he said.

Both of the young men approached the bed. Steinfinn held out his good hand toward Olav.

"Do you harbor so little anger toward me, my foster son, that you've kept vigil with me all night even though I refused to do as you wished regarding what we spoke of on that evening a short time ago? You have always been kind and obedient, Olav. May God bless you all your days. As surely as I need God's mercy, I want you to know that if I were able to manage things myself, I would have kept my word to Audun. If I was going to live, I would have been well pleased to have you as my son-in-law."

Olav knelt down and kissed his foster father's hand. He couldn't bear to reply. In his heart he was begging Steinfinn to say the words that could rescue him from all difficulties. But shame and guilt kept him from speaking.

That was the last time he spoke with Steinfinn Toressøn. Olav and Arnvid were still asleep in the afternoon when Haftor Kolbeinssøn came to wake them. Steinfinn's death throes had begun, and everyone on the estate went up to the loft room to be with him.

VII

Brother Vegard had given Steinfinn absolution in articulo mortis, and then the man had received a splendid burial. Steinfinn's kinsmen and friends spoke boastful words at the funeral feast. They swore that Mattias Haraldssøn would be judged unworthy of receiving any compensation for his murder. No one had yet heard from the dead man's heirs, but they all lived in different parts of the country. There was also a feeling of unrest in the air; rumors were flying over the villages about weighty events supposedly in the offing. And Steinfinn's kinsmen acted as if they were good friends with the men who would now hold the most power in the land while the king and duke were still children.

Only a small part of Steinfinn's debts and possessions were fully accounted for when the estate was divided among his underage children. His kinsmen behaved as if tremendous wealth were involved, yet in private they hinted otherwise.

Arnvid Finnssøn was to stay at Frettastein with the children until Haftor Kolbeinssøn celebrated his wedding at the new year. Then Haftor would move to the estate to take charge on behalf of Hallvard, Steinfinn's older son, until the boy came of age.

Steinfinn's brothers remained at Frettastein for a few days after the guests had departed following the funeral feast. The evening before they were to head south again, the men were drinking ale as usual after the food had been cleared away. Then Arnvid rose to his feet and motioned for Olav to come and stand before him.

"As you can see, Ivar and Kolbein, here is my friend, Olav Audunssøn, who has asked me to put forth a matter to discuss with you. Before he died, Steinfinn mentioned that Olav ought to travel home to his own estate and speak to his kinsmen regarding the bride's dowry and the groom's gift for Ingunn, now that he is about to wed her. Yet, as matters stand, we thought it would be best to settle this question at once and celebrate Olav's wedding here instead. Then neither we nor his kinsmen would have to travel long distances now that winter is approaching and our position is so uncertain. For that reason, Olav has asked me to tell you that he is offering a guarantee—and I am willing to vouch for him up to an amount of sixteen *mark* in gold—that he will put aside a portion of Ingunn's dowry so that she will become the owner of one-third of his estate, in addition to her bedclothes, clothing, and jewelry. He also offers an assurance that he will repay whoever hosts his wedding, either you, Ivar, or you, Kolbein, for the full amount of the costs, whether you wish to be paid in ready money or he sells you, at a reasonable price, Ingunn's share of Hindkleiv. Then he will compensate her for the property with lands of his own in the south."

Arnvid continued to speak about the terms that Olav was offering his wife's kinsmen, and they were particularly good terms. Olav promised to have a mass said for Steinfinn and Ingebjørg, and he vowed that the Steinfinnssøn kinsmen would always find him to be both loyal and compliant, willing to listen to the advice of his elders to the extent it was deemed suitable for a man of his young age. Finally, Arnvid asked that the Steinfinnssøn kinsmen accept this offer in the same manner as it was presented, with goodwill and a faithful heart.

Steinfinn's brothers sat there, looking as if the matter troubled them greatly. As Arnvid was speaking, Olav had stood before his friend on the outer side of the table, straight-backed and with his calm, pale face turned toward Ingunn's uncles. Occasionally he nodded agreement with Arnvid's words.

Finally Kolbein Toressøn spoke.

"It's true, Olav, that we know there was once talk between your father and our brother, that you should marry one of his daughters. And do not think that we are unaware of your goodwill in making such arrangements that would have pleased us all. Yet it's not certain that your kinsmen would now be as keen to see you marry our brother's daughter and would grant permission to accept what you're offering.

But of greatest import is that we now need to bind ourselves through marriage agreements to men who wield power and have powerful kinsmen, neither of which you have. We must seek alliances rather than wealth. We expect you to understand this, for you have shown through your offer that you are wise far beyond your years. Yet because Steinfinn once promised your father that he would help you make a good marriage, we would like to assist you in this matter. For Steinfinn's daughters we have other plans. But you need not lose heart. With God's help we will find for you a marriage that is just as good in every way and more suitable to a youth of your age. As young as you are, Olav, it would not serve you well to have an equally young bride. You should either take a wife who is older and more sensible, or become betrothed to a maiden who is younger and then wait to wed her until you are full grown."

Olav's face had turned bright red while Kolbein was talking. Before he could say anything, Arnvid quickly spoke.

"Here in this district, everyone has always considered Olav and Ingunn to be betrothed. I myself was present when Steinfinn offered his hand to pledge Olav to his daughter."

"Yes, I know," said Kolbein. "I've heard about that. But it was just a game they were playing. Later they spoke together, Steinfinn and Audun, and agreed it might be advantageous if one day they made the promise in earnest. And that could have happened, if our brother hadn't ended up in such unfortunate circumstances. But because this betrothal was never confirmed—"

"The betrothal ring I gave to Ingunn is in Steinfinn's chest. That I know," Olav interrupted.

"And well you should. Steinfinn has never squandered any of your property, Olav, my boy. Your kinsmen will see that not even a button is missing when they come to take everything into possession on your behalf."

Olav took several short, shallow breaths.

Kolbein went on.

"You must realize, Olav, that sensible men do not betroth their children in such a manner, on sudden impulse."

"But Steinfinn did make such a promise. I don't know how sensible a man he was."

"Everything is always carefully agreed ahead of time regarding property and possessions and such matters. You must know that if Steinfinn had made a binding arrangement with Audun Ingolfssøn, he would have told me no at once when I spoke to him in the spring about wedding Ingunn to the son of a friend of mine."

"What did he say?" asked Olav, holding his breath.

"He said neither yes or no, but he promised to consider this man. We spoke of it again when we discussed that other matter, agreeing that we might benefit greatly if Ingunn were to marry into such a lineage. But I stand by what I told you, Olav, that my kinsmen and I will gladly help you to find a good marriage."

"I haven't asked you for such help. I was promised Ingunn, and—"

Arnvid interrupted him.

"It was one of the last things Steinfinn said, Ivar. On the morning of the day he died, he said that if he were able to decide on Ingunn's marriage himself, he would have preferred to have Olav as his son-in-law."

"That may well be," said Kolbein as he stood up and stepped away from the table. "But as matters now stand, Arnvid, Steinfinn wasn't able to do that. Surely you are old enough and wise enough to realize that we can't turn away those men who would offer us the most support in our difficulties, just because Olav has believed the whole time that a game they once played with him when he was a little boy was actually meant in earnest. You were unwilling enough when you were ushered to the bridal bed, Arnvid. It's strange that you should be in such haste to urge your friend in that direction. Olav will likely thank us one day for refusing to allow such childish whims."

With that Kolbein and Ivar went over to the enclosed bed where Steinfinn used to sleep. They lay down and closed the door.

Arnvid went over to Olav. The youth stood in the same spot, unmoving and staring at the floor. Tiny tremors passed over his face. Arnvid told him it was time to sleep.

"It was fortunate you could restrain yourself enough that no un-kind words were exchanged between you and Kolbein," said Arnvid as they undressed in the dark behind the pillars.

Olav uttered what sounded like a snort.

Arnvid said, "Otherwise it would have been impossible to find a good resolution to this matter. Kolbein might have ordered you to leave the estate at once. Do not let him see that it's important to you whether you wed Ingunn or some other wife. That will make things easier."

Olav didn't reply. He usually slept on the outer edge of the bed, but when they were about to climb in, Arnvid said, "Let me sleep there tonight, my friend. The ale this evening was not the best, and I'm feeling ill after drinking it."

"It did me no good either," said Olav with a terse laugh.

Nevertheless he lay down next to the wall. Arnvid was on the verge of falling asleep when he noticed Olav had gotten up and was about to step over him.

"Where are you going?" Arnvid asked, taking his friend by the arm.

"I'm thirsty," muttered Olav. Arnvid heard him fumble his way over to the cask that held a mixture of milk and water. He scooped up some of the liquid and drank.

"Come to bed and sleep," Arnvid implored.

After a moment Olav quietly went back to the bed, climbed in, and lay down.

"It will be much better if you don't mention to Ingunn what sort of response we received tonight until we've decided how we're going to proceed," Arnvid whispered urgently.

Olav lay still for a while before answering.

"All right." He sighed heavily. "We will do as you say."

Arnvid then felt a little less anxious. But he didn't dare allow himself to doze off until he could hear that the young man was sleeping soundly.

VIII

It was snowing heavily when Olav went out to the courtyard after dark on the eve of Saint Catherine's Day. This was the first snowfall of the year. Slick black ice appeared in the wake of his footsteps as he ran down to the stable.

He paused at the stable door to turn and peer into the swirling whiteness. Olav blinked as the snowflakes landed on his long lashes; the snow felt like soft caresses against his skin. The forest, which stood below the estate to the north and east and thrust its eerie gloom into the autumn nights, had now come close, shining like a white and friendly wall through the drifting snow and ever-encroaching darkness. Olav stood there, happy to see the snow.

Someone was speaking loudly inside the stable. The door flew open behind Olav and a man came tumbling out as if he'd been thrown. He collided with Olav, and both of them ended up on the ground. The man sprang to his feet and shouted toward the person standing in the stable doorway, a towering dark figure in the faint glow from a lantern.

"Here's somebody else you might want to treat with brute force, Arnvid!" With that, the man ran off and vanished into the snowy night.

Olav shook himself and then ducked to enter the stable. "What's the matter with Gudmund?" he asked. Then he caught sight of a girl standing in the dark behind Arnvid and crying.

"Get out of here, you vile slut," Arnvid told her furiously. The young woman crouched low as she crept past the men and went out. Arnvid shut the door after her.

"What is it?" Olav asked again.

"Oh, nothing that you would think important," said Arnvid harshly. He picked up the small membrane-covered lantern at his feet and hung it on a hook.[20] Olav saw that Arnvid was so enraged he was shaking. "Nothing except that now every whoring fellow in service here on the estate seems to think he can mock me because . . . because . . . I've said that I won't have any womenfolk inside the horse stable. They don't belong in here. Gudmund told me that I should keep watch over the loft rooms and the women belonging to my kinsmen instead."

Olav turned away. In the dark the horses could be heard munching on their fodder and moving about in their stalls. The closest horse poked its head over the planks and snorted at Olav. The lantern light was faintly reflected in the animal's big, dark eyes.

"Did you hear what I said?" insisted Arnvid.

Olav turned toward the horse and didn't respond. He was embarrassed to find himself blushing fiercely.

"What do you have to say to that?" Arnvid asked angrily.

"What do you want me to say?" replied Olav in a low voice. "As matters stand for me now, after what Kolbein told me, it shouldn't surprise you that I took your advice."

"Advice? From me?"

"The advice you gave me that day when we talked up in the forest. You said that when two underage children have been betrothed to each other by their proper guardians, no one has the right to separate them. And if they agree with the arrangement that was made by their parents, nothing more needs to be done; they can live together as married folks."

"I never said that!"

"I don't recall the exact words, but that's what I understood you to mean."

"You thought that's what I meant?" whispered Arnvid, greatly agitated. "I don't think, Olav . . . what I meant . . . I thought you knew . . ."

"No. Then what *did* you mean?" asked Olav bluntly. He turned to face Arnvid. Filled with the utmost shame, he made himself speak coldly as he defiantly looked his friend in the eye, though his face was a fiery red.

Arnvid Finnssøn lowered his gaze before the youth, and he too blushed. He couldn't say what he'd been thinking. Right now he had a hard time coming up with any answer at all. Confusion and shame rendered him speechless. How could he have defended continuing a loyal friendship with a man who he knew full well had disgraced his kinswoman? Yet it was only now that he saw how badly that appeared to everyone else. Until now he hadn't fully recognized how ignominious and abhorrent it was. Olav seemed so thoroughly honorable, and because of that, Arnvid had been unable to see that dishonorable conduct *was* dishonorable—even when Olav was concerned.

Yet he couldn't believe that Olav would stand before him and lie. Olav had always seemed to him the most truthful of people. That's what Arnvid told himself now. He had to believe the truthfulness of what Olav was saying. This past summer he must have wronged his friend when he voiced such a mistaken notion. That must be what happened. Surely nothing improper had taken place between the two young people, even though they had been together at night during the summer.

"I have always thought well of you, Olav," said Arnvid. "You're someone who possesses great dignity."

"Then you couldn't very well expect me simply to submit," said Olav fervently as he continued to look his friend in the eye. "Not when the Toressøn kinsmen decided to stomp on my honor and deprive me of what is my right. I refuse to go back to my own district under these circumstances. Then every man will dare to mock me behind my back because I allowed those fellows to cheat me out of the marriage I was promised. You know they are trying to swindle me, both Kolbein and the others. Do you remember how I got back the ring?"

Arnvid nodded. When the estate was being settled, Kolbein had returned to Olav the chests containing the personal items that Steinfinn had held in safekeeping for his foster son. And the signet ring that had belonged to Olav's mother was included, strung on a ribbon with several other rings. It would have been impossible for Olav to say that when he last saw the ring, it had been among Steinfinn's own most precious possessions.

"In my mind, this seems to be about my father's honor as well," Olav went on heatedly. "Should I allow strangers to betray his last wishes and the promises that were made to him before he died? And what about Steinfinn? You heard for yourself what he said, though the poor man undoubtedly knew he wouldn't be able to exert his will against those arrogant brothers of his. Should both Ingunn's father and mine be regarded with such scorn as they lie in their graves that they're denied their right to decide on the marriage of their own children?"

Arnvid took his time before replying.

"Nevertheless, Olav," he said quietly, "you must not . . . Do not go to her in outlying loft rooms, nor meet with her so furtively that everyone here in the estate knows about it. God knows, I should not have kept silent for so long, but I found it hard to speak of this matter. And you have shown no hesitation to betray *me.*"

Olav didn't reply. Looking at his friend, Arnvid took pity on him.

He said, "What I think, Olav, is that if matters are such between you and Ingunn, then you are the one who should take charge here on the estate."

Olav looked up with a puzzled expression.

"Make it known to everyone here that you will not yield to these new marriage prospects. You will keep to the agreement that Steinfinn and your father made and take Ingunn as your wife. Climb into the master's bed with Ingunn and declare that you now deem yourself to be the closest kinsman to preside over the estate, on behalf of her brothers Hallvard and Jon, for as long as you and Ingunn are living up here in the north."

Olav stood there, biting his lip, his cheeks blazing. His first thought was that Arnvid's counsel was overwhelmingly tempting. It offered him a direct path out of all the sneaking about at night and all the hiding. Even he sensed that this was making him less of a man and diminishing his position. He could take Ingunn by the hand and boldly lead her to the bed and the high seats that had belonged to Steinfinn and Ingebjørg. Then everyone would have something else to whisper about—all those people here on the estate who were sneering and muttering behind his back, though they hadn't yet dared say anything to his face.

But Olav lost courage when he pictured himself doing any of this. He kept thinking about the disparaging comments, all those ugly little words. People here in the valley were so good at offering such remarks, and with perfectly innocent expressions, so that a man had a hard time responding reasonably or defending himself. They would calmly let drop a few little comments containing barbs that stung. Many times the malicious intent was so well hidden in what they said that it took a while before Olav realized what all the men were smiling about; that is, until he saw one of them fall silent, feign indifference, or leap to his feet. Without being aware of it, this was something Olav had been striving for the whole time he had lived on the estate: to behave in such a way that they would have no reason to make him the brunt of that type of ridicule. And until now he had more or less succeeded. He knew that he was well liked by the other household servants. They regarded him with a certain respect, because he was the type of person who said little, yet folks knew that he was not stupid; rather, he was soon reputed to be much wiser than he was. Yet no one had dared hint at what everybody knew about him and Ingunn—at least not as far as he knew.

But he cringed at the thought. Laughter and mockery would no doubt erupt if he were the one to make known the true nature of his bond with Ingunn, and then tried to take charge of things here on the estate where he'd always been considered a little boy up until this year. Olav's view of himself and his position on Steinfinn's estate had imperceptibly changed. He no longer regarded Frettastein as the home where he'd belonged as a child of the household. Because of the biting remarks that had seeped into his soul, because of the way in which Ingunn's kinsmen shunned him, and because of the terrible guilt and shame weighing on him after everything he'd done in secret, Olav had come to see himself as occupying a lower standing than he had before.

And then there was the fact that he was so young. All the other men on the estate were much older than he was. He was still used to the way in which they refused to regard either him or Ingunn as full-grown. And he was ashamed at the thought of living openly with a woman, when none of the adult men had stepped forward on his behalf and welcomed him as master of a household. Without that, he didn't think the marriage was truly valid.

Now he said, "That would be ill-advised, Arnvid. Do you think any man or woman here on the estate would obey me if I tried to take charge? Grim or Josep or Gudmund? Would Dalla willingly give up her household keys to Ingunn?"

"No, Ingunn would have to settle for wearing a married woman's wimple." Arnvid gave a laugh. "Until you hand her the keys to Hestviken, that is."

"No, Arnvid. They're all afraid of Kolbein, every last one of them. It would be impossible to do what you're suggesting."

"Then I can think of only one other way. And it's something I should have advised you to do long ago, may God forgive me. You must go to Hamar and place your case in the hands of the bishop."

"Bishop Torfinn? I don't think I can expect much mercy from him," said Olav grudgingly.

"You can expect him to acknowledge what is your right," replied Arnvid. "In this case only the Holy Church can decide. And the two of you can't marry anyone else."

"What if the Holy Father demands that we become monk and nun and retreat to a cloister as penance for our sins?"

"He will certainly demand that you pay a fine to the church because you took your bride without first having marriage banns read and without celebrating a wedding feast. But if you can present witnesses to say the betrothal was proper and binding, and I'm certain we can do that, then he will demand that the Toressøn kinsmen accept the offer of an honorable settlement—"

"I wonder whether it will matter much," Olav interrupted him, "even if Lord Torfinn makes such a demand. In the past the bishop of Hamar has had to concede to the wishes of the Steinfinnssøns."

"Yes, when it came to matters of property and such. Yet the Toressøn men cannot be so ungodly that they will dare deny the fact that in this case no one has the right to pass judgment other than the learned fathers of the church—they are the ones who will determine whether the marriage is valid or not."

"I'm not certain that's what will happen. No, I'm more inclined to take Ingunn and head south to my own land."

"Not as long as I'm able to wield a sword. In the Devil's name, Olav, do you expect me, because I've said nothing for so long . . . Do you think I would sit here and close my eyes while you stole my kinswoman from under my protection?" He saw that Olav was growing agitated. "Don't worry," he said curtly. "I know you're not afraid of me. And I'm not afraid of you either. But I thought that we were friends. Can't you see for yourself how poorly you've treated me, your loyal friend? Do what I'm now suggesting and seek to put an end to this matter in a reputable and honorable way."

When he saw that Olav was still hesitating, Arnvid said, "I will go with you to see the bishop."

"I do this with great reluctance," said Olav, sighing.

"Do you prefer things as they now stand?" asked Arnvid harshly. "With gossip flying here on the estate and throughout the countryside, about you and me and about Ingunn? Don't you see how the womenfolk are whispering and tittering behind her back wherever she goes? Secretly gawking at her? They're no doubt waiting to see if she is treading less lightly than she used to."

"There's no danger of that," muttered Olav angrily. "At least that's what she says." His face was again bright red. "Ingunn will have to come with us," he said pensively. "Otherwise it will be difficult even for Bishop Torfinn to wrest her out of Kolbein's hands."

"I will bring both Tora and Ingunn with us. Did you think I would let her fall into Kolbein's hands after this?"

"So be it," replied Olav, his expression bleak as he stared into the distance.

It was only two days later that they headed south, arriving in the town of Hamar late in the evening. The two young maidens slept a long time the following morning. Olav said he would go to see the blacksmith to reclaim his axe while the others got ready to attend the next mass, which was being held in Christ Church.

They had already left by the time Olav returned to the inn. He hurried along the narrow lane to catch up with them, the snow creaking under his feet. The weather had turned brisk and fair. The ringing bells sounded so beautiful in the clear, frosty air, and to the south the sky was fading to a lovely yellow above the white mountain crests and the dark blue water. He saw the others nearing the churchyard gate, and he ran after them.

Ingunn turned toward him, her face blushing as crimson as a rose. Olav saw that under her hood her face was framed by the white linen wimple of a young wife. He too blushed, and his heart began to pound. They were embarking on something of the utmost seriousness; only now did he seem to fully understand this. Young as he was and lacking in kinsmen and friends, he had taken on the task of insisting that she was his wife. Yet he also felt terribly shy about walking beside her in this manner. Side by side, as upright as candles, and with their eyes fixed straight ahead, they made their way up through the churchyard.

After the midmorning meal Olav followed Arnvid over to the bishop's palace. He was feeling apprehensive as they made their way there, and it didn't help matters when he was left to sit alone in the bishop's stone reception hall while a cleric took Arnvid up to see Lord Torfinn in the bishop's bedchamber.

The waiting seemed to go on forever. Olav had never been inside a hall made of stone before, and there was plenty for him to see. The ceiling was vaulted and also made of masonry, so that the only light seeping inside came from a small glass window on the back wall. Yet it was not particularly dark because the whole interior had been whitewashed, and high up where tapestries were usually hung, the walls had been painted with bright flowers and birds. There was no hearth in the room, but shortly after Olav arrived, two men had entered carrying a big basin of embers, which they set in the middle of the floor. Olav went over to the basin to warm his hands when he got tired of freezing as he sat on the bench. For the most part he was left on his own, but he didn't feel comfortable being in this hall. There was something church-like about it that made him uneasy.

After a while three men wearing travel clothes came in. They stood around the charcoal basin and conversed, seemingly unaware of the young boy seated on the bench. They were discussing a case they were presenting about fishing rights. Two of the men were farmers from somewhere near Fagaberg; the younger man was a priest and the stepson of one of the farmers. Olav felt suddenly very young and inexperienced. It was not going to be easy for him to assert himself in this place. After a while one of the bishop's servants came to get the three men. Olav would have liked to go outside to explore the courtyard of the bishop's palace, for there was so much to see. But he didn't think it would be seemly; he would have to stay where he was.

At last Arnvid came rushing into the hall. He grabbed his sword and fastened the belt around his waist while he explained that the bishop was going to ride over to an estate in Vang, and Arnvid had been invited to go along. No, he hadn't been able to speak at length about Olav's case; people had come and gone all morning, wanting to see the bishop. No, the bishop hadn't said much, but he'd invited both Arnvid and Olav to stay at the bishop's palace, so Olav needed to go over to the inn and bring back his horse and their belongings.

"What about the maidens? They can't stay at the inn alone."

"No, they can't," said Arnvid. They would go to a townyard and stay with two pious old women who had been granted corrody by the church.[21] And in a few days Fru Magnhild, Steinfinn's sister from Berg, would also come to stay with them there. The bishop intended to send her a letter by messenger on the following day. "He thinks it best that you don't meet with Ingunn until this matter has been resolved, although you should know that you can see each other in church and speak there." Arnvid dashed out.

Olav hurried over to the inn, but by then one of the corrodian women had arrived, and both Ingunn and Tora were ready to leave, so he wasn't able to talk to Ingunn. She looked sorrowful when he offered his hand in farewell. But Olav told Tora, within her sister's hearing, that the bishop had received them kindly. It was a gesture of great goodwill that all four of them were to be his guests.

When Olav went back to the bishop's palace, he was met by a

young priest who said that they were to be *contubernales*. Olav realized this meant he was to sleep in the room where the priest had his sleeping quarters. He was a tall, gaunt man with a big, bony face as long as a horse's head. Yet he was called Fat Asbjørn. The priest asked a servant to take charge of Olav's horse, and then he showed the youth to the loft where he was to sleep. After that, he said he needed to go down to the wharf. A ship had arrived with goods from the Gudbrandsdalen region earlier in the morning. Perhaps Olav might find it amusing to come along and watch? Olav gladly agreed.

He knew that a great deal of shipping went on at Hestviken, yet as things had turned out, it would be hard to find a man who knew less about ships and boats than Olav. Now he kept his eyes and ears open as he went on board the cargo vessel, and he also mustered enough courage to ask about one thing and another. Then he lent a hand when the men began unloading the ship; it was always better to help out instead of merely standing around with idle hands. The cargo mostly consisted of barrels of salted freshwater vendace and brown trout, but there were also casks of animal hides and a good many fur pelts, as well as butter and tallow. As the priest tallied up everything, Olav helped by making marks on a piece of wood. This was something he'd had practice doing at Frettastein, for he'd often helped Grim in this manner. The old man was no longer very good at reckoning.

Olav stayed with Asbjørn all day and accompanied him to prayers in the church choir as well as to the evening meal. Olav was invited to eat at the same table as members of the bishop's household. Later that evening, when he went with Asbjørn and another young priest up to the sleeping loft, he was in a better frame of mind. He no longer felt like such a stranger on the bishop's estate, and there were so many new things for him to see. Arnvid had not yet returned.

In the night Olav awoke and lay in bed thinking about everything he'd heard people say about Bishop Torfinn. And he discovered that he was in fear of the man, after all.

The bishop had supposedly said that it was better for ten men to lose their lives than for a young maiden to be taken by force. There was a case that had been much discussed throughout the villages during the previous year. The son of a wealthy man out in Alvheim had taken a liking to a poor farmer's daughter. He was unable to seduce her with promises and gifts, so one evening in the spring he arrived when the girl was out plowing, and this time he was set on using force. Her father had gone into the forest to repair a fence. He was old and feeble, but when he heard his daughter shouting, he took his axe and ran to her aid. Then he split open the man's skull. The dead attacker was found to be unworthy of any compensation from the farmer who had killed him, and his kinsmen had to be content with that. But, as was only reasonable, they demanded that the murderer should leave the district. At first they attempted to pay the old man to move, but when he refused, they besieged him with threats and vicious attacks. That's when Bishop Torfinn had taken the poor farmer and his children under his protection.

There was also the case of the man from Tonstad who was found murdered in the forest where he'd gone to fell trees for wood. His widow and children accused the other leaseholder on the estate of being the killer. The man had to flee to save his life, while his wife and underage children were subjected to both torments and abuse from the murdered man's kinsmen. It so happened that the dead man's own cousin then admitted that he was the one who had killed his kinsman after they had argued about an inheritance. But it was Bishop Torfinn who had forced the murderer to publicly admit to what he had privately confessed to the bishop. Torfinn said that no priest had the power to absolve the man of his sin until he had shown heartfelt remorse and won a reprieve for the innocent man who was now suffering for the evil deed.

Arnvid had said that this particular bishop treated poor and sorrowful folks with the gentlest kindness, beseeching them to turn to him as to a loving father. Yet he never relented in the slightest whenever he encountered obstinate and hard-hearted men, whether they were of noble or lowly birth, priest or layman. He would never cause any person to sin, but he welcomed with open arms all sinners who showed remorse and a willingness to repent, offering to guide, console, and protect them.

Olav had thought such conduct admirable, and much of what he'd heard about Torfinn had seemed to him quite favorable. This monk from Trøndlagen must be a fearless man, and someone of great conviction. But in the past Olav had never imagined that one day he'd have occasion to present a case for the bishop to decide. The fact that Arnvid said the bishop treated all people the same now seemed to Olav too much of a good thing. He couldn't help thinking that it did make a difference whether it was a leaseholder who killed his neighbor for some minor offense or it was Steinfinn taking revenge upon Mattias. And he wouldn't want anyone to think that he had turned to the bishop and asked him to protect his rights against the Steinfinn lineage because—well, because his standing was lesser than that of the other men. Also of concern was the fact that Bishop Torfinn led a life of such strict purity. Olav might assert to everyone else that what had gone on between him and Ingunn since the summer could be considered acceptable conduct because they were married. Yet that was not how he viewed things himself.

The following morning Olav again sat in the little hall to wait. It was called "little" because there was a larger hall or parlatory right next to it, though there was no access between them. Each of the rooms in the stone building had only one door, which opened out to the estate courtyard.

Olav had been waiting for a while when a short young man came in. He wore a gray-white monk's cowl that was slightly different from the robes worn by the Dominican brothers. The monk closed the door behind him and quickly came over to Olav, who jumped to his feet and then knelt on one knee. He knew at once that this must be Lord Torfinn. When the bishop reached out his hand, Olav humbly kissed the large stone on his ring.

"Welcome, Olav Audunssøn! It was a shame that I had to leave when you arrived yesterday, but I hope my servants have treated our guests well."

Olav saw that the man was not young, after all. His sparse fringe of hair gleamed as brightly as silver. His face was narrow and furrowed, his complexion almost as gray-white as his cowl. But he was slender and moved with surprising agility. He was not quite as tall as Olav. It was impossible to guess his age. When he smiled he didn't look old; his big yellow-flecked gray eyes shone, but the smile appeared only as the faintest shadow on the pale, thin lips of his mouth.

Olav managed to murmur his thanks and then stood there, feeling ill at ease. This man looked nothing like the zealous bishop he had expected. He vaguely recalled having seen the previous bishop—a man who filled any room with both his voice and his body. Olav suspected that this man would also fill a room, even as thin and silver-gray as he was, though in a different way. When Lord Torfinn sat down and invited Olav to sit beside him, Olav shyly took a seat on the bench, but not too close.

"As things are now, you will have to stay here for a good part of the winter," said Bishop Torfinn. "I hear that you are from the Oslo Fjord district, and all your kinsmen live far away, except for the Tveit folks out in Soleyar. It will take time for us to hear what they have to say about this matter. Do you know whether they lawfully relinquished their guardianship over you?"

"My father did that, my lord. And surely he was the one who had custody of me?"

"Yes, yes. But he must have spoken of it to his kinsmen, and then they would have agreed that in their place Steinfinn would have the benefit of the money set aside for your care."

Olav remained silent. He could see that this was not going to be a simple matter—something he'd been well aware of for a while now. As far as he knew, Steinfinn had never taken any payment for his care from the property that was his.

"I know nothing of this. I know very little about the law. No one has ever taught me such matters," said Olav dejectedly.

"No, I can't imagine they have. But we will have to determine the state of your guardianship, Olav. First, with regard to the undertaking that led to the murder and fire, did you participate as Steinfinn's son-in-law or as his hired man? Kolbein and the others who were outlawed have been granted dispensation and can remain in the land, but you were not included in this decision. You will have to speak to the bailiff about this matter so that you can remain here in Hamar without reprisal. The next concern is what Steinfinn said before he died. Arnvid tells me that it was Steinfinn's wish for you and his daughter to marry. But we need to know whether he was your guardian at that time, or whether these kinsmen of yours now have custody of you."

"I thought I was now considered of legal age," said Olav, blushing. "Since she was lawfully betrothed to me, and I have taken her as my wife."

The bishop shook his head.

"Did you children think you would have any rights under the law when you took it upon yourselves to go to bed together, without the presence of your kinsmen as witnesses and without having the banns read in church? The two of you now bear the responsibility, because you considered it to be a binding marriage. You are now bound, under threat of mortal sin, to live together until death. Or else you must each live alone if we cannot forge an agreement between those who decide her marriage and those who decide yours. But this marriage does not mean you are now of legal age, and your spokesmen cannot demand any dowry on your behalf until you fall at the feet of the Toressøns and pay them restitution. And it would be very unlike them to consent to giving you the sort of dowry for Ingunn Steinfinnsdatter that a man of your standing could otherwise demand when he takes a wife. These exploits may cost you dearly, Olav. You will have to pay compensation to the church for holding your wedding in secret, which is something all children are forbidden to do. A wedding must be celebrated in the light, in a seemly and sensible manner. Otherwise far too many young folks would do as you have done. You and this young woman are now bound by what you have promised before God, but no man is obliged to extend to you any rights or support, since no men were present as witnesses, nor gave you their pledge, nor vouched for you when you bound yourself in marriage."

"My lord!" said Olav. "I thought you would safeguard our right, since in our judgment we are compelled to keep the vows we made to each other."

"The right thing to do would have been to bring this matter to the attention of the church as soon as you understood that the maiden's uncles would dispute whether the betrothal was valid. You could have demanded that my official, Sir Arinbjørn Skolp, should refuse to allow Kolbein, under threat of excommunication, to betroth Ingunn to another man until it was made clear whether you already held the right to this marriage."

"Yet I wonder whether Kolbein would have paid any mind to that."

"Hmm. That much you do know, it seems. You may not have been taught the law, but you have seen unlawful acts." The bishop moved his clasped hands resting on his lap under the scapular. "You must remember that from now on Kolbein and Ivar will carry the stigma of outlawry, and perhaps they would not have been so ready to risk another matter that might result in banning."

"But I thought the betrothal was considered valid," Olav stubbornly insisted. "Her father shook hands with mine and promised the maiden would be my wife."

"No." The bishop shook his head. "As I said, you have now won responsibility and obligations, but no rights. If you had turned to Sir Arinbjørn about this matter while the girl was still a chaste maiden, you would have won more than what you can ever win now. Either the Toressøns would have had to give you both the woman and her belongings, or she and you could have parted and been free to marry someone else. As matters now stand, my son, we must pray for God's help so that when you come of age you won't regret in the light of day that you blindly bound yourself hand and foot in the darkness of night before you had even left your childhood behind."

"That day will never come," said Olav vehemently. "I won't regret refusing to allow Kolbein Borghildssøn to rob me of what was my right."

The bishop gave him a searching glance as Olav went on.

"No, my lord, Kolbein fully intended to break this agreement, and he would not be content with any other outcome. This I know." He told the bishop about the betrothal ring.

"Are you certain," asked Lord Torfinn, "that Steinfinn didn't return the ring to your chest before he died? He might have considered that the best thing to do, so you would be sure to get back all the belongings that he'd been safeguarding on your behalf."

"No. It was on the morning of the day he died that I saw Ingunn's betrothal ring. And at that time it was in the small box in which Steinfinn kept the most precious of his and his children's possessions."

"Was it Steinfinn who brought out the box? Was he the one who showed it to you?"

"No, it was Arnvid."

"Hmm. Then it looks as if Kolbein . . ." The bishop sat in silence for a moment before turning to look at Olav. "As matters stand between you two young people, the best way out—and I won't say it's a good way, but it's nevertheless the best—would be for your kinsmen and hers to give their consent. Then your marriage will fall under the law of the land and you will belong to each other and you will have the benefit of everything you own and bring to the marriage. Otherwise life will be very difficult for you. And if you are parted, then you may be tempted to worse sins than the first sin. But you must realize that even if we can present witnesses to say the betrothal was valid, the Toressøns can stipulate such terms for the agreement that the marriage will make you poorer than you were before."

"Yes, but that makes no difference to me," said Olav defiantly. "The promise that was made to my father shall not be broken merely because he's dead. I will take Ingunn home with me, even if it means she comes with only the shift she is wearing."

"What about young Ingunn?" asked the bishop quietly. "Are you certain that she is of the same mind? Would she rather keep to the old agreements than be given to another man?"

"Ingunn thinks as I do. We should not oppose the will of our fathers just because they are dead, and now strangers wish to challenge their right to make decisions for their own children."

Bishop Torfinn did his best not to smile.

"So you children crept into the bridal bed simply to obey your fathers?"

"My lord!" said Olav in low voice, blushing again. "Ingunn and I are close in age, and we were raised as brother and sister from the time we were small. From my seventh year I have lived far away from all of my kinsmen. And when she lost both her mother and father, she turned to me. That's when we agreed that we would not let them part us."

The bishop slowly nodded.

Olav said fervently, "My lord, it seems to me that it would be a great insult, both to me and to my father, if I should leave Frettastein without my bride, when for the past ten years everyone there has considered us betrothed. I also think that when I arrive back in my home district, where I am a stranger, I would most want to have as my wife the woman who has been my friend since my childhood days."

"How old were you when you lost your parents, Olav?" asked the bishop.

"I was seven when my father died. I'm told that I became motherless at the hour of my birth."

"Ah. And my mother is still alive." For a few moments Bishop Torfinn didn't speak. "I can see that it's reasonable you would not want to lose your childhood playmate." He stood up, and Olav sprang to his feet at once.

The bishop said, "You must know, Olav, that you are neither motherless nor without kinsmen. No Christian man is without such ties. You, like all of us, have the mightiest of brothers: Christ, our King. And his mother is your mother. And with her is your own mother, who gave birth to you. I have always thought that the Virgin Mary prays more to her son for those children who must grow up motherless down here than she does for the rest of us. No one should ever forget who our closest and mightiest kinfolk are. This is something you ought to remember even better. You shouldn't be as easily tempted to forget the power of kinship you possess in the Prince of Peace, because you have no earthly brothers or kinsmen to draw you into violent acts and arrogance or to urge you to seek revenge and discord. Yet young as you are, Olav, others have already drawn you into blame for murder, and you have embroiled yourself in quarrels and disputes. May God be with you so that you become a man of peace when it's time for you to take charge of your own life."

Olav knelt to kiss Bishop Torfinn's hand in farewell. The bishop looked down at his face and smiled faintly.

"I can see you're of a stubborn disposition. Well, well. May God and his gentle mother protect you so that you do not become hard-hearted."

He raised his hand to bless the youth. As Bishop Torfinn reached the door, he turned and said with a small laugh, "There's one thing I forgot. I meant to thank you for your help. My priest Asbjørn, the one they call Fat Asbjørn, told me that you have already taken it upon yourself to be useful here on the estate. I want to thank you for that."

Not until that evening, as Olav lay in bed, did a shudder pass through him. What he had told Bishop Torfinn about his bond with Ingunn was not completely truthful. But he pushed that thought away at once. Right now he was not of a mind to think about the past summer and autumn, with all those nights they'd spent together in the sleeping loft and everything else.

He was happy at the bishop's palace, and for each day that passed, he felt even happier to be there, solely in the company of men. Everyone was older than he was, and everyone had assigned tasks to do at specific times.

Olav constantly followed at the heels of Fat Asbjørn, wherever he went. Olav and Arnvid shared the sleeping loft with two priests. One of them was a young priest who had been at school with Arnvid; the other was Brother Asbjørn. At nearly thirty, he was a good deal older than his companions.

Arnvid went to the church to sing the hours with the priests. He'd found a copy of the study book he'd had when he was a postulant at the school, and during the midmorning rest he liked to amuse himself by reading it. He would sit on the edge of his bed and read aloud from the first entries in the book: *De arte grammatica* and *Nominale*. Olav would stretch out and listen. He thought it strange how many different names these Roman clerics seemed to have for a single word, such as "lake." In the back of the book were exercises meant to be used for practicing penmanship. Arnvid found it entertaining to copy the old sketches, words, and phrases. But it was cold working in the chilly loft room, and his fingers were not as nimble as they once were in his childhood. One day he finally wrote: *Est mala scriptura quia penna non fuit dura.* After he'd put the book down and gone out, Brother Asbjørn picked it up and printed in the margin: *Penna non valet dixit ille qui scribere nescit.*

Olav smiled gently when he heard what the words meant:

> The writing is ill with an unsharpened quill.
> The pen was to blame, says the one with no shame.

Fat Asbjørn usually went to mass early in the morning, and Olav would accompany him to the church, though the priest seldom attended other services on weekdays. For the most part Brother Asbjørn was exempt from serving in the choir, and he marked the canonical hours by reading from a book wherever he happened to be while carrying out his work duties. He was greatly involved with handling the bishopric's revenues and expenses, accepting tithes and leased-land payments, and speaking to folks. The priest taught Olav to examine goods and assess their worth, and told him how to determine the best way to store and preserve each of them. He explained the regulations that applied to purchasing and selling, the tithing law, and how to use a wax tablet for accounting purposes. Lake Mjøsa had not yet frozen over, so folks could still row and sail to Hamar. Several times Brother Asbjørn took Olav along on short business outings. He also bought two brooches from Olav, so that for the first time in his life, the young boy carried ready coins in his belt.

All of this meant that Olav didn't see much of Ingunn. He kept his promise to the bishop and did not attempt to meet her outside of church, yet she seldom appeared until one of the later services, and Olav preferred to go to early mass. Arnvid often went over to the townyard where the Steinfinn daughters were staying. From him Olav learned that Fru Magnhild had shown her niece little sympathy. She said that Ingunn had allowed herself to be seduced, and Ingunn had reacted with great anger. Bishop Torfinn had been very kind when he spoke to Ingunn and Tora on the day he asked them to visit. But Olav wasn't home when the maidens came to the bishop's palace; that day he had gone with Fat Asbjørn on an errand to Helge Island.

Nor did Olav and Ingunn have much time to talk on those occasions when they did meet in church and afterward he accompanied her the short distance down to the townyard near the Church of the Cross. Yet he thought this was for the best. Sometimes he would remember how it felt to hold her in his arms, so slender and soft, warm and loving. But he would put such thoughts out of his mind; now was not the time for that. They had so many years ahead of them to live together as good and loving friends. He was convinced that Bishop Torfinn would help him to win what was his right.

It was also true that Olav felt a certain distaste in recalling his life during the past few months. Now, when he thought back, the memory of those days seemed strangely unreal or somehow aberrant. Those nights he'd spent in the sleeping loft with Ingunn in utter darkness, experienced with all his senses wide awake except his sight; it was so dark that he might as well have been blind. In the daytime he was half-asleep and sluggish, aware only of a trepidation about all that was unknown and threatening from the outside, moving like a breaking wave inside his empty, dazed head. There was always an uneasiness deep inside him. He might not be able to tell at the moment what new torment was plaguing his conscience, but he knew something was wrong and would soon make itself felt. Even when he was alone with Ingunn, he couldn't fully forget that something was not as it should be. And then he would grow a little annoyed with her, for she never seemed to be bothered by either fear or doubt. And he would tire of her, for she demanded that he should always be happy and eager and shower her with caresses.

He wasn't the least bit sad that for a while he had to live a life in which there was no place for women or secret loving.

◆ ◆ ◆

As for the bishop, Olav seldom saw him. Without ignoring the obligations of his position, Lord Torfinn tried to live as much as he could in accordance with the rules set for the order of monks he had joined in his youth. His sleeping quarters were above the parlatory, and that was where he also worked, prayed the canonical hours, and received most of his meals. From this room a stairway led down to the chapel where the bishop said mass in the mornings. From the loft gallery, which was an external structure at the second level of the stone building, a covered bridge led to one of the side chapels of Christ Church. No doubt plenty of those living at the bishop's palace were not pleased that such a parsimonious monk had become their lord. Gilbert, the previous bishop, had kept house in the manner of a great chieftain, yet he had been a pious priest and an able and zealous spiritual teacher. Brother Asbjørn said he was very fond of the current bishop, but he'd liked the old one better. Bishop Gilbert had been a jovial man, a great storyteller, and the most fearless horseman and hunter.

Olav thought he'd never seen a man ride a horse with more grace and ease than Lord Torfinn. And the household was still maintained in a manner befitting a chieftain, even though the bishop himself preferred an ascetic way of life. Every guest who came to the estate was lavishly welcomed and hosted; every servant received strong, home-brewed ale on weekdays, and mead on the sabbath. Wine was served in the bishop's guest hall, and when Lord Torfinn dined with guests he particularly wanted to honor, he would allow a large silver goblet to be placed in front of him. During the entire meal, the man in charge of serving the wine had to stand next to Torfinn's high seat and refill the goblet every time the bishop motioned for him to do so. Olav thought it looked quite splendid when Lord Torfinn picked up the goblet and took a sip, bowing with charming courtesy at the one to whom he was drinking a toast. Each time the bishop would then have the goblet carried to the guest of honor.

On the evening when Tore Bring of Vik was present, it fell to Olav to drink with Lord Torfinn. After the evening meal, the bishop summoned the youth from his seat at the very end of the table. He had to come over and stand before the bishop's seat. Lord Torfinn lifted the goblet to his lips and then handed it to Olav. It felt ice-cold in his hand, and the wine was tinged almost a pale green inside the shiny silver goblet. The wine was sharp and sour and stung the boy's throat, yet he still liked the fresh taste. It seemed to him a drink meant for men, and afterward heat raced through his whole body with a strange and festive warmth. He shook his head when Bishop Torfinn smiled and said, "Perhaps you prefer the taste of mead, Olav?" Then he asked Olav what he'd thought of the service that day. A special mass had been celebrated, and there had been a procession in the morning. The bishop invited Olav to drink some more. "I assume that you're happy now? I think we can be well satisfied with what Tore has said."

The bishop had not been able to get any sensible answers from Fru Magnhild. She refused to give any opinion regarding what had happened at that ting long ago. She thought that her brother indeed might have considered a marriage between Olav Audunssøn and one of his daughters—yet his intention had never been settled or confirmed. But Tore Vik said he was certain it had. Steinfinn and Audun had agreed to an arrangement for their children on that night. They shook hands to seal their pledge, and Tore himself was the one who had announced the promise they'd made. Tore was also able to name three or four men who had been witnesses to the handshake and who were still alive, as far as he knew. He knew nothing about the decisions made regarding properties, but afterward he'd heard men discussing the matter. He recalled that Audun Ingolfssøn refused to hear any talk of an equally shared ownership of possessions unless Steinfinn offered to increase the amount of his daughter's dowry. Audun had supposedly said, "My son is going to be much wealthier than you may think, Steinfinn."

When Advent came, Arnvid returned home to his estate in Elfardal for a while, and Olav went with him. Olav hadn't been there since he was a child. Now he went about as the master's friend and equal, casting discerning looks and speaking of matters with the air of a man with authority. On the estate, Arnvid's mother, Hillbjørg, had charge of everything, and she received Olav with open arms because he had thwarted Kolbein's plans for Ingunn. She hated Kolbein and all the children who were the offspring of her brother-in-law and his paramour. Hillbjørg was a proud and beautiful woman, even as old as she was, but there seemed to be a coldness between her and her son. Arnvid's three children were bright and fair little boys. "They take after their mother," said Arnvid. Olav thought with pleasure about becoming the master of a household when he went to Hestviken.

Just before Christmas, the two friends traveled back to Hamar. That's where Arnvid wanted to celebrate the holidays.

IX

On the evening before Christmas Eve, Olav received word that the bishop wished to see him.

A candle was burning on the lectern in the deep-set window. The small, masonry chamber looked warm and cozy in the faint glow. There were no furnishings other than a chest for books and a bench along the wall. That was where the bishop slept and ate his meals. He wanted neither a bed nor a table. But there was a low chair where the scribe would sit, holding a tablet on his lap whenever the bishop dictated letters to him. On other occasions when Olav had been in the room, Lord Torfinn had invited him to take a seat on this chair, and Olav had thought it pleasant to sit at the bishop's feet. That made it easier to speak to him, as if to a father.

But tonight Bishop Torfinn merely came over to stand before Olav, keeping his hands under his scapula.

"The Toressøn kinsmen will arrive on the Epiphany Eve, Olav. I have summoned them here, and they have promised to come. Now, with God's help, we will put an end to this matter."

Olav silently bowed, giving the bishop an apprehensive look.

Lord Torfinn pursed his lips and nodded a couple of times.

"Truth be told, my son, they do not sound particularly willing to come to an agreement. They spoke to my men about the fact that I have accepted payments from you as atonement for your part in the murder and that I've allowed you to attend mass. They had wanted me to release them as well from the ban of outlawry before Christmas, but that's something else we will have to discuss at this meeting. You must realize that they're furious because I did not receive you as someone who was an assailant and a despoiler of women." He gave a brief, angry laugh.

Olav looked at the bishop, waiting.

"And you most certainly have done wrong; you must not think otherwise. But you are young and far away from the protection of your kinsmen, and these men who have murdered and burned and now wish to deprive two fatherless children of their right . . . I hope you will not lose heart," he said, giving Olav a little pat on the shoulder, "if you have to bow quite deeply before Ingunn's uncles. You must realize, my boy, that you have offended them. Yet you need not suffer injustice at their hands if I am able to prevent it."

"I will do as you say, my lord," said Olav, sounding a bit dejected.

The bishop gave him a fleeting smile.

"You will not find it easy to yield even a little. No, you won't. Now, if you're headed to the church, you can go through the high-loft gallery."

Then Bishop Torfinn nodded and stretched out his hand to Olav, signaling that the conversation was over.

The brothers who served as canons were in the midst of singing vespers. Olav knelt down in a corner, spreading the folds of his fur cloak under his knees and holding his cap before his eyes so he could better gather his thoughts.

He was filled with trepidation, yet it was good that a decision would soon be made. He longed to escape this uncertainty. He felt as if he'd been walking a path through the dark and at any moment he might stumble and end up with both feet in the soggy marsh. That was something he'd feared, but he was not afraid of Kolbein and the others. Now there would be an end to all the unresolved and half-hidden unpleasantness. And the case would be settled. He would soon be seventeen years old, and he enjoyed feeling that he was the instigator of a legal matter. It seemed to him that his bones had become sturdier during the weeks he'd spent here at the bishop's palace, after all those indolent years he'd lived at Frettastein among lazy hired men and prattling women as he played with the children. His self-respect had increased with every day he'd been allowed to stay in this place where neither women nor nonsense was permitted. Here, he found only grown men from whom he had learned and on whom he had bestowed all the affection contained in his youthful desire to meet those who were either his equals or his betters. His soul was warmed through and through by the thought that Brother Asbjørn had the greatest need for his help, and that Bishop Torfinn was sheltering him with fatherly benevolence.

When Olav finished his prayers, he sat down in a corner to listen to the end of the song. He thought about what Fat Asbjørn had told him lately about the art of numbers, about the way in which the essence of God was revealed in the very nature of numbers, in their inherent laws and rules. Arithmetica, he thought, how beautiful that word sounds. And then there was what the priest had explained about the ways in which numbers behaved, how they increased and split apart in accordance with mystical and unbreakable laws. It was like looking into one of the heavenly realms. All of creation hung from the golden chains made up of number sequences, with the angels and spirits flying up and down the links. And his heart rose, yearning for something that would make his own life rest in God's hand like one of those golden links—a balance sheet lacking any deceit, a time when what weighed on him now would be erased as false marks on a reckoning stick.[22]

Midnight mass—the angels' mass—was lovelier than anything Olav could have imagined. The entire, vast space of the church was pitchdark, but in the chancel surrounding the main altar so many candles burned, tapers both tall and short, that they seemed to form a wall of flickering flames. The light shimmered, gentle and muted, on garments woven with golden threads, and it gleamed on white linen. On this night, all the priests wore cantor cassocks made of satin and heavy silk, and the other singers wore linen surplices and held candles in their hands as they stood before the weighty volumes from which they sang. Arnvid Finnssøn was among them, as were many respected men from the villages who had attended the school in their youth. The air in the church was heavy with incense from the evening procession, and fragrant gray clouds continued to billow from the altar. When the entire choir of men and boys sang in unison the great *Gloria*, it was as if angels had joined in and were singing with them from the darkness beneath the roofbeams.

Bishop Torfinn's face shone like alabaster as he sat on his throne, wearing a golden cassock and mitre and holding a crosier. Now all the bronze bells began to toll, and everyone knelt down. They had been standing and sitting as they waited in breathless silence for the transformation that on this night would become one with the birth of Christ on earth. Olav waited, filled with yearning. His prayer became one with his longing for justice and a pure conscience.

He had caught a glimpse of Ingunn on the women's side, but after the mass was over he didn't follow her out when she left. While they sang the lauds, or dawn prayer, in the chancel, he found a place to sit at the foot of a pillar. There he stayed, wrapped in his fur cloak yet feeling the cold and dozing occasionally until the priests left the chancel.

Outside the churchyard there were still embers smoldering in the heap of torches that the worshippers had tossed to the ground when they arrived. Olav went over to warm himself. He was freezing, and he kept yawning after the long hours he'd spent inside the church. The snow had melted all around, leaving big bare patches, and a good, strong warmth gusted from the black and red embers. A great many people had gathered there. Olav caught sight of Ingunn. She was standing with her back to him, and she was alone. He went over to greet her.

She turned halfway around, and the light of the fire cast a crimson glow on the white wimple peeking out from under the hood of her cloak. He still found it strange to see her dressed as a married woman. He couldn't quite grasp the notion that she was able to look so womanly and respectable while he himself was struggling to win justice and recognition and the dignity of a grown man.

They shook hands as they wished each other a blessed sabbath. Then they talked a bit about the weather. It wasn't terribly cold. The sky was mostly clear with a few stars, though not many because of the slight haze from the lake, which hadn't yet frozen over near Hamar.

Tora came over to them, and Olav greeted her with a kiss. He could never bring himself to kiss Ingunn whenever they met now. She was both too close to him and too distant for him to embrace her as her foster brother.

Tora left at once to join some acquaintances she happened to see. Ingunn had hardly said a word, and she'd kept her face turned away the whole time. Olav thought he might as well leave; no doubt it wasn't good for them to be seen here together. Then she reached out and timidly took hold of his cloak.

"Could you accompany me, so we might talk?"

"I suppose I can. Are you heading home to the south part of town?"

Bulky, fur-clad shapes moved along, looming against the snow in the nighttime darkness of the lane. People were going to rest for a while in their townyard homes before the midmorning mass. Snow was piled high on the houses and fences and trees; the walls and branches were nothing more than small, dissonant black patches in the snowy night. Christmas darkness had settled over the small town, and everyone moved about as quietly as frightened shadows, hurrying inside wherever a door opened and a little light fell across the snow-drifts in the courtyard and street. But smoke rose up from the roof-top hearth vents, and the smell of smoke filled the air. Everywhere, women were setting pots over the hearths to cook the Christmas Day meal. Outside the Church of the Cross light stretched across the snow from wide-open doors, and several old folks from the *spital* were slowly making their way inside.[23] Mass was about to be celebrated.

Olav and Ingunn trudged along the narrow passage behind the church. They didn't meet a soul. It was pitch-dark beneath the trees, and they had a hard time walking because the snow had not been packed down.

"When we walked here in the summertime, we never imagined things would turn out to be so difficult for us," said Ingunn with a sigh.

"No, we couldn't have known."

"Could you come inside with me?" she asked when they stood in the courtyard. "The others are going to the Church of the Cross."

"I suppose I can."

They entered a room as dark as coal, but Ingunn raked the hearth embers and added more wood. She had taken off her cloak, and when she knelt forward to blow on the fire, her long, white linen wimple lay spread out over her shoulders and down her slender back.

"This is where Tora and I sleep," she said, turned away from him. "I promised to do this for them." She hung a pot on the trammel hook. Olav realized that this must be the townyard's cookhouse, for all around were items used in preparing food. Ingunn bustled about, moving in and out of the glow from the fire. She looked tall and slender and young in her dark gown and white wimple. It all seemed like some sort of play-acting and not real. Olav sat on the edge of the bed and watched. He had no idea what to say, and by now he was terribly sleepy.

"Could you help me?" asked Ingunn. She was cutting up meat and bacon on a wooden trencher over by the hearthstone. She was having trouble splitting apart a piece of saddle meat with a knife. Olav found a small axe and easily chopped the meat in half.

While they were doing this, she whispered to him as she knelt near the cookpots, "You're so silent, Olav. Are you unhappy?" When he merely shook his head, she whispered even more quietly, "It's been so long since the two of us were alone. I thought you'd like being here with me."

"You know I do. Have you heard that your uncles will be here on Epiphany Eve?" he asked. Then he realized she might think that this was his response to her question about whether he was unhappy. "There's no need to be frightened," he said firmly. "We have no reason to be afraid of them."

Ingunn had stood up and was now staring at him as a little gasp issued from her lips. Then she moved forward as if to embrace him. Olav held out his hands to show her they were soiled with fat and brine.

"Come over here. You can wipe your hands on the coverlet." She changed the position of one of the cookpots. "We can lie down on the bed for a bit while we're waiting for the food to cook."

Olav took off his boots and unfastened his cloak. Then he spread it over both of them when he lay down beside her. The next moment she was pressing close to him, with her face hot against his cheek, her breath tickling his throat.

"Olav, tell me you won't stand by and let them take me away to separate us."

"No, I won't. Nor will they be given the right to do so. But you must know that Kolbein's demands will not be insignificant before he and I can come to an agreement."

"Is that why?" she whispered, pressing even closer to him. "Is that why you're less fond of me than you were?"

"I'm as fond of you as I've been all my days," he murmured, his voice thick with emotion. He tried to slip his arm under her neck, but the wimple she wore was in the way.

"Shall I take it off?" she whispered eagerly.

"No, it will just be troublesome for you to put it back on again."

"It's been almost a month. We've hardly seen each other in all this time," she whispered plaintively.

"Ingunn. I only wish you well," he pleaded, realizing at once that he'd said the same thing before, though he couldn't remember when. Why does she have so little sense, he thought unhappily, that she can't see how she is tempting me by lying so close?

"Yes, but I have such a longing for you. They're very kind, those women who live here, yet I long to be with you."

"Yes. But this is a holy night. In a short time we'll be going to mass again." His own words made him blush with shame in the dark. Such things should not even be mentioned. Quickly he sat up and kissed her eyelids, feeling her pupils tremble as wet tears spilled out over his lips.

"Don't be angry," he pleaded quietly. Then he moved to the outer edge of the bed and lay down facing the room as he stared at the fire in the hearth. Tormented by a terrible agitation in his heart and his blood, he lay there listening, wondering whether she would move away or weep. But she was as quiet as a mouse. Finally he could hear that she'd fallen asleep. Then he got up, put on his boots, and took back his cloak before spreading the coverlet over her instead. He was freezing; he felt sleepy and ill and hollow after fasting for so long. The food in the cookpot smelled so good that it made his chest ache.

Outside it had grown colder. The snow screeched under his feet, and in spite of the dark, he could tell that there was more frosty mist in the air. People were gradually making their way up toward the church. Olav shivered under his fur cloak. He was so tired that he didn't have much desire to go to mass right now; he would have preferred to go home and sleep. And yet he had been looking forward with such joy to this Christmas Eve with the three church services. People said that each was even lovelier than the one before.

During the following days leading up to the meeting, Olav kept mostly inside the bishop's palace, going no farther than to the church. Day after day there were splendid church services, and guests came and went during this holy season. Both the priests and the layfolk had their hands full with all manner of tasks, which meant that Olav spent most of his time alone. He'd spoken to the bishop only once, when he thanked Torfinn for his new year's gift. The bishop had given him an ankle-length brown cotehardie, trimmed with beautiful black otter fur. It was the first garment Olav had ever owned that was both elegant and befitting of someone who should now be considered a full-grown young man. It helped his confidence to no end, knowing that he was well dressed in every way. Arnvid had loaned him money so he could purchase a handsome winter cloak lined with marten fur, along with hose, boots, and the like.

Olav learned from Fat Asbjørn that the bishop had heard back from the four men he had assigned to find out from Olav's own kinsmen what they thought of the matter. The bishop was not pleased with their replies. One thing was certain: Steinfinn had never taken over guardianship for Olav in a lawful and binding manner, yet none of his kinsmen had ever asked about the boy or demanded to have him back from Frettastein.

"This is causing our worthy Father a great deal of trouble and expense, all on your behalf, Olav," said Brother Asbjørn with a small laugh. "Now he has summoned your kinsmen from Tveit. Your kinsman at Hestviken seems to be both ill and bedridden. But the men from Tveit will have to consent to your marriage before it can be declared lawful. And they told their parish priest, who spoke to them at Lord Torfinn's request, that if these Toressøns want this marriage to take place, they will have to offer you a satisfactory dowry along with the seduced maiden—those were their words, not mine. But they will never agree to you paying a fine to her kinsmen more than the law requires for sleeping with a maiden before marriage. And you know that Kolbein and Ivar will refuse such terms of an agreement; it would bring shame upon them for as long as they live."

"It seems to me the shame would also be mine—and hers," said Olav angrily. "It would be the same as calling her a . . . paramour."

"Yes. That's why the bishop hinted at what might be your only resort. You could leave the country and stay away for four winters until you come of legal age. Then you would be able to handle the arrangements yourself. Lord Torfinn thought you might go to Denmark and demand protection from your mother's family there. Did you know that the kinsmen of your mother's lineage are among the most powerful of men in that country? Your uncle, Sir Barnim Erikssøn of Høvdinggaard, is supposed to be the wealthiest knight in all of Sjælland."

Olav shook his head.

"My mother's father was Bjørn Anderssøn of Hvitaberg," he said. "And her only brother was named Stig. They are said to be from Jylland."

"Fru Margrete was married twice. Bjørn was her second husband, but first she was married to a man named Erik Erikssøn. He owned Høvdinggaard in Sjælland. Do you think, Olav, that it would be the worst misfortune if you were to live abroad for a few years and had a chance to see some of the customs of other folks? Especially if you could live in the company of such exceptionally rich and powerful people?"

The priest's words had sent Olav's thoughts in a new direction. Ever since arriving at the bishop's seat in Hamar, he'd come to realize that what he knew of the world was only a terribly small and constrained portion of it. Here the men of the church sent off letters and messengers to the north and south, to the east and west. In less than six weeks they had managed to reach folks that Olav had found it impossible to locate. For him, these kinsmen of his might as well have been living in Iceland or Rome. The bishop here knew more about Olav's own maternal lineage than he ever had. In the church there were candlesticks and books from France, silk tapestries from Sicily that had been sent by a pope, weavings from Arras, the relics of martyrs and the faithful who had lived in England and Asia. Fat Asbjørn had told Olav about the important schools in Paris and Bologna where a man could acquire all manner of skills and wisdom. In Salerno it was possible to learn the Greek language and to discover how to make yourself invulnerable to steel and poison. Asbjørn was the son of a farmer from Oppland County, and the farthest he'd ever traveled was north of Eyjabu Church, yet he talked a great deal about venturing abroad. And no doubt he would eventually do just that, for he was a clever man and able to make himself useful in many ways.

Olav talked to Arnvid Finnssøn mostly when they went to bed in the evening and when they got up in the morning. He had grown somewhat estranged from his friend after they'd come to the bishop's palace. Arnvid was preoccupied with so many things that Olav didn't understand. And besides, being with Arnvid reminded the young man about so much that was difficult and reprehensible. Olav had a feeling of remorse or shame whenever he thought about all that he'd confided in Arnvid, who had accepted the role, partly out of goodwill and partly under duress. Yet Olav didn't see how he could have forced Arnvid to do anything, a man who was so much older than he was, and someone who was also a wealthy and powerful landowner, when he thought about it. Even so, Olav felt as if he'd somehow committed an offense against his friend, both when he'd persuaded him to search for the ring and afterward when Arnvid had kept quiet about what he knew of Olav's nighttime meetings with his young kinswoman. And it was the latter that the Toressøns and everyone else would roundly condemn. It was something that had cast an ugly stain on Arnvid's honor, and he was too good a man for that. Olav also knew that his friend took everything to heart. And for that reason, he no longer felt at ease with Arnvid right now.

Olav felt more secure and calm with Brother Asbjørn. The priest was always alone, a steady and industrious worker whether he was praying the canonical hours or examining salted hides. The expression on his narrow, gaunt horse-face never changed, and he was equally laconic and concise when he said mass as when he oversaw the weighing of goods or went to find out whether the support posts of a livestock shed were rotten on one of the leaseholder farms belonging to the bishop's estate. Olav would go along with the priest and think ahead to his own life, when he would return to Hestviken and travel on his own boats, with wharves and storehouses and livestock sheds to see to. Brother Asbjørn was the friend that he instinctively dreamed of emulating.

The memory of the hours Olav had spent alone with Ingunn on Christmas Eve had only served to sharpen his longing for her. He thought about her girlishly slender figure, wearing the garb of a married woman, as she knelt before the hearth to blow on the embers. She had moved in and out of the flickering light, bustling around the benches and cooking implements and hearthplace. Then he would picture himself lying in his own bed at Hestviken on dark winter mornings as he watched Ingunn making a fire in his hearth. He recalled the way she had lain close to him, so ardent and devoted, as they rested beside each other in the dark. When they lived at Hestviken they would sleep together in the marriage bed as the master and mistress of the estate. Then he'd be able to take her in his arms as often as he liked. And in the evening he would lie in bed and tell her about everything that had happened during the day and seek her advice about what he should do next. Then he would no longer need to fear what, until now, he had dreaded as a misfortune; instead, having a child would only increase their joy and social standing. Then he would no longer be the last fragile offshoot of a dying lineage; he would be the very trunk of the new family tree.

But Brother Asbjørn's words had abruptly stirred new and unimagined ideas inside him. He'd never thought it might be his lot to go out and see the world. Far, distant places—Valland, England, Denmark—were practically all the same to the young boy who, in all this time, could not recall ever traveling farther than from Frettastein to Hamar. And he had never dreamed of venturing beyond Hestviken except to fish and trade. He had been willing to accept the destiny that had been planned for him, and he was content to do so, but that was only because he'd never thought anything else was possible. Now . . . it was as if he'd been offered a gift. Four years in which to take a look at the world and try new adventures, to see different folks and countries. And this came just at the moment when he'd realized how small and remote a corner of the world was occupied by the villages he knew, this place that he thought was all he was ever meant to see. And there was also the news that he was descended from such grand folks on his mother's side—something that he learned just when the Stein-finnssøns were trying to treat him as a lesser man, and it looked as if his kinsmen of his father's lineage either had no interest in or lacked the power to protect his rights. But in Denmark he'd be able to ride directly to estates owned by the wealthiest and mightiest of knights in the land and say to the master: I am your sister Cecilia's son.

One evening Olav got out his mother's signet ring and slipped it on his finger. He thought he might as well wear the ring himself until he and Ingunn's kinsmen could reach an agreement. And around his neck he hung a gilded chain with a little gold cross, hiding it under his shirt. This was something his mother was said to have brought from her home. It would be wise to take good care of things he might use as talismans, if needed. Yet, in spite of everything, he did not feel help-less, even though his enemies might place hidden snares at his feet and his kinsmen here at home might offer him little support.

The Steinfinnssøns arrived in Hamar several days later than they'd promised. Kolbein brought both of his sons, as well as Ivar Toressøn and Hallvard Erlingssøn, who was the young cousin of the Toressøns. Hallvard's mother, Ragna, was the full-fledged sister of Kolbein; she too was an offspring of old Tore and his paramour. Hallvard had not visited Frettastein very often, so Olav hardly knew him, but he'd heard that Hallvard was supposed to be exceedingly stupid.

Olav was not allowed to be present when they met with the bishop. Arnvid said this was because his own spokesmen had not come, and Olav could not represent himself. And the bishop was not acting on his behalf but rather on behalf of the church, which had the sole right to determine whether a marriage was valid or not. Olav wasn't pleased to hear this, nor did he fully understand the difference. But both Arnvid and Brother Asbjørn were present at the meeting. They said that at first Kolbein and Ivar had been quite hostile. They were most bitter about the fact that Lord Torfinn had sent Ingunn away from Hamar to stay at an estate near Ottastad Church. Kolbein said that here in Oppland County it had never been the custom for the bishop of Hamar to rule like a minor king. It was clear that this man was from Nidaros,[24] because up there priests always did as they pleased. Yet even there it was apparently unheard of for a bishop to side with a seduced maiden who had run away from her kinsmen so as to hide her shame and escape punishment, or for him to raise his shield to protect a man who had abducted a woman.

Bishop Torfinn replied that as far as he knew, Ingunn Steinfinnsdatter had neither run off nor been abducted by Olav Audunssøn. Arnvid Finnssøn had brought the two young people to Hamar and asked the bishop to investigate a matter that fell under the auspices of the church, and to safeguard Olav and the girl in the meantime. The brothers themselves had asked Arnvid to stay at Frettastein to take charge of the estate and the children. When Arnvid realized that Olav had disgraced the older daughter, he had demanded that the man should take responsibility for his conduct. That was when it became apparent that these two young folks, who were in fact still children, believed that—because their fathers had made an agreement on their behalf when they were small—it fell to them, now that both Steinfinn and Audun were dead, and to no one else to ensure that the pledge was kept and the arrangements settled. For that reason they had conducted themselves as man and wife ever since Steinfinn's death; it had not occurred to them that they might offend anyone by doing so. Arnvid had then decided to bring the two to Hamar so that learned men might determine how matters stood.

One thing was certain: because Olav and Ingunn had given themselves to each other with the understanding that they were consummating an agreed-upon marriage, neither of them was free to marry anyone else. It was also certain that such a marriage went against the laws of the land and the teachings of the church. The woman had relinquished her right to a dowry as well as any inheritance and kinship support for herself and her child or children, if it should turn out that she had conceived. But the men who were in charge of arranging her marriage could demand payments from Olav because he had defied their right. And both young people were responsible for making amends to the church because they had failed to keep its laws regarding the posting of marriage banns and the proper establishment of a marriage.

Then the bishop asked the woman's uncles to remember that Olav and Ingunn were quite childish, with no knowledge of or instruction in the law, and they had grown up in the belief that they were meant to marry each other. Tore Bring of Vik and two other respectable farmers had told him, the bishop, that Steinfinn Toressøn had promised Audun Ingolfssøn with a handshake that his child Ingunn should be the wife of Audun's son. They were willing to swear on the Bible to this. And Arnvid had testified that Steinfinn, right before he died, had spoken to Olav about this matter and said it was his wish that the pledge should be honored. For this reason, the bishop asked that Ingunn's kinsmen agree to a reconciliation on such terms as would prove beneficial to all concerned. Olav and Ingunn would fall to the feet of the Toressøns to beg forgiveness, and for his stubbornness Olav would pay a fine they considered acceptable, however reluctant they might be. But after that, Bishop Torfinn thought it would be most seemly for the Toressøns to reconcile with Olav as good Christians and magnanimous men. They should allow him the benefit of providing his wife with a dowry sufficient that their future kinship with Olav would not bring shame upon them, nor would Olav suffer a diminished standing in his home district because his marriage had not increased his power or fortune. Finally, the bishop asked the Toressøn brothers to keep in mind that in God's eyes it was a particularly noble deed to care for fatherless children, but to ignore the rights of such young progeny was one of the worst sins. It was a sin that shouted for revenge even here on earth. And it had been the wish of the deceased men that their children should be given to each other in marriage.

But if it was now their intent to show that Olav and Ingunn had never been lawfully betrothed, and if they could not come to an agreement with Olav's guardians about how to proceed, it was clear that they could then lodge a claim of bedding without marriage against the lad. Then the bishop would hand over Ingunn to them, so they might punish her in whatever way they judged befitting, and they could divide her share of the inheritance among her siblings. After that her kinsmen would have to provide for her in whatever manner they thought she deserved. Bishop Torfinn would let it be known in all the bishoprics of Norway that for the rest of their lives, these two young people were not free to marry anyone else, so that no one else, neither a man nor a woman, might succumb to the sin of whoredom by taking a wife or husband who was already bound by marriage in accordance with God's commandments.

Both Arnvid and Asbjørn said that it was this last statement that provoked discussion. Evidently, neither of the uncles wanted to take in Ingunn if it meant they would have to provide for her and never be able to marry her off. Kolbein spoke for a long time about the fact that Olav Audunssøn had certainly known what he and his brother thought of the betrothal and that they intended something different for Ingunn. In the end, however, Kolbein promised, for the sake of the bishop, to reconcile with Olav. Yet he refused to discuss the terms until everything was resolved regarding the old agreement and he was able to meet with Ingolf Helgessøn of Tveit or whichever of Olav's kinsmen had the authority to act on the boy's behalf. The bishop then asserted that it was more or less certain that a pledge *sponsalia de futuro* had been made at the ting years ago, so if the Toressøns would give their consent to what had already taken place, then Olav could act on his own behalf. And they would no doubt find him to be most compliant. But Kolbein refused at once to hear of it. They would not take advantage of the boy's ignorance; they demanded to confer with Olav's kinsmen so that the matter would end with honor and dignity for them and their kinswoman.

X

The following evening Arnvid and Olav decided to go down to the monastery together. Arnvid had promised to present the monks with some wool, and Olav wanted to ask Brother Vegard whether there was a day when the monk might hear his confession. It was very dark outside, so each of them brought a weapon. Olav took his axe *Ættarfylgja,* which he carried whenever he had a chance to do so.

When they entered the cloister courtyard, they realized it was later than they had thought. One of the monks who had come outside to look at the weather told them that the lay brother had already left to ring the bell for compline. Nevertheless, Arnvid insisted he needed to have a word with Brother Helge. The monk told them he was in the guesthouse, so that's where they went.

As soon as they entered the house, they saw Kolbein's sons and their cousin, Hallvard, along with three other men. They were sitting on the bench against the wall, eating and drinking. Brother Helge and another monk stood near the table, talking and laughing with the men, who were already quite boisterous.

Olav remained near the threshold while Arnvid went over to Brother Helge. At that moment the monastery bell began to ring.

"Have a seat," said Brother Helge, "and taste our ale. This batch is especially good. I'll ask the prior to come and speak with you after the service. But stay here in the meantime, Arnvid."

"Olav is with me," whispered Arnvid. He had to repeat these words several times, speaking a little louder, because Brother Helge was hard of hearing. The monk finally understood and went over to greet Olav and invite him to sit down to have some ale. Then Kolbein's sons saw who had come with Arnvid. Olav told the monk that he'd rather go over to the church to listen to the singing, but that's when Haftor Kolbeinssøn shouted to him.

"No, come over here, Olav. Come and keep us company! We haven't seen you since you became our kinsman. Come, Arnvid, sit down and drink with us too!"

As Arnvid took a seat on the outer bench, Olav put down his axe and threw back the hood of his cloak. When Olav stepped forward, Einar clapped his hands and smiled as if to a small child.

"How big you've grown, my boy! I think I can see just by looking at you that you're now a married man!"

"Oh, when we were Olav's age, all of us were no doubt 'married' too," smirked Hallvard.

Olav's face turned bright red, but he gave them a disdainful smile.

Brother Helge shook his head, but laughed a bit. Then he asked that all of them remain peaceful. Haftor replied that they would, and with that the monks left. Olav watched them go and murmured that he would much prefer to go over to the church.

"No, no, Olav," said Einar. "That would be most discourteous. You seem to show little eagerness to become acquainted with the kinsmen of your wife. Let's drink," he said, picking up the ale bowl that the lay brother had set on the table. And Einar drank a toast to Olav.

"That's quite a thirst you have," said Olav in a low voice. Einar was already drunk. Aloud he said, "But we've known each other before. And I think it best that we wait to drink to our kinship until your father and I have come to an agreement."

"Surely it must be good enough that Father has acceded to the bishop's wishes," said Einar with feigned benevolence, "since Torfinn seems to have set you on his knee like an adopted child. But it's pleasant to see how quickly a youth can learn. Do you now realize that sometimes it's more seemly to wait? I've heard that Lord Torfinn spoke so eloquently on the subject of patience during Advent. Is that what you've been learning?"

"Yes," replied Olav. "But you must realize that this is a new notion for me, so I fear that I might forget it."

"Oh, I'll be certain to remind you," said Einar, with another mocking laugh.

Olav half-rose from his seat, but Arnvid pulled him back down.

"Is this how you keep the promise you made to the good brothers?" he said now to Einar. "Here on this estate we must remain peaceful."

"You don't think I'm peaceful? A man should be allowed to jest a bit in the name of kinship, my kinsman."

"I didn't know that I was among kinsmen," muttered Arnvid with annoyance.

"What did you say?"

Arnvid was not related to the offspring that Tore of Hov had had with his paramour Borghild. But he refused to be goaded. He looked at the men accompanying the Kolbeinssøns and at the lay brother who was listening with interest as he went about serving at the table.

"There are many here who are not kinsmen."

Haftor Kolbeinssøn now warned his brother not to speak. "And yet all of us here know Einar, and we're aware that he sometimes feels an urge to jest when he has been drinking. But you, Olav, must show that you're a grown man now that you're about to leave and play at being the master of a household. It wouldn't do for you to allow Einar to provoke you as he did that time when you were a small boy and wept with anger."

"Wept with anger!" Olav snorted indignantly. "That's not something I've ever done. And playing at being the master of a household? I don't imagine it will be any sort of game when I go home and take charge of my properties."

"Well, you know best," said Haftor quietly.

That made Olav feel as if he'd said something foolish, and again his face turned bright red.

"Hestviken is the chieftain's estate of that district. It's the largest of the noble estates in the parish."

"Is that right?" said Haftor with solemn composure. "That means you'll have a lot to contend with, Olav, my boy. But I'm sure you'll manage. You know what, kinsman? It seems to me things will be much worse for Ingunn. Do you think she'll be able to handle all the household duties on such a large estate?"

"I'm sure we'll find a way. And my wife won't have to do any of the strenuous work herself," Olav boasted.

"Well, you know best," Haftor said again. "It will be a lavish life for Ingunn, I see."

"Oh, that might be saying too much, even though Hestviken is not a small estate. Most of the effort goes into fishing and shipping."

"Is that right?" said Haftor. "So you also own many seagoing vessels down in the south, on the fjord?"

Olav said, "I don't know how things now stand. It has been years since I was last at Hestviken. But that was true in the old days. And I'm thinking of taking it up again. I've spent time here with Brother Asbjørn and learned quite a bit about ships and merchant voyages."

"It doesn't seem to me that would be necessary for the likes of you," said Einar, smiling. "Not after all the sailing we saw you doing— in Ingebjørg's goose pond."

Olav sprang to his feet and went to stand in the middle of the floor. He now realized that all of them, including Haftor, had been merely ridiculing him. The remark about sailing in the goose pond referred to a game he'd devised for Ingunn's brothers, Hallvard and Jon, during that summer when the children of Frettastein had been sorely neglected.

"I don't see that it makes me any lesser of a man," he said vehemently, "just because I whittled a few boats for the children. Nobody would think that I play such games myself." Then he realized how foolish and childish that sounded, and surly.

"No, that's true," replied Einar. "It would be a very childish game for a boy who's already grown-up enough and bold enough to seduce their sister. It was much more the conduct of a man when you played with Ingunn in the outlying loft rooms and in the barn, where you made her with child."

"That's a lie!" said Olav furiously. "You have the blood of a thrall in you, if you can utter such vile things about your own kinswoman. And I know nothing about any child. But if things are as you say, then none of you need fear that we would ask your father to raise the child. We know he would be reluctant to do so, and—"

"Say no more!" said Arnvid. He sprang to his feet and went over to Olav. "And that's enough from the rest of you." He turned to face the others. "The conduct of a man, you say? Do you consider it manly conduct when Kolbein has agreed to a reconciliation, yet you sit here yapping like dogs? And you, Olav—you should have enough self-respect not to be provoked to bark back."

Now Kolbein's sons and Hallvard had also got up and were standing in the center of the room. They were beside themselves with rage at what Olav had hinted. In his youth, Kolbein had sworn he was not the father of a certain child, but there had been much talk about it back then, and when the boy grew to be a man, most people found it scandalous to see how much he resembled Kolbein.

"You should keep your mouth shut too, Arnvid," said Haftor. He was quite sober. "It's true that your part in this matter is such that it's not to your benefit to have it discussed. But Olav will just have to stand for it, even though I might wish for him to be reconciled instead of receiving what he deserves. He can't expect us to embrace him as a man who is welcome to join our lineage."

"No, Olav, my boy, you will never be welcome to our clan," said Hallvard.

"Speak for yourself and not on behalf of your entire lineage, Hallvard," said Arnvid. "Otherwise Kolbein will offer to Olav your sister, Borghild, as his wife instead of Ingunn!"

"That's a lie!" shouted Hallvard.

"That may be," replied Arnvid. "But he told me that's what he intended to do."

"Shut your trap, Arnvid," Einar interjected. "We know all about your friendship with Olav. It would not be to your advantage for us to examine it too closely. You've refused him nothing, that favored boy of yours—giving him even your own kinswoman, who is still a child, to be his lover."

Arnvid leaned forward and warned, "Watch what you say, Einar!"

"No, the Devil take me if I'm going to be wary of a rotten novice cleric. It seems to me quite a fine tale, this friendship of yours with the fair-complexioned boy. We've heard a rumor or two about the sort of friendship you learn in school—"

Arnvid seized hold of Einar's wrists and twisted them until the man sank to his knees, cursing and gasping with fury and pain. Then Haftor stepped in.

The Kolbeinssøns' hired men stayed where they were, sitting at the table and seemingly not inclined to interfere in this quarrel between the noblemen. Einar Kolbeinssøn got back on his feet, turning and rubbing his hands and arms as he muttered fierce oaths to himself.

Olav looked from one man to the other. He didn't fully understand what they were saying, but it felt as if a hand were clutching at his heart. He had put Arnvid in a much worse position than he'd imagined; they were attacking his friend with bloodthirsty scorn, flaying him alive. He felt such pain when he looked up at Arnvid's face, mostly because he couldn't decipher his expression. Then anger surged inside Olav, a fiery blaze, and all other feelings were devoured in the flame.

Einar again found his voice, now that he had the support of his brother and cousin. He said something, but Olav didn't hear the words. Arnvid's face seemed to tense—then he drove his fist into Einar's throat so that the man fell backward and crashed full length onto the bench in front of the table.

The lay brother rushed over to separate the two men. He helped Einar Kolbeinssøn to his feet and wiped off the blood as he shouted to the others, "An offense that could get you outlawed, that's what this is, and you know full well that you're breaking the peace in our house. Is this conduct befitting of noblemen?"

Arnvid composed himself and said to Haftor, "Brother Sigvald is right. Olav and I will leave now. That would be best."

"We're leaving?" said Olav sharply. "But we weren't the ones who started this quarrel."

"Whoever has good sense must end it," said Arnvid curtly. "As for Einar, I will speak with him in some other place that is better suited to such things. And I say to you, Haftor, that I can fully defend my conduct in this matter, and I have already done so before both the bishop and Kolbein. This is no concern of yours."

"Oh yes, you say that you knew nothing," sneered Einar. "And that might well be true, if it's as folk say, that you were a married man for an entire year before you understood what your mother had given you a wife for."

Olav saw a tremor pass over Arnvid's face, the way it does when a man receives a sudden blow to an open wound. Arnvid turned around and ran back to grab his spear from the doorway, where he'd left it. Seized by a senseless fury on his friend's behalf, Olav leaped between the two men, and as Einar swung an axe in the air, Olav used both hands to raise Ættarfylgja. He struck Einar's axe with a great clang, knocking it out of his hand so that it grazed Hallvard, who was standing behind his cousin before it fell to the floor. Olav raised Ættarfylgja again and swung at Einar Kolbeinssøn. Einar ducked to escape the blow, causing the blade to land just below his shoulder blade and bury itself deep in his back. Einar dropped to the floor and lay there, curled on his side.

Now Kolbein's hired men came alive. All three of them leaped off the bench, waving their weapons in the air, but they were exceedingly drunk and they didn't seem to have much heart for the brawl, though they bellowed loudly. Hallvard sat on the bench, holding on to his wounded leg and groaning as he rocked back and forth.

Haftor had drawn his sword and now set upon the two men. It was quite a short little weapon, while Olav and Arnvid were armed with an axe and a spear, so at first they merely tried to hold Haftor at bay. But they soon realized that it required more effort than they'd thought. Haftor was now completely sober, and he wielded his sword with skill. Determined to avenge his brother, he sought his target with movements that were quick and agile, and with confidence surging through every joint and limb, with all his senses on alert.

Olav defended himself as best he could, inexperienced as he was in using a weapon in earnest, but there was a strangely sensual excitement about this confrontation, and he felt an indefinable yet strong impatience about the way in which Arnvid kept trying to protect him by thrusting his spear between him and Haftor.

Olav was vaguely aware that the door had opened and let in the night air, yet he was still tremendously surprised when the prior and several monks came storming in. The whole battle hadn't lasted long, but when it ended, Olav felt as if he'd been awakened from a lengthy dream, though he wasn't sure how that had happened.

The light in the parlatory was now quite dim because the fire in the hearth was burning low. Olav looked around at the group of monks dressed in black and white. He wiped his face, then let his hand fall and stood there leaning on his axe. What he felt now was a great astonishment about all that had taken place.

Someone lit a candle from the hearth and carried it over to the bench where Brother Vegard and one of the other monks were tending to Einar. He was still alive, though he sounded like a drunken man trying to vomit. Olav heard them say that most of the bleeding seemed to be inside his chest. For a moment Brother Vegard cast a strange glance in Olav's direction.

Then he heard the prior speaking to him, asking whether he was the first to break the peace in the room.

"Yes, I struck first and felled Einar Kolbeinssøn," said Olav. "But there has been little peace here in this room all night—and that was long before I broke what peace there was. Finally Einar cast such disparaging remarks upon us that we took to our weapons."

"That's true," said the lay brother. He was an old farmer who had only recently come to the cloister. "Einar spoke such words that in the past any man would have claimed that when he fell at Olav's hand, he was not worthy of any compensation for his death."

Haftor was standing near his brother. He turned around and said with a cold smile, "No doubt that is how this death will be judged here in this house, and at the bishop's palace—since these two are the bishop's men, through and through. But it may be that the chieftains of this land will soon tire of such abhorrent practices, seeing that every priest who thinks he holds some measure of authority tries to use it to take under his protection the worst assailants and lawbreakers."

"That's not true, Haftor," said the prior. "We who are God's servants will not protect an assailant longer than is his right under the law. But we are obligated to help so that breaches of the law are punished in accordance with the law and not avenged with more lawbreaking that will only give rise to further acts of vengeance, without end."

Haftor said scornfully, "To my mind, these new laws are as effective as a fart. The old laws worked better for men of honor, while the new ones are better for such fellows as Olav over there—men who rape daughters of the best lineage and strike down their kinsmen when they demand their rights for such misdeeds."

The prior shrugged.

"But such is the law. The bailiff will take Olav and hold him prisoner until judgment is passed in this matter. And here are the two men that I sent for." He turned toward two armed men. Olav knew that they lived on the farms closest to the church. "Bjarne and Kaare, you must tie up this young lad and escort him to Sir Audun. He has struck down a man, and it's not yet known whether or not this will be his bane."

Olav handed *Ættarfylgja* to one of the monks.

"You don't need to tie me up," he said fiercely to the two strangers. "No, don't lay hands on me. I'll go with you willingly."

"However it's done, you must leave this place," said the prior. "Surely you must know that you, of all people, cannot be here now that they are coming with *Corpus Domini* for Einar."

Outside it had begun to snow again, and there was a strong wind. The town had settled in for the night more than an hour earlier. The small group of men trudged through the dark, making their way through the swirling snow and powdery drifts between the churchyard wall and the low, black-timbered houses of the canons' estate. Everything looked dead and desolate, and the wind howled mournfully around the walls and whistled through the branches of the big ash trees.

One of the townsmen led the way, followed by an old monk Olav didn't know, though he realized this man must be the subprior. Next came Olav with a man walking on either side of him, and another man behind, keeping so close that he almost stepped on Olav's heels. Olav walked along, thinking that now he was a *prisoner*, yet he felt so drowsy, strangely sluggish and lethargic.

The bailiff's townyard was east of the cathedral. The men had to stand in the snowdrifts for a long time as they pounded on the gate while the snow seeped through their clothing and blanketed the whole group in white. Finally the gate opened and a sleepy-looking man appeared, holding a membrane-covered lantern in his hand. He asked them what was the meaning of all this commotion. Then he let them come in.

Olav had never been inside this townyard before. He could distinguish only darkness and falling snow between the black walls. The bailiff was away; he'd ridden out of town at noontime in the company of the bishop. That's what Olav heard as he stood there in a daze, on the verge of falling asleep. Staggering with fatigue, he allowed himself to be escorted to a small house in the courtyard.

It was bitterly cold inside and pitch-dark; there was no fire in the hearth. After a moment someone brought a candle along with bedding that was tossed onto the bedstead. The servant bade him good night, and Olav responded in kind, already half-asleep. Then the servant left, fastening the door from the outside, and Olav was alone—and suddenly wide awake. He stood there, staring at the little flame of the candle.

The first thing he felt was a piercing chill. Then rage flared up inside him along with a defiant, gleeful sense of satisfaction because he'd gotten the better of that insufferable Einar Kolbeinssøn. And he did not regret it, though God might strike him dead. He didn't care what his brash behavior might cost him. Kolbein and his kinsmen—how he hated them with all his heart! Only now did Olav realize how tormented he'd felt during the past months—the fear, the gnawing anguish of guilt, all the humiliations he'd suffered as he looked for some way out of the mire into which he'd sunk. It was Kolbein who had blocked him at every turn as he tried to regain a foothold on solid ground. If Kolbein and his cronies hadn't stood in his way, he would have long ago escaped all this agony and been a free and saved man. Then he could have put aside the terrible feeling that he was someone who had betrayed and furtively crept about. But Kolbein had held him under his thumb. And now Olav had taken revenge, and for that he thanked God with all his heart. It would do no good for Bishop Torfinn and his new friends here at the bishop's palace to say that this was a sinful way of thinking. The flesh and blood of a man *made* him think such things.

Olav's soul rose up, shaking with defiance against all the new teachings and ideas that he'd encountered here at the bishop's palace. They might be well and good, he did see that—but no, no, they were impossible and unnatural dreams. Never would all men become such saints that they would consent to having their concerns, both great and small, judged by their Christian peers. Nor would they be forever content with the law and willing to be *given* what was their right—and never *take* it for themselves. He recalled that Haftor had said something in the same vein that evening, something about the new laws being suitable only for the lowliest of men. He suddenly found himself in agreement with the likes of Kolbein and his sons, if only on this one score. He would rather settle this matter against them on his own, pitting one injustice against another, if need be. His place was among people like Kolbein and Steinfinn and Ingebjørg—and with Ingunn, who had thrown herself into his arms with no regard for the law, giddy and ardent, with headstrong passion. He didn't belong among these priests and monks whose lives proceeded with clear and serene regularity, who did the same thing every day at the same time. They prayed, worked, ate, sang, retired to their beds, and then got up again to say their prayers. And they studied the laws, writing them down and discussing each paragraph, then agreeing among themselves and arguing with the laymen about what they'd read. They did all this because they loved the law and dreamed of using it to tame everyone until no man would bear arms against his neighbor or use violence to claim his rights; instead, everyone would become tranquil and willing to listen to Our Lord's gentle words about the brotherhood that exists among all God's children. Olav now felt a vague and melancholy tenderness for all of this, as well as a respect for the men who could behave in such a manner. Yet he found himself unable to submit to the law in every instance, and he was filled with a terrible revulsion at the mere thought that he was the one on whom they now wished to fasten these bonds.

His rebelliousness was made worse because he dimly sensed that now they would certainly think of him as an outlaw. Bishop Torfinn couldn't possibly have affection for him any longer, considering how he had repaid the man's fatherly kindness. And all the monks had given him such strange looks; no doubt they were angry because he had sullied their parlatory with bloodshed. The old subprior had said something about remorse and repentance before he'd left. But Olav was not of a repentant mind.

He would simply have to accept whatever the cost might be. He should never have listened to Arnvid, should never have come here, should never have allowed himself to be separated from Ingunn.

Ingunn, he thought. A yearning for her surged inside him like a restless torment. She was the only person on this earth whom he truly knew, the only one he felt close to. Ingunn, precisely the way she was and not in any other way. She was weak and willful, overly impetuous, lovely and tender and warm. She was the only one he could be certain of, the one constant he could trust. Of all that he owned, it was she alone he had touched and possessed and seen as something other than unreal dreams and words and hazy memories. She was as real as his own body and his own soul, and now he was soundlessly shouting for her as he curled up, gnashing his teeth and clenching his fists so tight that his nails cut into his skin. He thought about how far away from her he now was, and about how things might go in order for her to be his. And all his desire for her blazed up, making him whimper aloud and bite his own fists. He wanted to go to her, he wanted to have her right this minute, he could have gladly torn her limb from limb and devoured her, out of fear that someone might tear them apart. "Ingunn, Ingunn," he quietly moaned.

He had to find her. He had to tell her what had happened and hear what she thought about the fact that he had killed her cousin. Because Einar was going to die, he was certain about that. There was now blood between them—but, Holy Mary! What did that matter when the two of them had already become one flesh? She was not fond of those Kolbeinssøns, but kinsmen were kinsmen, so his poor Ingunn would no doubt mourn and weep. Yet he had no urge to wish that what he'd done could be undone. And he also needed to find out if things stood with her as Einar had said; if so, she was going to suffer, and suffer terribly. A dry sob racked Olav's body. Kolbein had demanded that she be given to him so he might punish her. But if she fell into his hands, and she was carrying the child of his son's murderer . . . Then they would certainly torment her to death.

He needed to speak to Arnvid about this. Surely Arnvid would seek him out tomorrow. Arnvid had to send Ingunn someplace where Kolbein couldn't find her.

The candle was merely a thin wick wrapped around an iron spike. Olav wasn't usually afraid of the dark, but right now he didn't want the candle to go out and leave him alone in the dark with his thoughts. Cautiously he tended to the wick.

Then he swiftly took off his cloak, boots, and the fine cotehardie he was wearing and climbed at once into the bed. He burrowed into the ice-cold bedding, burying his face in the pillow as he cried for Ingunn. He thought back to Christmas Eve and felt a great anger against Providence. Was this to be his reward because for once he had insisted on doing what was right?

He pulled the coverlet up over his head; that way he wouldn't see the candle burn out. But then he tossed it aside again and, leaning his face on his hand, he lay there and stared at the little flame.

Yes, Arnvid was the only one he could ask to protect Ingunn, now that he couldn't do it himself. But he suddenly felt such a strange reluctance to think about Arnvid.

He hadn't understood what Einar meant by the scornful words he'd flung at Arnvid, but this much Olav did know: the remarks had struck Arnvid like a vicious kick to an open wound. Each time Olav thought about this, he at first felt disgusted and ill, and then beside himself with fury. It was as if he'd been witness to some sort of vulgar and cruel abuse.

He'd now come to see that there was much he needed to learn before he could say he knew Arnvid well. He trusted him more than anyone else he'd ever met. He relied on Arnvid's high-mindedness and loyalty, and he knew that Arnvid would not be afraid of anything when it came to helping a friend or kinsman. But there was something about Arnvid Finnssøn that made Olav think of a tarn with unfathomable holes on the floor of the lake. Or . . .

One evening Fat Asbjørn had told a story about an exceedingly learned doctor in the southern countries who had tried to seduce a woman, the loveliest in all the land. Finally she pretended that she would submit to him. In secret she led him to her bedchamber, where she unfastened her clothing and invited him to look at her breasts. One was white and fair, but the other was nothing but a suppurating wound.

The others had praised this tale, calling it wise and instructive, because after witnessing such a sight, Raimond, the learned man, had turned away from the world and entered a monastery. But Olav thought it was the most awful story he'd ever heard, and he had lain awake far into the night, unable to get the tale out of his mind. There was something about Arnvid that frightened him. He worried that one day he might see something in the man that was like a hidden wound. And Olav had always secretly felt repulsed by the sight of illness or suffering; nor could he bear to cause anyone harm. He wondered vaguely whether what he feared was to be struck in a wounded place, as Arnvid had been in the autumn, making him strangely unable to act. Now Olav almost wished that Arnvid had not been so meek but had instead demanded earlier that he should assume responsibility. He didn't like thinking that he'd taken advantage of his friend's weakness. And here he now lay, knowing that he would have to ask Arnvid to take care of Ingunn and protect her in the face of whatever consequences his reckless behavior might bring, since God alone knew when he himself would be in a position to look after her.

In a sense, Olav did understand something of what ailed Arnvid. Arnvid had never concealed the fact that his deepest wish had always been to devote himself in service to God by joining an order. And after spending time in Hamar, Olav could now better grasp why a man might want to do this. But he had a feeling that Arnvid had a more complicated nature than . . . well, than what he'd seen of Fat Asbjørn or Brother Vegard. Arnvid longed to submit, to obey, and to serve—but he also felt a certain affinity for those men who demanded that another law should apply: the laws for men with hearts of flesh, volatile blood, and vengeful spirits. It was as if Arnvid had been crushed between these two types of law.

Olav had noticed that Arnvid never spoke of the years when he'd been married. From others he'd heard a few things about Arnvid's marriage. His wife, Tordis, had first been promised to Magnus, who was the eldest of the Finnssøns. He was a brash but jovial man, well-liked and handsome. Tordis must have been bitterly disappointed with the husband she was given instead. Yet Arnvid hadn't been overly fond of his wife either. Tordis was a proud and obstinate woman who never hid the contempt she felt for her husband because he was so young and reserved and somewhat shy around people. And she openly squabbled with her mother-in-law. Arnvid must have had an unhappy youth, living as he did with those two controlling and quarrelsome women. No doubt that's why he now seemed to keep away from all women—except for Ingunn. Olav saw that Arnvid felt a deep affection for her. That was probably because Ingunn was so weak and in need of the protection and support of men; it never occurred to her to try to rule or manipulate them. Arnvid often seemed lost in thought as he sat and looked at Ingunn, his expression strange and somber, as if he felt such compassion for her. One of Arnvid's weaknesses was this tendency of his to feel compassion—too deeply and too often, especially when it came to animals. Olav was kind to animals too, but Arnvid could make such a fuss about animals that had fallen ill. Yet it was odd how frequently the animals would recover and thrive after Arnvid had taken care of them. The two or three times that Olav had heard Arnvid mention his deceased wife, it was clear that the man felt compassion even for her.

But lately Olav had felt a growing aversion toward Arnvid because his friend was so quick to sympathize. Olav knew that he shared this weakness himself, but he had now realized what a shortcoming it actually was. It could so easily make a man unable to act and cause him to fall victim to those of a more callous nature.

◆ ◆ ◆

Olav sighed, tired and bewildered. It was disheartening to think of all those for whom he felt affection: Bishop Torfinn, Arnvid, and Ingunn. Yet when he thought about Einar Kolbeinssøn and those who were his enemies, he was pleased about what he'd done. No, it was impossible for him to feel remorse. But he wouldn't be able to bear it if he was separated from Ingunn now. Through his own actions he had backed himself into a corner.

The candle had almost burned out. Olav crept out of bed and carefully unwound the last of the wick. Then he took the candle with him as he went over to examine the door. Not that he had any hope of escaping, but he still had to try.

It was a heavy and sturdy door, yet there was a gap around the edges. A great deal of snow had drifted inside. He shone the candlelight on the door. No doubt there was a big lock on the outside, as well as a wooden latch, but there were no such fastenings on the inside. A willow handle was merely nailed to the wood. Olav pulled out his dagger and slipped it into the gap in the door. That's when he noticed that the lock had not been attached. The latch was the only thing holding the door closed, and he was able to wiggle it a bit with his dagger, but only a little because the latch was big and heavy, and the dagger blade quite thin.

Yet it caused a fiery heat to pass through him. His hands trembled as he put on his boots and outer garments. He couldn't very well give up when it turned out that he'd been left in a house that wasn't even locked. He gripped the haft of his dagger with both hands and tried to force the latch up. At his first attempt, the dagger blade broke in half. Olav clenched his teeth and stuck through the gap what remained of the blade and the haft as well. But then he couldn't budge the dagger in the narrow crack. Sweating with exertion, he jiggled the dagger until he figured out how far in he was able to slip the blade. Then he pried at the latch, trying to lift it. Several times he thought he'd managed to get it out of the slot, but it fell back down when he let go with one hand so he could tug at the door handle. Finally he succeeded. Snow came pouring in. Quietly he stepped across the threshold and peered into the night.

No sign of any dogs; they must have been taken inside because of the weather. Not a sound except for the hushed whistling of the hard granules of snow as they were whipped about by the wind. Slowly and cautiously Olav worked his way in the dark through the unfamiliar courtyard. A number of skis had been set in a snowdrift in front of one of the houses. Olav took two of them and then continued on.

The gate facing the lane was closed, but a heap of timbers had been left nearby. If he climbed to the top, he should be able to slip over the stave fence. He was starting to believe that this was a portent. He clambered up on the timbers and dropped the skis over the fence, hearing the quiet sound they made as they fell into a snowdrift. Mother, he thought. Maybe it's my mother who is praying for me, asking that I might get away from here.

The wide cloak and ankle-length cotehardie he wore made it more difficult, but finally he climbed over the fence and landed in the snow in the lane. He hitched up his clothing and belt as high as he could and fastened the skis to his boots. Then he leaned forward and set off through the falling snow that glinted with white streaks and stripes in the dark.

As soon as he reached the end of the street, the way forward disappeared, covered in snow. Only occasionally did he glimpse the tops of fences now that his eyes had grown accustomed to the dark. But he continued on, heading directly into the driving snow almost the whole time. It was impossible to make out any landmarks on such a night as this, though he was familiar with the estate where she was staying. He had passed it several times when he rode with Asbjørn along the main road, but that made no difference in this weather. He was just as good on skis as the best of skiers, but it was snowing heavily. Yet he wasn't worried as he blindly battled his way onward, for he was convinced that on this night he would receive help. It didn't occur to him that he carried no weapon—his dagger was now useless—or that he had no money other than five or six ørtuger.[25] He felt no fear at all.

◆ ◆ ◆

Olav had no idea what time it was when he finally made it to the entrance of the estate where Ingunn was staying. Here the dogs were awake. A whole horde of them came rushing toward him, furious and ravenous. He held them off with a post that he had picked up along the way and then began shouting. At last someone came to the door.

"Is Ingunn Steinfinnsdatter here? I must speak with her at once. I am Olav Audunssøn, her husband."

The short winter day was already coming to an end. Twilight was closing in over the snow-covered land when the two sledges, pulled by exhausted horses, drove into the small estate near Ottastad Church. The three fur-clad men got out to speak briefly with the owner.

"Yes, she's here inside the house," he said. "Her husband is apparently still in bed. He arrived in the early hours of the morning and then the two of them lay in bed, talking and whispering. Only Our Lord and Saint Olav can know what must be worrying them, the way they were carrying on. As for me, I went to sleep." He scratched his head as he gave the three men a slyly questioning look. He knew Brother Asbjørn well, and the two others were Arnvid Finnssøn of Miklebø—the woman's kinsman who had been here several times to speak to her—and his old manservant.

The three men went into the house. Ingunn was sitting on the step to the bed farthest away. On her lap she held some mending, although it was too dark for her to do any sewing over there in the corner. She stood up at once when she recognized who had come in, and she came forward to greet them. She looked tall and slender in the dark gown she wore; her face was pale and her eyes dark beneath the wimple of a married woman.

"Hush," she pleaded softly. "Tread quietly. Olav is sleeping."

"It's about time for you to wake him, my dear woman," said Brother Asbjørn. "I never thought that boy was in possession of much sense, but now things have gone from bad to worse. Surely he must know this is the first place they'll look for him, yet here he is, lying in bed fast asleep!" The priest snorted angrily.

Ingunn blocked their way.

"What do you want with Olav?"

"We mean him no harm," said Arnvid. "But considering the fine mess he has made of things . . . You will have to come with me, Ingunn, and stay with me at Miklebø, for you must see that now Lord Torfinn can hardly refuse to return you to your kinsmen."

"What about Olav?" she asked in the same tone of voice.

The priest groaned with resignation.

"This woman . . . It's sheer madness that he has come running here! Now this woman will never be able to keep quiet about what she witnesses."

"Yes, she will, when she realizes that it's for Olav's best," said Arnvid. "Ingunn, you must understand that it's no small risk for this priest here, and for me as well, to side with a murderer and help him to escape."

"I promise not to say anything," said Ingunn solemnly. Then she turned away and went over to the bed. She paused for a moment, looking at the sleeping man the way a mother might if she was reluctant to wake her child.

The priest thought to himself: she certainly is beautiful, all the same. In his view, the women that caused young boys to behave sinfully and foolishly were rarely the sort that a sensible and level-headed man would regard as respectable in any way. And he had harbored an unusual aversion toward this particular woman. This Ingunn Steinfinnsdatter looked like an indolent and frivolous woman, helpless and pampered, of little use for anything but sparking discord and difficulties for men. Now Brother Asbjørn thought that perhaps she was a better person than he'd judged her to be; she might, in fact, become a good woman when she was older and more settled in temperament. In any case, she had conducted herself as a reasonable person would, and she was gazing at Olav as if she held loyal affection for him. And she was indeed beautiful; he had to agree with those who said as much.

Olav looked so young and innocent as he lay there with his white, muscular arms raised, his hands clasped behind his neck, and his fair hair spread out on the brown woolen pillow covering. He was sleeping as soundly as a child. But the instant that Ingunn touched his shoulder to wake him, Olav jolted up, wide-awake, and sat on the bed with his legs drawn up and his arms wrapped around his knees. He looked calmly at the two men.

"Are you here to take me back?"

"Arnvid is here to take your wife home with him," said Asbjørn. "I . . ." He glanced at the others. "I think that first you must let me speak to Olav alone."

Arnvid took Ingunn by the hand and led her to a seat at the far end of the room. Fat Asbjørn sat down on the edge of the bed.

Olav asked him somberly, "What does Lord Torfinn say about all this? It's woeful that I should repay his hospitality with such misfortune."

"Yes, those words are truer than even you could know. And that's why you must be on your way and leave this country."

"You want me to run away from here?" said Olav slowly. "Without a judgment? Does Lord Torfinn say this is what I should do?"

"No, it's what I'm saying you should do. As yet, the bishop and the bailiff know nothing of the murder. Yes, Einar is dead. We don't expect them back until tomorrow. And I convinced the servants at Audun's townyard that since they weren't able to hold you captive any better than they did, they ought to wait to inform Kolbein until the bailiff himself can speak to the man. They've gone out searching for you now, but in this heavy snowfall, it's doubtful they'll manage to get this far, and it will soon be night. At least that's what we dare hope, in God's name. We'll stay here until the moon comes up a little after midnight. Then the weather will be clear and freezing. Old Guttorm will go with you to show the way. Since both of you are skilled skiers, you should be able to reach Solberga in Sweden on the night of the third day. There you can stay in hiding with my sister, but only as long as is needed, just until Sven Birgerssøn can find you somewhere else to stay in the districts over there."

"But would it be wise for me to flee the land before I've been sentenced as an outlaw?" asked Olav.

"Since you've already taken flight, it would be best for you to continue on," said the priest. "Do you want folks to say of you that you broke out of captivity merely so you could come out here and caress your wife? There's no need to look at me like that, just because I say such things. You are young and shortsighted, and you give little thought to anything but your own concerns; that's the nature of your youth. No doubt you haven't considered that a man like Lord Torfinn may be dealing with many matters that are far more important than whether you're allowed to live in peace with your Ingunn and be granted her dowry. You arrived here with this case of yours at an inopportune time. You could hardly have decided on a worse time to bother the bishop with your—."

"It was Arnvid who made that decision, not me," Olav interrupted him.

"Ah, Arnvid. His timing is just as poor as yours when it comes to this fragile grass-blade of a woman. But as I told you, Olav, you must ensure that the bishop doesn't have to concern himself with this murder as well. Your kinsmen must come forward, and it will then be up to them to win dispensation for you so that you might be granted peace for yourself here in the country of the Norwegian king."

"I don't know," said Olav pensively. "I don't think Bishop Torfinn will be pleased if I run off like this."

"No, he won't," said the priest curtly. "And that's why I want you to go. These new men who have taken charge on behalf of our young king are preparing to make open war against the Holy Church. And Lord Torfinn must wash his hands of cases such as yours. If you had ended up imprisoned in Mjøskastellet,[26] he would have done his utmost on your behalf because you sought help from him and because you have few friends. And Lord Torfinn is so pious and such a true and holy father to all those who are fatherless. He is also as stubborn and obdurate as a billy goat; that's his greatest fault. But I expect you to understand that after you sought his protection, which you received, you then behaved quite recklessly. It would not be manly conduct for you now to demand more from him, when you know that such a request would only cause him added trouble."

Olav nodded silently. He stood up and began to get dressed.

"I suppose it will be more difficult for us now," he said quietly. "For Ingunn and me to be together."

"In the long run, her kinsmen will probably tire of keeping her and having to provide for her, when she's neither unmarried nor properly married," said the priest. "But the two of you will certainly have to wait several years now."

Olav frowned as he stared straight ahead.

"That's what we promised each other last night—that we would be true to the pledge we've made, and I will come back to her, whether it be dead or alive."

"That is an ungodly promise," said Asbjørn dryly. "But I am not surprised. It's easy to be a good Christian, Olav, as long as God makes no more demands upon you than inviting you to church to listen to beautiful songs and asking you to obey Him while He pats you with His fatherly hand. But a man's faith can be tested on the day when God does not want the same thing as he wants. Let me tell you what Bishop Torfinn said the other day when we were speaking of you and your case. "'May God grant,' he said, 'that the boy learns to understand over time that for a man who insists on doing what he wants to do, there will soon come a day when he sees he has done what he never intended to do.'"

Olav solemnly gazed into the distance. Then he nodded.

"Yes. That's true. I know that."

They ate some food, and a little later they lay down to rest, fully clothed—all except Arnvid, who offered to keep watch. He sat down in front of the hearth and quietly read from a book that he'd brought along in his travel bag. Occasionally he would get up and step outside to ascertain the time. By now the weather had cleared and a dense blanket of glittering stars covered the vault of the sky; a freeze had set in. Once he knelt down to pray with his arms stretched out in the form of a cross.

Finally, when Arnvid went outside again, he saw the light of the rising moon come streaming over the mountain ridge. He went back inside and over to the bed where Olav and Ingunn lay, sleeping cheek against cheek. He woke the man, saying, "It's time now for you to leave."

Olav opened his eyes, gently pulled himself free from Ingunn's arms, and climbed out of bed at once. He was fully dressed, lacking only his boots and outer surcoat. Now he put on different footwear and a tunic made of reindeer hide. Arnvid had brought him garments that were more suitable for a long ski journey than the ankle-length surcoat and the red boots made from fine goat leather, which had become badly damaged the previous night.

"My old Guttorm knows his way everywhere in these districts and on both sides of the border," said Arnvid. He was referring to his old manservant, his so-called foster father, who was to be Olav's guide. Arnvid handed his sword to Olav, along with a spear and a money pouch. "We'll say that you sold me your horse Elgsblakken; you know that I've always wished he was mine."

"All right."

"That vile slander Einar was spouting . . ." muttered Arnvid hesitantly as he stared down at the fire. "He was always so malicious and such a liar. And a dissolute devil himself, so he could never see that other men might . . . might be repulsed by what he . . ."

Olav lowered his eyes, mortally embarrassed. He had no idea what this was about.

"I wanted you to have Ingunn, because I thought you would be good to her. Do you swear to me, Olav, that you will never betray my kinswoman?"

"I swear. And can I trust that you will take care of her? If I couldn't be certain she will be safe when you take her into your care, then I'll be damned if I would do as Asbjørn wants and escape to Sweden. But I know that you are fond of her."

"I will keep her safe." Then Arnvid burst out laughing. He tried to stifle the laughter, but he couldn't stop. He sat there, shaking with barely suppressed chortles until the tears poured down his cheeks.

Finally he bent forward and laughed so hard that his whole body shook, his head buried in his arms that were resting on his knees. Olav stood next to him, feeling terribly ill at ease.

"So. Now you and Guttorm need to leave." Arnvid pulled himself together, wiped the tears of laughter from his face, and stood up. Then he went over to wake the other three.

Olav and Old Guttorm stood outside in the courtyard with their skis securely fastened to their boots; they were well armed and outfitted with everything they would need. The three others stood in the doorway to the house. Then Ingunn went over to Olav and held out her hand. He shook her hand firmly, and they spoke to each other for a moment, just a few words. She was quiet and utterly calm.

The waning moon had risen high enough in the sky to cast long, indistinct shadows across the windblown snowdrifts heaped on the ground.

"I think the skiing conditions will be good inside the forest," the priest reassured them.

Olav turned around and slid on his skis back toward his two friends standing in front of the door. He shook their hands as well and courteously thanked them for their help. Then he turned away. Arnvid Finnssøn and Brother Asbjørn stayed where they were and watched Olav Audunssøn and his guide head across the expanse of fields toward the forest, skiing with steadfast vigor until they slipped into the shadows at the edge of the woods.

"Ah yes, *Laus Deo*," said the priest. "Given the grave state of things, this is the best solution. I was afraid that Ingunn would behave badly, screaming and sobbing at the last moment."

"No, no," said Arnvid. He looked up at the moon with a strangely resigned smile on his face. "It's only small concerns that cause her to complain. When it comes to serious matters, she is as good as gold."

"Is that so? Well, you know her better than I do," said Brother Asbjørn indifferently. "Now it's just the two of us, Arnvid. The fact that we've helped Olav to escape is going to cost both of us dearly."

"Yes, but there was no other way."

"No, there wasn't." The priest shook his head. "But I wonder whether Olav truly understands how much you and I have risked by helping him like this."

"Have you lost your wits?" said Arnvid, and laughter again overtook him. "You can be sure that, young as he is, he has no idea what anything might cost."

Fat Asbjørn laughed briefly. Then he yawned.

And all three of them, the priest, Arnvid, and Ingunn, went back inside to return to bed.

Part II

Ingunn
Steinfinnsdatter

I

After Olav Audunssøn fled, Bishop Torfinn said that he no longer had the right to keep Ingunn Steinfinnsdatter from the guardianship of her uncles. But Arnvid Finnssøn replied that the woman was ill, and for that reason he couldn't send her away. Lord Torfinn grew quite irate when he learned that Arnvid, too, was unwilling to comply with the law unless it suited him. Now the bishop wanted to make arrangements for Ingunn to stay with her father's sister in Berg, but Arnvid said her health was too poor for her to travel anywhere at all.

Kolbein Toressøn, as well as his son Haftor, were beside themselves with fury because Olav had managed to get away. They claimed that the bishop must have had a hand in his escape, even though Lord Torfinn had not been in town when the murder was committed and he hadn't returned home until after the murderer had fled. And Arnvid Finnssøn had also admitted he was the one who had helped Olav flee to Sweden. When it became known that Fat Asbjørn had aided Arnvid in this matter and that the fugitive had been taken in by the priest's married sister, who lived in Sweden, Lord Torfinn was so angry that he sent Asbjørn away for a while, after the priest had paid restitution for the part he had played. Even though no one seriously believed that the bishop had been aware of Olav's escape, there were still many men who blamed him because one of his priests had broken the law, had consorted with an outlaw, and had helped him flee.

The bailiff declared Olav an outlaw. After that, Helge of Tveit and his sons finally came forward and offered, on Olav's behalf, to pay compensation for the murder in accordance with whatever decision was reached by the participants at the *ting.* But these men were not Olav's closest kin; they were related through a brother of his great-grandfather, and the two branches of the lineage, one at Tveit and the other at Hestviken, had had little contact over the years. The old man living at Hestviken was Olav's rightful guardian. For that reason, Olav's spokesmen found it a difficult and prolonged process as they tried to settle this matter. In the spring Bishop Torfinn had to travel to Bjørgvin on other business, and he invited Jon Helgessøn of Tveit to accompany him so that the man might petition the king for dispensation for Olav.

Kolbein demanded that Olav should remain an outlaw, ineligible to pay any fines that would permit him to stay in Norway peacefully. He claimed the killing was the act of a dishonorable man. Olav had raped Kolbein's niece at her father's estate and then felled the girl's cousin when Einar insisted that Olav should make right his misdeed. Kolbein had chosen as his spokesmen in Bjørgvin the knight Gaut Torvardssøn and his son Haakon. Sir Gaut was a kinsman of the baron Andres Plytt; and Sir Andres was a member of the State Council, which was in charge of governing Norway until the king came of age. Sir Andres was one of the leaders of the noble chieftains who now intended to do battle with the prelates regarding church freedoms and rights. It turned out that these were the men the Toressøns had been counting on for support, and Haakon Gautssøn was the one who was supposed to have married Ingunn.

Then the bishop of Hamar once again took it upon himself to defend Olav. He maintained that it would be impossible to accuse Olav of rape if he had bedded Ingunn in good faith, based on an old betrothal pledge. And Ivar and Kolbein had already promised to reconcile with Olav regarding this matter when the man had the misfortune to kill Einar during a quarrel while they were drinking with several other men in the guest quarters of the Dominican monks in Hamar. The bishop said that it would be the worst injustice if Olav were not shown the same mercy as any other man who had murdered someone—which meant granting him dispensation and guaranteed peace for his property, if he was willing to pay the necessary fine to the king as well as restitution to Einar Kolbeinssøn's heirs. In every district in Norway there were now men who had committed a murder or some other crime resulting in banishment, yet they were living securely on their estates with a royal document of dispensation in their possession. Those who considered themselves powerful enough did not even bother to seek such a document. So anyone could see it would be the greatest injustice to dole out harsher treatment for Olav, who was so young that if not for the latest change in law made by his blessed majesty King Magnus, no one would have demanded more of Olav than that he should leave the country and stay away until he came of age. And through Arnvid Finnssøn and Fat Asbjørn, Olav had immediately conveyed to Kolbein that he was certainly willing to pay the required fine as restitution for the murder.

During Whitsun, Olav had returned to Norway at Elvesyssel, near the Mariaskog cloister. There he owned a small estate by allodial right as well as several smallholdings. This estate had been passed down to the Hestviken men through the wife of Olav's paternal grandfather, Ingolf Olavssøn. No one tried to detain Olav, and the king's local representatives allowed him to remain there in peace until well into the autumn. The estate was far away from those places frequented by Olav's enemies. But in the fall, it became known that Olav Audunssøn's properties in the north had been confiscated, including the household goods he had left behind in Oppland County and his property in Vik, except for his allodial lands. Then Olav again left Norway, and this time he sailed south to Denmark.

At Miklebø, Fru Hillebjørg had warmly welcomed Ingunn Steinfinnsdatter. She had developed a fondness for Olav during the few times she had seen him, and she was no less fond of him now that he had felled a man who was the offspring of Tore's paramour. She greeted her son with more tenderness than usual, and when a demand for banishment was raised against Arnvid because he had helped Olav, she laughed and patted him on the shoulder. "It's none too soon, my son, for you to be the subject of such a case as well. I never liked the fact that you were so submissive."

She was gentler toward the ill young woman than Arnvid had ever seen her behave toward anyone else. Ingunn's health was only passable. She suffered such dizziness that when she got out of bed in the morning, she had to stand still for a long time and hold on to something while the room spun around and around and black spots appeared before her eyes, making it impossible for her to see. If she had to bend down to pick up something from the floor, this hazy state would overtake her, blinding her for a long time afterward. She was unable to eat anything, and she grew so thin and pale that her face took on a pallor all the way up to the corners of her eyes. Hillebjørg brewed special concoctions for her to drink that were supposed to ease these symptoms, but Ingunn couldn't keep them down. The old woman laughed and consoled her. It was well known that such an illness would soon run its course and then she would feel much better. Ingunn didn't reply when the mistress jested in this manner. She would bow her head and try to hide that her eyes were brimming with tears. Otherwise she never wept; she was always exceedingly quiet and uncomplaining.

Ingunn didn't have the strength to undertake even the smallest amount of work. She would sit with a band-weaving loom and make trim with exquisite flowers and animals. Or she would continue sewing the linen shirt that she'd cut out while she was in Hamar. She had always been skilled at delicate handiwork, and now she put all her artistry and diligence into this shirt, which she intended to give to Olav when he returned. But the work progressed very slowly. She also made toys for Arnvid's sons, plaiting coats of mail for them out of straw, attaching feathers to their arrows, and making bats and balls that were better than any they'd ever had before. Ingunn told Arnvid that she was good at such things because she had always played with boys. Olav had taught her. She sang for the children and told them stories and recited maxims. She seemed to find the most solace when she spent time with the three small lads. She would have liked nothing more than to hold one of the children on her lap at all times. Magnus was now in his fifth year, while the twins, Finn and Steinar, were almost four. Magnus and Finn were unruly and robust little fellows, and they didn't care to have women fussing over them. But Steinar was meeker and showered all his love on Ingunn. So she took this boy with her wherever she went, carrying him in her arms, and he slept in her bed at night. Steinar was also his father's favorite. Arnvid would often sit with Ingunn in the evening as the child played on her lap, and he would sing for them until the boy fell asleep with his head resting against Ingunn's chest. Then she would whisper to Arnvid to hush, and she would sit in silence, staring straight ahead and occasionally glancing down at the sleeping child. She would gently kiss the boy's hair, then go back to staring straight ahead.

But as summer neared, it became clear that there was no natural cause for Ingunn's poor health, and no one could understand what ailed her.

Arnvid wondered whether it was sorrow alone that had broken her so utterly, for her health did not improve; in fact, it seemed to grow worse. The fainting spells took over, and many times she would fall unconscious. She couldn't keep down any of the food she attempted to eat, and she said she had constant pain in the small of her back, as if she'd suffered a hard blow in that area. She also had such an odd feeling in her legs, as if they had withered. She hardly had enough strength to walk anymore.

Arnvid could see that she longed for Olav day and night, and now her grief over her parents came rushing back. She had almost forgotten about them for a while because of Olav. But now she reproached herself bitterly for this neglect, saying that she fully deserved the unhappiness it now looked like she would have. "It was on the night Mother died that I became Olav's wife!"

Arnvid's face took on a strange expression when she mentioned this, but he didn't say a word.

She was also sad about being separated from her siblings. Tora was at Berg, staying with their aunt, and even though the two sisters had never been close, Ingunn now longed to see Tora. It was much harder to think about her two young brothers; she had always been good friends with them, but now they were at Frettastein with Haftor and his young wife. And Hallvard and Jon would no doubt be taught to feel hatred toward Olav Audunssøn and anger toward her.

Ingunn talked of all these things to Arnvid, though she shed few tears; it was as if she felt too downhearted and hopeless to cry. Arnvid wondered whether she might die of sorrow.

But Fru Hillebjørg hinted that the affliction that had befallen Ingunn was quite strange; it was almost as if some sort of *treachery* might be the cause.

One evening in early summer Arnvid managed to persuade Ingunn to take a walk with him down the slope to look at the grain that was growing so beautifully in the lovely weather. He had to support her as they walked, and he noticed that she moved her feet as if they were fettered with an invisible chain. They got as far as the edge of the woods when she suddenly collapsed and lay unconscious on the ground. It took some time before he was able to revive her; he didn't think she'd ever been insensible for so long before. She couldn't stand, so he had to carry her the way he might carry a child. It frightened him to feel how thin she was and how little she weighed.

The following morning it turned out that she couldn't move her legs. Her entire lower body was paralyzed. For the next few days she whimpered quietly because the pain in her back was so severe. But it gradually eased, and then her body seemed to lose all feeling from the waist down. And that was how she remained. She never complained, rarely spoke, and often seemed removed from everything around her. Her only request was to have Steinar nearby, and she seemed content whenever he climbed up onto her bed to play and tumble over her half-dead body, which had now wasted away so much that only a skeleton remained.

During this time no one knew where Olav was. Arnvid thought that Ingunn would die soon, but he was unable to send word to Olav about her failing health.

Yet Fru Hillebjørg didn't hesitate to tell anyone who would listen that she was firmly convinced somebody had cast a spell over Ingunn to make her so ill. She had stuck needles in the young woman's thighs and legs, and she had burned her skin with a glowing hot iron, but Ingunn felt none of it. Hillebjørg could present witnesses to this effect, respected men and women as well as her parish priest and her own son. Kolbein and Haftor were the only ones who could be suspected of such a misdeed. And here lay this unfortunate young child, wasting away and slowly dying. Now the mistress urged her son to insist that the bishop should investigate this matter.

Arnvid was almost willing to believe that his mother was right, and he promised to call on Lord Torfinn as soon as the bishop returned home from his rounds of the diocese. In the meantime, Arnvid persuaded Ingunn to speak with the priest and allow him to hear her confession. He also had masses said for her. In this way time passed until the celebration of the Virgin Mary's birthday, on the eighth of September.

On that day Arnvid had gone to confession and received *Corpus Domini*. During the mass he prayed so long and so fervently for his ill kinswoman that his garments became soaked with sweat. It was past noon before the churchgoers from Miklebø returned home. Arnvid was talking to Guttorm about his horse Elgsblakken, who had started to limp on the way home, when he heard loud screams for help coming from the house where Ingunn lay in bed.

Arnvid and Guttorm raced head over heels to the house and rushed inside. There they found Ingunn running around, barefoot and wearing only her shift, as she stomped on the floor. The room was filled with smoke, and the straw spread over the floor was burning at the edges of the cushions she had tossed on top. In her arms she held Steinar, who was wrapped in the coverlet from the bed. He was shrieking and wailing.

When others arrived, Ingunn sank down on the bench and began kissing and soothing the boy as she rocked him back and forth. "Steinar, Steinar, my precious boy, everything will soon be better. I'm going to take such good care of you, little one!" She called to the servants, saying that Steinar had burned himself and they needed to bring ointment and linen cloths at once.

She had been lying in bed, and only Steinar was with her. He had been sitting near the hearth, where the tiniest of flames burned. Even though she had warned him not to, he had started playing with the fire by poking dry little twigs into the embers. It was a warm day, and the boy wore nothing more than a shirt, which all of a sudden caught fire. Without knowing how it happened, Ingunn found herself standing at the hearth and holding the child in her arms. She had put out the fire on his shirt by wrapping him in the coverlet. But then she saw that the juniper branches and rushes spread on the floor were burning, so she threw cushions from the benches onto the fire and began stomping on them as she shouted for help.

The boy had suffered burns to his stomach, while Ingunn had bad burns on her legs and the inside of both arms. But all her attention was focused on Steinar. She refused to let anyone bind up her wounds until the child had been tended to. Then she placed the boy on her bed and began to fuss over him while she caressed and consoled the poor little thing. For as long as the boy's fever and pain lasted, she gave no thought to anything but Steinar.

The paralysis seemed to have completely vanished, though she herself hardly noticed. Without thinking, she would eat and drink whatever meals they brought to her; the ghastly vomiting and dizziness had stopped altogether. Arnvid sat with Steinar day and night, and no matter how terrible he found it to see the boy suffering so badly, he still thanked God for the miracle that had occurred for Ingunn.

From that day forth, her health swiftly improved. By the time Steinar had recovered enough that he could be carried out into the sunlight to have a look at the snow that had fallen overnight, Ingunn had regained the lovely fullness of her face and body, and her cheeks turned a delicate crimson in the frosty air. She stood there holding Steinar in her arms and waited for Arnvid, who went over to the piles of stones to gather icy rosehips in his hat. Steinar had insisted that his father should find some berries for him.

The prospect of a reconciliation between Arnvid's family and the rest of Ingunn's kinsmen was not helped by the fact that Fru Hillebjørg had been spreading rumors about Kolbein. She claimed he had used trickery to afflict his niece with a deadly illness. And when the marriage ale celebration was held at Frettastein for Haakon Gautssøn and Tora Steinfinnsdatter a short time before Advent, no one from Miklebø attended. The wedding then took place just after New Year's in 1282, and afterward the newly married couple traveled around to visit the young wife's kinsmen, for Haakon was the youngest son of many brothers and therefore had no estate of his own in Vestlandet. No doubt the intention was for him to settle in Oppland.

Now a message arrived from Fru Magnhild at Berg, saying that she would like Ingunn to come and stay with her. Ivar and Kolbein had promised to leave the girl in peace if she agreed to live there quietly and behave in a seemly manner. Arnvid uttered a stream of curses when Brother Vegard told him of this, but he couldn't deny that he had no lawful right to serve as Ingunn's guardian. And his mother was beginning to tire of their guest. Now that Ingunn had regained her health, Fru Hillebjørg had lost patience with the young woman who seemed merely decorative and of no earthly use to anyone. And what Fru Magnhild had said was no more than reasonable: she was caring for her old mother, Aasa Magnusdatter, who was the widow of Tore of Hov. The old woman was in poor health, and it would be good for her to have the company of her granddaughter to lend a hand and help pass the time.

Just before Easter, Arnvid set off for Berg, taking Ingunn with him.

Fru Magnhild was the eldest of Tore's lawfully born children and now in her fiftieth year, the same age as her half-brother Kolbein Toressøn. She was the widow of the knight Sir Viking Erlingssøn. She had never had children, and so she had generously taken in young maidens, the daughters of kinsmen and friends, who would stay with her for several years while she taught them courtly manners and various skills befitting noblewomen. Fru Magnhild had spent a good deal of time at the king's palace when her husband was alive. She had also offered to take in her nieces from Frettastein, but Steinfinn—or perhaps it was Ingebjørg—had not wanted to put the young maidens in her care. Fru Magnhild had been terribly offended by their refusal. When it became known that Ingunn had allowed herself to be deceived by her foster brother, Fru Magnhild said it was no more than she had expected. Those children had been poorly brought up, and their mother had disobeyed her father and spurned the man to whom she'd been betrothed, so it was not surprising that Steinfinn's daughters should bring shame upon the lineage.

Ingunn felt worn out and downcast in spirit as she sat in the sledge during the last stretch of the way through the forest. The journey had taken them many days because just after they'd left Miklebø it had started to snow and then milder weather had set in. Now, toward evening, it had begun to freeze, and Arnvid walked beside the sledge to guide the way, for the road was terrible. In places it passed over bare rock, slippery with ice; in other places it wound through tightly packed snowdrifts, because no one had traveled this way since the last snowfall.

When they emerged from the forest, the sun was low in the sky, hovering just above the mountain ridge in front of them. It shone red-gold in the fog, and the dark, rough ice on the bay glittered with a dull and dirty gleam of copper. The frosty mist had covered the snowy woods and marshes with rime, turning everything an ugly gray as dusk fell. Arnvid's men were struggling to make their way across the field below. They and the sledge loaded with belongings were heading straight through the mountain gorge. The estate stood down by the water, in a somewhat remote spot in the district, with the forest blocking it from view. From Berg it was impossible to look up and see any of the other large estates in the surrounding area.

Ingunn had not seen her aunt since she'd visited Hamar almost a year and a half ago, and back then the mistress of Berg had treated her with great sternness. Nor was Ingunn expecting much kindness from Fru Magnhild on this occasion either.

Arnvid flung himself onto the side of the sledge as it dropped into the first hollow.

"Don't look so sad, Ingunn," he pleaded. "I will find it hard to part with you when you look so disheartened."

Ingunn replied, "I'm not disheartened. You know that I haven't complained. But I am not about to enter the embrace of friends. Pray to God for me, my kinsman, that I might remain steadfast in spirit, for I expect to be tested during all the time I must stay here at Berg."

When they drove into the courtyard, Fru Magnhild herself came out to welcome Ingunn. She led her brother's daughter over to the women's house and told the maidservants to bring her dry footwear and something warm to drink. Then she helped the young woman take off the heavy, shaggy hide boots and fur surcoat she was wearing. But when she plucked at a corner of Ingunn's wimple, she said, "You can put this away now."

Ingunn blushed. "I have worn a married woman's wimple ever since I went to Hamar. The bishop asked me to cover my hair. He said it was not proper for a woman to go about bareheaded when she was no longer a maiden."

"That man!" sneered Fru Magnhild. "He says so many things. But a long time has now passed and all the talk about you has died down here in the villages. I don't want to see you sparking new life in the rumors about your shame if you go about like a fool, dressed in the garments of a married woman. Put away that wimple and cinch your belt tighter. In the midst of misfortune, it was nevertheless fortunate that you never had to fasten it to the side."

Ingunn wore around her waist a leather belt embellished with silver studs and beautifully adorned on the end that hung down. Fru Magnhild reached out to adjust it so that the fastening sat in front. Again she told Ingunn to remove her wimple.

"But everyone knows this about me," Ingunn protested. "They'll have an even worse opinion of me and think I'm an immodest wife if I go about bareheaded when I have no right to do so, the way loose women do."

Fru Magnhild said, "Ingunn, you also need to consider your grandmother. She is old now. She remembers clearly everything from her youth, but anything new she forgets as soon as she hears it. Each day we would have to explain to her again why you are dressed as a married woman."

"Surely it would be easy enough to tell her that my husband is away."

"And then it would soon come to Kolbein's attention that you are stubbornly holding to the old demands, and his hatred toward Olav will never lessen. Be reasonable, Ingunn, and give up this foolishness."

Ingunn unfastened the wimple and folded it up. It was the loveliest one she owned: eight feet in length and trimmed with silk. Fru

Hillebjørg had given it to her in the spring, saying that she could wear it to church and later when she accompanied Olav to mass for the first time after he returned home.

Then she pulled the pins out of her hair and let the heavy, dark-golden tresses tumble down.

"What lovely hair you have," said Fru Magnhild. "Most women would be happy to display such hair for a while longer, Ingunn—if they were not to have any joy from their husband, and possessed neither the power nor the authority that goes with wearing a wimple. You must wear your hair loose tonight."

"Oh no, Aunt," said Ingunn, on the verge of tears. "You must not ask that of me!" She gathered up her hair and tightly plaited it into two severe braids.

Arnvid was already seated at the table when Fru Magnhild and Ingunn came into the room. He looked up and his expression darkened.

"So that's how they want things here?" he asked later, when he bade Ingunn good night. "You're not to be granted the respect that is owed a married woman?"

"No. As you can see," Ingunn merely replied.

Aasa Magnusdatter had a house and a loft storeroom to herself at Berg. She had two maidservants to perform the household chores and do the cooking. They also saw to all the spinning and weaving of linen and wool that their mistress might need from the estate. Grim and Dalla, the two old caretakers from Frettastein, tended to her animals that were kept in stalls in Fru Magnhild's cowshed. These old servants had been given a little hovel in which to live, right next to the barn for larger livestock, but they were considered part of Aasa's household.

For this reason there was nothing for Ingunn to do at Berg other than formally oversee her grandmother's housekeeping and provide amusements for the old woman. This mainly entailed sitting with her grandmother whenever the maidservants were out doing chores.

As Fru Magnhild had mentioned, Aasa had now reverted to her childhood and recalled little of what was said to her anymore. Every single day, she would ask about the same things again and again. Sometimes she would ask about her youngest son, Steinfinn, and whether he had visited recently or whether they were expecting him to arrive soon. Yet she often did remember that he was dead. Then she would ask whether he had four children who were still alive. "And you are the eldest? Of course I remember you. Your name is Ingunn. You were named after my mother, for Ingebjørg's mother was still alive when you were born, and she had renounced her daughter for running off with Steinfinn. Oh yes, he was so trusting and merry, my Steinfinn. It ended up costing him dearly that he was so particular about his choice of paramour that he carried off a knight's daughter by force." Aasa had never been fond of Ingebjørg, and she often talked about Steinfinn and her son's wife, failing to recall that it was their daughter she was speaking to. "But what happened? Didn't one of Steinfinn's little maidens land in great misfortune? No, I must not be remembering properly. Surely they can't be old enough yet."

"My dear grandmother," said Ingunn with some distress. "I think you should try to get some sleep for a while."

"Oh yes, Gyrid, that might be best for me." Aasa often called her granddaughter Gyrid, mistaking her for Gyrid Alfsdatter, a kinswoman who had stayed at Berg fifteen winters earlier.

Yet Fru Aasa remembered perfectly everything that had happened in her youth. She spoke of her parents and her brother Finn, who was Arnvid's father, and she talked about her sister-in-law Hillebjørg, whom she both loved and feared, even though Hillebjørg was much younger than she was.

At the age of fourteen winters Aasa had been wed to Tore of Hov. Up until then he had spent more than ten years living with that woman Borghild, and only reluctantly did he send his paramour away. She didn't leave Hov until the morning of the day when Aasa was escorted inside as a bride. Borghild continued to wield great power over Tore until she died—and that was twenty years after his marriage. He consulted her on all matters of importance, and he often took his lawfully born children to see her, so that she might foretell their future and judge whether she found them promising. But Tore's greatest efforts and love were directed toward the four children he'd had with his paramour. Borghild was the daughter of a thrall woman and a nobleman. Some said he was one of those kings that seemed to abound in Norway at the time. She was a beautiful, wise, and self-assured woman, but she was also arrogant, greedy, and unkind to poor folks.

All the while, Aasa Magnusdatter lived at Hov. She gave her husband fourteen children, though five died in the cradle, and only five lived to be full-grown.

Aasa remembered all of her deceased children and often talked about them. She grieved most for a daughter named Herdis, who lost all movement because she'd slept outside on the dew-covered ground. She died four years later, when she was eleven winters old. A half-grown son had been kicked to death by his horse, and another son named Magnus had lost his life during a brawl on board the ship carrying him home from a feast out in Toten, along with other drunken young men. Magnus had recently married, but he left no children, and his widow then married someone from a different part of the country. She was the daughter-in-law for whom Fru Aasa had felt the most affection.

"But tell me, Grandmother," said Ingunn, "have you had nothing but sorrow your whole life? Were there no good days you might think about now?"

Her grandmother looked at her as if not understanding. Now that she was waiting for death, she seemed to take as much pleasure in recalling her sorrows as her joys.

Ingunn was not unhappy with this life she shared with the old woman. She was not strong, even though she had now regained her health, and she'd never enjoyed doing anything that required her to exert herself or that demanded all her attention. She would sit with some delicate handiwork that she didn't need to finish in haste and sink into her own thoughts as she listened with half an ear to what her grandmother was saying.

As a child, Ingunn had been restless and found it hard to sit still for any length of time. But that had changed. The strange ailment that had befallen her after parting with Olav seemed to have left behind a shadow that refused to dissipate; she felt as if she were always wandering in a dreamlike state. At Frettastein she'd had the company of all the boys, with Olav first and foremost, and they had brought her games and excitement and lively amusements, since she was not inclined to think of such things herself. Here at Berg, there were only women: two old mistresses and their servant women, along with a few elderly hired men and workmen. They couldn't rouse her from the dreamlike stupor into which she'd slipped while she lay in bed, unable to move, waiting to waste away altogether until she was no longer to be counted among the living.

When Olav disappeared, it was as if Ingunn didn't have the strength to believe that he would ever come back. Far too many important events had overwhelmed her in the short time between her father's departure to seek out Mattias Haraldssøn and her arrival in Hamar when Arnvid took her there. She felt as if she'd been carried off by floodwaters, and the time in Hamar seemed like a shallow eddy, where she and Olav had been spun in circles, slowly but steadily moving farther and farther away from each other. Everything had been new and unfamiliar, and Olav had changed until he too seemed a stranger to her. She could understand that it was right for him not to find some opportunity to meet with her in secret while they were in Hamar. But that he had behaved as he did when she arranged the meeting with him on Christmas Eve . . . That had frightened her beyond all measure. Afterward she had felt so ashamed and lost that she didn't dare even think about him the way she'd done before, lingering over the sweet, ardent yearning she'd felt for his love. It was as if she were a child who had been chastised and rebuked by a grown-up, even though she had never thought there was anything wrong with her longing for him.

Then he'd come to her on that last night, appearing out of the darkness and blizzard, covered in snow, worn out and agitated, alternating between exhaustion and suppressed frenzy—an outlaw with the blood of her cousin still warm on his hands. She had remained oddly calm. But when he left, it felt as if all the floodwaters closed in upon her.

During the early days of her illness, Ingunn had thought it might be caused by what Fru Hillebjørg had hinted. But as time passed and it became clear she was not carrying a child, she had no strength even to feel disappointment. She was so drained that it would have been too much to bear if she'd had to face anything more, either good or bad. She patiently accepted that she was very ill, that no one could understand what ailed her, and that there seemed to be no cure for her. If she tried to look ahead in time, she saw only a shifting black mist, much like the darkness that had swirled before her eyes when she had suffered fainting spells.

Then she immersed herself deeply in memories of everything she had experienced with Olav during the previous summer and autumn. She would close her eyes and kiss her own braid and hands and arms, pretending it was Olav doing so. But the more she surrendered to dreams and desire, the less real it all seemed to her, as if none of these things had ever happened. She had believed that the case they were pursuing would undoubtedly bring them together at last, to live peacefully and lawfully, though she could never fully imagine how it would be—just as she believed everything she'd heard from the priests about the bliss in the heavenly world, yet she could not picture it.

She lay in bed, not expecting that she would ever be able to move her body again. With that the last mooring line broke, cutting her off from daily concerns and chores and the lives of other people. She lost all hope of ever being lawfully married to Olav Audunssøn, of taking charge of his estate, or of giving birth to his children. Instead, she allowed herself to be lured into games and dreams that she couldn't imagine would lead anywhere.

Every evening, when the candle in the room was put out and the fire banked, she would pretend that Olav came and lay down beside her. Every morning when she awoke, she pretended that her husband was already awake and had gone out. She would lie there, listening to the sounds of the day reaching her from the large estate, and she pretended she was at Hestviken, and it was Olav who was bringing in the hay, it was his horses and sledges she heard, and he was the one who was sending his servants out to work. When Steinar lay quietly in her bed for a moment, she would put her thin arms around the boy and press his fair head to her chest. In her mind she called the boy Audun, and he was her son and Olav's. Then Steinar would want to get up, struggling to free himself from Ingunn's embrace. She would persuade him to stay by giving him tasty bits of food that she had hidden in her bed and by telling him stories, all the while pretending that she was a mother talking to her own child.

When Ingunn arrived at Berg, the first thing to wake her, at least partially, from this dreamlike state was the fact that Fru Magnhild took away her wimple. Never before had she considered it shameful to know that she now belonged to Olav. At Frettastein she'd given herself over to love without thinking. It was only when both Olav and Arnvid were suddenly in such a hurry to go to Hamar and request that Olav's right to her be formally acknowledged that something resembling confusion had stirred inside her. But when the good bishop sent her a respectable white wimple and bade her bind up her hair, she again felt calm. Even though she had defied her uncles, who should have been the ones to decide about her marriage after her father's death, Lord Torfinn would no doubt find a resolution and then she would have the standing of a wife just like all the other married women.

She shivered with humiliation at the unfamiliar sensation of going about bareheaded after wearing the wimple of a married woman for a year and a half. It felt as if she had been immodestly exposed by rough hands, as was done to thrall women at the slave markets in the past. She avoided going over to Magnhild's house whenever strangers were present. And she did not willingly spend time with others, except in church, for that was the one place where all women had to cover their heads. Ingunn would pull the hood of her cloak forward to hide her face and ensure that not a single strand of hair was visible. As a small token of penance for dressing in a manner that she did not find seemly, she put away all jewelry, wore only dark and unadorned gowns, and plaited her hair in tight, severe braids without ribbons or any sort of finery.

◆ ◆ ◆

Then spring arrived. One day the ice sank in the bay and the waters lay open and clear, reflecting the green emerging on the hills on either side. Berg was now beautiful. Ingunn led her grandmother out to the sunlit wall and sat with her as she sewed the shirt for Olav Audunssøn. Olav had told her that Hestviken stood near the fjord.

She found some small chores to keep her busy up in the loft room that belonged to Aasa. She spent morning after morning up there, rummaging about and cleaning. Ingunn would remove the shutter from the small window and stand there, peering out.

Below the opposite shoreline a boat rowed past, causing the dark reflection of the mountain ridge to be splintered by long ripples. Ingunn pretended it was Olav and their son in the boat. They were rowing in this direction. Ingunn could picture it all so well. They put in at the dock, and Audun helped his father tie the mooring line. Olav stood on the planks of the dock, while the boy busied himself in the stern of the boat, gathering up their belongings. Last of all he picked up his little axe as Olav held out his hand to help the boy climb out. He was now as big as Jon, Ingunn's youngest brother. Then the two walked up the path toward the estate, the father first, followed by his son.

She also had a little daughter named Ingebjørg. The child was out in the courtyard. She had come from the storehouse, carrying a big wooden plate of flatbread. She broke off a chunk and crumbled the bread for the chickens—no, for the geese. Ingunn remembered that they'd had geese at Frettastein when she was a child, and there was something pompous about the bulky, motley white-and-gray birds. There should be geese at Hestviken.

Cautiously, as if she were doing something wrong, she crept over to the door and shoved the latch closed. Then she took a wimple out of the chest that was hers and wrapped it around her head. Ingunn turned her belt until the fastening sat at her side and hung from it whatever she could find of heavy objects: a sheep shears and several keys. Thus attired, she sat down on the edge of the empty bedstead there in the loft. She clasped her hands in her lap and again considered everything she needed to tend to before her husband and children came back inside.

Only intermittently did news reach Berg about all the extraordinary events taking place in Norway during that year. Ingunn heard almost nothing over in her grandmother's house. For this reason it felt as if a bolt of lightning had struck from a clear sky on the day she learned that Bishop Torfinn had been declared an outlaw and was thought to have left the country.

It was their parish priest who brought the news to the estate on the first day of winter. Lord Torfinn had spent several months making his rounds in Norddalen, and from there it was undoubtedly his intent to meet with the archbishop somewhere out in the headlands. But before this could happen the barons, who now held all the power in the realm, had declared both the archbishop and many of the other bishops outlaws and hounded them so zealously that they were forced to flee, each going his own way. It was said that Bishop Torfinn had boarded a ship, but no one knew where he had ended up or when he might be expected back at his bishop's seat in Hamar. The parish priest felt no sorrow at this news. The bishop had reprimanded him for his indolence and for not castigating the sins of the noble-born folks sternly enough. The priest thought himself an adequate shepherd, and it would do no good to handle his flock as the bishop wished. He had become quite indignant about this unyielding bony monk, as he called Lord Torfinn.

It was clear that the strife between the bishops and the councilors to the young king concerned issues of monumental importance, while the marriage case of Olav Audunssøn was a petty matter of no significance whatsoever—although it was put forth as an example of the Bishop of Hamar's intolerable stubbornness, and his desire to ignore the established laws and regulations of the land. But the parish priest wanted to remain friends with the wealthy mistress of Berg, and perhaps even he didn't realize how little this matter of the marriage of two young people meant beyond the districts where their kinsmen were known. So he spoke as if Bishop Torfinn had been outlawed mostly because he had held a protective hand over the worst enemy of the Steinfinnssøn lineage.

Ingunn was seized by a terrible dread. Again she lay wide awake, frightened about the true nature of her position. All her dreams abruptly collapsed the way a flower-strewn meadow darkens and sinks on a night of frost. Shivering with cold, she realized that she was nothing more than a defenseless, abandoned, and fatherless child, neither maiden nor wife, and not a single friend did she have who would uphold her right. Olav had disappeared and no one knew where he was; the bishop was gone; Arnvid was far away, and she was unable to send word to him. There was no one to whom she could turn except her old paternal grandmother, who had now retreated into childhood, if her ruthless kinsmen should decide to take their revenge on her. A small, quivering, and trembling thing, she curled herself around the only scrap of determination within her weak and instinct-driven soul: she would steadfastly trust in Olav and remain faithful to him, even if, because of him, they should torture the very life out of her.

It was at about this same time, during Advent, that Tora Steinfinns-datter and her husband, Haakon Gautssøn, came to Berg. Haakon had not yet found a place where he wanted to settle permanently, and Tora was already expecting a child before Christmas. For this reason, the young people intended to stay at Berg over the winter. Ingunn hadn't seen her sister in two years, and she'd never met her brother-in-law until now. He was not unpleasant looking. He was a big, tall man with handsome features and curly, reddish-brown hair, but he had small brown eyes that sat too close to the high, narrow bridge of his beaked nose, and he was quite cross-eyed.

From the very first day Haakon took a disliking to his wife's sister. Through both his words and his behavior he made it perfectly clear that he considered Ingunn to be no more than a seduced woman who had brought shame upon herself and the entire lineage. He was immensely satisfied with his own marriage, proud of Tora's beauty and her sound intelligence, proud that she would soon present him with an heir. He allowed his wife to advise him on all matters, and that proved to be to his benefit. Even though poor Ingunn had been unaware of the honor and happiness she was casting aside when she surrendered to Olav

Audunssøn, the truth was that she could have been married to Haakon Gautssøn. And for that reason Haakon harbored a hatred toward her because she had chosen a young boy—her father's servant, and a man whose lineage and fortune were little known to anyone here in the villages of Lake Mjøsa—instead of him, the knight's son from Harland.

Ingunn's younger sister went about so amply fecund and glowing pink and white, proud of her wifely dignity even though she owned neither a house nor an estate over which she could take charge. The white wimple of a married woman, which she wore both honorably and rightfully, nearly reached to her feet and at her belt clinked a heavy key ring—although God only knew what the wife of a landless farmer might use those keys to open and close. But Tora had managed to get every living soul, including Fru Magnhild, to practically stand on their heads in their desire to pay their respects to both her and her husband. And the women were already preparing to welcome the child they were awaiting with all the honor befitting the son of such a nobleman.

Throughout their entire childhood, Ingunn had no doubt known that Tora, in her heart, had rarely been happy with her older sister's behavior. She found Ingunn to be unloving toward their parents, thoughtless, and lazy. She should have sat quietly with their mother and the maidservants in the women's house rather than always going off to run about and play with Olav and his friends. But Tora had never said a word. She was two years younger, and for children that was a significant difference in age. And Ingunn cared little what Tora might think. During that last autumn at Frettastein, Tora had also kept quiet about what Ingunn knew she suspected and feared. It was only when they were staying at the pious old women's townyard in Hamar that her sister spoke of the matter. That was when Tora had been unexpectedly gentle in her judgment of how Ingunn and Olav had conducted themselves, and she had treated her sister kindly while they were there. One reason for this was that Tora had always felt a genuine, sisterly love for her foster brother. She was more fond of Olav than of her own flesh-and-blood siblings, for he was quieter and more even-tempered. And the bishop, after all, had lent his support to Olav and Ingunn, and everyone the two sisters met in town had agreed and judged as Lord Torfinn did. Even though Olav had countered injustice with injustice, it was a far greater wrong to want to sever a betrothal pact that had been sealed with a handshake merely because the groom was young and lacked powerful spokesmen. No one doubted that the bishop would eventually negotiate a resolution to the case that would prove honorable for Olav. Back then Tora had not thought that Ingunn's impulsive behavior might bring shame upon them all.

Now things had changed. Tora could not forgive Olav for killing her close kinsman, and she spoke harsh words about the way in which he had repaid her family, after they had taken him in as a foster child of the Steinfinnssøn lineage, a child with no kin of his own. Tora was not unkind toward Ingunn. Nevertheless, Ingunn could tell what her sister thought of her: from the time she was a small child she had behaved in such a way that her younger sister was not surprised she had now landed in misfortune. But Tora wanted to be gentle, and she had no wish to make it harder for her poor sister to bear the fate she had brought down upon herself.

Ingunn silently endured Tora's quiet, little words of sympathy, but when talk turned to Olav's misdeeds, she tried to defend him. Yet it did little good, for Tora now had the upper hand. The fact that Ingunn was older didn't matter because it was Tora who was married. She had the experience and right to pass judgment on other full-grown folks. Ingunn had her own experiences, which she had no right to possess. She knew of a love for which everyone seemed to want to punish her; she knew of taking charge of a household and raising children, because she had pretended about such things in her dreams, though she'd never actually set her hand to these tasks. She felt diminished and dispirited as she kept to her corner and watched Tora and Haakon fill the entire estate with their life. Dressed in the dark clothing of a penitent, with her two heavy braids hanging straight down in front so it looked as if their weight were causing her to stoop forward and bend her head a bit, Ingunn resembled a poor maidservant when compared to the young and lavishly clad mistress.

Tora gave birth to a son, just as she and Haakon had anticipated. Everyone who saw the infant said he was a big and promising child. It was Ingunn's task to sit with her sister while Tora convalesced, which meant that she also spent time tending to her nephew. Ingunn had always held great affection for little children, and now she grew dearly fond of the young Steinfinn Haakonssøn. When she had to take him into her own bed at night so that his mother might rest, she couldn't stop herself from pretending that he was her own son. She found some measure of solace in imagining again that she was at Hestviken, on her own estate, where she lived with Olav and their children, Audun, Ingebjørg, and this new little infant. But this time she was bitterly aware that she was merely wrapping herself in a paltry web of dreams, while she saw her sister warmly and securely enfolded in very real riches with her husband and suckling child and an entire entourage of servants who took up so much space at the estate, along with all the chests and sacks containing their belongings that had been piled up inside the houses and storerooms.

Haakon wanted to host a grand ale feast to celebrate the birth of his child, and Fru Magnhild offered to pay for half the costs. The guests included not only Haftor Kolbeinssøn, who had become Haakon's good friend, but also the uncles Kolbein and Ivar. All of them stayed on for several more days after the other guests had departed.

One evening the kinsmen were taking their meal at the table in Fru Magnhild's house. Aasa Magnusdatter was there too, sitting in the high seat with Ingunn beside her so she could help her grandmother eat and drink, for the old woman's hands shook terribly. Otherwise her health had been much improved over the winter. She was overjoyed to have a great-grandchild; this was news that she never forgot, and she often asked about the boy and wanted to see him.

On this evening the men began discussing the strife between the barons and the bishops, and the Toressøns declared that it was certain who would win. The bishops would have to give in and content themselves with the authority to which they were entitled, as the spiritual fathers of the people, while they would have to let stand unchanged the old laws about the way in which lay folks dealt with each other. As for Bishop Torfinn, many of the priests in his own diocese thought he had gone too far. "I've spoken with three parish priests, learned and decent men of God," said Kolbein, "and all three told me that they would be willing to celebrate the wedding mass the day we give our Ingunn away."

Fru Magnhild replied, "It's clear that the bishop's interpretation of the situation cannot possibly be right. It cannot be God's will that His priests should side with impulsive and headstrong youths, or that the Holy Church should aid wicked children in disobeying their parents to win their own way."

"Yes, that's true," the others agreed.

Ingunn's face had turned bright red as she sat there, but she straightened her back as defiance grappled with fear inside her. Her eyes looked exceedingly big and dark as she stared at her uncles.

"Yes, it's you we are talking about," said Kolbein in response. "You have been a burden to your kinsmen long enough, Ingunn. It's time for you to take a husband who can rein you in."

"Can you find a man who would have me?" asked Ingunn scornfully. "As wretched a wife as you think me to be?"

"We will not speak of that," said Kolbein furiously. "I thought you'd had time to come to your senses. Surely you can't be so shameless as to want to live with a man who has stained his hands with the blood of your cousin, even if you were allowed to wed him."

"This is not the first time that a man has come to harm because of his wife's kinsman," Ingunn ventured, speaking quietly.

"We'll hear no more of that," replied Kolbein irately. "Never will we give you to the man who killed Einar."

"That may well be your resolve," said Ingunn. Now she saw that everyone was staring at her. She felt strangely incited by the fact that she had now stepped out of the shadow of her submissive position. "But if you want to give me to someone else, you'll soon find that it's not your decision!"

"And who do you think will decide?" asked Kolbein derisively.

Ingunn gripped the edge of the bench where she was sitting. She could feel how pale her cheeks had grown. But this was real; she wasn't dreaming. And she was the one speaking, as everyone stared at her. Before she could reply, Ivar spoke up, seeking to mediate.

"In God's name, Ingunn. This Olav . . . No one knows where he is. Even you can't know whether he's alive or dead. Will you perhaps spend your whole life waiting for a dead man?"

"I *know* he's alive." She reached into the linen covering at her bodice and drew out a small, silver-clad knife that she wore on a string around her neck. She took off the knife and placed it in front of her on the table. "Olav gave me this as a talisman before we parted. He asked me to wait as long as the blade remains shiny. He said that if it rusts, that means he is dead."

She took several deep breaths. Then she noticed that a young man who sat at the table some distance away was staring at her with an enthralled expression. Ingunn knew this was Gudmund Jonssøn, the only son on a large estate in the neighboring parish. She had seen him here at Berg several times, but she had never spoken to him. Now she suddenly understood. This was the bridegroom her uncles had chosen for her; she was quite certain of that. She looked the young man in the eye, feeling how her own expression was as hard as steel.

Then Ivar Toressøn said in a conciliatory voice as he scratched his head, "A talisman like that . . . I don't know how much meaning should be assigned to such things—"

"I think you'll soon discover, my Ingunn, who will make the decision about your marriage," Kolbein interrupted him. "Are you saying that you would object if we give you to a man whom we consider to be of equal standing? Who will you turn to then, now that your friend the bishop has rushed off and left the country, so you can no longer hide under his cloak?"

"I will turn to God, my Creator," said Ingunn. Her face had taken on a deathly pallor, and she half rose from her seat. "I will put my trust in His mercy if you force me to commit a sin in order to avoid one that is even greater. I will not allow you to threaten me to become an adulterer and take to the bridal bed with another man while my rightful husband is still alive. Before that happens I will throw myself into the fjord out there!"

Both Kolbein and Ivar were about to reply, when old Aasa Magnusdatter placed her hands on the table and with great effort stood up, tall and thin and hunched forward. She peered around at the men with her old, watery red eyes.

"What are you trying to do to this child?" she menaced them, setting her knobby claw of a hand heavily on the back of Ingunn's neck. "I can tell that you wish her harm. Ivar, my son, are you acting on behalf of that harpy Borghild's offspring? I see that they want to torment Steinfinn's children. Are you going to aid them in this pursuit, Magnhild and Ivar? If so, I fear it's my misfortune that you are the two who have been left to me!"

"Mother!" pleaded Ivar Toressøn.

"Grandmother!" said Ingunn, moving closer to the old woman and slipping under her fur cloak. "Oh, Grandmother, please help me!"

The old woman put her arm around Ingunn.

"We must leave now," she whispered. "Come, my child, let's go."

Ingunn stood up and helped her grandmother to cross the room. Aasa Magnusdatter fumbled her way forward while leaning on her staff with one hand, the other resting on her granddaughter's shoulder. She headed for the door as she murmured, "Go ahead and help Borghild's brood, my children. I can see that I've lived too long!"

"No, oh no, Mother." Ivar followed and took the staff from Aasa, offering instead the support of his shoulder. "I have always said it would be better if they accepted a reconciliation with Olav, but . . . And now that he has disappeared . . ."

By this time they had reached the door of Aasa's house. Ivar said to his niece, "You must know that I mean you no harm. But I think it would be better for you to get married and have your own household to manage. Better than going about here and withering away."

Ingunn gently pushed him aside as she practically lifted her grandmother over the threshold and then closed the door behind them, leaving Ivar outside.

She helped the old woman to undress and lie down. Then they said their evening prayers together, with Ingunn kneeling at the side of her grandmother's bed. Fru Aasa was utterly exhausted after such unusual exertions. Ingunn bustled about the room a little while longer before she too prepared to retire.

She was standing in her shift and was about to go to bed when she heard a quiet knock on the door. Ingunn went over and drew back the latch. She saw a man standing outside in the snow, a looming dark shape against the starry sky. Before he even opened his mouth, she knew this must be the suitor, and she felt a strangely festive mood come over her, though she was also frightened. But at least something was happening!

Just as she'd thought, it was Gudmund Jonssøn. He said, "Have you already gone to bed? I wondered whether I might talk to you for a bit this evening. There is some haste, as you can imagine."

"Come inside, if that's the case. We can't stand here in the cold."

"Go ahead and climb into bed," he said when he stepped inside and saw the thin clothing she wore. "Perhaps you'll allow me to lie down on the edge of the bedstead so we can better talk."

At first they spoke about the weather and about Haakon Gautssøn, who was apparently thinking of settling at Frettastein. That meant Haftor would have to move back home with his father. Ingunn liked Gudmund's voice and his calm, amiable manner. And she couldn't help admitting that she enjoyed lying there in the dark, warm and snug, as she chatted with a suitor. It had been a long time since anyone had sought her out or cared to speak with her simply because they wanted her company. Even though she would have to tell him that his courtship was in vain, it felt like a form of exoneration that a man of Gudmund's standing should cast his sights on her, when her own kinsmen had banished her to a neglected corner.

"There's something that I'd like to ask you," her guest said at last. "Were you in earnest when you spoke earlier this evening?"

"Yes, I was."

"Then I had better tell you," said Gudmund, "that my father and mother wish for me to marry this year. And we have agreed that we will ask Ivar Toressøn for you to be my wife."

Ingunn didn't reply. Gudmund went on.

"But if I ask my father to seek a wife for me elsewhere, he will no doubt comply. If, that is, you meant everything you said this evening."

When she still did not speak, he said, "For you must know that if we do ask Ivar and Kolbein, they are certain to agree. But if that is not what you wish, then I will make sure you are no longer bothered with this matter."

Ingunn said, "I don't understand, Gudmund, why you and your kinsmen would consider a woman like me, when you have every right to expect a worthy marriage. You must know everything that has been said about me."

"Yes. But it's not necessary be too stern or harsh. Your kinsmen will allow you to take the full inheritance you share with your siblings, if an agreement can be reached for the two of us. As for myself, I am pleased with the way you look, and how lovely you are."

Ingunn didn't reply at once. It felt so nice to be lying there, talking with such a genial young man, feeling the warmth of his body lying close and his breath caressing her cheek in the dark. She had felt a cold and empty space inside her for so long. Then she said very gently, "You know what I think of this matter. I cannot allow myself to be married off to any man other than the one to whom I belong. Otherwise, I can tell you that I realize you would offer me good fortune."

"Ah," said Gudmund. "But don't you think, Ingunn, that the two of us could have lived well together?"

"I am certain of that. Any woman would have to be a troll if she wasn't able to live well with you. But now you must understand that I am not free."

"Yes, I see that," said Gudmund with a sigh. "I will ensure that you are no longer tormented for our sake. I would have liked to have you as my wife, but I suppose I will find someone else."

They lay there chatting for a little longer, but Gudmund finally said it was no doubt time for him to leave, and Ingunn agreed. She walked with him to the door so she could close it after him, and they parted with a handshake. Ingunn was filled with a strange sense of warmth and elation as she went back to bed. Tonight she was bound to sleep well.

During Lent Ingunn was allowed to ride into town so that Brother Vegard might hear her confession. He had been her father confessor ever since she was confirmed at the age of eight and up until the time when Arnvid had taken her to Miklebø.

It was not easy for her to tell the monk about all her troubles. Never before had it been necessary for her to make a confession that required anything more than naming each sin. She had prayed without proper reflection, she had spoken rudely to her parents, she had been angry with Tora or the maidservants, she had taken things without permission, she had told a lie—and then what had happened between her and Olav. Now she felt it was mostly her thoughts that she needed to talk about, and she found it hard to comprehend them and put them into words. Of greatest concern was that she might allow herself to be frightened or threatened into breaking the promise she had made to Olav Audunssøn before the eyes of God.

Brother Vegard said it was right for her to refuse to be married off to any other man as long as there was no proof that Olav had died. The monk judged the willful behavior of Ingunn and Olav much more harshly than had the bishop, but he also said that now they were bound to each other for the rest of their lives. Yet she must pray to God to free her from any thought of taking her own life; that was a mortal sin of no less import than allowing herself to be forced into a marriage when she was not a widow. And he warned her, in the most solemn terms, against thinking too much, as she had reported, of living with Olav and the children she would have with him. Such thoughts would only serve to weaken her will, awaken desire, and incite defiance toward her kinsmen. And she must have realized that she and Olav had brought misfortune upon themselves with their undisciplined loving and their disobedience toward those whom God had set to watch over them in their youth. Now it would be much better if she strove to acquire the virtue of patience, bearing her fate as the rebuke of a loving father, and dedicating herself to prayer, doling out alms, and displaying a subservient fondness for her kinsmen, as long as they did not demand that she should obey them when it would be a sin to do so. Finally, Brother Vegard said that he thought it would be best if she could enter a nunnery and stay there as a pious widow while she waited to hear whether Olav would be permitted to return to his homeland and take her as his wife, if it was God's will that they be allowed such happiness. If she heard it confirmed that he was dead, then she could decide whether to return to the world or to take the veil and devote herself to prayers for the souls of Olav and her parents and all the souls that had been led astray by their own willfulness and excessive love for the power and joys of this world. The monk offered to speak with her kinsmen about this and accompany her to a cloister, if that was what she wished.

But that frightened Ingunn. She feared that once she entered a cloister, it would not be easy for her to leave, even though Brother Vegard said that as long as Olav was alive, she could not take the veil without his permission. Then Ingunn mentioned that her grandmother was old and weak and needed her, and Brother Vegard agreed that as long as Aasa Magnusdatter had need of Ingunn, she should stay with her grandmother.

By the time Ingunn went back to Berg after Easter, Haakon and Tora had left with their entire entourage. It had been decided that they would live at Frettastein. A great silence settled over the estate after they'd gone. Time continued to pass in the company of the old women, with each day so like the next that Ingunn might as well have been living in a cloister after all.

And she couldn't help herself: after a while she again took up her pretend life with a husband and children on an imaginary estate that she called Hestviken. But occasionally certain feelings would stir inside her, those feelings that Gudmund Jonssøn's courtship had aroused: fear but also a measure of satisfaction. Apparently she hadn't ruined her reputation as badly as she'd thought if a wealthy young man from a noble lineage had wanted to marry her. She dreamed about handsome and powerful suitors whom her uncles would threaten her to accept—but she would show them her courage and her steadfast will, and there were no torments or humiliations they could think up that would make her put at risk her faithfulness to Olav Audunssøn.

II

Each day was much the same at Berg. Time flew by, and Ingunn could hardly keep track of the years. But when she saw how much had happened in the lives of other people, how everything had grown and changed for them, she would feel a jolt of fear. Was it all so long ago?

Tora came to visit from Frettastein, bringing both of her children. Steinfinn dashed about, as uncontrollable as a bad cough. He was big and more than capable for his age of two and a half. His little sister could already crawl over to a bench or some other such object; then she would grab hold and pull herself up to a standing position. Tora dearly wanted Ingunn to go back to Frettastein with them. Ingunn was so good with children, and now that Tora was expecting her third child before Saint Olav's Day,[27] she thought it only reasonable that her sister should come to stay with her and help to care for all these children. But Ingunn said that her grandmother could not manage without her. In her heart, she thought she would never see Frettastein again—not unless she and Olav could go there together.

She didn't know where he was now. The only time she'd heard any news from him was the previous summer, when Arnvid had visited Berg. Fat Asbjørn, the priest, had come back to Norway that same spring. He had accompanied Bishop Torfinn into exile, staying with him in Rome, and keeping vigil with him when he died in Flanders. On his way home, Asbjørn had passed through Denmark and sought out Olav, who at the time was living with his mother's brother and doing well. After that, Asbjørn had been appointed parish priest somewhere in Trøndelagen. When he'd traveled through Østerdalen, he had stopped to see Arnvid at Miklebø, bringing him greetings from their friend.

Arnvid had brought his son Steinar with him to Berg, for Ingunn's sake. But the boy had grown too big for the games she'd played with him in the past. Arnvid told his son that Ingunn had once saved him from a fire, but that seemed to make little impression on the child.

Ingunn took Steinar out in a boat in the bay so they could do some fishing. She used the oars to steady the boat right next to the dock, because she didn't have the strength to row the heavy skiff any distance, and Steinar had never been in a boat before. Nevertheless, they both found it amusing even though they didn't catch many fish.

Gudmund Jonssøn had married long ago, and he and his wife had a son. Once in a while he would come to Berg and borrow a boat so he could row across to the other side of the bay to visit his maternal grandfather.

Ingunn was the only one who spent day after day with the two old women, and by now she was already twenty winters old. Her uncle Ivar had once called her "withered." Yet she had a vague sense that she had never been lovelier than she was now. Spending so much time indoors with her grandmother had turned her cheeks pale, but her complexion was as delicate as a flower. And she was no longer so thin; her flesh was firmer, and she didn't stoop or hunch as she had before. She had a lovely way of walking, and she carried her tall, slender form with a distinctively lithe and gentle grace. Whenever, on rare occasion, she did go out among people, she noticed that many men would stare at her. It was something she could sense, although she never returned their gaze. She always went about in such a quiet manner, her eyes virtuously lowered, and with an air of placid melancholy.

One evening when several strangers had come to Berg to conduct business with Fru Magnhild, one of the men had forced his way into Ingunn's bedchamber after she'd gone to bed. He was quite drunk. Ingunn managed to roust him out, and old Aasa was never even aware that an intruder had been present. The man was almost sober when he slinked out, cowering like a whipped dog under the icy words Ingunn angrily hissed at him.

But after she had chased the fellow out, she collapsed completely, her body shaking and her teeth chattering with terror. What frightened her the most was the strange way she had reacted, though she was certain he couldn't have noticed anything. While she was fending the man off, acting cold and composed and much too indignant and outraged to be afraid, deep inside Ingunn had been tempted to give in, to surrender. She was so tired, so very tired. She suddenly felt as if she had been defending herself for years. She was tired of waiting. Olav should have been here, he should have been here by now! She didn't close her eyes all night. Distraught and miserable she lay in bed, weeping and whimpering as she burrowed under the coverlet. She didn't think she could bear this any longer. But the next day, when the man came to apologize for his behavior, Ingunn responded to his stammered speech with a few words of quiet dignity as she gave him an unwavering glare. Her big dark eyes were filled with such sorrowful contempt that the man seemed almost to crawl rather than walk when he departed.

Ingunn heard nothing more about Olav. More and more often she would lie in bed and weep until far into the night, tormented by worry and longing, as well as a hollow sense of fear. How long would this go on? She would clutch his knife talisman to her chest. The blade had not lost any of its shine, and that was the one thing to which she could cling.

It was a Sunday at the end of summer, and Ingunn was the only one from Berg who had gone to mass, along with some of the servants. She was on horseback. Old Grim walked alongside, leading her horse Blakken. They entered the courtyard of the estate, and the old man was just about to help Ingunn down from her horse, when she saw a young, fair-haired man duck his head in the doorway as he came out of Magnhild's house. After what felt like a strangely long moment, filled with hesitation, Ingunn recognized him. It was Olav.

He came toward her, and at first it seemed to Ingunn that everything turned gray and dull, the way it does when you've lain on the ground with your face hidden on a summer day with blazing sunlight, and then you open your eyes and look around. The sunshine and the whole world seemed to have faded, and all colors were paler than expected.

She had always remembered Olav as being much taller, a looming presence, and much bigger. And more handsome. She remembered a glow to his pallor and fairness.

He came over and lifted her out of the saddle, setting her down on the ground. Then they greeted each other with a handshake and walked side by side over to the house. Neither of them said a word.

Ivar Toressøn had appeared in the doorway. He greeted Ingunn with a big smile.

"Are you content now, Ingunn? Are you happy with the guest that I've brought to the estate this time?"

Then Ingunn's whole face seemed to awaken, flushing pink all the way down her throat. She broke into a smile that reached her eyes as well as her lips.

"The two of you came here together?" She looked from her uncle to Olav, who now smiled too—revealing the quiet radiance that was so dearly familiar to her. His lovely pale lips gently turned upward, though without parting. He closed his eyes halfway, and beneath his long, silky-white lashes his eyes shone blue and joyful.

"So you've finally come home?" she asked him, smiling.

"Yes, I thought it was about time for me to head home," he said, returning her smile.

She sat on the doorstep with her hands clasped in her lap and looked at Olav, who was standing nearby, conversing with Ivar. It was odd how swiftly everything had grown calm inside her. Happiness was a feeling of tranquillity that had now settled over her, complete tranquillity.

Ivar wanted to show something to Olav, so the two men walked away. Ingunn remained where she was, taking in Olav's familiar form as he left. She had never seen any man move with such poise, carrying himself with such calm grace. He was not especially tall; she remembered that now. In fact, she was no doubt slightly taller than he was, but he was so incomparably well built—his shoulders suitably broad, with a narrow waist, his body firm and muscular even though he was slender and straight-backed, with finely shaped limbs.

His face had grown leaner, his skin dry and weather-beaten. And his hair was darker, no longer a gleaming white-gold; now it was more ashen in color. But the longer Ingunn looked at him, the more familiar he became. When they had parted, there was still a sheen of childish softness about his good looks. Now he was a full-grown young man, yet still remarkably handsome.

Savoring her deep-felt happiness, Ingunn sat at the table that evening and saw with astonishment how friendly both Ivar and Magnhild were toward Olav. He had returned to Norway a week earlier, arriving in Oslo.

"It seems to me that you ought to have gone home to see to your estate first," said Ivar. "That shouldn't have entailed any risk, now that you've become the earl's man."

"No doubt I could have ventured there, but I had decided not to go to Hestviken until I regain charge of my property. That will happen soon enough," he said with a smile. "Then I can make everything ready there in the south so that Ingunn can move home with me."

From the conversation Ingunn gleaned that Olav had not yet been granted dispensation and guarantee for his safety in Norway. But neither he nor Ivar seemed to consider this of great concern. Earl Alf Erlingssøn of Tornberg was now the most powerful man in the country. Olav had met him in Denmark and joined his retinue. The earl had promised to obtain a peaceful resolution for him, and it was with the earl's permission that Olav had come to Norway to find a man who might negotiate on his behalf and seek a reconciliation with Einar's kinsmen. Olav had thought it best to act boldly, and for that reason he had gone straight to Ivar Toressøn at Galtestad. The two men had quickly reached an agreement.

"I've known you since you were just a lad," said Ivar. "And I've always been fond of you. As you know, I was angry when we heard you had helped yourself to the bride, and it was only reasonable that I—"

"Certainly it was reasonable," said Olav, laughing with him.

Ingunn asked fearfully, "So you haven't come home to stay, Olav?"

"I mean to stay in Norway . . . perhaps. But I can't stop here in the north for long. By Saint Bartholomew's Day, I must rejoin the earl at Valdinsholm."

Ingunn had no idea where in the world Valdinsholm might be, but it sounded as if it were far away.

It was easy to see that Olav had learned how to behave among folks. The sullen and taciturn boy who had never been far from home had now become a courtly young nobleman who spoke with ease. Olav presented himself in a lively and assured manner whenever he spoke, but he also listened attentively to the older folks, mostly replying to questions from Ivar and Magnhild. Rarely did he direct his words to Ingunn, and he hadn't tried to speak with her alone.

Olav said there was much strife in Denmark now. The great chieftains were dissatisfied with the king in every respect. Yet they had more freedom and rights in that country than here in Norway; perhaps that was why they were even more inclined to complain. In Olav's opinion, his own maternal uncle, Barnim Erikssøn, did whatever he liked, and he'd never seen the knight pay any attention to the laws that no doubt were in force in Denmark.

"Haven't you been granted part of the inheritance from your mother's kinsmen?" asked Ivar. "Surely you're entitled to that?"

"My uncle says no," replied Olav with a slightly mocking smile. "And that may well be true. It was the first thing he explained to me when I arrived at his estate of Høvdinggaard. First, he said that my maternal grandmother had made arrangements for her children's inheritance from Sir Erik before she married Bjørn Anderssøn. And my mother had lost all right to any inheritance from her kinsmen in Denmark when she left the country and was married in Norway without seeking their counsel—that was the second reason. The third was that the king had declared my mother's full-fledged brother, Stig Bjørnssøn, to be an outlaw. He is now dead, his sons reside abroad, and the king has confiscated Hvidbjerg, their estate. Duke Valdemar has now taken up the Stigssøns' case, and if he's able to get the estate back for them, then Uncle Barnim thinks I ought to step forward. Perhaps then a slice of the bacon might fall to me." He laughed. "This was something my uncle told me after we'd gotten to know each other better. We've been good friends from the start, and he has always provided for me in a seemly manner and been most generous. He just doesn't want me to demand anything as *my right*."

Olav smiled as he spoke, but Ingunn could tell that something unfamiliar had settled over his countenance. She saw an air of loneliness that had always been present, but now it appeared in a much sharper light, and there was something hardened about it that was new. She sensed that he hadn't been embraced solely with delight and joy when he arrived as a poor outlaw seeking refuge with his powerful Danish kinsmen.

"Otherwise I have to say that Barnim Erikssøn has been kind to me. Yet I was a happy man on the day I reached an agreement with Earl Alf. When I gripped the hilt of my sword and swore him fealty, I felt as if I'd come home."

"You're fond of him?" asked Ivar.

"Fond of him!" Olav's face lit up. "If you'd met the earl, that's not how you would describe what his men feel. Every one of us would follow him even if we had to sail straight through the reeking, sulfurous pools of Hell—all of us men whom he chooses to look upon when he laughs. His yellow eyes gleam like gemstones. He's a small man, and short—I must be a head taller than he is—and he's as broad as a storeroom door, with curly brown hair both on his face and his head. They say that the Tornberg lineage is descended from a king's daughter and a bear. Earl Alf has the strength of ten men and the wisdom of twelve. And I think most men would be happy and grateful to follow him— many women too," said Olav with a laugh.

"Is it true what they say about our queen, that she wants to marry him?" asked Ivar.

"How would I know about that?" replied Olav merrily. "But if what they say is true, that she's a wise woman, well . . . But it would put an end to her ruling the country and the realm, once she fell into those bear-paws of his."

In Ivar's opinion, it was at Queen Ingebjørg's command that Earl Alf sailed the Danish waters, laying waste to the coastal areas and attacking the German merchant ships that were trying to slip north through the inlets.

Olav said that was true enough. The earl wanted to obtain for Queen Ingebjørg the inheritance that was hers from her kinsmen in Denmark. At the same time he was punishing the German merchants for their assaults on Bjørgvin and Tunsberg during the previous year. But he was carrying out these actions because he wanted to do so, and not at the behest of the queen. Apparently an agreement had now been reached between the earl and the Danish noblemen. He would support them in their dispute with the king of the Danes, and in return Count Jacob and the other noblemen would pressure the king so relentlessly that he would take his hands off Queen Ingebjørg's properties in Denmark.

They had been sitting at the table and drinking after the evening meal, and Ivar had begun to hint that it might be time for him to go to bed. Then Olav stood up and took from his finger the big gold ring with the green stone. He showed it to Ivar and Fru Magnhild.

"I wonder whether the two of you recognize this ring? With this ring my father pledged me to Ingunn. Don't you think it might be fitting for me to give it to Ingunn, so that she might wear it now?"

Ingunn's kin agreed to this, and Olav put the ring on her finger. Afterward he took from his saddlebag a gilded chain with a cross and silver emblems for a belt. These items he also gave to Ingunn. Then he produced suitable gifts for Ivar and Magnhild, along with three gold rings, which he asked Ivar to give to Tora, Hallvard, and Jon. Both Fru Magnhild and Ivar were well pleased, praising the gifts and treating Olav with great friendliness. Fru Magnhild had more wine brought in, and all four of them drank from the Christmas horn.

When Fru Magnhild said that it was time for Ingunn to go to her grandmother's house to sleep, Olav stood up. He mentioned that he wanted to go and see the old servants Grim and Dalla, to have a talk with them. Magnhild offered no objections.

The sky was overcast, but the evening light, cold and brass-colored, shone through occasional rifts in the cloud cover. The evenings were already growing chilly, with a tinge of autumn.

Olav and Ingunn walked between the outbuildings. When they reached a fence surrounding a field, he rested his arms on the rail and stood there to peer across the land. The grain was ripe, gleaming white beneath the heavy gray sky; below was the bay, the water motionless and reflecting the approaching dusk. On the other side of the bay the image in the water of the blue-black wooded mountain slope merged with the shore.

"It looks the same," said Olav quietly. "Just as it used to look in the autumn. In Denmark the wind is almost always blowing."

He turned halfway toward the girl, put his arm around her shoulder, and pulled her close. With a deep sigh of happiness, she leaned heavily against him. At long last she felt herself home, now that she was in his arms.

Olav cupped her face in both hands, then pushed her hair back and kissed her temples.

"You used to have such curls here, along your hairline," he whispered.

"It's because I comb my hair so hard to make it lie straight," she replied softly. "I've combed away the curls. When they took my wimple from me, I plaited my hair as smooth as I could."

"Oh, I remember now. You wore the wimple of a married woman that winter in Hamar."

"Are you angry with me because I did as they wished and put the wimple away?"

Olav shook his head and laughed a bit.

"I had nearly forgotten about it. Whenever I thought of you, I always pictured you the way you used to look."

"Do you think I'm much the same as I was back then?" Ingunn whispered anxiously. "Or have I lost my looks?"

"No!" He wrapped her tightly in his arms. For a while they stood there, holding each other close. Then he let her go.

"We must go in. It will soon be dark." But he let her braids slide through his fingers, then twined them around his wrists and tugged her gently this way and that as he stood a few steps away from her.

"How lovely you are, Ingunn," he said fiercely. Again he let her go, this time with a strange laugh. Then he asked abruptly, "So it's more than a year since you last saw Arnvid?"

Ingunn replied that this was true.

"I would have liked to see him this time. He's the only friend I ever had in my youth—Arnvid and you. The folks you meet later in life, after you've grown older, are never friends in the same way."

Olav was twenty-one and she was twenty, but it didn't occur to either of them that they were too young to have such thoughts. So much had happened to both of them before they'd even left their childhood behind.

Then Olav turned on his heel and began heading up the slope. Ingunn followed him along the narrow path between the livestock sheds. Grim and Dalla were sitting on the doorstep in front of the barn. The two old people were overjoyed when Olav stopped to speak to them. After a moment he took some coins from his belt and gave them the money. Then their delight was beyond all measure.

Ingunn stood there, leaning against the wall of the barn, but none of them spoke to her. When she realized that Olav was going to stay with the old caretakers for a while, she bade them good night and went back to her grandmother's house.

Olav stayed at Berg for five days. On the morning of the sixth day he said that in the evening he would have to ride to Hamar. He'd been promised passage on a boat heading south to Eidsvoldene, if he could be ready early the next morning.

He had become good friends with Ivar and Magnhild, and everyone on the estate thought Olav had grown up considerably during the years he'd spent abroad. But he and Ingunn had not spoken much to each other.

On the day he was to depart, she asked him to accompany her up to the loft room where Aasa's belongings and her own were kept.

There she unlocked the chest that was hers and took out a big, folded linen garment. She handed it to him as she turned her face away.

"It's your wedding shirt, Olav. I wanted to give it to you now."

When she finally looked at him, he was standing still, holding the shirt. His face had turned red, and his expression was strangely defenseless and vulnerable.

"May Christ bless you, my Ingunn. May Christ bless your hands for every stitch you have sewn on this shirt."

"Olav, don't go!"

"You must know that I have to go," he said quietly.

"Oh no, Olav! I never imagined that when you came back home you would leave me again so soon. Stay here, Olav. Just three more days. Just one more day!"

"No," said Olav with a sigh. "Don't you see, Ingunn? I am still an outlaw. It was reckless of me to come here, but I felt that I had to see you and talk to your kinsmen. Today I own nothing in Norway that I can rightfully call mine. It's the earl, my lord, who has promised me . . . And if this were not the case . . . Since he has summoned me to appear at a specific time, I cannot stay away. As things stand, I must travel swiftly so as to reach him in good time."

"Can't you take me with you?" she whispered, her words barely heard.

"You must know I can't do that. Where would I take you? To Valdinsholm, where all the earl's men are staying?" He laughed.

"I've had such sad days here at Berg," she whispered again.

"I don't understand what you mean. They're both so kind, Fru Magnhild and Fru Aasa. While I was out there in the south, I thought so many times that if Kolbein managed to arrange things so that you had to stay with him . . . I was frightened for you, my dear. But here you've been treated as well as anyone can hope to be treated."

"I can't bear to stay here any longer. Can't you take me with you? Find me somewhere else safe to stay?"

"I can't ensure your safety as long as I have no authority over my estate," said Olav impatiently. "And how do you think Ivar and Magnhild would react if I took you away? Ivar is going to be my spokesman in negotiating with Kolbein. You mustn't be unreasonable, Ingunn. And Fru Aasa can't manage without you here."

Neither of them spoke for a while. Ingunn went over to the small window.

"Whenever I've stood here and looked out, I've always thought what I saw must resemble Hestviken."

Olav went over to her and caressed the back of her neck.

"No, not at all," he said absentmindedly. "The fjord is much wider at Hestviken, let me tell you. It's saltwater. And the estate is higher up the slope, if I remember correctly."

He moved away, picked up the shirt, and folded it.

"This must have taken you a great deal of work, Ingunn. There are so many seams."

"Oh, I've had four years to work on that shirt," she said harshly.

"Come. Let's go out," said Olav sternly. "Let's go out and have a talk."

They walked down through the fields until they came to a meadow near the water. Juniper bushes and other small shrubs grew on the dry, stony ground. In between were patches of short, sun-scorched grass.

"Come, sit down here," said Olav. Then he lay down on his stomach in front of her. He lay there for a long time, looking as if he were far away in his own thoughts.

She felt that in a sense they drew closer to each other now that he'd fallen silent and was lost in thought the moment the two of them were out here alone. She was so used to this from their childhood. She stared affectionately at the tiny scattering of freckles on the bridge of his nose; she thought they were so endearing.

Big clouds drifted across the sky, casting shadows that turned the forest land below a dark blue, with spaces of green meadow and white fields gleaming brightly in between. And the fjord was gray with shiny dark currents on the surface that reflected slivers of the autumn landscape. Occasionally the sun would come out, and the sharp golden light would sting their eyes and bring a blazing heat, but as soon as a cloud moved in front, the sun's warmth would quickly disappear. And the ground was cold and raw.

At long last the girl asked, "What are you thinking about so intently, Olav?"

He sighed as if aroused from sleep. Then he took her hand and pressed her palm to his face.

"About whether you could be more sensible," he said as he again took up their conversation from the loft room. After a moment he went on.

"I left Høvdinggaard without showing the proper gratitude."

Ingunn gave a little gasp of alarm.

"Yes, I know," said Olav. "It was wrong, and I should not have done so, because in many ways my Danish uncle has treated me well."

"Did you quarrel?"

"No, that was not the reason. But he happened to do something that displeased me. He had one of his hired men punished, and I can't say that the punishment was harsher than the man deserved. But my uncle could often be cruel when he was overcome with rage, and you know I've never liked to see folks or livestock tormented without reason."

"And because of that you quarreled?"

"No, that's not what happened. This fellow was a traitor. They had been drinking in the main hall, my uncle and some kinsmen and friends—they were my kinsmen too, for that matter. They had come to the estate to celebrate Easter, and it was the evening before Easter Sunday. They were talking about the king, and none of them had anything good to say about him, when they blurted out plans that were being devised against King Eirik. Many strange intrigues are being wrought down there in Denmark at the moment, let me tell you. And we were all drunk and reckless in our speech. This man, Aake, left the table and raced straight over to the king's officer at Holbekgaard, and, in return for payment, he reported the news he had heard. When my uncle found out about this, he had the fellow led out to a grove near the women's house where he was tied to the biggest oak tree. Then

Barnim raised the traitor's right hand, the hand with which he had sworn fealty to my uncle, and he nailed the man's hand to the tree with a knife.

"I'm not saying he didn't deserve such punishment. But as night fell, I thought Aake had stood there long enough. So I went out to free him, and then I loaned him a horse. I told him to send the horse back to a house in Kalundborg, where I was known, as soon as he found a chance to slip away from Sjælland. But I thought that my uncle would undoubtedly be furious when he learned how I'd defied him, and it would do little good to try to talk to him. I'd heard that the earl was staying at a place north, near the promontory, so I gathered up as many of my belongings as I could carry and rode north that same night. And that is how I happened to travel with the earl to England this year.

"It was a poor way for me to thank my uncle, and I pray to God each day that he will not suffer more trouble because I decided to free Aake. I made him swear not to tell, of course, but there's little difference between a sworn oath and a belch for that sort of fellow. If only my uncle had hanged him, I would have said it was a just punishment. But when Aake stood out there with his hand nailed to the oak . . . And this was right after Easter, you know. We had gone to church every day, and I had crawled on my knees to the Cross and kissed it on Good Friday. And so it seemed to me that the man was standing out there as if he'd been crucified."

Ingunn nodded gently. "What you did was a good deed."

"God only knows. I just wish I could believe that. But if I go to Denmark again with the earl's retinue, I suppose I could send word to my uncle and perhaps find an opportunity to visit him and ask his forgiveness. Because the way in which I left showed a terrible lack of gratitude."

He lay still, staring pensively at the dark blue of the forest.

"You say things have not been pleasant for you here, Ingunn. My life has not been like drinking Christmas ale every day either. I have no complaints about my wealthy kinsmen, but they are rich and proud men, and I came to them as a poor stranger and an outlaw. They considered me a boy and not a lawfully born member of their lineage because they were not the ones who had arranged my mother's marriage. Yet I cannot say that they should have welcomed me more warmly than they did, given how matters stood.

"You must not be unreasonable," he again begged Ingunn. He moved a little closer and let his head rest heavily on her lap. "If I had my way, I would stay here right now, or I would take you with me, if only that were possible. Do you wish that I hadn't come here at all, now that I can't stay?"

Ingunn shook her head as she ran her fingers through his hair, tousling it affectionately.

"But it's strange," she said softly, "that your uncle wouldn't do more for you, since he has no children of his own still alive, other than that daughter who is a nun."

"He would have done more if I'd been willing to stay in Denmark. But I always said that I wouldn't stay. And I suppose he could see that I was longing to return home."

After a moment Ingunn asked, "Those friends of yours, in the town that you spoke of, what sort of people are they?"

"Oh, they're nobody," replied Olav a bit curtly. "They own an inn. I often went into town for my uncle, to buy and sell oxen and conduct other business."

Ingunn continued stroking his hair.

"Surely you can at least let me have a kiss," said Olav. He got up onto his knees, threw his arms around her, and kissed her on the lips.

"You can have as many kisses as you like," she whispered to him. Tears spilled from beneath her lashes as he pressed ardent kisses all over her face and throat. "As many as you like. I would have gladly given you kisses every day!"

"I'm afraid that would have made me far too bold." He gave a deep laugh. "My Ingunn!" He dipped her backward until her neck nearly touched the ground. "But it won't be long now before . . ." he murmured.

"I suppose we should go back," he said, letting her go. "It must have been mealtime long ago. I wonder what Fru Magnhild would say if she knew we'd gone as far from the grounds of the estate as we have."

"I don't care," mumbled Ingunn defiantly.

"Nor do I!" Olav laughed as he took her hand and pulled her to her feet. He used his cap to brush off her clothes. "But we should go back home, nevertheless."

He kept holding her hand in his until they climbed to a spot on the path where they could be seen from the estate.

III

After Olav left, Ingunn was unable to rid herself of a slightly bitter sense of disappointment. It seemed as if his visit had had very little to do with her.

She knew full well that it was wrong of her to have such thoughts. Olav had behaved wisely when he pretended to have given up his old claims on her—and did nothing to show that she was his to possess and enjoy. Besides, they could never have been together in that manner on the estate. And he had won; both Ivar and Magnhild now let it be known that she and Olav were lawfully betrothed.

Fru Magnhild gave Ingunn presents for her dowry chest, which had been sadly empty until now. The gifts included a cloak of green velvet, lined with beaver pelt, and as good as new; a tablecloth and a hand towel with blue patterns; two shifts made of linen and one of silk; everything needed for a cradle; three bench cushions covered with tapestry weavings; a cast iron cookpot; a drinking horn with silver mountings; and a big silver pitcher. All this was given to Ingunn over the course of two months. Magnhild also persuaded Aasa Magnusdatter to give her granddaughter the good bedclothes she had kept in the storeroom, along with bed curtains and coverlets, pillows, and sheets made from both hides and cloth. "Is Ingunn about to marry?" asked Aasa with surprise every time her daughter managed to wrest something more from the old woman's possessions. But she forgot about all of it from one day to the next.

Ivar promised to give Ingunn a saddle and horse, along with money to purchase six good cattle; it would be too difficult to move the livestock from Oppland to Hestviken. And he invited her to come south to Galtestad so she could select garments from the clothing that had belonged to his deceased wife. "I would rather give the clothes to you than to Tora. She has grown so haughty ever since she married that Haakon Thunder-Fart, and she acts like a king's mother to those sons of his."

Ivar even went to the trouble of inquiring as to the whereabouts of Olav's clothing chest, which had been sold in Hamar when the youth was declared an outlaw. The chest was made from the white wood of a linden tree and was of unusually fine workmanship, with the loveliest carving on the front. Ivar bought the chest back and had it sent to Ingunn at Berg.

The axe called Ættarfylgja had been kept at the Dominican monastery in Hamar all this time. Brother Vegard had hidden it away when the bailiff confiscated Olav's belongings. The monk said this was no great sin on his part, for the axe, which had stayed with the same lineage for more than a hundred years, should not fall into the hands of strangers while Olav was still alive. When Olav now went back to Hamar, Brother Vegard was in Rendalen, preaching to the farmers there about the Paternoster and the Angel's greeting to the Virgin Mary. He had put together four excellent sermons on these topics, to be used on his tour of the bishopric during the summer. But Olav had sought out the prior and presented an official payment to the church for the murder he'd committed in the monastery. Afterward the prior had returned the axe to Olav. But when he once again headed south, he left the weapon with the monks for safekeeping.

Kolbein flew into a terrible rage when Ivar approached him and tried to negotiate a reconciliation on Olav's behalf. Never would he accept any payments for Einar's murder. Olav Audunssøn would remain an exiled man, and Ingunn would stay where she was, without inheritance or honor, if she refused to consent to whatever marriage her kinsmen might be able to arrange for a disgraced woman—most likely to a servant boy or tenant farmer.

Ivar merely laughed at his half-brother. Kolbein must have lost his wits, since he failed to see what sort of times he was living in. If the king granted Olav dispensation so he could peacefully live in Norway, then Kolbein, if he so wished, could refuse to accept the offered compensation—and merely leave the silver lying on the church hill for the crows and vagabonds to pick up. No matter what Kolbein did, Olav would be living securely at Hestviken. And as far as his betrothal to Ingunn was concerned, it was simply stupid to deny it was the result of a binding pledge made long ago. Ivar now took a favorable view of the fact that Olav had acted without their consent when they were planning to marry off his bride to Haakon Gautssøn. He thought it admirable that his kinsman Olav had already shown in his earliest youth that he was a man who would not allow himself to be cheated out of his lawful rights.

Haakon Gautssøn was now quarreling with his wife's kinsmen over an inheritance he was claiming on Tora's behalf, but Ivar had no intention of praising that particular kinsman for his actions. It was this very case that had prompted Ivar to give Haakon such a derisive nickname. For this reason, Haakon and Tora were staying at home this autumn as Ivar and Magnhild made preparations for Ingunn's wedding.

Haftor Kolbeinssøn met with Ivar at Berg to discuss the matter. Haftor was a hard and cold man, but right-minded in his way, and much more intelligent than his father. He understood full well that if Olav Audunssøn had acquired powerful friends who wished to support his case, then it would do no good for Kolbein to cause difficulties for the reconciliation. The only way they might win anything at all was by demanding that the payments be set as high as possible.

All this raised Ingunn's spirits. She accepted each gift as proof that she would soon have Olav back, and then he would take her home with him. She longed for him terribly, and the last time he'd been at Berg, he'd said so little to her. She realized that it was reasonable for him to spend most of his time trying to win over her kinsmen and secure the property that belonged to both him and her. And when he finally won her, she was certain that he would be as fond of her as he'd been in the past, although he was no longer as blind or impulsive as he used to be. He was different now that he'd grown up. It wasn't until she saw how he'd changed that she fully understood how many years had passed since they were children together at Frettastein.

♦ ♦ ♦

Haftor Kolbeinssøn was the one who brought the news to Berg when he arrived after Whitsun the following spring to claim the second part of the restitution payment for Einar.

Olav had already paid out half of the fine during the middle of Lent at Hamar. A German merchant from Oslo had brought the silver, and Ivar had met with him. Haftor then accepted the money on his father's behalf. More of the sum was to be paid now, after Whitsun. Then Olav himself would put the rest in the hands of the heirs at the summer *ting*, which was held in Hamar every year after the Eidsiva *ting* concluded. Afterward, Ingunn's kinsmen would give her to Olav.

But this time Olav had sent no representative, and Haftor brought unsettling news about the earl, who was Olav's lord. Queen Ingebjørg Eiriksdatter had died in Bjørgvin early in the spring, and with her passing Earl Alf had no doubt feared that his influence in Norway would be over. Ever since he was a small boy, the young duke Haakon had hated his mother's adviser with all his heart. Now he ordered the earl to send to Oslo the mercenary soldiers he had hired in England during the previous summer. This had been done in the name of the Norwegian king, but Earl Alf had then kept the men with him at Borg, causing great turmoil and discontent among the folks living in the surrounding villages. Earl Alf's response to the duke's command was to sail into Oslo Fjord with an entire fleet and then march into town with more than two hundred men. He and his personal retinue took lodging at the royal palace with the knight Sir Hallkel Krøkedans, the duke's official. One evening some of these Five-Port soldiers, as the English mercenaries were called, broke into an estate near town, robbing the place and beating the owner half to death. Sir Hallkel demanded that the malefactors be turned over to him. When the Englishmen refused to surrender those who were guilty, he took a group of the soldiers captive, then chose five men at random and had them hanged. After that the Englishmen launched an assault on the royal palace, which resulted in open warfare between the earl's men and the townspeople; the town was plundered and the whole section between

Saint Clement's Church and the river, down to the royal palace and the wharfs, was burned. In the end, the earl sailed out of the fjord with all his troops, and he took Sir Hallkel along as his prisoner, intending to cast all blame for the fiasco on the man. But the duke received word of what had happened while he was on a ship off the south coast, on his way home from his mother's funeral. In all haste he now gathered a large army and persuaded his brother, the king, to accompany him. They made their way to Borgesyssel. Sarpsborg and Insegran were taken by storm, and nearly three hundred of the earl's men reportedly fell or were killed afterward by the farmers in the villages. The duke had the chieftain at Alf's castle in Insegran executed along with several men in his retinue. People said this was revenge for the death of Hallkel Krøkedans, who, on orders from the earl, had been killed there at the castle. Earl Alf and what was left of his army had supposedly saved themselves by fleeing to Sweden. King Eirik had declared him an outlaw in Norway along with all the men in his company.

A heavy silence ensued when Haftor finished telling everyone at Berg about these events, speaking in a calm and laconic voice. He made no mention of Olav, but after a lengthy pause, Ivar asked Haftor directly whether he'd heard anything about him. Was Olav among the earl's men who had fallen?

With some reluctance Haftor said no, he wasn't. It turned out that the men who had first told him of all this—two Cistercian monks from Tunsberg—were able to give him precise news about Olav Audunssøn because he'd been at their sister cloister of Mariskog when the Oslo fire occurred. Before setting off for Oslo, the earl had granted leave to Olav, who had then gone to Elvesyssel to sell some land he owned there to the monks at Dragsmark. When he heard of the end to the earl's glory, Olav supposedly said that he owed Earl Alf everything he now owned and had regained. He refused to part ways with the first lord to whom he'd sworn fealty without first obtaining his permission. He then rushed off to Sweden to seek out the earl.

"Olav has had remarkable bad luck, that he has, when it comes to the men he chooses to ask for support," said Haftor dryly. "They end up as outlaws—first the bishop and now the earl. No doubt it comes with his lineage. I've heard that in his forefathers' day, Hestviken was a hotbed of Baglers, those followers of the party that fought King Sverre."

"In the past both Hov and Galtestad were called Bagler-lairs and Ribbung-dens,[28] and the same was said of other estates belonging to our lineage, Haftor," ventured Ivar, though without much conviction.

Haftor shrugged.

"Olav may well be a fine fellow, even though it's his fate always to side with those who lose. But he will never be a friend of mine. I do realize that his friends are fond of the man, but if Ingunn means to wait for him, she will have to practice patience."

Ivar objected, saying that this time Olav's case might be resolved swiftly. Haftor merely shrugged again.

It was Ivar who told Ingunn there was little chance that Olav would be able to take her home with him that summer. It didn't occur to him to recount all the details of Earl Alf's rebellion to the young woman, whom he considered naive and frivolous. For this reason Ingunn didn't understand at first that Olav's position was now just as bad as before he'd gained the support of Alf Erlingssøn.

But after that no more was said of her marriage.

Ivar and Fru Magnhild felt somewhat at a loss. They had thrown all their support behind the case and embraced Olav in such a way that they couldn't very well turn against him now that, quite unexpectedly, he had landed in new difficulties. And so they chose to say nothing at all about the matter.

Kolbein Toressøn was at home on his estate and for the most part bedridden; he had suffered a stroke. For that reason Ingunn heard very little about his response. And Haftor said nothing more. He had received half of the restitution payment in good English coin, and he didn't think it would be worthwhile to attempt rescinding the reconciliation after the fact. Besides, he felt a bit sorry for Ingunn, and he thought it might be just as well if the end result was that she married Olav, who would then take her away to another part of the country. She was of no use to her kinsmen and brought them no honor. When old Fru Aasa passed away, Ingunn would be nothing but a burden to her siblings. And Haftor was now the foster father for Steinfinn's sons, Hallvard and Jon, and a good friend of the boys, while Haakon Gautssøn had quarreled with his young brothers-in-law.

Ingunn was once again on her own, left to sit in silence in a corner of her grandmother's house.

During the first autumn she continued her work of spinning, weaving, and sewing items for her dowry. But gradually she lost all interest in the task. No one ever said a single word about her future. She stopped hoping that Olav might return soon, and with that, it seemed as if she'd never fully believed he'd come back at all. The days they'd spent together when he was last at Berg had left a vague feeling of disappointment in her heart; Olav had seemed almost like a stranger to her.

In her mind, the way he looked now didn't fit with her old dreams about living with him on his estate where the two of them had charge, and where they would fill it with young children. Yet she and Olav were the same people as when they had loved each other at Frettastein.

Then she seized upon the memory of the only time when they'd been alone, face-to-face, and lips to lips—that last day when they'd sat together in the meadow. In her thoughts she embroidered further on their conversation and the one, ardent and urgent, caress he had given her, when he had kissed her so passionately and leaned her back toward the ground. She dreamed that he had surrendered to his desire and her pleas, and taken her with him. She remembered what her mother had told her on the night before she died, about her own bridal journey over the mountains. Ingunn now reshaped that tale for her own purposes.

The following summer, the second since Olav had visited Berg, Ingunn accompanied Fru Magnhild far north in Gudbrandsdalen to Ringabu to attend a wedding. They stayed several weeks at Eldridstad with kinsmen who took them up to their mountain pasture so that Fru Magnhild might see their large herd of livestock. For the first time in her life, Ingunn found herself on a ridge so high that she was above the forests. She looked out across bare mountain plateaus with nothing but willow thickets and scrub birches and expanses of grayish-yellow reindeer moss. Across from her arched one summit after another, all the way to the northern horizon, where snow-covered peaks towered with clouds nestled in the clefts.

At the wedding celebration she had been forced to don bright, colorful clothing with a silver belt, and she'd worn her hair loose. At the time she'd felt merely embarrassed and confused. But afterward she couldn't stop thinking about it. When she once again sat in her grandmother's house at Berg, new images drifted through her mind. She pictured herself wearing jewelry and looking radiantly beautiful as she walked with Olav. Perhaps, judging by their appearance, they were in some royal palace abroad. It felt to her like a form of exoneration after all the years she'd spent sitting in the corner. And in her dreams she traveled over the mountains with the outlawed man. They rode through the mountain streams that roared with a stronger and brighter tone than the streams farther down the slopes. It sounded more like a song, less like thunder, and the water was clear, with round white stones on the bottom. All the sounds beneath the sky, as well as the light and the air, were different in the mountains than below in the countryside. She traveled with Olav toward the distant blue peaks, through deep valleys and over more plateaus. They rested in stone huts like the one at the Eldridstad mountain pasture. And the thought of these mountains caused a wildness to surge in her mind. She had longed with such quiet surrender, submitting to her fate and merely weeping softly under the coverlet on nights when she felt she was being pressed too hard. Now she felt something uncontrollable stirring inside her. And her dreams became more varied and adventurous, encompassing events that she'd heard about in ballads and tales, and she imagined all those things that she'd never seen: stone castles with roofs of lead, soldiers wearing blue coats of mail, ships with silken sails flying gilded pennants. These imaginings were far grander and more brilliant than the old pictures of the estate where she lived with Olav and their children, but they were much airier and less orderly, more like true nighttime dreams.

Arnvid Finnssøn had visited Berg a couple of times over the past years, and he and Ingunn had spoken of Olav, yet of his friend he knew only that Olav was alive and in Sweden. During the winter following the summer when Ingunn had gone to the mountains—this was at the new year, written as 1289 after the birth of Christ—Arnvid arrived at Berg in a state of great elation. Almost every year he would go to a trade meeting in Serna, and there he had met Olav in the autumn. They had spent four days together. Olav said that the earl had personally released him from his oath, saying that he wanted Olav to think of his own well-being. The earl had given him a token to bring to Tore Haakonssøn in Tunsberg, who was married to Alf's sister. Olav had then entered into service with a Swedish nobleman in order to support himself until he could return home, but it was his intention to leave for Norway at the new year. He might have already arrived at Hestviken.

Ingunn was pleased, and as long as Arnvid stayed at Berg, she felt her courage reawakening. But afterward her hopes again seemed to fade and then disappear. She couldn't allow herself to expect that something was truly going to happen. Even so, there was a lighter mood underlying all her thoughts and dreams that winter, aware as she was that spring was approaching. And perhaps Olav would come, as Arnvid had said.

In the summer the women at Berg would go outdoors when it was time to smoke meat or fish. There were some big rocks in the birch grove north of the estate, and there they made a fire in a crevice of the stone and placed on top a chest with no bottom. Under the chest's lid they hung whatever was going to be smoked, and then one of the women had to sit there all day to tend the fire.

A few days before Saint Hallvard's Day, Aasa Magnusdatter wanted some smoked fish, so Dalla and Ingunn went out to the smoke site. The old woman lit a bonfire and made sure that it was burning and smoking properly, but then she had to go back home to keep watch over a cow. Ingunn was left there alone.

In the grove the ground was almost bare and pale brown in color, but the sun was good and warm on the rocks. Fair-weather clouds sailed high overhead on the silky sheen of the blue sky. But the bay, which she could glimpse below through the naked white trunks of the birch trees, was still covered with disintegrating and brittle ice, and snow gleamed white inside the forest on the opposite bank, reaching almost down to the shoreline. Water dripped and trickled everywhere here on the sunny side, but spring had not yet found its full, rushing voice from the thawing snow.

Ingunn found it pleasant to sit in the sunshine and tend to the smoking fire. She'd already been there several hours. She had just stood up, thinking she might have to go and find more juniper branches, when she heard someone come riding along the path that headed into the mountains across from where she'd been sitting. She glanced up. It was only a man riding a small and somewhat shabby-looking dun horse. The next moment she happened to bump into the water vessel, which stood unsupported between the stones, and it toppled over.

She realized with annoyance that now she'd have to get more water, and Dalla had taken the wooden bucket. The water vessel was made of soapstone with a wooden handle stuck through two ears on either side of the rim. As she picked it up, the man up on the path called out to her. He had jumped off his horse and came running down through the withered heather.

"No, no, my dear maiden, let me do that for you."

He threw his arms around her waist to slow his descent, hastily pulled her close, and then grabbed the water vessel from her hand and kept on dashing toward the stream. Ingunn couldn't help laughing as she stood there and watched him run. He had shown so many white teeth when he laughed.

He had a dark complexion and curly hair. The hood of his cloak had fallen back so he was bareheaded. He was very tall and slender and agile, though a bit loose-jointed in the way he moved. And he had the merriest voice.

He came back with the water, and she saw that he was exceedingly young. His dark face was narrow and bony, but not unsightly; his eyes were big and either amber or light brown in color, lively and clear. His mouth was large, with a fine, arcing row of teeth, while his nose curved attractively. The young man was decently dressed in a moss-green knee-length tunic and a big brown cloak. He wore a small, short sword at his belt.

"So!" he said with a laugh. "If you'd like more help, all you have to do is ask!"

Ingunn laughed again. She told him she was not in need of any other help, and what he'd already done for her was of great service, since the water vessel was quite heavy.

"Much too heavy for such a fine and young maiden like you. Are you from Berg?"

Ingunn said she was.

"That's where I'm headed. I'm carrying messages and letters from my lord to your mistress. But I'll stay here a while and help you. Then I'll arrive so late that Fru Magnhild will have to give me lodging for the night. Might I be allowed to lie with you tonight?"

"I suppose you may," said Ingunn, thinking only that he must be jesting. She saw that he was no more than a boy, and she laughed when he did.

"But I'll stay here and talk to you for a bit," he said. "Such tiresome work you have, and it must be so desolate for you to sit out here in the woods all alone, as young and beautiful as you are."

"It would be worse to sit here if I were old and ugly. And it's not desolate out here in these woods. I haven't sat here more than four hours, and you've already appeared on the road."

"So I must have been sent to shorten the hours for you. Let me help you. I'm far better at this task than you are." A bit perplexed, Ingunn accepted, for she disliked getting smoke in her eyes and throat. The boy dipped the juniper branches in the water and placed them on the embers, then jumped aside when the smoke billowed up toward him. "What's your name, my lovely girl?"

"Why would you want to know?"

"Because then I will tell you my name. It might be useful for you to know what it is, seeing as I am to sleep with you tonight."

Ingunn merely shook her head and laughed. "So you're not from this district?" she asked. She could hear that he spoke with a strange accent.

"No, I'm an Icelander. And my name is Teit. Will you tell me your name now?"

"Oh, my name isn't nearly as unusual as yours. I'm simply called Ingunn."

"That suits you fine . . . for the time being. It's as lovely as the loveliest name I know. If I find a better one, I will write it with gilded letters and give it to you, Ingunn with the rosy cheeks."

He helped her to take out the fish that had been smoked long enough and then hung more inside the chest on the fire. He stretched out on the ground, chose a trout, split it open, and began eating.

"I see you take the fattest and the best for yourself," said Ingunn with a laugh.

"Is she so stingy with the food, your mistress Fru Magnhild, that she would begrudge us poor folks the spine of a fish?" Teit laughed in turn.

Ingunn realized that he assumed she was a maidservant. She had on a brown gown made of rough wadmal with a plain leather belt around her waist, and she wore her hair as she always did, in two braids without adornment, merely wrapped with blue woolen yarn.

Teit seemed in no hurry to leave. He tended to the smoke for her, dipping juniper branches in the water and then placing them on the fire. In between he would stretch out beside her and chat. She learned that he was a scribe for the bailiff's sheriff in these districts. He was the son of a priest named Sira Hall Sigurdssøn,[29] and he'd attended school in Holar. But Teit had not had any desire to become a priest. Instead, he wanted to travel the world to seek his fortune.

"And have you found it?" asked Ingunn.

"I'll answer your question tomorrow." He smiled slyly.

She couldn't help liking this merry boy. And then he asked permission to kiss her. That took her by surprise, but surely it would do no harm. So she said neither yes nor no as she simply sat there, laughing. Then Teit put his arms around her and kissed her on the lips. After that he refused to let her go and slipped his hands under her clothing, behaving in a manner much too bold and improper. Ingunn was starting to feel frightened, so she fended him off and told him to stop.

Vows

"This is unmanly behavior on your part, Teit," she told him. "Here I sit, tending to my work that I can't very well leave, as you can see!"

"I didn't think of that." He let her go at once, looking slightly shamefaced. "I'll go and see where that nag of mine has wandered off," he said then. "Shall I see you at Berg?" he called after her from up on the path.

When Ingunn and Dalla went down to the estate in the evening, there was no one in the courtyard, but when the door to Fru Magnhild's main house opened, laughter and loud voices could be heard inside. Fru Magnhild had guests: two young maidens named Dagny and Margret, who were the twin daughters of one of her foster daughters. This evening a number of youths had come to Berg, kinsmen of the maidens and friends of the kinsmen.

Ingunn went into her grandmother's house. Holding a bowl on her lap, she sat next to the bed to give the old woman some porridge and milk, occasionally eating a spoonful herself. Then she picked up a basket and knife and went out. The evenings were already lovely and light. On the sunny hill facing the bay and below the bridal field, as they called the biggest and best field on the estate, caraway and wild cabbage had already sprouted. She wanted to dig up enough to fill her basket so she could make soup for her grandmother. The old woman no doubt needed to cleanse her body of phlegm and unhealthy fluids after the winter.

The plants were so tiny and fragile. Before she had gathered enough in her basket, the gray-blue dusk of a spring evening had firmly settled over the land. When she neared the estate, she saw a tall and slender man coming toward her in the twilight. It was Teit, the Icelander.

"My dear maiden, must you go out and toil and strive so late in the evening?" he asked her gently. He reached into the basket and lifted up a handful of the greenery, breathing in the scent. Then he took hold of her wrist and lightly stroked it up and down.

"They're dancing inside. Won't you come and join us, Ingunn? Come and I'll sing the loveliest song I know."

Ingunn shook her head.

"Surely your mistress can't treat you so sternly. Everyone else in the household is there."

"They would be startled if I came in," said Ingunn quietly. "It has been a long time since I joined in with the amusements of the young people. Dagny and Margret would be surprised if I wanted to be with them and their friends."

"That's only because they begrudge the fact that you're more beautiful than they are. Most likely they're not pleased that the maid-servant is lovelier." He slipped his arm around her, making the woven basket creak as she held it in front of her. "I'll come to you later," he whispered.

Ingunn stood for a moment on the doorstep, looking out at the gray-blue spring night and listening to the muted sounds of voices singing and stringed instruments playing at Fru Magnhild's house. She didn't want to go over there; they were young and lively. But it wouldn't hurt to let Teit in tonight. She too had an urge to talk with a stranger once again. She left the door slightly ajar and then lay down on the bed, fully clothed.

She waited and waited, and she tried to deny that she was disappointed he hadn't come after all. Finally she must have fallen asleep. She was jolted awake when the man leaped onto the bed and lay down on top of her in a most unseemly manner. But when she shoved him off, he turned meek at once.

He excused himself by saying there had been so much ruckus in the house where everyone had been dancing. But when Ingunn lay still and gave only chilly replies to everything he said about the entertainments they'd enjoyed, Teit grew more and more subdued. Finally he pleaded, "But you must know that what I wanted most was to talk with you. And now you seem to be angry with me. My sweet Ingunn, what do you want me to tell you? What would you like to hear?"

"You'll have to come up with something yourself," said Ingunn, and then she had to laugh. "If you want to please me, you can't ask me how you should proceed."

"No? But if I could win your heart, would you like to leave Berg behind, Ingunn?"

"Oh . . . That could be."

"Would you like to move to Iceland and live there?"

"Is it very far to Iceland?" asked Ingunn.

Teit said it was. But it was a good country to live in, better than Norway; at least better than Oppland County, for here the winter was horribly cold. Back home in Iceland the snow often didn't last the whole winter, and the sheep and horses could stay outside all year round. Ingunn thought that sounded tempting, for she also found the wintertime to be vile, with the livestock starving in their stalls, and the bedclothes frozen to the timbered wall in the morning. Her feet were always cold, and they had to chop a hole in the ice for every drop of water that was needed in the house.

Teit spoke eloquently about his fatherland. Ingunn thought it must be beautiful. The heights where they went to get the sheep in the autumn must look like the mountain ridge she'd climbed when she was north in Gudbrandsdalen. The world was big and vast—for the men who were able to travel widely, that is. She happened to think of Olav and how far he had roamed in England and Denmark and Sweden. Teit had seen only Iceland and Norway. She wished Olav had also wanted to tell her about everything he'd experienced, but Olav rarely spoke of what had happened to him. No doubt Teit was the way he was because he was so well educated. She'd never thought that a man with book learning could be so young and lively and carefree. And she'd never met a layman who'd had priestly training, other than Arnvid, and he was much older and had such a serious disposition.

At last they both grew sleepy and several times their conversation came to a halt. Then the boy crept closer to Ingunn, wanting to grope and caress her. She fended him off, her efforts at first somewhat drowsy and half-hearted. But then she grew frightened as Teit became more insistent. She told him to think of Fru Aasa, who was asleep in the other bed. If she awoke and saw that Ingunn had taken in a nighttime guest, there would be trouble for her.

Teit protested a bit, whining as if in jest, but then he relented, thanking her and bidding her good night. Ingunn went with him to the door to close it behind him. That's when she saw that it was already past midnight.

She slept late the next morning, and it was midday by the time she went out to the courtyard to carry out a chore. She caught sight of the Icelander as he stood loafing near the stable door, looking as if he'd sold some butter but received no payment. Ingunn went over to bid him good morning and to thank him for his company.

Teit pretended not to see her outstretched hand, and his expression was surly.

"No doubt you've found it all very amusing. Did you think I was such an idiot that you could fool me as much as you liked?"

"I don't know what you mean."

"I suppose you thought it a clever trick to entice the poor young lad to court you, the daughter here at Berg."

"I'm not the daughter at Berg, Teit. I'm the niece. There is a big difference."

Teit looked at her suspiciously.

"I thought you were the one who was jesting," said Ingunn. "With all your words of courting and your attempts to caress me. I didn't think you were in earnest. Nor did I think you were trying to ridicule me—for being naive, I mean. And I must tell you that because I've never been beyond these districts where I was born, there is so much I don't know. I found it pleasant to talk with you, such a clever and learned and well-traveled man as you are."

She smiled at him, her expression gentle and imploring.

Teit lowered his eyes. "You don't truly mean that."

"Yes, I do. And I thought you might stay here a few more days. I thought it would be agreeable to listen to you some more, and learn from you."

"No, I have to head home now. But I expect that Gunnar Bergssøn will send me here again at the sabbath," he said, a bit shyly.

"Then you will be most welcome." Ingunn shook his hand in farewell and went back to her house.

IV

As Saint Jon's Day approached, Arnvid Finnssøn came down to visit his aunt. The state of Fru Aasa's health changed from day to day; she might die at any moment, yet she might also live for a good while longer, God willing. Arnvid had heard nothing more about Olav since the last time he'd come to Berg.

The day after he arrived, he was walking with Ingunn in the courtyard when Teit Hallssøn dashed past and went into Magnhild's house. Arnvid stopped and stared after the young man.

"He seems to have business here quite often, that clerk."

Ingunn said he did.

"I don't know whether you ought to talk so much with him, Ingunn."

"Why? Do you know something about him?" she asked after a moment.

"I've heard about him in Hamar," said Arnvid brusquely.

"What did you hear?" Ingunn asked, a little anxiously. "Is there some fault they claim he has?"

"Gambling," said Arnvid quietly and a bit grudgingly. It was Master Torgard, the cantor, who had first taken the vagabond into his service, and he had also praised the fellow. The Icelander had the most beautiful handwriting, and he wrote with both speed and accuracy. He was also proficient at illuminating texts, so Master Torgard had entrusted him with drawing and coloring the initial capitals in an antiphonary and in a transcription of the laws of the land. And he had done beautiful work. When the bookbinder's wife, who usually helped her husband, fell ill, Teit had assisted the man in her place. And he turned out to be as skilled a bookbinder as the bishop's own man. So Master Torgard had reluctantly allowed the fellow to leave his service.

But Teit's weakness was that he lost all reason and sense whenever he got his hands on dice or some form of board game. And a great deal of that sort of gambling went on in the town. The fellow was capable of gambling away his very hose and shoes, and then he would come home to his master wearing borrowed clothing. In general, Teit had no idea how to tend to his own well-being, and he bought on credit from women selling ale and from peddlers. Although he was reluctant to lose such a clever scribe, Master Torgard had decided that for the boy's sake, he needed to send him away to a place where such temptations were not as close to hand. Teit was otherwise an amiable fellow; that much the cantor had also said. But when the sheriff in Reyne had need for a clerk who was skilled at both reading and writing, Master Torgard had sent the Icelander to him.

Teit had also been involved in some troubles with womenfolk, but this was not something Arnvid thought he needed to mention to Ingunn. As it was, he took little pleasure in spreading rumors about the boy. But he felt it necessary to share what he had learned about Teit, since the Icelander had, among other things, borrowed money from Master Torgard's old sisters.

The day before Saint Jon's Day, the folks at Berg had attended the morning service—it was the annual mass for Fru Magnhild's late husband, Sir Viking—and when they were on their way home from church a terrible thunderstorm swept in. It rained so hard that it seemed as if the earth hadn't seen the likes of such a deluge since Noah's day. The churchgoing folks sought refuge under several big overhanging cliffs, yet they were as soaked as crows by the time they reached home late in the day.

Tora Steinfinnsdatter was visiting her aunt, and she'd brought along her two eldest children. This time she had been most friendly toward her sister, and later in the afternoon she went over to Fru Aasa's house to invite Ingunn to join them in the main house, where the guests included several strangers.

Wearing only her shift, Ingunn sat hunched near the hearth, with her hair hanging loose so it would dry faster. At first she objected that she couldn't leave her grandmother, but Tora thought Dalla could certainly come and sit with the old woman. Then Ingunn said that she had nothing suitable to wear. The only Sunday gown she owned had been soaked through on the way back from church.

Tora walked about the room, humming to herself. She was still a very beautiful young woman, although she had grown quite heavy over the years. But she was elegantly attired in a blue velvet cotehardie and silk wimple. And the silver filigree brooches and gilded belt she wore looked lovely on such an expanse of fabric. Now she opened the chest belonging to Ingunn.

"Couldn't you wear this?" Tora stepped into the light of the hearth, carrying the leaf-green silk gown that Ingunn had been given by their mother for the celebration after Mattias Haraldssøn was killed.

Ingunn bent forward, as if embarrassed.

Tora went on. "I can see you haven't worn it much. I remember I begrudged the fact that Mother gave the gown to you. Have you ever worn it after that evening?"

"I wore it to the wedding at Eldridstad."

"I heard you looked so lovely when you were there," Tora sighed. "I lay in bed, feeling quite vexed that I couldn't attend, and it was the grandest wedding this valley has seen in twenty years. Come, my sister," she pleaded. "I have such an urge to dance and frolic tonight. This is the first summer I'm free to do so since I married. Come, my Ingunn. Arnvid is here to sing for us, as well as the Icelander, that friend of yours. I don't know which of them has the more beautiful voice."

Ingunn reluctantly stood up. Laughing, Tora pulled the gown over her sister's head and helped her to arrange the folds under the silver belt.

"My hair is still damp," murmured Ingunn self-consciously as she gathered the tresses in her hands.

"Just let it hang loose," said Tora with a laugh. Then she took her sister's hand and led her outside.

◆ ◆ ◆

"Oh look! It's Aunt Ingunn, it's Aunt Ingunn!" shouted Tora's little daughter when Ingunn stepped forward into the light and then picked up the child to hold her. The little maiden threw her arms around her aunt's neck, burying her nose in Ingunn's hair that was still warm from the fire and wrapped around Ingunn like a cloak made of some sort of dark golden threads, reaching below her knees. "Mother!" shouted the child, "I want to have hair like this when I'm a grown maiden."

"That's something you might well wish."

Ingunn set the girl down on the floor. Tonight she was so aware of her own beauty that it seemed to dazzle her eyes. Olav, she thought, and she felt her heart pounding hard. It seemed to her that he had to be here. She rubbed her face and pushed her hair back on both sides as she looked around. She met Arnvid's strange dark gaze; she saw Teit's amber eyes shining toward her like two lit tapers. But the one she sought wasn't there. She pressed her hands, crossed at the wrists, to her chest. He was the one who should have been here tonight to see that she was the most beautiful woman in the room. For a moment all she wanted was to run back to her grandmother, take off all the fine clothing, and weep.

Later that evening the conversation turned to line dances. They spoke of the graceful old sword dance known as the "Lay of Kraka." Arnvid admitted that he was familiar with it, and Tora said that both she and her sister had learned the steps. Teit jumped in eagerly, his face flushed, saying that he knew the words to the whole ballad and would gladly sing it. Fru Magnhild said, laughing, that if the young people would find it amusing to see the old dance performed, she was willing. "And what about you, Bjarne?" she said, turning to an old gentleman who had been her childhood friend. Then a couple of older servants stepped forward, a bit bashfully. It was clear they had an urge to try out the pastimes of their youth.

Arnvid told Teit to lead the dance, since he was no doubt the best to do so, and then Fru Magnhild and Sir Bjarne would follow. But the old people declined the place of honor. It ended with Teit standing at the head of the chain with Ingunn, and then Arnvid with Tora. Altogether there were seven men with drawn swords and six women.

The dance proceeded well, for Teit was an excellent leader. His big, bright voice was a bit shrill, but it was clear that he was an accomplished singer. Arnvid's lovely full voice offered good support, and Sir Bjarne and two of the old hired men also had very commendable singing voices. Everyone was filled with enthusiasm because of the superb way in which Teit led the ballad and dance. None of the women sang along, but that only seemed to enhance the gravity and power of the old sword dance. It was the weapons that ruled, along with the rhythmic steps of the men and their voices that sang with ever-increasing fervor. The women merely glided in and out beneath the clanging swords that were raised and crossed again and again.

Ingunn danced as if entranced and possessed. She was tall and lithe and had to dip her head lower than the other women. She kept her eyes half-closed as she grew pale and breathed heavily. Whenever she leaped forward beneath the blades, the cloak of her flowing hair would billow out a bit, as if she were trying to lift heavy wings. A strand had fluttered onto Teit's chest, where it became entwined with the brooch he wore. It tugged at Ingunn as she stepped out and in, but it didn't occur to her to stop the dance to free her hair.

They had danced fifteen or sixteen of the verses when Fru Magnhild gave a loud shout that caused the whole chain to pause for a moment. Sweat was pouring down her flushed face. She pressed her hands to her bosom and cried with a laugh that she could go no further.

Arnvid tossed his small, tight-looking head toward Teit, his eyes glittering wildly. He shouted something and then all the men joined in as he sang:

> With the sword we struck—
> All of Aslaug's sons
> would with sharpened blades
> awaken Hild if they knew—

The men insisted on singing the last stanzas of the ballad, even if they had to skip over the ten or twelve verses in between.

> A mother I chose for my sons
> to make their hearts most bold!

The men were so lost in the dance that their voices burned with zeal, and in unison they sang so the words reverberated:

> With the sword we struck—!
> Now I wish to be done!
> Invited home am I
> by those Odin sent to summon me
> to the halls of Herjan.
> Gladly will I sit in the high seat
> to drink ale with the Æsir;
> weary of life's hopes:
> laughing will I meet death!

Then the dancers let go of each other's hands and tumbled backward to land on the benches. The men put down their swords and wiped the sweat from their faces, laughing with joy. And the young people who had been watching called out, saying how lovely the dance had been. Fru Magnhild held her hands to her sides, panting with exhaustion.

"Oh yes, it's a different sort of dance than when all of you jump and leap about. Take over now, Margret, and dance one of the sweet love ballads that you are all so fond of:

> It was Eirik the king
> riding north through the mountains—

"For it's as fine and sweet as honey, and no doubt the old ballads are too harsh for the silken dolls that you are!"

The young people didn't wait to be asked a second time. They probably thought the old dance had lasted too long, even though they found it quaint to see the old sword dance.

Teit came over to where Ingunn was sitting, huddled against the wall and wrapped in her lovely hair. Her face had not grown flushed during the dance; instead, it seemed damp with a waxen pallor.

"No, I can't manage to dance another step. I just want to sit here and watch," she said.

Teit dashed back to the others. He was tireless and seemed to know all the words to both the old ballads and dozens of new songs.

Ingunn paused in the courtyard. She had left the amusements behind to return to her grandmother's house and go to bed.

It was close to midnight. The sky was pale and clear along the whole horizon, with a shimmering whiteness that deepened to a sulfur-yellow in the north. Only above the ridge on the other side of the bay was what seemed to be a grayish-blue veil of thin clouds, and within was the moon, about to sink, its radiance blurred and wet.

Even though the night was so clear, darkness lay heavier across the land than was usual for this time of year. The fields and meadows and leafy groves were still saturated with moisture from the storm earlier in the day. A damp and cold mist hovered low over the ground in every direction. Thin wisps of brownish smoke drifted across the water, but all the bonfires had been put out except for one that gleamed big and red on a distant promontory, casting its reflection like a slender, glowing blade on the steel-blue surface of the water.

Teit came out, looking for Ingunn. She knew he would. Without glancing back, she headed toward the field down by the fjord. When she came to the fence opening and stopped to take down the guardrail, he caught up with her.

They didn't say a word to each other as they continued, she leading the way and he following, both of them walking along the little footpath through the tender young grain. At the end of the field was a stream; the path ran alongside it, beneath the dense thickets of alder trees and willow bushes, heading down to the estate's boat landing.

Ingunn stopped as soon as she entered the shadows of the leafy trees. It was pitch-dark, and she was frightened of going any farther.

"Oh, how cold it is tonight," she whispered so softly her words could barely be heard. She shivered. She could hardly see the man at all, but the warmth of his body felt gentle and sweet in the midst of the icy, acrid scent of wet leaves and raw soil. He didn't speak, and his silence suddenly seemed to loom with an awful menace. She felt a sudden, ungovernable fear and thought that if only she could make him say something, the danger would pass.

"That verse you sang back at the house," she whispered, "about the willow tree. Recite it again."

In a low, clear voice, Teit spoke into the dark:

> Blessed are you, willow,
> standing there by the lake,
> with lush and lovely leaves.
> Men shake from you
> the morning dew.
> And I long for Thegn
> both day and night![30]

Ingunn raised her arms and pulled into her embrace some of the bitter-scented leafy branches; a shower of rain and dew poured over her in the darkness.

"You'll ruin that lovely gown of yours," said Teit. "Did you get wet? Let me see."

But when his hands brushed against her bodice in the dark, Ingunn pulled away, as fast as lightning, from his outstretched arms. With a low shriek of alarm, she raced up the path. Gathering her skirts in both hands, she ran through the field as if fearing for her life.

Teit was caught so off guard by this turn of events that it took a moment for him to collect himself and take off after her. By then she had such a head start that he didn't catch up with her until she reached the gate. At that spot they could be seen and heard from the courtyard, where the guests were now crossing through on their way to bed. Teit stopped there and let Ingunn go.

He wore a surly and offended expression the next day when they met. Ingunn's greeting was almost humble.

With some embarrassment she murmured, "I think we both must have lost all sense last night. Why would anyone think of going down to the lake at so late an hour?"

"Oh, is that what you were thinking?" asked the Icelander dryly.

"And the only bonfire seemed to be the one we saw up at the estate. So it would not have been worthwhile to go down to the boat landing."

"No. We would undoubtedly have enjoyed each other's company better if we'd stayed indoors," said Teit, sounding annoyed. With a nod of farewell he went on his way.

On an autumn afternoon three months after Midsummer Eve, Ingunn walked through the gate where the rails had been taken down now that the livestock had been brought home from the lower mountain pastures. They were allowed to graze freely in the nearby grounds.

Today the cattle were in the meadow below the grain field. It would be impossible to imagine a more beautiful sight than those animals, fattened up from their time in the mountain pastures, with the sun gleaming and glinting off their coats. Their colors were as varied as livestock can be, and the grass stubble that had sprouted after the harvest was so lush and green that it seemed to have swollen in size, with large clumps of silver-shimmering mayweed nestled in the grass. The sky was blue, with small, gentle fair-weather clouds drifting high overhead. The blue fjord mirrored the land that glittered with autumn colors, and the leafy groves surrounded the nearby pastures with red and yellow. Beyond stood the forest, shadowy and blue-green, with the crown of every single spruce tree clearly visible and seeming to drink in the light from the dazzling chill air.

The joyful radiance of the day made Ingunn cringe, burdened as she was by anxious dread and misery. She dared not stay away when he had asked her to meet him. She was frightened to death of being alone with him, yet she had no choice. Otherwise he might seek her out at the estate and someone might hear them talking.

The grass stubble gleamed like pale gold on either side of the path. Now, after the harvest, it was possible to see far across the open fields. His small, dun-colored nag was grazing in the grove down by the stream.

Ingunn silently said a prayer that was no more than a gasp issuing from her deep distress, the same way she'd prayed on that night when he'd stood outside the door to her loft room, knocking quietly and calling her name. In the pitch dark she had knelt at the headboard of her bed with her arms thrown around the carved horse's head and inwardly cried for help, without making a sound, as she trembled with fright. If the misfortune had occurred, if she had now descended into the worst of the worst . . . She wanted no more of it, she had no wish to sink even deeper. But then it had seemed to her that he was able to force her against her will, and she felt compelled to cross the room and let him in.

When she saw that he was no longer standing at her door, she sobbed with sheer gratitude. For it was not the tiny spark of her own will that had held her back, but rather an invisible force, strong and stern, that had filled the darkness between her and the terror at the door. Exhausted, she curled up under the coverlet, humbly thankful that she had been saved. And she thought no punishment for her sin would be so severe that she wouldn't accept it with gratitude, if only she might never again fall under Teit's power.

And when they met the following day and he teased her about sleeping so soundly that he had to leave, unconsoled, from her door, she had replied, "I was awake. I heard you." She was utterly calm, for she was certain that the benevolent forces that had held her back in the night would not allow him to gain control over her again.

He asked her why she hadn't opened the door. Was it that she didn't dare, or was someone else inside?

She had boldly replied, "No, but I didn't wish to let you in. And you mustn't come here anymore, Teit. Be good enough not to seek me out again!"

"Never have I heard the likes of this! 'Be good enough' you say! Yet the night before—"

"Yes, I know," she interrupted him with a groan of pain. "Things are bad enough as it is, things are sinful enough."

"Sinful?" he said, overwhelmed with astonishment. "Is that what you're thinking?"

It occurred to her then, and it occurred to her now as she walked along, that she felt some sympathy for the young man. He couldn't know how great a sin was committed when she allowed him to possess her. She had broken a pledge that she couldn't yet bear to think about in this section of Hell where she had now taken up residence.

Six weeks. Six weeks had already passed since that day and that night which she, deep inside and beyond all conscious thought, had started to hope might be forgotten—at least eventually. She could confess and atone and then she could set about forgetting what had happened with Teit. For she had neither seen nor heard from him since then. Not until today when he arrived at Berg, having found some reason for visiting Fru Magnhild. That's when he had asked her to come and meet him. And she had no choice but to go.

Now Ingunn saw him. He was sitting on a rock among the thickets. And she silently cried: help me, don't let him frighten me so that I fall into his hands again!

There he sat, at almost the same spot where they'd stood in the dark on Midsummer Eve, when he recited for her the verse about the willow. But that's not what she was thinking about now. Today this place was a bright and airy bower beneath the yellowed foliage of the trees. Sunlight and blue sky shone down upon them through the slender branches that had begun to lose their leaves. Tiny glints of light danced on the stream beyond the bushes. Drops of dew sparkled on the pale, broken straw and on the coarse vegetation already cracked and withered by frost. The path was bright with fallen leaves.

Even the moss-covered rock on which he sat looked so lovely with the green tendrils hanging off the surface. She felt quite confused at being all alone with her fear and distress in such a beautiful and radiant world.

"Christ save me! What's wrong?" Teit had jumped to his feet and was now staring at her. Then he moved forward, as if to embrace her. She raised her hands in a half-hearted gesture, making a feeble attempt to defend herself as she shrank away. Swiftly he helped her to sit down on the rock, and then he stood there, looking at her. "I can see you haven't been very happy during these weeks I've been away. Has someone caught wind of things?" he asked.

Ingunn shook her head. She was shaking as she sat there.

"Then it's best I tell you the good news I've brought," he said giving her a little smile. "I've been to Hamar, Ingunn, and I spoke to Master Torgard about the matter. He has promised to speak on my behalf to your kinsmen. He and Gunnar Bergssøn. As you can see, I'm not so badly off when it comes to spokesmen who are willing to support my courting of you."

She felt as if she'd once been knocked down by an avalanche, but she had clawed her way out, injured and bloody. And now this new landslide had come along to bury her.

"What do you say to that?" he asked.

"I've never thought this would happen," she whispered, wringing her hands. "That you would . . . seek to marry me."

"I've thought about it before, in the summer, several times. I was fond of you from the very first moment I saw you. And when you didn't hide the fact that you were as fond of me as you were, well . . . But it's not certain," he said as he looked down at her and gave a sly laugh, "that I would have made the effort to move so quickly if you hadn't refused to let me come in on that second night. I realized afterward it would have been reckless to continue playing that game at Berg. And I was loath to lose you. So now you'll soon be released from worrying about the sin, if that's what has been weighing on your mind!" He smiled and stroked her cheek.

Ingunn hunched forward as she sat there, looking like a dog expecting to be beaten.

"I never thought that would be such a burden for you. But now you can take comfort, my poor dear."

"Teit . . . It's impossible for the two of us to marry."

"Neither Gunnar nor Master Torgard was of that opinion."

"What is it you told them?" she whispered, her words nearly inaudible.

"I told them everything that has happened between us—well, more or less, you know," he said with a laugh. "But I did tell them that the two of us have the greatest affection for each other. And that at last you let me know that you wished for us to be together. But you must know I haven't said anything that would make them think you've given me anything more than your *word*." He gave a giddy laugh as he lifted her chin, trying to make her look up. "Ingunn?"

"I never said that."

"What do you mean?" Teit's expression darkened. "Perhaps you think I'm too lowly to marry you? Gunnar and Master Torgard did not think so. You must know that I don't intend to remain in Gunnar's service after I marry. We've already agreed that I will leave him at Christmastime. Nor is it my intention to stay in this part of the country, unless that should be your wish and your kinsmen would give us land on which to build. Yet I don't suppose they will. But Master Torgard is willing to give me a letter to the archbishop, and to some of his friends in the chapter, and he'll write that I'm a most skillful scribe and painter of images on calfskin. Contrary to what all of you farmers may think, I can provide for myself much better with my handiwork when I'm somewhere like Nidaros. There will be plenty of prospects for me there, Ingunn, plenty of ways for me to increase my wealth when I have goods that I can trade. And later we can travel back to Iceland. You spoke so much about it in the summer. You said you would dearly love to go to Iceland. I think I can promise that I'll be able to take you there, and under favorable conditions as well."

When he looked down and saw her pale, terrified face, he grew angry.

"You have to consider that you're not so young anymore, Ingunn. You've passed your twentieth year. And I've heard of late that very few men have been thronging the courtyard of your guardians in the hopes of wooing you." He glanced away, a bit ashamed of his own words.

"Teit, I can't!" She clasped her hands tightly on her lap. "There's someone else, someone to whom I gave my promise, years ago."

"I wonder what he'd have to say about such a promise if he knew everything that has gone on," Teit said tersely. "I would never abide by such a promise if it were *my* betrothed who carried on with some stranger and bantered with him so freely, the way you have, showing me how much you enjoyed the game the two of us played this summer. No, the Devil take me if I would—not even if you withheld from me that which you did not withhold, the first day we were alone at the estate!"

Ingunn put her hand to her face, as if he had struck her.

"Teit, I didn't want to!"

"No, of course not!" He gave her a scornful grin.

"I didn't think . . . It didn't occur to me that was what you wanted."

"Surely, you jest!"

"You're so young. You're younger than I am. I thought it was just the reckless behavior of a young boy."

"That's what you thought?"

"I struggled and tried to defend myself."

Teit laughed a bit. "Yes, that's what most women usually do. But I'm not too young to have learned that there's nothing that angers women more and there's nothing for which you reproach a young and gullible fellow more afterward than when he allows himself to be deterred by such . . . resistance!"

Ingunn stared at him, her face rigid with fear.

"If you'd been a young and pure maiden . . . I would never have forced myself on a young maiden. I am not that sort of fellow. But surely you can't expect me to believe that you didn't know full well where the dance was heading after you'd been leading me in that direction all summer long?"

Ingunn continued to stare at him. Slowly a flush crept up to the gray pallor of her face.

"You must realize," said Teit coldly, "that I've heard a good deal about you, so I know about that boy who served on your father's estate—the one with whom you had a wayside bastard when you were fourteen years old."

"He was not a servant boy. And I've never had a child." Then she bent low over her lap, wrapped her arms around her knees and hid her face as she began to weep quietly.

Teit smiled uncertainly. He stood there looking down at the weeping young woman.

"I don't know whether he's the one you're waiting for, believing that he'll come back to marry you. Or perhaps you've found someone else after him? However that may be, he doesn't seem to be in any haste, this friend of yours. I'm afraid, Ingunn, that it won't do any good for you to keep waiting for him. If you do, far too many others might easily appear in the meantime."

She stayed as she was, weeping quietly with heartbreaking despair.

Teit went on in a gentler tone, "It would be better for you to take me, Ingunn. Someone you already know. I'll be . . . I'll be a good husband to you, as long as you put aside this . . . inconstancy of yours, and behave in a reliable and sensible way from now on. I . . . I'm fond of you," he said, awkwardly, lightly stroking her bowed head. "In spite of everything."

Ingunn shook off his hand.

"Don't weep like this, Ingunn. I have no intention of abandoning you."

She sat up and stared straight ahead. She realized it would be useless to try and tell him the truth behind the stories he'd heard. These rumors must be what people had been saying about her here in the village where no one knew Olav. And few knew her as other than the neglected woman sitting in the corner, a disgrace to her lineage, a woman whom her kinsmen held in such disfavor that they'd sent her away.

That was something else she couldn't bear to mention. But as for what had gone on between her and Teit . . . She thought she needed to tell him how that had happened. And so she spoke.

"I know this is punishment for my sin. I knew that I was committing a grievous sin when I refused to forgive Kolbein, my father's brother. I rejoiced when he died. I thought of him with hatred, I was filled with a desire for revenge, and I refused to attend the funeral feast for him. He was the person, first and foremost, who had caused me to be separated from the one to whom I was pledged as a child and the one I wanted most. Not a single prayer was I willing to say for Kolbein's soul, although I thought he could certainly use all the prayers anyone might offer. When they said De profundis in the evening, I left the room. And I refused to travel north with the others for his burial.

"May God forgive me. I know that it is sinful to hate an enemy after he has been called to judgment. Then you arrived, and I wanted to think of other things. I was pleased when you wanted to keep me company up in the weaving loft. I had no thoughts other than that you were a mere boy. And given my state of mind, I wished only to revel and carouse with you, for I didn't want to give any more thought to the dead man. And when we pulled wool out of the sacks and began throwing it at each other . . . But I didn't think—no, I didn't think that because you were so importunate and uttered such improper words . . . I thought it was simply because you were so wanton and young."

Teit stood there looking at her with the same uncertain little smile.

"So be it. We'll say that's how it was. I took you first against your will. But later, in the night?"

Ingunn hopelessly bowed her head. That was not something she could explain away. Even to herself she could hardly make sense of what had happened.

She had lain awake hour after hour, crushed by horror and shame. And yet it was as if she couldn't fully grasp the truth—that now she was lost and disgraced. For it already seemed like the memory of a dream or a moment of dizziness. That was how she thought of her own wild and frenzied merriment that afternoon in the weaving loft. And the fact that Teit had taken her . . . Yet the whole time his image appeared to her as she'd pictured him after Midsummer Eve, when the next day she had regretted her own foolish fear of him. He was only a boy, an amiable, clever, and lively boy, with whom she'd always felt comfortable; a bit too bold in his speech, but he was so young, after all. Yet she knew, as she lay in bed, that she had brought misfortune upon herself along with eternal damnation, and now she was a whoring woman.

Finally she fell asleep.

She was awakened by Teit pulling her into his arms. She hadn't thought to latch the door; they never did when they slept in the loft during the summer. She no longer remembered clearly why she hadn't tried to fend him off. Perhaps she thought the shame would seem even worse if she now said she wanted nothing more to do with this man who had already possessed her, if she told him that she would rather not see him ever again, that she hated him. But when he appeared in the loft and she heard his lively young voice, perhaps she thought that her hatred for him was not as fierce after all. He was so trusting and had no idea what distress he had caused her. He didn't know that she was bound to another or that, in the eyes of God, she was married.

Only the next morning, when she saw her misfortune in the clear light of day, did she realize that she needed to escape from this situation at once. She mustn't allow herself to be dragged down even deeper. Yet she seemed to lack all strength to do so. On her own she wouldn't be able to break away. In her woe and misery she had cried for help: *whatever may become of me, I will not complain if only I might be saved from sinning further.*

Teit now stood and looked at her. And when she still said nothing, he reached out his hand toward her.

"It would be better for us to reconcile, Ingunn. We must try to resolve this matter and live as good friends."

"Yes. But I will not marry you, Teit. You must tell your friends they should not speak of courting me on your behalf."

"That I refuse to do. And what if your kinsmen say yes?"

"Even so, I will say no."

Teit was silent for a moment. She sensed the anger surging inside the youth.

"And if I do as you ask? What if I decide not to court you, and I never come here again? What if your kinsmen should see for themselves, after some time has passed, that you have taken up your old ways?"

"Even so, I will not marry you."

"You must not think that you can easily find me and lure me back if you should have need of me in the winter. I *have* offered to do what is right by you, but you've greeted me with scorn and cruel words."

"I won't have need of you."

"Are you certain of that?"

"Yes. I would walk into the fjord before I would send word to you."

"I see. Then that will be your concern and not mine—and your sin is not mine. You seem to think that we have no more to say to each other. Am I right?"

Ingunn nodded silently. Teit hesitated for a moment. Then he turned on his heel, leaped across the stream, and ran toward his horse.

She remained where she was, standing motionless, as he came riding up the path. He reined in his horse to stop next to her.

"Ingunn . . ." he pleaded.

She looked him in the eye. Beside himself with fury and agitation, Teit leaned forward and, with all his might, he struck her just below the ear, making her stagger.

"Evil are you! A cursed and frivolous bitch!" Sobs racked his body. "May you suffer the punishment you deserve for the false way you have toyed with me!"

Then he dug his heels into the horse's sides, and the old nag took off at a trot, but only for a short distance. As soon as it began climbing the slope, the horse slowed to its usual pace.

Ingunn stood there, watching the rider go. She pressed her hand to her burning cheek, but she felt no anger toward Teit for striking her. With remarkable clarity and pain, she realized that he must think she truly was what he had called her. And that added to her sorrow. Even now she was able to recall that she had been fond of him. And she felt sorry for him, because he was so young.

She thought she should see about heading back home, but she felt close to collapse when she pictured the estate. There was nowhere she could turn without being reminded of the boy.

And yet it occurred to her that in a few months' time everything would be easier for her, when she no longer had to think about all of this. Suddenly her mind was filled with a fiery bolt of fear. Yet that hardly seemed likely. If only Teit hadn't mentioned anything. She had already suffered enough trepidation on her own. As ill as she was now, from both sorrow and worry, she knew nevertheless that when enough time had passed so she could be completely certain such a consequence, at least, was not going to happen, then she would not feel quite as wretched. Then she wouldn't think, as she did now, that her whole life had been ruined by this misfortune and this sin.

◆ ◆ ◆

Old Fru Aasa's health declined rapidly during the autumn, and Ingunn lovingly and tirelessly tended to her. Fru Magnhild was astonished by the girl. For all these years she had watched her niece dragging herself around the estate, often looking as if she were sleepwalking and doing as little work as she possibly could. Even the small tasks she chose to carry out were done with great reluctance. Now Ingunn seemed to have awakened, and her aunt saw that the girl was, in fact, capable of working when she set her mind to it. She was not lacking in ability when she made an effort. Occasionally a certain thought occurred to Fru Magnhild: perhaps the poor thing feared what would happen to her when the old woman passed away. Her unusual diligence might be a plea for them not to view her too harshly when they no longer needed her help in caring for her grandmother. Perhaps they had been less than kind toward the poor, delicate child.

Ingunn seized upon anything she could find to keep herself busy. When she didn't have her hands full nursing the ill old woman, she would look for other tasks to perform—anything that might divert her attention from the one thought that, against her will, kept returning to her mind. Breathless with dread, she was waiting to ascertain that her fears would prove groundless.

Over the years she had grown accustomed to amusing herself by picturing her shared life with Olav at Hestviken, imagining Olav arriving to take her away, and envisioning their children. Now if she came anywhere near her memories of these dreams, it felt as if she were touching the angel's flaming sword. She could hardly keep herself from whimpering aloud.

She threw herself into all the tasks that required her full attention, tasks that would exhaust her body. She refused to surrender to any hints of illness she noticed that autumn; she was not nearly as feeble as she'd been during that first period of time she'd spent at Miklebø.

It had always been her habit, whenever something had badly frightened her, to suffer such violent nausea afterward that she would grow quite faint. All it took was for her to think about that time when she and Olav had ridden in the sledge down the mountain. It was during the Christmas festivities, during one of the last years of their childhood. They had decided they were finally going to attend mass down in the main church. So they set off on a dark winter morning, even though no one else at Frettastein wanted to go to church that day. A strong southerly wind had swept in, bringing rain and milder weather. Ingunn recalled so clearly the slow, dizzying panic that seemed to sink through her, dissolving her whole body, when she felt the sledge swerve outward and sink backward down the shiny, ice-covered rocks. It moved at an angle from the horse that was struggling so hard to find a foothold that sparks and splinters of ice flew up, but the animal was pulled around and downward. Olav, who had jumped out to try and stop the sliding, was flung backward and fell to the slippery ground. Then Ingunn was aware of nothing more. When she again came to her senses, she found herself kneeling in the buttery-soft snow, bending over Olav's arm as she vomited so violently that it seemed everything inside her would be squeezed out. With his free hand, Olav was pressing clumps of snow and ice to the back of her head, which she had bruised when she fell on the ground.

And now, fear was once again the only thing ailing her.

On the Eighth Christmas Day, Ingunn was home alone with her grandmother. Everyone else had left to attend a feast. She had put plenty of wood on the hearth, for her feet were very cold. The flickering glow of the fire seemed to lend a liveliness to the countenance of the old woman asleep in the bed—bone-white and wrinkled though her face was. Ingunn had often thought that in the pale daylight of winter Fru Aasa's face had already taken on the peaceful visage of the dead.

Grandmother, don't die! she cried silently. By now she and her grandmother had been companions for a long time. The two of them had been left to themselves in this out-of-the-way spot, while the lives of other people had raced past outside. And in the end she had grown quite fond of the old woman, inexpressibly fond of her, Ingunn thought. Now it seemed to her that she was the one who had gained support. The only support she knew had come from her grandmother, as she had accompanied the tottering old woman, as she had helped her to dress and to eat. And soon it would all be over. If only she could have lain down at the old woman's side. That was sometimes the end that Ingunn had dared to hope would be hers—that she would be allowed to die here, in the dim twilight of her corner, hidden away in the protective presence of her grandmother, and no one need know a thing.

But the old woman would soon die, and Ingunn would have to rejoin the others. Then she would be in constant terror that one day someone would notice.

Yet it wasn't certain; even now it wasn't certain at all. It was merely fear that kept chasing and pressing the blood in her body. She had felt such strong jolts to her heart that she had nearly lost all sense. Sometimes the veins at her throat would abruptly start throbbing, and she would feel the pulsing that seemed to race through her head behind her ears. And then there was the sensation she'd noticed last evening—and again in the night—and several times today as well, deep inside her abdomen on the right-hand side. It felt like a sudden blow or shove. Perhaps that was just her blood pounding hard in a vein.

For even if something had once been there, it was impossible for any life to have taken hold, considering how thin she had grown and how tightly she cinched her belt.

The weeks passed, and a few times Fru Magnhild mentioned to Ingunn that she must not work quite so hard. The unaccustomed toil seemed to be too much for her. Ingunn said little in reply as she continued to tend to her grandmother, but the zeal with which she had bustled about the estate and carried out all manner of tasks appeared to have left her. She seemed to have slipped back into herself.

To her, it felt as if her soul had sunk down into an impenetrable darkness where it was blindly waging a battle with the alarming, strange creature residing within her. Day and night it tumbled around, demanding more room and trying to burst open her aching body. Occasionally she thought she could bear it no longer. She had such pain in her whole body that she could hardly see, for not even at night did she dare loosen the bindings that caused her such agonizing torment. But she could not surrender; she had to make it stop until it moved no more.

A certain memory kept whirling through her mind during this time. Once, when she and her sister were small, Tora's tabby cat had killed a bird that Olav had caught for Ingunn so she might tame it. The cat had just had kittens, so Ingunn stole two of them and ran down to the pond and held them underwater. She expected them to die as soon as they went in, but for the longest time the tiny animals kept on kicking and flailing for their lives as she held them in her hands, while little air bubbles rose to the surface. At last she thought they were dead; but no, there was still some movement. Then she pulled them out and ran back to place them next to the mother cat. But by then they were finally dead.

She never thought of it as her own child, this mysterious life that she could feel growing inside her and moving about with increasing strength, defying all her attempts to subdue it. It was nothing more than some shapeless, wild, and painful living thing that had forced its way inside to gorge itself on her marrow and blood—a terrifying thing that she had to conceal. How it would behave when it eventually came into the light, and what would happen to her if anyone found out she had carried such a creature—those were things she dared not even think about.

Six weeks after Christmas Aasa Magnusdatter finally died. Her children, Ivar and Magnhild, hosted a grand funeral feast in her honor.

During the last seven days of her grandmother's life, Ingunn hardly slept, merely dozing off now and then when she lay down, fully clothed. And when the old woman's body was carried out, Ingunn wanted only to be allowed to rest. She crept into her own bed, occasionally falling asleep, occasionally staring at the ceiling, unable to think at all about the future that lay ahead of her.

Yet she had to get up and join the guests at the feast. No one was surprised that she looked like a ghost of herself, dressed in a dark blue mourning gown and swathed in her long black veil. Her face was a sallow gray, her skin was stretched shiny and taut over her bones, and her eyes were big and dark and weary. The men and women who were her kinsmen came over to greet her, and nearly all of them offered kind and appreciative words. Fru Magnhild had said that for all these years, Ingunn had been a loyal companion to the deceased woman.

Master Torgard, the cantor, and the sheriff from Reyne were among the guests at the funeral feast. And all of a sudden Ingunn happened to think of him—of Teit! She had almost forgotten him. It was as if she were unable to see the connection between him and her misfortune. Even now, when she recalled him, it was merely as if she were thinking about an acquaintance for whom she had once felt affection, but then something had come between them and she had no desire to think of him again.

Now it occurred to her to wonder what he might have said to his spokesmen when he retracted his request. If he had betrayed her to them, then she was truly lost. She had to try and find out whether they knew anything. Yet she felt as ill at ease, as if she were a poor farmer's wretched and worn-out nag, an animal that had been harnessed to a cart holding an excessively heavy load, and she was nearly done in, but now more weight was going to be heaped on top.

"You haven't brought your clerk with you?" she asked Gunnar of Reyne, trying to sound as indifferent as she could.

"Is it that fellow Teit you mean? No, he has left my employ. But he's the one you're inquiring about? He seemed to be constantly running over here to Berg. Is it true that you were the one he came to see?"

Ingunn tried to laugh.

"I don't know whether that's true. He did say . . . He said he wanted to court me, and that he intended to ask you to speak on his behalf. I discouraged him from doing so, but . . . Might it be true?"

The sheriff winked at her. "Yes, he said the same thing to me as he said to you. And I too discouraged him, just as you did." Gunnar laughed so hard his stomach quivered.

"What became of him after he left Reyne?" she asked with a little laugh. "Do you know, Gunnar?"

"We'll have to ask the cantor; Teit was planning to go to him. Master Torgard, would you favor us with your company? Listen, my dear sir, do you know what became of that fellow, the Icelander, my scribe? The maiden here is asking about him. You must know that he had intended to honor her to such an extent that he wanted to marry her, Ingunn Steinfinnsdatter."

"Is that right!" said the priest. "He was always coming up with one thing or another, my good Teit. You're not missing him and mourning for him, are you, my child?"

"As well I might. For I've heard he was such a remarkably clever man that you gentlemen wanted to send him to the archbishop. It seems there was no one else in the land who might make better use of such skills. And I suppose that must be true, since he said as much?"

"Ha! I wouldn't put it past him to say such a thing. That boy was half-mad, even though he could write better than most. He did come to see me not long ago, but I refused to take him into my household again. He may be a skillful clerk, but he's a lunatic. So it will do you no good to mourn for him, my little Ingunn. Is it true then? Was the boy so brash that he dared talk of courting you at Berg? No, no, no, no." The old priest shook his little, birdlike head.

Then Ingunn realized that it wasn't true at all, what Teit had said to her when they last spoke. Yet now she had something more to worry about, on top of everything else. Had she done something terribly foolish when she let these men know she'd been thinking so much about Teit that she would bother to ask about him?

When the guests departed after the funeral feast, Tora stayed behind with her two eldest children and old Ivar Toressøn of Galtestad. One evening they were all sitting together; they had taken out the precious items they had inherited from Fru Aasa and were looking at them. That's when Tora mentioned again that her sister ought to move to Frettastein.

Fru Magnhild said Ingunn should do whatever she pleased. "If you'd prefer to go to Frettastein, Ivar and I will not stop you."

"I'd rather stay here at Berg," replied Ingunn quietly. "That is, if you will allow me to stay, now that Grandmother is gone."

Tora kept trying to persuade her sister. She now had five children of her own, and she had taken in the motherless twins of Haakon's sister as foster children, so she needed Ingunn's help.

Fru Magnhild noticed the miserable expression on Ingunn's thin and worn face. She reached her hand toward her and said, "Stay here with me, my dear. For as long as I live, you will have shelter and food and clothing. Or at least until Olav comes back to take you home. I do think he will return one day, God willing, provided he's still alive." Then she said scornfully to Tora, "Do you think Haakon would show his sister-in-law the respect at Frettastein that Steinfinn's daughter rightfully deserves? Should she live at her father's estate as a nurse-maid for the offspring of Haakon and his sister Helga Gautsdatter? Neither Ivar nor I would consent to that. I was thinking of giving this to you," she said to Ingunn now. She picked up the big gold ring that she had inherited from her mother. "As a memento because you tended to our mother and served her with such loyalty all these years."

She grabbed Ingunn's hand, wanting to put the gold ring on her finger.

"But what have you done with your betrothal ring? Why have you taken it off? You poor thing. It seems to me that you've toiled so hard that your hands have swollen terribly," she said.

Ingunn noticed that Tora gave a start. She didn't dare look at her sister, yet she couldn't help a quick glance. Tora's expression did not change, but a flicker of concern appeared in her eyes. For her part, Ingunn couldn't feel the floor under her feet. Her only thought at that moment was: if I fall down senseless now, they'll find out everything. Yet it was as if she were listening to someone else speaking when she thanked her aunt for the costly gift. And she had no idea how she managed to find her way back to her usual place to sit down.

Later in the evening Ingunn was standing at the estate's gate, calling and whistling for one of the dogs. That's when Tora came over to join her.

The moon had not yet risen, and the black sky was glittering with a profusion of stars. The two women stood there, drawing their hooded cloaks tighter around them as they stamped their feet in the powdery snow and talked about the wolves that had grown exceedingly bold over the past few weeks. Every once in a while Ingunn would whistle and call out anxiously: "Tota! Tota! Come, Tota!" It was so dark that they couldn't see each other's face.

Then Tora said quietly, her voice strangely hesitant, "Ingunn, you're not ill, are you?"

"I can't say that I'm well," replied Ingunn quite calmly. "Even though Aasa was so thin and frail toward the end, you mustn't think it was easy to lift her and tend to her day in and day out for all these months. And there was very little sleep to be had. But no doubt my health will soon improve."

"And you don't think there is something else ailing you, my sister?" asked Tora, again timidly.

"No, I don't think that is the case."

"In the summer you were so pink and white, and just as lithe and slender as when we were young," whispered Tora.

Ingunn managed to give a sad little laugh.

"I suppose that sometime it has to become clear from my appearance that I'm now in my third decade. Just look at those big children of yours, my Tora. Don't you remember that I'm a year and a half older than you?"

Up in the darkness between the fences a black shape came rushing toward them. The dog leaped up at Ingunn, nearly knocking her over into the snowdrifts as it licked her face. She grabbed for the dog's snout and forepaws, fending the animal off as she laughed and uttered endearments. "It's a good thing the wolf didn't get you tonight, either, Tota, my Tota!"

The sisters said good night to each other and went their separate ways.

But Ingunn lay in the dark, unable to sleep, trying to endure this added fear that Tora might have become suspicious. And she was sorely tempted. What if she told Tora about her distress and asked for her help? Or perhaps she could speak to her aunt Magnhild. She thought about the unusual kindness her aunt had shown to her this evening, and she felt tempted to give in to weakness and surrender. Or what about Dalla? Ingunn had also thought of the old servant woman when she found it unbearable to go on carrying this secret torment all on her own. Perhaps, if she turned to Dalla . . .

Breathless with worry, Ingunn kept an eye on her sister during the days when Tora remained at Berg. But she didn't notice any sign. Nothing in Tora's expression or her manner or her words gave any hint that she knew how things stood with her older sister. Then she left, and Ingunn was once again alone with her aunt and the old house servants.

She counted the weeks. Thirty had already passed; now only ten were left. She simply had to hold out. Nine weeks. Eight weeks. Yet for what purpose was she persisting and remaining steadfast while she struggled and suffered her way forward, as if she were being smothered in a dark gloom filled with formless horrors, and her whole body was nothing but one heavy and oppressive pain, and there was only one thought in her mind: that no one must have any inkling of the misfortune that had befallen her; this was something she had never clearly acknowledged even to herself.

The end that she pictured ahead . . . When she thought about that, she was filled with a terror that approached the rigid stillness of death. But she saw it as the end of the road, and she had no choice but to continue on, though she was traveling the last part with her eyes closed. Even when she sought some sort of solace by playing with the notion that she might scream for help, might speak to someone before it was too late . . . She never thought in earnest that she would be able to do so. She had to keep going, heading toward what she saw up ahead.

This late in the spring the ground was nearly always clear of snow here in the countryside. They would not be able to follow her tracks. The big birch grove north of the estate reached from the fish smoking site nearly all the way down to the water. Far below it, the land narrowed until it was no wider than a stone's throw between several mountain crags. No one from the estate would be able to hear or see anything down there, and almost no one ever went there. The ice didn't leave the bay this early. Yet up on the barren ridge on the south side and spilling down into the cleft lay the enormous piles of rocks that had been cleared from the fields in bygone days. That was where the folks at Berg were accustomed to disposing of the bodies of horses as well as any animals that had not been slaughtered and bled properly.

VI

On a morning in the waning days of winter, Ingunn had gone up
to the loft room where she kept her belongings after Fru Aasa died. It
was several days before the Feast of the Annunciation. She sat there
freezing, though she wore shaggy hide boots on her feet and a big
sheepskin surcoat over her clothing. Right now it was colder indoors
than outside. Streams of water fell and fell from the eaves past the
small open window, and the air trembled and steamed above the bit
of white rooftop that she could glimpse against the shimmering blue
sky. She had taken down the shutter from the window to let in some
fresh air. She could hardly draw breath anymore, and it felt as if a
heavy leaden hood were covering her entire brain inside her skull. It
squeezed so hard that the blood hammered and pounded in her neck
behind her ears, and it pressed on her eyes so that flickerings of red
and black blurred her vision. She had sought refuge up here, for she
feared someone might speak to her, and she had no wish to talk. But
she found some relief in sitting here and sinking inward.

Afterward she always believed that she had known what was
about to happen as soon as she heard the horsemen up at the entrance
to the estate. She stood up to look out. The first man to ride through
the gate was Arnvid. He was riding his black horse with the little bells
on the bridle, which he favored whenever he set out on visits. She
also recognized the other horse as one of his. It was a large-boned,
red-and-white animal that Arnvid's manservant usually rode. The
third man, who rode a tall horse the color of apple blossoms with its
leather harness dyed red, was Olav Audunssøn. She knew it was him
even before he drew close enough for her to recognize him.

He looked up as he reined in his horse and saw her there in the little window. He raised his hand in greeting. He wore a big black travel

cloak, its voluminous folds draped over the horse's flanks; in front the cloak covered his legs all the way down to his feet in the stirrups. He had pushed back the hood, and on his head he wore a foreign-looking black hat with a high crown and narrow brim. His flaxen hair billowed out from underneath all the way around, reaching to his eyebrows in front. He had smiled at her when he raised his hand.

Afterward she always thought that she had been awakened from a nightmare at the very moment she saw him. Olav had come home. To misfortune, that was true, and he would no doubt crush her in one way or another; she realized that at once. But it felt as if the blinding gloom now came pouring out of her in every direction, along with all the demons, those shifting shadows of darkness that had swarmed around her so closely that they kept jostling each other's elbows and knees as they surrounded her and led her blindly forward. She seemed to know, even as she walked down the stairs of the loft, that now that Olav had arrived, she had no choice but to tell him everything and accept his judgment.

Olav was standing in the courtyard with the hired men who had come out to tend to the visitors' horses. Now he turned to face her. With a twinge of pride, she saw how handsome he was, this man who was now lost to her. The black garments suited his radiant fair looks. He held out his hand to her. "Well met, Ingunn." Then he caught sight of her haggard face. And impetuously, paying no mind to the accepted customs or to all the others who stood there watching, Olav threw his arms around Ingunn, pulled her close, and kissed her on the lips.

"You've had to wait such a long time for me, my dear Ingunn. But that's over now, and I've come to take you home!"

He let her go, and then she and Arnvid greeted each other with a kiss on the cheek, as befitted kinsmen.

She watched as the young men next offered their greetings to Fru Magnhild. Laughing, they said that Ivar was accompanying them, but they'd left him behind as they rode past the church, for neither the Galtestad nag nor the Galtestad farmer was particularly inclined to travel with haste.

"Yes. You know how angered he was when you acted with haste

in your youth," said Fru Magnhild with a laugh. "But after you gave up that bad habit, Olav, I think my brother has grown more and more fond of you."

Have I ever seen a more beautiful day? thought Ingunn. Across the fields and out on the bay, the crusted snow gleamed silvery-white in the spring sunlight. After the mild weather at the beginning of the week, all the snow had been licked off the forest, and the conifer sprigs glistened a springtime green, as if newly washed. Out in the fields stood the slender, pale green trunks of the aspen trees amid the bluish-brown groves still bare of leaves.

And she felt delight bubbling up in her heart, elated that the world was filled with sunshine and beauty and joy. Even though she had caused her own downfall and condemned herself to sit in the corner, it was still good to know there could be such joy in being alive—for other people, for all those who had not deliberately landed in misfortune. At that moment she felt the fetus flailing about inside her, and it seemed to her that something was fumbling in her own heart in response: no, no, I no longer mean you any harm.

After eating, they stayed seated at the table, and Ingunn silently listened to the men's conversation. She understood that Arnvid and Ivar intended to continue on the next morning, heading north to visit Haftor Kolbeinssøn so as to put into his hands the third of four payments for the killing of Einar. Olav thought it most seemly if he did not personally meet with Haftor until he was ready to pay the last sum, which would happen at the same time as Ingunn's kinsmen gave her to him along with her dowry.

"I see that you have no wish to travel with us any farther," said Ivar Toressøn with a gleeful laugh. "I don't think you have any intention of budging from Berg until you're chased off the estate!"

"As long as Fru Magnhild is willing to grant me shelter and feed for my horse . . ." Olav laughed with the others as he cast a quick, sidelong glance at Ingunn. "Truth be told, I would much prefer to stay here and put an end to the trouble between me and Haftor. And then take Ingunn with me at once, when I head south to Hestviken."

"It might be possible to do just that," said Arnvid.

"I understand what you mean, and I give you my thanks, but I don't want to ask for any more help from you, Arnvid, now that I can manage without it. And I will do as I explained to you at Galtestad. I will travel south and see how things now stand at Hestviken, before I bring my wife home. And I will go to Oslo to collect the money I have left there in safekeeping. After we've reconciled, it will be much easier to gather the men who are to be witnesses if the wedding feast is held during the days when everyone is headed home from the tings—no matter whether you wish me to receive Ingunn here or at Galtestad. Ivar is right in saying that as drawn-out and complicated as this case has been, it ought to be resolved as openly as possible."

When everyone was leaving the tings? That would be in the middle of summer. The thought passed through Ingunn's mind like the whispering of the demons who had held her in their power all winter. It was not possible for her to continue on the same path, now that she'd seen Olav again. She vaguely recalled everything she had imagined about her life with him and their children at Hestviken. That was not somewhere she could ever go again, even if she tried to free herself from her secret in the gloom of night and hide it in the heap of rocks. It would do no good. She could never again go to Olav.

Ivar told the others with a show of scandalized merriment that Olav had not yet set foot at Hestviken. Had anyone ever heard the likes of such a man?

Olav laughed contritely. He blushed at the teasing from the old man, and he suddenly looked quite young. He looked younger now and more like himself from years earlier than when he was last at Berg. Yet several furrows now marked the erect fullness of his throat, and when he craned his neck, a red scar was visible below the neckband of his shirt. His face was also more weather-beaten and gaunt. Even so, he looked very young. Ingunn realized this was because he was so happy. Her heart sank, heavy with despair. She wondered whether she would cause him terrible sorrow when he learned that she, through her own actions, was now lost to him.

But he had been granted *grid*, a guarantee for his own safety in

Norway, and he had regained his estate. She realized that he was now a man of high standing. He had sold Kaaretop, the estate he had owned in Elvesyssel and where he had stayed after being granted dispensation to return to Norway. It would not be difficult for Olav to find a better marriage match than she would have been. She knew that after the reconciliation with her kinsmen, she would not have brought him much wealth.

Olav walked with Ingunn to the door when she was about to leave for the night.

"Do you sleep alone in Aasa's house? Then I suppose it would not be seemly for me to come to you after you have retired to bed," he said with a sigh and a laugh.

"No, it would not be right to do so."

"But tomorrow night? Could you ask one of the maidservants to stay with you so we might speak to each other alone in the evenings?"

Swiftly and shyly, he pulled her close, embracing her so tightly that she gasped. Then he kissed her and let her go.

Ingunn lay in bed, unable to sleep, trying to think ahead. But it was as if she sought to clear a path through a scree-covered slope with rocks so heavy that she couldn't even budge them. She could not imagine what was to become of her. Yet she had managed to come this far, staggering her way forward through utter darkness, a darkness that was alive with swarming, unseen terrors. And now she could see daylight up ahead, although it was as gray and hopeless and impassable as a rainy day in the middle of winter. She had to continue forward. She could not escape what she had brought down upon herself unless she should seek refuge in Hell.

She knew she had no rights. She had already lost all rights back when she gave herself to Olav without the knowledge and consent of her lawful guardians. They had made that eminently clear to her. It was for Olav's sake that her kinsmen had later agreed to grant her an inheritance and rights. Upon reconsidering their opinion of him, they had decided the most beneficial action was to accept his offer of reconciliation and allow him to marry her in the lawful manner. She could hardly think about what they would do when they learned how she had behaved so that Olav could not now take her as his wife. What would happen when they found out that she was carrying a child? And that the father was a man whom her kinsmen might seek out but without hope of ever collecting any remuneration. They should just let Teit go. They would gain nothing useful from him, and if they sought to punish him, the shame would only be worse when it became known what sort of man she had allowed to seduce her.

She had no idea what they would do to her—or to it. But as soon as tomorrow, or in two or three days' time, she would surely find out. And as impossible as it was for her even to imagine, it was as certain as death that when the birches were a leafy green, she would be sitting here with the wayside bastard on her lap. And then she would have to endure everything her kinsmen wished to heap on her in their fury because she had brought such shame upon them all, and because they would have to provide for her and for the child.

She had now submitted so utterly to her fate that she could barely even comprehend that a day earlier she had thought she might be able to cast aside this burden. Now her only thought was that she would have to drag this child along with her for the rest of her life. She still felt no tenderness or kindness toward it, but it was there, and she would have to suffer its presence.

Just for a moment, at the thought that Tora might again request that she come to stay with her, Ingunn pictured herself walking about with her own child, both of them outcasts, at Haakon's estate among his wealthy children. That's when something entirely new awoke inside her, the first tiny stirring of an urge to protect the offspring that was hers.

Ingunn's siblings were the ones who would be obliged to offer them safe haven. It would fall to Haakon to act on Tora's behalf in providing support, along with her two younger brothers, whom Ingunn had hardly seen in the years since they'd become full-grown men. Yet perhaps she dared hope that Fru Magnhild would be merciful enough to allow her to stay here at Berg until she had given birth to the child.

Arnvid. She thought about him. Would he offer to take them in?

He would be kind to both of them. Even though he was Olav's best friend, he was a friend to *everyone* who needed help. What if she told Arnvid? Arnvid and not Olav? He could then speak to Olav and Magnhild, and she could avoid what seemed like walking through blazing flames.

Yet she knew that was not something she would dare. She had no idea how she would find the courage to speak to Olav, but it was more important than anything else for her to tell Olav the truth. He was the one who was her master, and it was to him she had given her pledge. All of a sudden she realized that after she had undertaken this conversation with Olav, she would instinctively need to fall to her knees before God, repenting for her sin and all the sins she had committed in her life—*quia peccavi nimis cogitatióne, locutióne, ópere et omissióne, mea culpa.* The words rose inside her of their own accord. In spite of all the times she had repeated these words as she knelt before Brother Vegard, they were now illuminated and alive, just as when the dim glass in the church windows was suddenly lit by the sun. I have sinned greatly in thought, word, deed, and omission, and the fault is mine.

She sat up and then knelt in bed to say her evening prayers. It had been a long time since she'd dared to do so. *Mea culpa.* She had feared she might be saved from what she meant to do and then have to accept the misfortune she had brought upon herself. Now it occurred to her that when she received God's forgiveness for the great harm she had caused herself and Olav, she would not wish that she might be free of punishment. The mere sight of Olav had been enough for her to understand the very essence of Love. She had caused him the worst possible sorrow. And when he was suffering terribly, she could not wish that things might be better for herself. Beyond she glimpsed what seemed the image of the origin of Love. In the cup that Our Lord had been forced to accept on that evening in the Garden of Gethsemane, he saw all the sins that had ever been committed and that ever would be committed here on earth, from the birth of humankind until the final Judgment, as well as all the need and suffering that people had brought upon themselves and each other. And because God had suffered, because she was going to suffer so much through her own fault, she would yearn to be punished and allowed to suffer each time she recalled what she'd done. She understood that this was a form of suffering that was different from anything she had previously endured. Before, it had seemed as if she were plummeting down a steep scree-covered slope to land, at last, in a bottomless marshy pit. Now it seemed as if she were climbing upward, but with a helping hand. She was moving heavily and with great effort, but there was joy in the struggle itself. It was leading her toward something. And she realized what the priests meant when they said there was healing in penance.

The next day at noontime Olav and Ingunn stood together in the courtyard, waiting for Ivar and Arnvid to depart. The weather was as lovely as it had been the day before, causing everything to thaw and drip. The sun-drenched drifts of snow were slowly sinking, making tiny, brittle sounds. Little rivulets streamed across the courtyard, washing shiny the ice-covered culverts in the carpet of horse manure and woodchips that had piled up over the winter. Ivar was grumbling because Arnvid wanted to ride across the ice. He claimed it would no doubt be unsafe in many spots far from the Ringsaker shoreline. Several years ago Ivar had once ridden his horse into a break in the ice, and ever since he had been the worst coward. But Arnvid merely laughed at him. In full daylight? No, my kinsman! They would reach Haftor's estate before it was fully dark. Should they instead slog up the mountains and down the slopes through the countryside in this thaw? Arnvid said he was damned if he would do such a thing. "If you can get your men to do that, then you're welcome to ride wherever you like, but my man Eyvind and I will set our own course."

But Ivar's three hired men were already far down in the field. The wintertime track from several farms up in the village led via Berg and down to the bay. From there folks would head south to town or go north and west over the heights on the other side and down to ice-covered Lake Mjøsa.

Olav and Ingunn walked down the slope as Arnvid and Ivar slowly kept pace on horseback. Here the snow had melted away from the upper section of the track, and water rushed downward. Arnvid said something to Olav about getting splashed. Olav was bareheaded and wore no cloak over a knee-length, sky-blue cotehardie, light-colored leather hose, and low shoes with long points. These fine shoes of his had turned dark with water. "Ingunn is better dressed than you are to go out walking."

"I don't know how she can bear it in this heat."

Ingunn had on the same calf-length, sleeveless sheepskin surcoat she'd worn the previous day, and as she walked along she stomped her feet in their shaggy hide boots. She'd made no effort to adorn herself, other than to add several red silk ribbons to her hair.

On the slope the air gusted like lukewarm breaths, flickering and trembling in the distance wherever they looked.

"Over there is where we sat that time. Do you remember?" Olav whispered to Ingunn. Today big bare patches of grass were visible, even though the day before the entire expanse had been a glittering silvery-white, with only one or two rocks and a few juniper bushes sticking up. "The sowing season will probably be late this year, with the snow melting so much before the Feast of the Annunciation."

They stopped at a dip in the track to watch the riders continue on. Arnvid turned in his saddle to wave, and Olav raised his hand in reply. Then he broke off a briar rose twig and offered it to Ingunn, but she shook her head. He plucked off several of the rosehips and sucked on them before spitting the pulp into the snow. "I suppose we should head back up."

"No. Wait a moment. There's something I must talk to you about."

"Oh? You don't look at all happy, Ingunn."

"I'm not," she managed to say.

Olav looked at her. First with surprise, but then his expression grew solemn as well, and he turned slightly away.

"Is it that you think I've been away a long time?" he asked in a low voice.

Too long. That was what she wanted to say, but could not.

"I thought about that," he said quietly. "I thought about you, when I left to seek out the earl. I knew full well that I would be sharing his banishment. But he was my lord, Ingunn. The first lord to whom I'd ever sworn fealty. It wasn't easy for me to decide what I should do. But I lost all appetite, Ingunn, whenever I thought about settling down at Hestviken, eating bread and drinking ale, while the man who had helped me to regain all I owned would have to wander as an outlaw in another country, having lost everything here at home. Yet I want you to know that I never realized so many years would pass.

"Do you think I abandoned you because I followed the earl?"

Ingunn shook her head.

"You know full well that such matters are not for me to judge, Olav."

"I thought . . ." Olav took a deep breath. "Now that I've become such good friends with Ivar, and some of the payments to Kolbein have been made—in good English coin—and you received the betrothal ring and gifts from me . . . I thought you would be better off staying where you were. Have things not been good for you, here with your kinsmen, Ingunn?"

"Oh, that's not what I have reason to bewail."

"Bewail?"

She heard the first faint inkling of fear in his voice. She gathered all her courage and looked at him. He was holding the briar rose twig in his hand and staring at her, as if dreading what was to come, though he didn't know what it might be.

"Do you have something to bewail, Ingunn?"

"Things were such that I . . . I did not have the strength to . . . I'm no longer suited to be yours, Olav."

"You're no longer . . . suited?" His voice gave no hint of emotion.

Again she had to gather all her forces before she could look at him. The two of them stood there, staring at each other. She watched as Olav's fair face seemed to grow pale and stiffen before it turned gray. He moved his lips a few times but it took a moment before he managed to speak.

"What do you mean by that?"

They kept on looking at each other. Finally Ingunn could bear it no longer. She raised her arm to hide her face.

"Don't look at me like that," she pleaded, her voice quavering. "I am carrying a child."

After what seemed an eternity, when she thought she couldn't stand it another second, she lowered her arm and looked at Olav. She hardly recognized his face anymore. His jaw had fallen open like a dead man's, and he was standing as motionless as stone, just staring. This went on and on.

"Olav!" she cried at last, quietly moaning. "Speak to me!"

"What do you want me to say?" he replied tonelessly. "If someone else had said this about you . . . I would have killed him!"

Ingunn whimpered, low and shrill, like a dog that is being kicked.

Olav shouted, "Quiet! Evil bitch that you are! You're worthy only of death!" Now he leaned toward her. Again she cried out like a whipped dog. When he moved, she fled a few paces back and put her hand on the trunk of an aspen tree for support. The dazzling light reflecting off the crusted snow all around suddenly seemed to converge before her and she couldn't bear it, she had to close her eyes. She felt her body shrivel with pain, the way meat shrivels when tossed onto the fire.

When she again opened her eyes to look at Olav . . . no, she didn't dare look at him. She looked down at the briar rose twig with the red rosehips that he had dropped on the snow at his feet. And then she began to wail. "It would be much better, much better, if you did it."

Olav's face contorted fiercely so he no longer looked human. With both hands he grasped the haft of his dagger in its sheath. Then he yanked the knife away, ripping off the sheath and belt along with it, and hurled it as far away as he could. Somewhere in the distance the knife plunged deep into the melting snow.

"Oh, I wish I was dead. I wish I was dead," Ingunn kept on moaning.

She felt his wild, red bestial eyes on her. As frightened as she was, her greatest wish was that he would kill her. She raised her hands to clutch at her neck, whimpering quietly.

Olav stood there, glaring at her and the tensed white arc of her throat as she leaned against the tree. He had done it once. The sword had been knocked out of his hand, leaving him defenseless, so with one hand he had seized the combatant around the waist and with his other hand he grabbed the man's throat and shoved him backward, noticing that never before had he used all his strength to such extent. And as she stood there, he now saw it: the shameless change in her face and her body, the mark of another man.

With the loud bellow of an animal he tore his eyes from the sight and fled up the road.

He heard her calling after him, calling his name. He didn't know whether he shouted the words aloud or silently to himself, saying: No, no, I dare not stay near you.

She sank to the small patch of bare ground at the foot of the aspen, rocking back and forth and moaning. A good amount of time passed, and then Olav was back.

He bent over her, panting as he asked, "Who is the father? To the child you're carrying?"

She looked up and shook her head.

"Oh . . . It's nobody . . . He was a scribe for the sheriff at Reyne. Teit was his name. An Icelander."

"It's a shame you happened to be so particular," said Olav with an odd laugh. He grabbed her arm and squeezed it so hard that she whimpered loudly. "And Magnhild? What does she say about this? She laughed with such amusement last night along with all the others." He clenched his teeth. "No doubt they were laughing at me, the utter fool who was so merry and glad, when I had no idea that my joy had multiplied so greatly. Oh . . . may God curse the whole lot of you!"

"Magnhild knows nothing of this. Not a soul have I told until I spoke of it to you."

"How kind of you! That I should be the first to hear the news! I had otherwise thought that I'd be able to make my own children, but—"

"Olav!" she cried desolately. "If you hadn't arrived before it was . . ." Her voice broke. "Then no one would ever have known about it."

For a moment they stared into each other's eyes again. Then Ingunn's head fell forward.

"Jesus Christ! What a monster you are!" whispered Olav in horror.

He straightened up and stretched a few times, giving her a glimpse of a red scar on his chest at the base of his throat.

Then he said, mostly to himself, "If they'd brought word to me that you'd been afflicted with leprosy, I would still have longed for the day when I could receive you as my wife. 'Will you cherish this woman in sickness and in health?' asks the priest at the church door. But this? No, not this! May God have mercy on me, but this I cannot accept!"

He gripped her shoulder hard.

"Do you hear me, Ingunn? This I cannot accept! Magnhild will have to . . . You will have to tell Magnhild. I cannot. And since she has not safeguarded you better . . . This happened while you were under her guardianship, so she will have to . . . I can't bear to see you again until you have parted with this . . . Do you hear me?" he repeated. "You'll have to be the one to tell Magnhild."

Ingunn nodded.

Then he headed back up the slope.

The ground was soaking wet where she sat, and she could feel the cold making her body stiff and numb, which was a relief. She wrapped her arm around the aspen trunk and rested her cheek against the bark. Now she needed to seek inside herself for the solace she'd expected to find when she revealed her secret. But it was not to be found. She felt only eternal remorse, but not the sort of remorse that is redemptive. Her only wish was to die at once. She couldn't bear to think of getting up and continuing on, having to face everything she would now be forced to endure.

She recalled all the consoling words she had wanted to say to Olav: that he should give no more thought to her; that when he went out into the world, he should enjoy his good fortune and not think of her, for she was not worthy of his attention. She now realized this was true, and it was no consolation. The worst thing of all was that she was not worthy of his thoughts.

She didn't know how long she had been there when she heard someone coming up the road. With great effort she pulled herself up. She was stiff with cold and her whole body ached when she moved. Her legs had fallen asleep so she could hardly stand or walk, but she managed to make her way over to the bushes, where she pretended to be eating rosehips as the two sledges loaded with goods passed by.

The workmen called out a quiet greeting, and she responded in kind. They were from up in the village.

The sun was now low in the west. The light on the snowy surfaces was yellowish-red, and the steam rising up from the ground had taken on the appearance of a bright, hovering mist. Irresolute, Ingunn wandered about on the road for a while. Then she caught sight of several horsemen out on the ice of the bay; it looked as if they were heading in this direction. She grew frightened and turned on her heel to head back up to the estate.

She was just about to slip inside her own house when Fru Magnhild came toward her from the main house. Given the agitated state of Ingunn's senses, her aunt's appearance seemed to her quite horrifying. The woman's fleshy, reddish face was framed by the linen wimple, and her stomach bulged beneath her silver belt, from which hung heavy keys, a dagger and scissors, all of them clanking at her side. She looked like that ferocious, long-horned ox of theirs when it had rushed straight for her. Ingunn put her hand on the doorframe for support. Yet it suddenly felt as if her capacity for fear had been stretched too far.

"Holy Mother of God, where have you come from? Have you been out wandering all day? You look as if you must have fallen on the road. Your clothing is covered with water and horse manure all the way up to your bodice! What is this all about? And Olav? What is wrong with him?"

Ingunn didn't reply.

"Do *you* know why he was in such haste to ride to Hamar? He came back here and took his horse from the stable, and Hallbjørn could make no sense of him. Olav said he had to go to Hamar, but he left without his travel bag, and he rode off as if Satan himself were both behind and in front of him. Hallbjørn said it was dreadful to see how he used his spurs on his horse."

Ingunn said not a word.

"What is it?" Fru Magnhild now asked, her eyes flashing with anger. "Do *you* know what was wrong with Olav?"

"He's gone," said Ingunn. "He didn't want to stay here any longer, after he heard . . . After I told him how things stand with me."

"How things stand with you?" Fru Magnhild stared at the young woman, at her soaked and soiled clothing, at her braids coming undone and covered with bark and debris from the ground, at her face that was as dirty gray and gaunt as scraped bone. She looked hideous; there was no question about that. And the way she was clutching at herself underneath the wet and filthy sheepskin she wore . . .

"How things stand with you?" cried Magnhild. She grabbed Ingunn's upper arm and yanked her so hard into the house that she almost fell across the threshold. Then she flung the girl across the room so she collapsed in a heap next to the hearthstone. Fru Magnhild latched the door behind them.

"No! No! No! I simply can't fathom it! What have you done?"

She grabbed hold of Ingunn and pulled her to her feet. "Take off your clothes. You're as wet as a drowned corpse! It's no more than what I've always thought about you! Half a fool, that's what you are. You can't possibly possess all your wits!"

Ingunn lay in bed, lethargically listening to her aunt chattering as she hung up the wet garments on the rack over the hearth. This was the first time, in all these months, that Ingunn had lain down after removing all her clothes; it was a relief to be free of all the tight bindings and she could simply rest. She gave hardly any thought to the fact that Fru Magnhild would have been within her rights to treat her with much greater harshness. Her aunt had not cursed at her or struck her or yanked at her hair. And she said very little about her own thoughts on the matter.

Fru Magnhild's response was to demand the complete truth about how this could have happened. Then they would find a way to keep the whole thing secret.

She asked about the father, but when Ingunn told her who it was, Fru Magnhild sat motionless for a long time, utterly dumbfounded. This was so beyond what she could ever have imagined happening that she felt she had no choice but to believe it was true. The poor girl was clearly lacking in sense. Ingunn had to describe everything that had gone on between her and Teit. She gave brusque, terse replies to Magnhild's grimly voiced questions. Six months had passed since Ingunn had last seen him. No, he knew nothing about how things stood with her. She expected to give birth in six weeks' time.

It would be best to let the bird fly, thought Fru Magnhild. And it must be possible to keep the girl hidden here in Aasa's house during the time she had left. They would say she had fallen ill, though there were few who ever asked after Ingunn. In the midst of this misfortune, it was fortunate that she'd spent so much time living in the shadows over the past years. Magnhild sternly forbade her niece to venture outside the house during the hours when folks were awake on the estate. Dalla would come to stay with her for now, and when her time neared, they would send word for Tora.

Ingunn lay there, allowing weariness to overtake her. It almost felt good to be alive. Her feet had warmed up between the covers, and sleep swept through her like sweet, warm water. As if in a daze, she heard Fru Magnhild pondering half-aloud how they might best smuggle out the child as soon as it was born.

When Ingunn awoke, she realized it must be late in the evening. The fire had nearly burned out in the hearth, though it was not yet smoldering embers. Dalla was sitting on a stool nearby, nodding and spinning. Outside the wind had come up; Ingunn could hear it blowing around the corners of the house, and occasionally something wooden pounded against the wall outside. Ingunn still felt enveloped in deep contentment.

"Dalla," she said after a moment. The old woman didn't hear her.

"Dalla," she repeated a few minutes later. "Could you go out and see what keeps striking the wall? See if you can move it away."

Dalla got up and came over to the bed.

"So you're still so high-and-mighty that you send folks out to do your bidding, lazy-snout that you are? I'm here to keep watch over you but not to run around at your command. Fie on you, you wretched hag!"

◆ ◆ ◆

Fru Magnhild stopped in to see her niece once or twice a day. She had no more harsh words for Ingunn, and in fact she said very little to her. Yet one day she did tell Ingunn that she had found a foster mother for the child. It was the wife of a man who had cleared a patch of land in the woods to farm. The couple lived far north in the forest. It had been agreed that Fru Magnhild would send for the woman as soon as Ingunn felt the first birthing pangs; that way they could be rid of the child as soon as it was born. Ingunn said nothing to this news, nor did she ask for the name of the woman or the farm. And Fru Magnhild thought again that the girl must be lacking in wits.

And so Ingunn was left alone with Dalla, day and night. She withdrew into herself, staying as quiet as a mouse. If she happened to move or even breathe too loudly, she was afraid that Dalla would assail her with scorn and disdain, using the ugliest and nastiest words she could find.

Dalla and Grim had never been thralls in the same way that folks in the past used to be owned by their masters, as if they were livestock. But in many places it had made little difference either to those who were freeborn or to those who were children of thralls, that the latter were now entitled to rights under the law. This was especially true when it came to descendants of the old noble lineages and their servants who were the offspring of the old thrall clans. It would never occur to such a master or mistress to part with such a servant, no matter how burdensome or inept or sickly or enfeebled the person might be. Nor had it ever been the custom among these families to sell their thralls. A particularly handsome or promising thrall child might be given to a young kinsmen or godchild. And a thrall who was of more trouble than use, or who had committed some misdeed, might be sent away. The servants who were born into thralldom rarely considered any option other than working and living out their lives on the estate where they were born—especially in the inland villages. Any honor ascribed to their master's lineage was also their honor; the noble family's happiness and prosperity were also theirs. They took enormous interest in their master's fate. Among the thralls, the topic of conversation—matters they were constantly discussing and rehashing as they scraped together every detail they could uncover—was the life of the noble family in the main hall and the bedrooms and the loft rooms.

Grim and Dalla had been with Aasa Magnusdatter ever since all three of them were children. When Aasa sent them to Steinfinn, it was as good as any gift from mother to son. Steinfinn's fortune and misfortune had been theirs. And since it was Aasa's opinion that her son's marriage was the cause of much trouble, the two servants harbored a hatred for his wife, although they didn't dare show it openly. Even though Ingunn did not resemble her mother in the slightest, she had been allotted a share of their loathing, however groundless it might be. Olav and Tora had always been their favorites among the children, for they were both calm and thoughtful in manner, also toward the old servants. Ingunn was impulsive and flighty, and Dalla and Grim maligned her all the more so that they, by comparison, might heap greater praise on the two other children. It so happened that in all these years Dalla had been beside herself with envy because Ingunn was the one who stood closest to Aasa instead of her, and she could tell that the old woman was very fond of her young granddaughter. Then Ingunn had brought this unspeakable shame upon the Steinfinn lineage and betrayed her promise to Olav. She had been left in Dalla's care, and, as helpless and unable to defend herself as Ingunn was, the thrall woman now took her revenge any way she could.

Speaking in the most coarse and vile of manners, Dalla talked on and on about everything Ingunn had only vaguely sensed in the semidarkness. She talked about Teit and about Olav, until the young woman sat there, burning with shame and wishing the floor might open up so she would be allowed to sink into the earth. No matter whether Ingunn was sitting, standing, or walking about, Dalla would shower her with spiteful words for being so hideous. The old woman also tried her best to frighten Ingunn out of her wits with talk of what lay ahead when she would give birth. She predicted the most arduous childbirth and said she could tell by Ingunn's appearance that she would certainly die.

Ingunn had always known that Dalla found her to be stupid and unworthy of her affection, but she'd given this little thought. She had never imagined that the old thrall woman would set about tormenting her so tirelessly and with such spiteful malice. Ingunn couldn't understand the reason for this behavior. It seemed to her the only explanation must be that she was so disgraced and sullied and repulsive that anyone who had to spend time with her felt an urge to stomp on her, the way a person might roundly stomp on some loathsome vermin.

So Ingunn gave up any thought of peace or salvation. That she would be allowed to die was the best she dared hope. If only she could be freed of this foreign creature inside her. She still had no feelings for it other than horror and hatred, and her only wish in the world was that she might die.

Ten days passed in this manner. Late one evening Ingunn and Dalla were sitting in separate corners of the room when someone opened the door. Dalla leaped to her feet. "No one is allowed in here!"

"Oh yes, I'm coming in," said the man who ducked to cross the threshold. It was Arnvid.

Ingunn stood up and went over to him. She wrapped her arms around his neck and leaned close. She knew he was the only person in the world who would be kind to her, even now. Then she noticed that he pulled away a bit as he reached up to remove her hands from around his neck. And that hurt her more than all of Dalla's disparaging remarks. Even Arnvid was repulsed by her. Was she so defiled? Then Arnvid caressed her cheek and took her hand to lead her over to the small bench with room enough for two to sit near the fire.

"Leave us now, Dalla," he said to the old woman.

"The Devil himself must have caused Magnhild to give you that half-mad troll woman as a helper," he told Ingunn. "Or perhaps it was your wish to have her here?"

"No, it wasn't," Ingunn said faintly.

Gradually Arnvid learned a little about Dalla's behavior over the past few days, although there wasn't much Ingunn could bring herself to reveal. He took her hand and placed it on his knee. "You mustn't worry. I don't think she will be tormenting you any longer."

Yet there was so little he felt capable of saying. He wanted to hear from her directly how Olav had reacted to the news, and whether she knew what he was going to do, or where he was now, or what was to become of her. But it was impossible for him to be the first to broach such topics.

And so neither of them mentioned Olav at all, even though Arnvid stayed for quite a long time. As he was about to leave, he said, "This is a bad state of things, Ingunn. I cannot help you. But you must send word to me as soon as matters are such with you that a man might be of use. I will gladly speak my mind when they meet to discuss how to provide for you and your child."

"No man can be of any help to me."

"I suppose that's true. You must put yourself in God's hands, Ingunn. Then you'll know that, in spite of everything, all will turn out well in the end."

"Yes, I know that. And you may say as much, but you are not the one who has to endure this situation." Anxiously, she clung to his hand. "I can't sleep at night. And I have such a dreadful thirst. But I dare not get up to find something to drink, because of Dalla."

"Well," said Arnvid softly. "None of us has ever known what it must feel like to hang from a cross. Yet that thief did, and it was right that he hung there. And you know full well what he did."

A little while after Arnvid left, Magnhild came over to rebuke Dalla. She told the old woman to remember that Ingunn was Steinfinn's daughter, no matter what she may have done, and she should not be plagued with the unseemly talk of a servant. After Ingunn had gone to bed, Dalla brought over a big bowl of sour milk mixed with water. She set the bowl down so hard on the footstool next to the bed that the mixture splashed over the side. But during the night, when Ingunn took a drink, she got a mouthful of sweepings; it seemed to be straw and debris from the floor.

Arnvid came to see her the following day before he departed, but they said very little to each other.

Ivar had arrived at Berg with Arnvid, but he did not go over to see his niece. Ingunn didn't know whether he was so embittered that he refused to set eyes on her, or whether someone had asked him to spare her by not visiting.

Arnvid arrived at the Dominican monastery at midday, and the porter was the first to tell him that Olav Audunssøn was there. He had arrived over a week ago. He was not staying in a guest room but instead in a small house that had been built in the vegetable garden on orders from the new prior. He had decided that men and women should not sleep in the same guesthouse. Women would have to stay outside the monastery grounds. But the women refused to stay in a place where they would be separated from their traveling companions and in a house that stood next to the cemetery. Besides, the house was poorly built and excessively drafty in the wintertime. Instead of a hearth, Prior Bjarne had ordered a stove to be erected in the corner next to the door, but it gave off little heat, and the smoke refused to be drawn up through the vent hole.

It was cold in the shade behind the church and chapter house. Icy shards crunched beneath Arnvid's feet in time with the jingling of his spurs as he walked through the garden. Here the snow had melted away so much that furrows planted with peas and beans lay like black mounds topped with pale, rotting vines. The women's house stood close to the churchyard fence. Dark shadows surrounded the house from several large old trees, though their branches were now bare.

The house had no antechamber, so Arnvid stepped directly inside. Olav was sitting on his bed with his legs dangling and his head tilted back against the wall. Arnvid was shocked to see how changed his friend was in appearance. His ashen-blond hair seemed to have faded because his complexion had turned the same color, a grayish yellow. And he hadn't shaved in so long that the lower part of his face seemed literally overgrown. Olav looked thoroughly miserable and ill. The freshly cut wall timbers were still yellow, and there was some smoke in the room, but only a few smoldering embers in the stove. Arnvid felt as if he'd entered a place where everything was sallow and frozen.

Neither of the men noticed that they neglected to greet each other properly.

"You've come here?" said Olav.

"I have," replied Arnvid foolishly. He decided to mention what Olav already knew, that he had always intended to visit his son Finn, who was a postulant at the school. Then it had occurred to him that Olav might want to hear about the meeting with Haftor Kolbeinssøn.

"So how did it go?" asked Olav.

"Haftor was quite pleased with the money."

"How long did you stay at Berg?" Olav gave a little icy laugh. "I can tell you've been there."

"I stayed there last night."

"And how were things there?"

"As you might well imagine," said Arnvid curtly.

Olav said no more. Arnvid sat down, and neither of them spoke. After a while a lay brother brought ale and bread for the newcomer. Arnvid drank the ale but couldn't bring himself to eat anything. The monk stayed for a brief time, talking with Arnvid. Olav merely sat and stared. After the lay brother left, silence again settled over them.

Finally Arnvid mustered his courage to speak.

"What will you do about the reconciliation now, Olav? Will you grant me and Ivar the authority to act on your behalf so that we can bring the matter to a close? Doubtless you have no desire now to come north yourself to meet with Haftor this summer."

"I don't see how I can avoid it," replied Olav. "She can't very well travel unescorted across half of Norway to come home to me. Then there would be a risk she'd have another child on the way by the time she arrived." He smiled spitefully. "No, the safest thing is for me to take charge of her myself, as soon as that can be done."

After a moment Arnvid, clearly shaken, said quietly, "What do you mean by that?"

Olav laughed.

"Do you intend to take her as your wife after all this?" asked Arnvid softly.

"Surely you must know, since you've had some priestly learning," said Olav scornfully, "that I am forever bound to her."

"I know," replied Arnvid in a low voice. "I wasn't certain whether you knew that yourself. But you must realize that no one would force you to take her into your house and live with her after what has happened."

"I suppose even I have to live with someone," said Olav in the same disdainful tone. "From my seventh year I have constantly lived among strangers. It's about time for me to settle on my own estate. But you must know that it's more than I'd bargained for, that she should bring a fully formed child as part of her dowry."

"Magnhild has already arranged for a foster family," said Arnvid quietly. "The child will be taken away the moment it sees the light of day."

"No. I want nothing to do with making any arrangements here in the valley. I want nothing to do with anyone from here at all. Neither she nor I will ever set foot up here in the north once we've left it behind. In the Devil's name, if my wife has become a whore, then surely I can take in the whore's child too." He clenched his teeth.

"She is suffering such shame and distress, Olav," Arnvid pleaded with him.

"Yes, well, we will both have to suffer, she and I, for the beneficence she decided to show that Icelander of hers, that fellow who has now run off."

"Never have I seen a child weighed down by such misery. Remember, Olav, that you had to leave her behind when you left Norway. And things were already hard for Ingunn back then. She has been weak all her days, with neither the strength nor the sense to make wise choices for herself."

"I know that. I haven't ever thought her to be wise or brave. Yet it's still asking much of a man to accept what happened. Have they . . ." His voice suddenly failed him. "Have they dealt terribly harshly with her? Do you know?"

"No, they haven't. But it takes very little to cause her to feel despondent. I'm sure you know that."

Olav didn't reply. He leaned forward with his hands draped over his knees as he stared at the floor.

After a while Arnvid said, "I can well imagine that everyone at Berg expects that you will spurn her."

Olav sat motionless. Arnvid didn't dare say what was in his heart. All of sudden Olav spoke.

"I told her I would come back. That's what I told Ingunn. She has always had a half-heathen disposition, but I thought she was fully aware that we are bound to each other for as long as we shall live."

Arnvid said, "When they wanted to give her to Gudmund Jonssøn— and you know that would have been an exceedingly good marriage for her—she spoke her mind, without reservation."

"Ha! But now, when she's the one who has broken her pledge, does she expect that I too should betray everything I've promised before both God and men?"

"I think she is expecting to die."

"That would certainly be the easiest way out, for both of us."

Arnvid didn't reply.

Then Olav asked, "I once gave you my word that I would never betray your kinswoman. Do you remember that?"

"Yes, I do."

Finally Arnvid broke the silence.

"I suppose they ought to be told—Ivar and Magnhild—that you wish to have her, in spite of everything."

When he received no answer, he persisted, "Will you give me your consent so that I might tell them what you intend to do?"

"I can tell them myself what I intend to do," replied Olav curtly. "I left behind some of my belongings at Berg," he added, as if to soften the tone of his reply.

Arnvid didn't say a word. He thought that given Olav's present state of mind, it wasn't certain that anyone at Berg would feel any sort of consolation when he went back there. But Arnvid didn't think it was his right to intervene in this matter any more than he'd already done.

By afternoon Olav was ready to leave. He asked Arnvid, "When are you planning to continue on toward home?"

Arnvid said he hadn't yet decided.

Olav didn't look at his friend as he spoke, seeming to be both ashamed and distressed by what he now said.

"I'd rather we didn't see each other again, not until the wedding feast. When I return from Berg, I'd rather you weren't . . ." He clenched his fists and gritted his teeth. "I can't bear to see anyone who knows of this!"

Arnvid's face flushed dark red, but he didn't show how offended he felt and replied calmly, "As you wish. If you should change your mind, you know how to get to Mikleb∅."

Olav shook hands with Arnvid, but he refused to look him in the eye.

"All right then. You have my thanks. It's not that I'm ungrateful, but—"

"I realize that. I suppose you'll then head south to Hestviken?" Arnvid couldn't help asking.

"No. I plan to stay here in Hamar, at least for a while. I need to find out whether I should make plans for a homecoming celebration or not." He tried to laugh. "If she's no longer alive, there will be no need for that."

Ingunn sat huddled in the corner next to her bed. It was so dark, both indoors and outside, that she couldn't make out who came into the room, but she thought it was Dalla, who must have finished her chores in the cowshed. But there was no further movement after whoever it was closed the door. She suddenly grew terribly frightened, even though she had no idea who the person might be. Her heart would always lurch and begin pounding like a sledgehammer if anyone so much as spoke to her. Now she struggled to keep her breathing subdued as she backed farther into the corner, staying as quiet as a mouse.

"Are you in here, Ingunn?" said the person.

When she recognized Olav's voice, her heart seemed to burst. It stumbled, then stopped, and the same sensation passed through her whole body, making her feel as if she were suffocating and coming apart and dying.

"Ingunn, are you in here?" he asked again. He stepped forward

shame and despair. "Go!" she begged. "Olav, have mercy on me and leave!"

"All right, I'll go. But you must realize that we will do as I've said. Oh, don't weep so, Ingunn," he pleaded. "I mean you no harm. Though we may never have much joy from each other." He couldn't hold back the words as bitterness surged inside him. "God knows that during all these years, I've often thought about being a good husband to you, and how I would do my utmost to be kind to you. Now I dare not make any such promises. I may find it difficult on many occasions not to treat you harshly. But with God's help, I think our life together may not be so bad that we can't at least endure it, both you and I."

"Oh, how I wish you had killed me on that day," she lamented, as if she hadn't heard what he'd just said.

"Keep quiet," he whispered, greatly agitated. "You speak so much of killing—first about your own child, and now you say I should kill you. In my mind you're more beast than human. You lose all reason every time you can't escape. Yet humans have to endure whatever they have brought upon themselves."

"Go!" she begged. "Go, go!"

"Yes, I'll go now. But I'm coming back. I'll come back here after you've given birth to your child, Ingunn. Perhaps by then you'll have regained your wits enough that it will be possible to speak sensibly with you."

She heard him come a few steps closer, and she curled up even more, as if expecting to be beaten. Olav's hand fumbled to find her shoulder in the dark. Then he leaned over her and kissed the top of her head, pressing so hard that she felt his teeth against her hair.

"There's no need to behave like this," he whispered above her. "It's not my intention to . . . You must believe me when I say that I will find a way out of this."

He withdrew his hand, and a moment later he was gone.

The following morning Fru Magnhild came in to see her. Ingunn lay in bed, staring up at the ceiling. Fru Magnhild grew angry when she saw that today the girl looked just as disconsolate as she always did.

"You've brought this misfortune upon yourself, yet now you're going to be spared and your life will be much easier than you had any right to expect. We must all get down on our knees to thank God and the Virgin Mary that Olav is the man he is. But I say: may God reward Kolbein as he deserves, for he refused to allow Olav to have you, and he also duped that stupid ox Ivar! If only they'd let Olav have you nine years ago!"

Ingunn neither moved nor spoke. Fru Magnhild went on.

"I'm not going to send at once for Hallveig, after all. As weak as you are, it's not certain the child will live," she said hopefully. "If it does live, then we can talk about what would be best."

On the fourth day after Easter Tora Steinfinnsdatter arrived. Ingunn stood up to greet her sister, but she had to hold on to the bedstead to stay on her feet. She dreaded terribly what Tora would say.

Yet Tora took Ingunn in her arms and patted her back. "Poor you! My poor Ingunn!"

Then she began talking about how magnanimous Olav was and how bleak things would have been if he had wanted to do what most men in his position would do—which meant trying to get rid of a woman whom he had never received in a lawful manner. "Truth be told, I never thought Olav was so pious. He has long looked for support from the priests and the church, but I thought it was mostly because they were of use to him. I didn't think it was because he was so God-fearing or had such strong faith.

"And he will not demand that you give up the child," said Tora, beaming. "That must be such a comfort to you. Aren't you elated that you won't have to send your child away?"

"Yes. But let's not talk any more of that," Ingunn finally said, for Tora wouldn't stop extolling this good fortune in the midst of all the misery.

Tora didn't mention that she'd had her suspicions, or fears, earlier in the winter, and she refrained from uttering too many condemning words about Ingunn. She tried instead to instill some courage in her sister. Soon, when Ingunn was relieved of her burden, she would see that everything in the world would appear much brighter, and good days would come to her too. But she mustn't give up as she now seemed to be doing. She sat there in the corner all day long, refusing to move and saying not a word unless spoken to. She merely stared straight ahead, filled with dark despair.

Dalla had reacted to Fru Magnhild's rebuke by declining to speak to Ingunn again, yet she still found plenty of ways in which to torment the ill woman. Ingunn never dared get into bed in the evening until she felt under the coverlet to see if hard or sharp objects had been placed there. And all of a sudden both her bed and her clothing were crawling with vermin; previously they had been utterly clean. She was constantly finding ashes and wood splinters and mouse droppings in the food and drink that Dalla brought her. Each morning the old servant would bind Ingunn's shoes so tightly that they hurt her feet terribly. While Ingunn laboriously tried to loosen them, Dalla would hover nearby, laughing scornfully. Ingunn never said a word.

But Tora was aware at once of a great many things that had been going on, and she took it upon herself to give Dalla a stinging earful. And the old thrall woman groveled before her young mistress like a whipped dog. When Tora saw that Ingunn couldn't hide her terror if Dalla so much as came near her, she sent the old woman away from Aasa's house for good. She helped her sister to get rid of the vermin, brought her clean clothing and good food, and placated her aunt when Fru Magnhild grumbled that Ingunn was ungrateful. She said the girl had only herself to blame for her misfortune, and they had certainly treated her with greater kindness than she had any right to expect. Magnhild was no longer willing to tolerate Ingunn's sullen and morose demeanor. But Tora urgently pleaded with her aunt, saying they should take good care of Ingunn during these last days before she gave birth. When she was back on her feet after her confinement, that would be another matter. Then Ingunn would have to listen to some serious words from both of them.

VII

After Olav Audunssøn had paid the fine for the murder he had committed in the Dominican monks' guesthouse, he'd grown quite close to the members of the cloister. Brother Vegard had also been Olav's father confessor ever since he was a child, and the monk was good friends with Arnvid Finnssøn, who was one of the monastery's benefactors. Before Olav learned of what happened to Ingunn, he had considered joining the Dominicans as a brother *ab extra*. When the monks saw that something was weighing on his mind, they left him in peace and avoided as much as possible asking him to share with other guests his lodging in the women's house. There was a great deal of coming and going at the monastery estate during Lent, for many folks from the surrounding villages were accustomed to making their Lenten confessions there and celebrating Easter at the cloister church.

Olav kept putting off his confession. He didn't know how he could do it properly. Ingunn could not have confessed yet, for Olav knew that Brother Vegard was still her confessor as well, and the monk had not been away from the cloister in six weeks. So Olav sat in the women's house and didn't venture out, except to go to church.

But on the Wednesday before Easter Olav decided he couldn't put it off any longer, and Brother Vegard promised to be in the church at the specified time.

It felt cold and dark when Olav entered through the small side door from the cloister courtyard. Springtime weather had suddenly set in. Brother Vegard was already sitting in his place in the chancel. He was reading a book that he held on his lap, and he wore the purple-blue stole over his white monk's cowl. From a little window high above, a ray of sunlight fell on the pictures that were painted on the monks' chancel seats, illuminating the image of Our King at the age of twelve among the Jewish *doctores*. My Lord God, prayed Olav in his heart. Give me the wisdom to say what I have to say and neither more nor less. Then he knelt in front of the priest and gave his confession.

Clearly and carefully he listed his sins with regard to the ten commandments, stating the ones he had broken and the ones he had obeyed, as far as he knew. He'd had plenty of time to consider this confession of his. Finally he came to the most burdensome part.

"I confess that there is someone toward whom I harbor the bitterest rancor, such that it seems to me terribly difficult to forgive this person. It's someone for whom I have felt the greatest affection, and as soon as I found out what this friend of mine had done to me, I felt so betrayed that an urge to kill rose inside me along with impure and vile desires and evil wishes. Then God saved me so that I was able to restrain myself. But I find it exceedingly hard to show forbearance toward this person, and I fear I'll never be able to forgive my friend fully, unless God should grant me the grace to do so. Yet I'm afraid, Father, that this is all I can say about the matter, and no more."

"Is it because you fear you might otherwise reveal another person's sin?" asked Brother Vegard.

"Yes, Father." Olav took a deep breath. "And that's why it seems to me so difficult to forgive. If I could have spoken to you of everything about this matter now, in this place, I think that would have made things easier."

"Give this careful consideration, Olav, my son. Are you of this mind because you think that if you could speak freely about what your fellow Christian has done to you, then your own injurious thoughts, your urge to kill, and your hatred might be justified in accordance with what we sinful humans call righteousness?"

"That is true, Father."

The monk then asked, "Do you hate this enemy of yours so much that you might wish for him unhappiness every day that he lives on this earth and eternal damnation in the beyond?"

"No."

"But you do wish that he might suffer for what he has done to you, enduring frequent and deep-felt torment?"

"Yes. For it seems to me that I too will suffer for this as long as I live. And I fear that unless God performs some miracle on my behalf, I will never again have peace in my soul. The anger and evil wishes will rise up inside me time and again, because from now on my circumstances, both my well-being and my standing, will only grow worse for as long as I live on this earth."

"You must know, my son, that if you pray will all your heart, God will give you the strength to forgive this person who has wronged you. Never has it been heard or said that God has not answered such a prayer. But you must pray without reservation. You must not be like the man Saint Augustine tells of—the one who prayed that God would grant him the grace to live a pure life, but not until sometime later. That is the way men often pray for the grace to forgive their enemies. And you must not be discouraged even if God waits until you have fervently prayed for a very long time before He grants you this gift."

"Yes, Father. But I fear that I may not always have the strength to restrain myself while I'm waiting for my prayer to be answered."

When the monk did not at once reply, Olav said urgently, "For you see, Father, what my friend has . . . done to me—it has destroyed everything for me. I dare not say any more, but there are now such difficulties that . . . If I could say more, you would realize that . . . This person has placed such a heavy burden on my neck, and—"

"I see that it does weigh heavily on you, my son. But you must persist and pray. And on Good Friday, when you step forward to kiss the Cross, pause to take a long look at it. Then look into your heart and ask yourself whether your own sins have added to the burden that Our Lord took on when he shouldered sins for us all. Do you think then that the hardship this friend has caused you is so great that you won't have the strength to bear it? You being a Christian man and His man?"

Olav bowed so deeply that his forehead touched the monk's knee.

"No. No, I don't think so," he whispered uncertainly.

In the night between Good Friday and the Saturday before Easter, Olav awoke, drenched in sweat. He'd been dreaming. As he lay there in the pitch dark, struggling to rid himself of the disturbing sensation this dream had left with him, he suddenly recalled their childhood so vividly. In his dream he and Ingunn were a small lad and maiden. But when he thought about this—how everything had seemed so promising back then, and how the future now looked for them—it all seemed to slip through his fingers like smoke, everything he thought he'd managed to understand through fervent prayer over the past few days. He pulled the coverlet over his head, and, in order not to weep, he lay there the way a man lies on the rack, focusing all his efforts on a single aim: that the torturers will not be able to force even a whimper out of him.

That summer, that summer and autumn, when she had waited in her bedchamber for him every night . . . He had been so restless. His own young and naive heart had trembled with excitement and agitation from the moment he awoke and saw that he was naked. But he had been so certain of her. That she might willfully fall out of his hands and give herself to another man? No, that had never occurred to him. That last night, when he went to her as a murderer and an outlaw, when he had placed the cold knife blade against her warm chest and asked her to keep the knife as a talisman—that was not something he'd done because he thought she might be unfaithful. No, he was thinking of himself, someone who now had to meet an unknown fate, as young and untried and uncertain as he was.

Whenever he'd moved close to her he would bury his face in her wheat-brown hair that smelled like a haystack. And her flesh was so soft and supple that it always made him think of grain that hadn't yet fully ripened. Never had he taken her in his arms without thinking: I must treat her gently, for she is so weak and slender. She needs me to protect and defend her from any scratches and blows, for this flesh of hers is too delicate to heal on its own. And he had refrained from speaking to her of anything that troubled him, for he thought it would be wrong to shift any of his burden onto her fragile shoulders. Uncertain in his conscience and uneasy about the future—how could she understand any of that, as childish as she was? She had insatiably demanded that he caress and embrace her and would playfully cajole him to do so again if he even for a moment seemed lost in thought or happened to speak of something other than the two of them. All this he'd regarded as a form of childish behavior. She didn't understand much more than a child or animal did, the poor thing. He had often thought that she resembled a gentle and timid animal, a tame fawn or a tender young heifer, affectionate and easily startled.

He recalled that this was what he'd understood as soon as he became aware that she was a woman he was to possess and enjoy. He'd seen quite clearly that she was a weak and fragile creature, and he needed to shield and protect her.

It now seemed to him that this dream had been sent to him as a message and a gift, although at first it had brought such distress and torment to his mind. He'd thought it was only right for her to suffer greatly for her weakness. But that was far from what ought to happen. He should instead do all he could to help her escape as leniently as possible.

My little fawn, you've certainly allowed yourself to be chased into a hollow, and now you're lying there, wounded and debased, a poor little animal. But I will come to find you and carry you off to a place where you will not be stomped on and crushed. It now seemed to him that what had occurred—back when he'd taken her in his arms, when he'd been allowed to pluck the flower from her and breathe in the fragrance and sweetness—all of that had mostly fallen into place along the way. Of greater importance was the fact that she had been put into his arms so that he might carry her over everything, lift any burdens away from her, and protect her. That was what true happiness was; all the rest was merely pleasure.

All during Easter he walked about as if he'd just recovered from a terrible illness. Not that he'd ever been ill in his life, but that must be how it felt. "My soul has been healed. Ingunn, you must know that I only wish you well."

He considered telling his dream to Brother Vegard. But in the nearly twenty years that the monk had been his father confessor, Olav had never spoken to him of anything personal outside of confession. Brother Vegard Ragnvaldssøn was a good man and an intelligent man, but he had a detached and wry disposition, which made it possible for him to speak of folks in a droll and witty manner. That was something that Olav greatly appreciated, as long as it had nothing to do with him. In the past he'd never felt an urge to climb over the fence that existed between him and his father confessor. In fact, he had thought it only proper that outside the church the man seemed like a different person than the priest who listened to his self-reproaches and acted as his spiritual guide.

Olav had earlier considered confiding in the monk, outside the confessional, about what had happened to Ingunn. But that would seem as if he were trying to exonerate himself while accusing her. And so he decided not to do it. No doubt Brother Vegard would soon be summoned to Berg. The poor thing must be preparing now to face what might well be a mortal danger.

It was the Wednesday following *Dominica in Albis,* which was the first Sunday after Easter. As Olav reached the threshold of the church after midmorning prayer, someone touched his arm from behind.

"Greetings, sir. Are you not the man they call Olav Audunssøn?"

Olav turned around to see standing behind him a tall and slender young man with a dark complexion.

"That might well be my name. But what is it you want of me?"

"I would like to speak with you, just a few words." Olav could hear from the way the man talked that he was not from the area.

Olav stepped aside to allow the throng of people to continue leaving the church. Then he moved into the portico. Through the arches that were supported by pillars, he saw the morning sun as it abruptly rose above the blue-black ridges to the southwest and glinted on the dark open waters between the island and the mainland at Stange, shining over the brown countryside, now bare of snow.

"What is it you want? I don't recall ever seeing you before."

"No, we've never met. But you undoubtedly know my name. I am Teit Hallssøn. I'm from the Varmaa valley on Sida, in Iceland."

Olav was dumbfounded. Teit. The boy's clothing was tattered, but he had a handsome, thin face with a brown complexion beneath the leather cap of a *skald* that he wore. He had clear, amber eyes and a wide mouth with a great many shiny white teeth.

"So perhaps you understand now why I have sought you out."

"No, I can't say that I do."

"If you know of a place where we could speak in private," said Teit, "that might be for the best."

Olav didn't reply, but he turned on his heel and led the way along the portico on the north side of the church. Teit followed. Olav was aware as he walked that no one could see them. The roof of the passageway reached so far down that it was too dark for anyone outside to be able see who was moving behind the small archways.

At the place where the passageway ended and the choir section of the church jutted out, it was possible to enter a corner of the cemetery. Olav led the other man diagonally across the churchyard and then jumped over the fence to the vegetable garden. This was the route he usually took from the church. It was the shortest way for him.

When they went inside the women's house, Olav latched the door behind them. Without waiting to be invited, Teit sat down on the bench, but Olav remained standing and waited.

"I'm sure you know full well that I wish to speak to you about her, Ingunn Steinfinnsdatter," said Teit, with a little embarrassed smile. "We were friends last summer, but I haven't seen her nor heard from her since early autumn. Yet there's talk that she is carrying a child and is already far along. If so, it must be mine. And I know that she was yours before she was mine. For that reason I thought I'd talk to you about what we now should do."

"You don't seem to have any fear," said Olav.

"Well, no man is in possession of all possible faults, and that is not one of mine," said the boy with an easy smile.

Olav said nothing further, merely waited. Instinctively he cast a quick glance toward his bed, where his weapons were hanging on the wall.

"Back in the autumn," Teit now went on, "I already let her know that if it could be arranged, I would gladly marry her."

"Marry you!" Olav laughed, just a few brief snorts, with his lips pressed tightly together.

"Yes, I know," said Teit calmly. "Yet it didn't seem to me such an unequal match. Ingunn is no longer young, and she had already been the topic of gossip. No one had heard from you in ten years' time, and it hardly seemed likely that you would ever come back, though she spoke as if she believed you would. And that's why she gave me short shrift. I was offended, as would be only reasonable, when treated with such capriciousness. I told her I would leave if that was what she wanted, but then it would do no good for her to send word for me later on. Nor has she done so. Not a word have I heard from her about the distress in which she now finds herself. And I don't know whether I would have gone to her, even so. I did not treat her gently when we parted.

"But then I discovered that you had returned and had gone to Berg, and then you took your leave as soon as you found out how things stood. And I felt sorry for her, all the same. Now they say that she has been locked up in one of the outlying houses and is living on nothing but filthy water and porridge mixed with ashes, and they've tied her up and dragged her by the hair, so it's a wonder she is still alive."

Olav had listened to all this with a frown on his face. He was about to reply brusquely that these were lies, but he stopped himself. This was not a matter that he could possibly discuss with Teit. And it occurred to him that when such rumors got out, their difficulties would increase tremendously. He wondered how many people this fool had boasted to about being the father.

Teit asked, "Isn't it true that you are good friends with that rich man Arnvid of Mikleb in Elfardal, the one who is her kinsman?"

"Why do you ask?" Olav replied curtly.

"Everyone says that he is so helpful and kind—a friend to any man in need of help. So I thought it might be better if I turned to him first, instead of to the Steinfinnssns or the old man at Galtestad. What do you think? And you could give me a token to present to your friend, or you could have a letter written to him and then place your seal on it."

Olav sank down onto the bench.

"This is beyond belief! Is that what you're asking? For me to support your courtship?"

"Yes," said Teit placidly. "Do you find that so strange?"

"It does seem strange to me, yes." And Olav gave a brief, harsh laugh. "I've never heard the likes of it."

"But it happens every day," said Teit. "A man of your standing often marries off his paramour when he no longer wishes to keep her."

"Watch what you say, Teit," Olav warned. "Watch what words you say about her!"

Then, as if carelessly, Teit took the small, short sword from his belt and placed it across his lap, putting one hand on the sheath and the other on the hilt. He gave Olav a little smile.

"Ah, I see. Is it here in this room that you usually strike down your enemies?"

"It was in the other guesthouse. And I wouldn't use the term 'strike down.' We had ended up fighting—" He stopped himself there, regretting that he'd allowed himself to say as much as he had to this man.

"As matters now stand," said Teit with the same smile, "I seem to have a greater claim on her than you do."

"There you're wrong, Teit. Never can you have any claim on her. Ingunn belongs to us, and no matter what she may have done, we will never give her away to someone not of our own standing."

"Nevertheless, the child is mine, the one she's carrying."

"Don't you realize, Icelander, learned man that you are, that the child of an unmarried woman stays with the mother and inherits her rights, even if she's a freeborn woman who has allowed herself to be seduced by a thrall?"

"I am not a thrall," said the Icelander indignantly. "Both my father and my mother are descendants of the best families back home in Iceland, even though they were poor folks. And you need not fear that I won't be able to provide for her, as long as you give her a reasonable dowry." Then he expounded on all his future prospects. He would become a prosperous man, if only he could go to a place where he'd have the opportunity to practice all his skills and talents. And he would teach Ingunn to assist him.

Olav sat there, thinking back to his youth when a bookbinder had lived in Hamar. He was a master bookbinder whom the bishop of Oslo had sent to Lord Torfinn when he was ready to have bound the books that had been written during the year. Fat Asbjørn had taken Olav to visit the man and his wife in the room where they worked. The bookbinder's wife helped out by boring holes in the parchment, through many layers at once. Occasionally she would use her elbow to give a gentle shove to the baking trough she was using as a cradle and had hung by a rope nearby. Her child cried and whined the whole time and kept spitting out the mouthful of food it had been given to suck on. Asbjørn finally told her to rest for a bit and tend to the child. The monk said he felt sorry for the woman. When the bookbinder and his wife finished their work, the bishop had sent her a winter sur-coat, calling her a clever woman. Olav had seen them the day they left Hamar. The master rode quite a fine horse, while his wife rode a small, stubby-legged, and sway-backed nag as she held the infant in her arms. All their traveling sacks were piled up behind her.

Should Ingunn be pushed out into such a life? Holy Mother of God, no! Such a thing was unimaginable. Should Ingunn be cast out of the social standing into which she had been born and bred? Such a thought was both preposterous and wrong. He simply could not fathom how a fellow who was a complete outsider had even managed to meet her.

Olav sat there, looking at Teit and callously assessing him as he talked. In the midst of everything, he could see there was something appealing about the boy, who seemed quite fearless and was used to making his own way in the world. That's what Olav saw. It would take a good deal to upset Teit or thwart his cheerful audacity. And he smiled so easily, which suited him. No doubt he'd become coarse in manner from the wandering life he'd led among strangers, all those unfettered men and loose women. And yet. Olav himself had spent the last nine years roaming the world, and he'd been involved in one thing or another that he had no intention of remembering once he was settled in his own home. But to think that something from that world had come between him and Ingunn, had touched her.

Touched her, so that she was now out there at Berg, waiting for the hour when she would have to kneel on the floor to suffer the indignity and throes of birth.[31] It was Nobody's child. Nobody's. That's what she'd said when he asked her who the father was. He remembered that he too had said "Nobody" when she wanted to know who had helped him escape to follow the earl when he fled. And during those years when he was accompanying the earl, he had met so many people, both men and women, whom he knew would become Nobodies when he one day was back home at Hestviken. He'd known many boys like this Teit. He'd been their comrade and enjoyed their company. But he was a man, after all, just a man. When something from outside crossed a man's path to get to his wife, then life was forever tainted for both of them. A woman's honor—that was the honor of all the men who had the obligation and right to act as her guardian.

"Well, what do you say?" asked Teit a bit impatiently.

Olav was startled out of his thoughts. He hadn't heard a word Teit had just said.

"I say you need to banish such nonsense from your mind. And see about leaving Oppland as quickly as you can. Head for Nidaros, and do so today. Don't wait for tomorrow. Don't you know that she has two grown brothers? The day they hear of their sister's disgrace, you are a dead man."

"Oh, I'm not so sure about that. I'm quite skilled at wielding a sword, if I do say so myself. And Olav—she was once yours, after all. Don't you wish to do something to help her so she can regain her honor and marry?"

"Do you truly believe I would consider her circumstances improved if she should marry you?" Olav replied vehemently. "Shut your trap, I tell you. I have no wish to hear any more of your foolish talk."

Teit said, "Then I will go to Miklebø alone. I will at least try to speak with this Arnvid. In my view, she will be better off as my lawful wife than if she stays with her rich kinsmen until they have tormented both her and our child to death."

That's what I once said myself, thought Olav, now exhausted. Torment both her and the child. But as it happened, we did not have a child.

"I've seen for myself how she was treated at Berg even before this occurred," said Teit. "In my view it may well be that she would count it an improvement if she had a husband who could take her far away from this part of the country and all of you. It's true that as soon as she allowed me to have my way with her, she turned against me and behaved like a witch toward me. But perhaps she did so out of fear. That's not as unreasonable as I thought at first. And up until that happened, we were friends and always on good terms. And she never hid the fact that she was fond of me, just as I was fond of her."

Fond of him? So she'd felt affection for him. Up until that moment Olav hadn't felt jealousy, not the sort that he could pin on this man Teit. It was Ingunn and the misfortune that had infuriated him to the very core of his being. For him, it was again "Nobody" who had been the cause of it all. But hearing that she had favored this fellow and been good friends with him all summer . . . And by Devil, he certainly was a handsome boy, both lively and merry. She had been so fond of him that she'd let him have his way, yet afterward she grew frightened. Out of the goodness of her heart, she had given herself to this boy with the black curls, to this Icelander.

"So you will not give me any sort of token or message to take to Miklebø? Something that might be of use to me?" asked Teit.

"It's strange that you don't ask me to accompany you so I might speak on your behalf," said Olav scornfully.

"No. I thought that might be too much to ask," replied Teit guilelessly. "But I did think that if you happened to be of a mind to head up there, then we might keep each other company along the way."

Olav gave several abrupt snorts of laughter.

Teit stood up, said goodbye, and left.

The next moment Olav leaped to his feet, as if he'd just awakened. He went over to the door and then noticed that he'd picked up his small axe, a tool that had lain on the bench in front of him among the knives and chisels and the like. Olav had taken it upon himself to fashion several footstools to be used in the church. The prior had mentioned they were in need of such items, and Olav had offered to make them.

He walked through the monastery's courtyard and over to the gate. There he found the lay brother who was the porter hanging about. Olav went to stand beside him.

"Do you know anything about that fellow you can see heading off?" he asked. Teit was striding up the hill toward the cathedral. There was no one else in sight.

"Isn't that the Icelander?" replied the porter. "The one who was a clerk for Torgard the cantor last year? Yes, that's him all right."

"Do you know anything about that fellow?" Olav again asked.

Brother Andreas was known for his dutiful life, but his piety was of the sort that might be compared to a lamp without oil; he showed little forbearance toward other poor sinners. Right then and there he recounted for Olav every chapter of Teit Hallssøn's saga that was known in the Hamar bishopric.

Olav gazed upward, at the spot where the youth had disappeared beyond the churchyard wall.

Could there possibly be any great harm done if that man should vanish for good?

The next day the sky was again clear, and the air trembled with heat and damp around the bare, brown treetops. When Olav entered the monastery's courtyard late in the morning, stout Brother Helge, who was the cook, was there tending to the pigs that were fighting over the fish guts he had just tossed on the ground.

"Where were you?" he asked. "Why weren't you at mass today, Olav?"

Olav replied that he hadn't fallen asleep until the early hours of the morning, and then he'd overslept. "But I wonder, Brother Helge, whether you could find some skis that I might borrow." Arnvid had invited him to come north to Miklebø after Easter, and he was thinking of going there today.

But wouldn't you prefer to ride? asked the lay brother. Olav said that given the road conditions he would make faster time by taking the ski trails through the forest.

He had just finished shaving when Brother Helge came to the door of the women's house, carrying in his arms all the skis he could find at the monastery. Slung over his shoulder was a knapsack with provisions. Olav had cut himself on the jaw so that blood was running down his neck and staining the opening of his shirt. His hand was dripping with blood. Even Brother Helge was unable to stanch the blood, and he was surprised that such a little cut could bleed so heavily. Finally he dashed out and then returned with a cup of oat flour. He pressed a fistful of flour to the wound.

The sweet smell of flour and the cool feel of it against the skin of his face caused an abrupt stirring of longing and desire in Olav—a yearning for a woman's caress, tender and sweet without a trace of sin or pain. That was the very thing that had now been stolen from him.

The monk saw the veiled look that had come over Olav's eyes. He said anxiously, "I think you should give up these travel plans of yours, Olav. At least find out in town whether anyone else is headed that way. It's not natural for such a tiny cut to bleed so badly. Look at your hands. They're covered in blood."

Olav merely laughed. He went outside and washed himself in the puddles of water under the eaves. Then he chose a pair of skis.

Back inside and fully dressed, he was speaking to the lay brother about his horse and the belongings he would leave behind when they heard the loud clang of steel from somewhere. Both men turned at once to look toward the bed. That's where Olav's axe *Ættarfylgja* hung on the wall, and it seemed to both of them that it was swaying on its hook.

"That was your axe singing," said the monk quietly. "Olav, don't go!"

Olav laughed.

"So you think that was the second portent? Perhaps I'll take heed if there's a third, Helge."

Hardly had he spoken before a bird flew in the door and began darting this way and that in the room, beating its wings against the wall. It was unbelievable how much noise its little wings were making.

The cook's ruddy, plump face turned white as he stared at Olav, whose bright lips now seemed a pale blue. But then Olav shook his head and laughed. He caught the bird in his cap and carried it outside to let it go.

"These titmice climb on the wall timbers, scratching and pecking for flies at this time of year. They make a great commotion every morning. You'll be seeing portents everywhere, my dear Brother Helge, if you consider it an omen when titmice fly into a house!"

He picked up the little axe he used as a tool and hung it on his belt.

"You don't intend to take Ættarfylgja with you?" asked the cook.

"No. It would not be advantageous to take her along this time." He asked the lay brother to hide the horned axe along with his sword. Then he picked up his ski staff that was topped by a small spear point. He bade Brother Helge farewell and departed.

It was midday by the time Olav reached the foothills below Furu Mountain. The sunlight had paled, and the air suddenly seemed a bit clammy and cool, heavy and gray-tinged to the north. It looked as if it might snow. Olav paused, his skis resting on his shoulders, and looked back.

In the fading sunshine the flat countryside looked merely black and withered-gray. Only a few small patches of snow remained. The dried thatch and black shingles on the town's rooftops, as well as the bare tree crowns, surrounded the light-colored masonry walls and heavy, lead-covered towers of Christ Church, visible against the restless, leaden-colored waters. Olav silently cursed the ominous feeling that came over him. It would have been better, after all, if there was no new snowfall now that he would have to make his way through the forests. He'd gone this way once before, but that was with Arnvid, and they had set off swiftly, taking shortcuts through the worst of the rugged terrain. Arnvid was the most skillful skier of any man he'd ever known.

It so happened that Olav knew about the small hut at the edge of the forest where the Icelander had chosen to stop. A vicious murder had been committed there during the time when Olav was a guest of Bishop Torfinn. A man and his two underage children, a son and a daughter, had killed and robbed a prosperous old beggar. Ever since, no one had wanted to stay there. But this man Teit owned nothing worth stealing.

Olav convinced himself that he had no plans. He would let fate determine what happened. Teit might have taken off for the north the day before, or he might have changed his mind and given up the whole idea. If so, Olav realized he would have to make Teit reconsider; he couldn't have this man wandering about the countryside. He had to find a way to get him to Nidaros, or to Iceland—either way, Teit had to go north and to Hell.

He tried the door. It wasn't latched. The hearth vent was covered, so it was very dark inside. The small room felt desolate and black and cold, with a raw smell of earth and mold and filth. But Teit sprang up, fully clothed, from the bench where he was sleeping and seemed as alert as ever. When he recognized who had come in, he gave Olav a fleeting smile.

"Take a seat on the bench against the wall here. I can't offer you anything else to sit on. As you can see, there's not even a stool to be found."

Olav sat down on the middle of the bench. As far as he could tell, there were no household items whatsoever in the hut, nothing but firewood scattered across the floor. Teit put wood on the hearth, blew on the embers, and opened the smoke vent.

"Nor can I welcome you with something to drink, for good reason. But you didn't offer me any yesterday either."

"Did you expect me to do so?" Olav laughed harshly.

Teit laughed too. Again Olav sensed there was something appealing about the youth. He might be impudent and unabashed, but he hadn't been cowed by poverty or isolation.

"I've changed my mind, Teit," said Olav. "I'm on my way to Miklebø now. And if you still think it might benefit you to speak to Arnvid Finnssøn, you're welcome to keep me company."

"Well, I have to tell you that I haven't brought my horse along. I don't suppose you could find one I might borrow?" He laughed, as if his words were a merry jest.

"I'm heading through the forest on skis," said Olav curtly.

"Ah. Then I do have a means of travel. I saw a pair of skis outside in the cowshed." He dashed out and came back with the skis. The back end of the left ski had cracked and bent forward. The hide covering on the other, shorter ski was almost worn off.[32] Teit fastened his belt and sword around his waist and threw on his cloak.

"All right, I'm ready anytime you want to leave!"

"Haven't you brought any food with you?"

"No, I thought I'd spare myself having to lug such things with me—for good reason."

Olav felt strangely ill at ease. Should he share his food with a man with whom he might afterward . . . break peace? There was something inside him telling him to offer all his provisions to the youth. It was clear that Teit hadn't had much to eat of late. But that could at least wait until they reached the ridge.

"Consider well this decision of yours, Icelander," he said, his voice almost menacing. "Don't you think it might be ill-advised for you to accompany me through the forest?" It occurred to Olav that with these words he was trying to assuage his own conscience a bit. This warning might be taken as a way for him to avoid responsibility. It was uncertain what would happen, but just in case . . .

Teit merely gave him a cold smile as he patted his sword.

"I seem to be better armed than you are, so I think I'll take my chances, Olav. And besides, a nobleman like yourself would never send his falcon after all the little flies."

As they were about to leave the hut, Olav looked back over his shoulder. The fire was now burning brightly in the hearth.

"Aren't you going to put out the fire?" he asked.

"No, why should I bother with that? And besides, it won't be any great loss if the hut should burn down."

The moment they stepped outside, Olav noticed that the haze had grown so thick that he couldn't see the sun. It was now hidden behind a gray veil.

The skiing was good once they were up on the ridge. Olav kept to the slopes on the backside of the mountain, standing between Ridabu and Fauskar. As far as he could remember, he should head due north and then veer a bit to the northeast, and by late afternoon he should reach a stretch where he'd see quite a few mountain pastures that belonged to farms in the Glaama valley. There they could no doubt find shelter for the night. The days were already staying light longer.

The snow was six to eight feet deep in this area. After all the warm weather of the past few weeks, the thawing snow had sunk down, but then a sudden frost had set in, making their skis slide smoothly over the icy surface. Yet Olav sometimes had to wait for Teit, who would flounder about after plunging into the snow. He fell often, no matter whether he was clambering up a slope or skiing at the bottom of a hollow.

"I think we ought to exchange short skis," Olav offered.

The hide covering on Teit's ski was so tattered that Olav simply scraped it off. But it didn't help matters for Teit to use Olav's ski; he kept on falling. Occasionally he would even lose his skis and plunge through the crusted snow up to his waist. Then he would laugh at his own lack of prowess as he sat there flailing.

"Do you have much practice on skis, Teit?" asked Olav. He'd had to go far down a scree slope covered with brush in order to retrieve the youth's skis.

"A little." Teit's exertions had turned his face bright red, and he'd scraped both his face and hands on the icy snow, but he just laughed. "Back home in Iceland I never did any skiing, not even once. And here in Norway, I've only tried this sport two or three times before today."

"Then it's going to be hard for you to ski the whole long way to Miklebø," said Olav.

"Oh, I'm sure I can manage. Don't worry about that."

God knows, thought Olav, he doesn't seem at all aware what a torment it is for me to keep backtracking like a she-dog to pull out both him and his skis. Aloud he said that perhaps they should rest for a while and have something to eat. Teit was more than willing, so Olav broke off some branches and laid them on the snow.

He sat there with his face turned away as the young man ate.

"I can see that no one is going to starve if they've been given provisions from a cloister!" said Teit.

The day had turned gray. From where they sat, high on the back-side of the mountain, they could see nothing but one forest-covered ridge after another, now dark blue beneath the threatening sky. In the valley right below them, the coal-black trees seemed to surround a small white area that was either an icy lake or marsh.

Yet all around them the birds began chirping and whistling their springtime songs, slightly hesitant and uncertain, in anticipation of the approaching season. Occasionally a rushing and sighing sound passed through the forest, moving from ridge to ridge. To the north a snowstorm cloaked the ground, hiding beneath it the solid blue-gray rock and the forested mountain. The snow was headed toward them.

"We need to continue on, Teit."

Olav helped the Icelander to fasten his skis securely. That sword of his, worn by someone who kept on falling. Olav couldn't help saying that swords and skis did not belong together.

"But it's the only weapon I own," said Teit. He drew the sword and rather proudly handed it to Olav. It was a good sword with a plain hilt and fine blade. "I inherited it from my father. It's the only possession I have from him. It's not something I will ever give up."

"Your father's dead?"

"Yes. He died three years ago. That's when I came up with the idea to try my luck in Norway, though I first went down to Fljotshverv to visit my mother. She left me and my father when I was seven winters old, and I hadn't seen her in ten years. She'd met a man she wanted to marry, but she all of a sudden felt guilty because she'd been a priest's paramour for so long. Yet she made it clear that she would rather see my heel than my toe. Those were lean years in our part of the country, and there were children swarming all over their place. I never managed to find out how many were my mother's and which of them belonged to the other women."

"Time to go, Teit." Olav leaned forward and set off.

Making one swift turn after another, he raced downward. The terrain was rough, and he had to duck under the trees. The sun had been shining here, so he left a high ridge of loose snow in his wake. The Icelander would just have to manage as best he could.

Down by the ice-covered lake, Olav paused to listen. A strong wind was gusting off the ridge, sending through the forest a muted groaning and squeaking along with a rushing sound. Then, at last, he heard the creaking of skis on the crusted snow above.

Teit made his way down the last short slope to the lake. He was completely covered in snow from the falls he'd taken, but his white teeth gleamed in his red, scraped face.

"I'll soon be as good a skier as any Norwegian!" He showed Olav what he'd done with his cumbersome cloak. It had ended up so ripped that he'd simply stuffed his arms through two of the holes and then fastened his belt on the outside. Now it was no longer a hindrance.

"Are you worn out?" asked Olav.

"Oh no." Teit put his hand to the back of his neck and bent his head forward a bit. Only the sinews in his neck were stiff and tender. It felt as if the Devil himself had grabbed him there.

Olav's neck also ached a bit, for this was the first time he'd gone out skiing this year. He could only imagine what Teit must be feeling. All of a sudden he was remembering the boat trip to Hamar with Ingunn. He'd been only a boy back then. He had strained and pulled on the oars, and the back of his neck had hurt worse and worse. He had gritted his teeth, rowing with a great deal of splashing but refusing to give up and reveal how exhausted he felt. He was utterly despondent and thought they would never reach Hamar.

Now he looked at Teit and clenched his teeth. He had to hold back what was surging up inside him. He wanted to think about *her* and how she was doing right now—about the hatred and loathing that had filled him when he found out about her disgrace, about all the promises that had been broken. And we will have to live in the shadow of this sorrow and shame, forever and ever, thought Olav. Yet here was this fool of a boy who had caused their misfortune, and he was completely unaware of any of it.

Side by side, they skied across the icy surface of the lake, with Teit talking ceaselessly as he panted and huffed and groaned. He asked Olav about the animal tracks they saw, old prints that glittered atop the crusted snow, and fresh ones from elk that had left deep imprints.

And he bragged about his newfound skill as a skier. He was putting his trust in Olav, much like a boy would do with his father. And more than anything Olav felt a certain pity for this misplaced sense of trust. No! This was all too much for him.

The first hard little snowflakes began coming down when they entered the forest on the other side of the lake. And the daylight was starting to wane. They didn't make it very far up the ridge before they were in the midst of a snowstorm. Olav kept on. He would pause to wait for Teit, who was lagging behind, and then continue on. Now he was impatient to put an end to this trek and find shelter. At the same time he dreaded thinking about what would happen then. From up on the heights where they'd paused to rest, he'd seen that beyond the mountain where they were now skiing, there was an even higher ridge, and at the very top were several white patches with what looked like houses that might be farmsteads. If so, they could spend the night in the company of other folks. But what he'd seen might also be huts in mountain pastures, and that seemed more likely. Whatever happened, it would be a matter of fate.

Higher up, a fierce wind blew toward them. Big, wet snowflakes had been coming down for a while, but now the wind was whipping dry, hard flakes right into their faces. The whistling sound of the snow seemed to fill the entire forest with a low, sharp tone that pierced through the droning and howling of the wind in the spruce tops. And the weather seemed even worse because dusk had set in so fast.

The ski trail had vanished long ago. So much new snow had already fallen that their skis cut deep into the snow wherever it had been swept into drifts.

Again Olav had to stop to wait for Teit. The Icelander pulled up alongside him, gasping as if his chest might burst. Out of breath, but still sounding as cheerful and undaunted as ever, he said, "Wait a bit, friend. Let me go on ahead and break the trail."

Olav felt his will weaken and sink, confronted as he was by what now surged inside him, what he would need to forcefully stifle before he could do this boy any harm. He threw himself forward and began skiing with all his might. Now and then he would pause to listen, wanting to know if his companion was still behind him, but he never paused long enough for Teit to catch up with him.

It was almost pitch dark by the time they reached the meadow, which looked to be a little mountain hamlet. Through the swirling snow and the darkness, Olav glimpsed small black patches up ahead. Some might be huge rocks, but others were huts.

Olav dropped the sack he was carrying the moment they came inside the dark space. He got out his pouch with the flint and began working to make a fire. He knelt over the hearth, blowing on the tiny flames that were trying to take hold on the slightly damp twigs. He listened to Teit's pleased exclamations as the youth wandered around, inspecting the little hut. There was hay on the bedstead, along with a hide coverlet and several sacks for pillows. And the boy dashed into the dark alcove at the back of the hut, which turned out to be an attached storeroom made of stone and sod. There's flatbread, Teit called to Olav, and a tub of whey and water. He appeared in the opening, with a ladle in his hand, wanting to offer Olav some of the half-frozen drink.

"Of course, Teit. We live in a Christian country, after all, and folks don't depart a mountain hut without leaving behind supplies, in case some forest traveler should have need of them."

While they ate their meal, Teit stretched out on the bedstead with his knees drawn up and his head down because of the smoke. They weren't able to create a cross-draft because the little room was so cramped that the fire might then spread to the bedstead or set alight all the kindling that was heaped on the floor. Olav sat on the opposite bench even though the smoke tore at his throat and stung his eyes. He sat with his arms crossed, staring from under half-closed eyelids at the fire, keeping as silent as a stone while he listened to the young man's chatter—all of it utter nonsense. Neither the weather nor the trail they'd taken was worth mentioning. If he hadn't had to drag along this fellow who skied like a newborn calf, he would have made it here in half the time. But the fool talked as if they'd become stalwart companions, making it through the most arduous of adventures and treks.

"Are you tired?" asked Teit. He was suddenly aware that Olav hadn't said a word while he'd talked nonstop. He shifted position. "Or perhaps you'd rather take the side next to the wall?"

Never, thought Olav. Share a bed with this guest tonight? No. There was a limit to everything.

"No, I'm not tired."

He tried to collect his thoughts. What he meant to do seemed to keep slipping away from him. He and Ingunn were *married*, after all. That's what he needed to remind himself, and that's why Teit had to go. This boy had ruined her out of sheer stupidity. But what he kept prattling about, saying he would redeem her from disgrace—that was something this lustful devil could never do. Olav had to do it himself. He had to hide the shame. Folks could believe whatever they liked as long as they knew where he stood and that her kinsmen stood with him. He would acknowledge the child as his own, and he intended to defend his assertion against anyone who dared doubt his claim.

"When did you hear those rumors?" Olav asked abruptly. "That she had ended up in . . . difficulties? Such gossip must be quite recent."

Teit said yes, it wasn't long ago that he'd heard this news. Some acquaintances of his in town had a daughter who was married to a man from one of the small leaseholdings that belonged to Berg. Both they and their daughter had seen her wandering about on the slope below the estate in the evenings, and it now stayed light far into the night. Teit expounded further on what they'd told him.

Olav sat there frowning as he listened. Blood began rushing in his ears. But this was better. Let the boy keep talking. That would help him to overcome more quickly these unmanly feelings of his, the kindliness that was on the verge of weakening him.

"What about you?" asked Olav, his lips twisted into an odd smile. "Could you resist telling them that you were the one who had been there?"

"I did say something of the sort."

"Have you told anyone else?"

Would it be possible to pretend it was merely idle hearsay that had been spread by poor folks, both men and women? That was something he could live with. He could hold his head high among his peers, look them defiantly in the eye, and pretend that he knew nothing about what was being whispered behind his back. It was merely vulgar gossip that the maidservants had brought to their mistresses.

Teit said with some embarrassment, "I was so angry with her that I felt she deserved it when I heard she was now walking with such a heavy tread. The Devil knows she was both nimble and agile enough last summer, the way a tabby cat rubs up against you and then slips away if you try to set her on your lap. When I finally managed to get my clutches on her . . ."

Olav wasn't properly listening to what Teit was saying, for the blood was making such a rushing and ringing sound in his head. But it was enough; all of this was enough. He'd regained his sense of determination to take revenge. Yet it would be a costly revenge, for he would have a hard time forgetting what he'd now heard.

"By the next night she'd changed her mind and locked me out. And when I went to her to speak of marriage, she drove me away as if I were a dog."

"I think you'd best give up all thought of this marriage, Teit."

Hearing the warning tone in Olav's voice, Teit looked up. Olav was on his feet, holding the small axe in his hand. Quick as lightning the boy grabbed his sword and drew it from the sheath as he leaped up. Olav was seized by a wild surge of joy when he saw that Teit now fully understood what was happening. The boyish face seemed to grow dark with rage. He realized that he'd been duped, and he confronted Olav's unspoken challenge with the ferocious cry of a youth ready to do battle.

Teit didn't wait to see how Olav would react. Instead, he launched his attack at once. Olav remained standing in the same spot, and three times he used his axe to fend off the boy's blows. When Teit lunged at him a fourth time, Olav unexpectedly stepped to the right so the sword struck his left arm. In confusion, the boy then paused for a moment, and Olav's axe struck him on the shoulder, causing him to drop his sword. He bent down to pick it up with his left hand, and that's when Olav brought his axe down on the boy's skull. He collapsed at once.

Olav waited until the last spasms in the body subsided, and a few more minutes after that. Then he turned the corpse onto its back. A little blood trickled through the hair, making a diagonal stripe across the forehead. Olav lifted the body under the arms and dragged it over to the attached milk storeroom.

Then he stepped out of the hut and into the night, where the wind was blowing snow and rushing and roaring through the trees. He would have to stay here until daylight. Olav went back inside and lay down on the bench.

So many men who had fallen by his hand were more worthy than this one.

Olav put more wood on the hearth. He needed to shake off this unhealthy feeling of remorse, or whatever it was. Teit had brought this upon himself. Bishop Torfinn himself had stated that a man who disgraced a woman and was then killed by the maiden's kinsmen must be largely regarded as a suicide, as if the man had been seeking his own violent death. And Teit? He had also been asking to die violently. It was meaningless for Olav to consider this death any worse than killing a man in battle. Teit had fallen with his sword in hand. The sword now lay there on the floor between the bench and bedstead.

He would never have been able to make a secure life for Ingunn as long as that miserable fool was running to the east and west, babbling about his misdeed, which he hadn't had sense enough to fully understand.

Olav was so cold that his teeth chattered even though the fire was roasting the front of him as he lay on the bench. But the back of his elk-hide tunic was sopping wet and stiff and ice-cold, and his boots were soaked through. He now noticed the wound on his left arm; he'd forgotten all about it, but it had started throbbing painfully.

He added plenty of wood to the fire. If the hut burned down, let it burn down.

No. For Ingunn's sake, he had to stay alive. She had waited long enough for her husband. He couldn't disappear now, not when she needed him most.

No, Teit, my boy, you're the one who has to give up, for that's not something I'm willing to do. Olav struggled to hiss these words as the full weight of the youth settled on his chest, crushing him. And he couldn't throw him off, for he felt drained of all strength. Teit showed the wide expanse of his white teeth, smiling as merrily as ever, in spite of the fact that the back of his skull had been split in half. *You don't realize, you poor fool, that the woman is mine, so you have to give up and take yourself away from here.*

Olav was awakened by his own hoarse scream as the nightmarish figure tumbled off him. It was almost pitch-dark in the hut, with only a slight glow from the embers in the hearth. The wind and snow were seeping through the walls, and his elk-hide tunic felt like an icy coat of mail.

Olav got up and went into the milk storeroom, fumbling his way in the dark. The dead man lay there, rigid and motionless and ice-cold. It must have been a dream. Olav seemed to have slept for several hours. He put more wood on the fire, intending to sit down so the heat would warm his back. But he couldn't bear to sit with his back to the black opening to the storeroom, nor did he want to sit facing it. So he was going to have to lie down on the bench again. He piled the hay sacks underneath him, then pulled the coverlet over him as best he could.

Occasionally sleep would overtake him like a heavy fog. Every time his thoughts became shrouded in this way, he would be startled awake by the dull, thudding pain inside him. The throbbing in his wounded arm was merely an echo of some agony deep inside. Then he would lie there, wide awake, with his thoughts again going round and round.

That fellow had merely got what he'd deserved. Olav had been forced to kill many better men in battle, and it had never weighed on his heart. There might be reason to pity Ingunn, but not this man. No. And if no one happened to mourn him, either here in Norway or back home in his own country, so much the better. Then no innocent person would grieve because this guilty fellow had been given his rightful punishment. All the past years that Olav had spent first with his uncle and then with the earl should have been enough to harden him. This was not the proper reaction. The man had got what he'd deserved. But then Olav's thoughts would circle round again.

He jolted up. No, he'd only dreamed that Teit was standing in the doorway holding a ladle and offering him milk. His body was still lying in the storeroom where it was supposed to be. No, Teit, I'm not afraid of you. If I'm frightened, you've never had sense enough to understand what it is I fear. My poor, little Ingunn—you mustn't be frightened of me.

And then Olav was once again wide awake.

There was now a new burden he needed to consider: what his next step should be. Should he announce the killing at the first farm he passed when he reached the village? Should he bring upon himself the blame for another murder before he was freed of the old one, and again be forced to pay fines and surrender property as restitution for his actions? And know that folks would be feverishly gossiping behind his back, wondering what a man such as himself could have had against that Icelandic vagabond? Oh, they'd no doubt say, it must be because of Ingunn Steinfinnsdatter. No, he couldn't do that.

But then there was the matter of how he should get rid of the body.

He'd watched the bodies of so many better men be tumbled overboard to vanish into the sea. And the bodies of many good farmer sons in Denmark had been left to the wolves and eagles after the earl's raids. But that was a matter for the earl, not Olav. He himself had never caused a dead man to be left behind without a Christian burial. And yet, if he was so weak that the killing of someone such as this Teit, the seducer of his wife, should weigh on him so heavily, then it was unlikely he'd be able to bear what he was now considering—something that was truly a sin. It would be an inescapable sin.

But if he announced that Teit had died at his hand, they would never be able to pretend that Ingunn's honor was untarnished.

Finally Olav must have dozed off, falling into a dreamless sleep that lasted for hours. The sun was shining through the cracks in the timbers when he opened his eyes. The fire in the hearth had gone out. He didn't hear any wind—not a sound except for the mating calls of black grouse both near and far, along with a few chirps from songbirds belatedly greeting the day.

Olav got up, stretched, and rubbed his face. His arm felt stiff and a bit sore, but not too bad. He went over to the door to peer outside.

White everywhere. The sun was high overhead in the blue, cloudless sky. The fog had settled like a white sea over the ground, gilded by sunlight, with the crests of forested ridges and higher crags sticking up, golden with new-fallen snow that sparkled in the sun. Flashes of red and blue glinted across the white carpet of the meadow; hares and birds had already left their tracks in the new snow, and black grouse were calling and cackling from the forest.

Here he stood in this endless white world of desolation and snow, the only person in this wilderness, yet he had no idea where to hide that poor wretch of a dead man. Should he break through the snowy carpet to bury him? No. It had be done in such a way that animals couldn't get to the body. He refused to allow that to happen. Should he just leave the corpse here, to be discovered when folks moved up to their mountain pasture? That was impossible. Then it would come out who the dead man was. And the rest of the story would follow.

The two pairs of skis stood in a drift next to the wall, covered in snow. Olav took the good pair that he'd borrowed from the monastery, wiped off the snow, and laid them down. He clenched his teeth hard, and his face took on a rigid, closed expression.

He went back inside the hut and smoothed out the hay sacks and coverlet where he'd slept. Then he brought the body from the milk shed and placed it on the bed, trying to straighten out the man's limbs. There was dried blood and brain matter in the hair, but not much on the gray-frozen face. He was grinning wickedly, that Teit. Olav couldn't close his mouth or his eyes. Then he covered the dead man's face with the old, worn, blood-stained leather cap.

He dug in the hearth to stir up a few sparks. On top he placed pieces of birch bark, twigs, and plenty of wood. The fire was soon burning steadily. In the milk shed he found a bundle of hay. Olav carried it into the room and scattered it between the hearth and the bed. When he stumbled over Teit's sword, he picked it up and placed it on the boy's chest. Then he tore up bunches of bark and an armful of twigs and tossed them on top of the hay on the floor.

Now the fire in the hearth was a regular bonfire. Olav pulled out a burning piece of firewood and tossed it onto the hay. With a roar and a whine as the birch bark caught fire, flames shot into the air. Olav dashed outside, stuck his skis under his arm, and then waded up the slope through the newly fallen snow.

At the top, where the wind had swept bare the old crusted snow, he paused to kneel down and securely fasten the skis to his boots. Then he picked up his staff. But he stayed where he was until he saw wisps of gray smoke seeping out of every crack in the walls. Quietly he said the Christian prayers he knew, for terror was about to overpower him. Was this blasphemy? But he felt as if he were being forced to say these words. A dead man was inside that hut, so he had to pray.

Then he remembered that he'd forgotten his axe inside, along with the provisions sack, though it was empty. By now the wooden tub with whey would be burning, along with the flatbread. Petty things in the midst of everything else, and yet . . . He had never before shown disdain for God's gifts. He would pick up even the smallest scrap of bread that he'd dropped on the floor and kiss it before he ate it. That was practically the only thing he recalled from his great-grandfather's teachings.

To hell with that. In wartime he'd seen loft rooms and farmers' homes, many of them packed with people, go up in flames. And better men than this one had been consigned, both living and dead, to the flames. Why should he consider this instance to be so much worse?

In the past they used to burn fallen chieftains in this way. You've been given a cremation befitting a minor king, Teit, my boy, with your sword in your arms and food and drink beside you.

The smoke kept trickling out, completely shrouding the hut. The fire gleamed from inside, and the first flames now reached the eaves. Olav set off swiftly, skiing downhill where there was no trail.

He tried to console himself by imagining that when folks came up to their mountain pasture in the summer, they would no doubt find bones among the ashes. And finally Teit's body would be given a Christian burial.

He skied down toward a streambed, making the snow spray up around his ears, then flew across the hollow and paused for a moment on the opposite bank to look back. The crest of the ridge where he'd come from formed a long, graceful curve, the white snow glittering with sunlight against the blue. In one place a little dark cloud of smoke was billowing.

I took revenge for the defilement of my marriage bed. Shouldn't a man be able to answer to God for such a deed? He fell with sword in hand, Lord. You saw that yourself.

An hour later Olav raced between the tops of a snow-covered fence along several white meadows. There he saw a house. In many places the drifts on the rooftop had merged with the ground, but smoke was coming out of the hearth vent. Someone had made a path from the house to the cowshed, and manure had recently been added to the heap outside.

Olav gazed across the countryside as he turned his skis and came to a stop. The world was a spotless white, with blue in all the shadows. Far to the north he could see down to the bottom of a wide valley, scattered with large farms.

He could say that he had quarreled with his companion last night, and they'd ended up taking to their weapons. And then fire from the hearth had spread to the hay.

With a start he pulled himself together and continued skiing across the meadow.

Late in the afternoon he arrived at Miklebø. Arnvid was away. The day before he'd gone out to the forest with both of his sons to hunt for mating wood grouse. But the household servants gave their noble master's best friend a hearty welcome.

The next day at sunset Olav was standing outside in the courtyard when Arnvid and his sons returned home. Magnus was leading the horse, which wore snowshoes, as did the men. The horse was loaded down with sacks and other provisions, as well as several bunches of colorful dead birds. Arnvid and Steinar were carrying skis and crossbows and big quivers, now empty of arrows.

Arnvid quietly and warmly greeted his guest, and his sons added a friendly and polite welcome. They were now half-grown, two handsome and promising young men with fair complexions.

"As you can see, I changed my mind."

"And well you did," said Arnvid with a faint smile.

"But did you travel through the forest with no other weapon but that little spear point?" asked Arnvid as they sat at the table and talked while the food was being brought in.

Olav said that he'd also had an axe, but he'd lost it in the night. He'd used it to cut some branches to lie on. And yes, he'd found a hut where he could sleep. No, he didn't know what the place was called. The Graadal hut? Yes, that could be it. No, in the dark and with new fallen snow, he hadn't been able to find the axe. And he had a small cut on his upper arm, caused by the axe when it flew out of his hands.

Arnvid wanted to take a look at the wound before they went to bed. It was a clean, straight gash and looked as if it would heal quickly. But Arnvid couldn't understand how Olav happened to cut himself in such a spot. Oh, those old axes with a long point at both the top and bottom were certainly temperamental, and not the best of tools for cutting down spruce branches.

VIII

Ingunn gave birth on the third day after the Feast of Saint Hallvard. When Tora picked up the newborn infant from the floor, the mother wrapped her arms around her head and screamed as if afraid of what she might hear or see.

After Ingunn had been put to bed, Tora brought the newly swaddled child over to her.

"Take a look at your son, my sister. He's so lovely," Tora pleaded. "He has long black hair."

But Ingunn merely screamed and pulled the coverlet over her head.

Tora had sent for the priest the night before when things seem bleak for the child. But now that she could see there was a little life in the boy after all, she asked the priest to christen the infant before he left. They asked the mother what his name should be, but she merely groaned and hid under the covers. Neither Magnhild nor Tora had any wish to name the boy after a man from their lineage, so they asked the priest to choose his name. He replied that on this day the church commemorated Saint Eirik, king and martyr, and so he would name Ingunn's child after him.

Tora Steinfinnsdatter was both angry and sorrowful as she sat with this tiny bird of ill omen on her lap. He was the son of her own sister, yet the mother would have nothing to do with him.

On the third day after giving birth, Ingunn fell terribly ill. Tora thought the cause was the milk that was now bursting in her breasts. Ingunn couldn't bear to move, nor could she stand to have anyone touch her. She couldn't swallow even a morsel of food, but she complained constantly of an unbearable thirst. Tora said it would only make matters worse if she had anything to drink; then the milk would rise all the way up into her head. "I don't dare give you a drop to drink unless you let me put Eirik to your breast," Tora told her. Even then Ingunn refused to receive her child.

That evening, when Tora was readying the child for bed, she happened to topple over the water basin, and she had no more warm water in the room. For a moment she hesitated. Then she threw a cloth over the naked child and carried him over to the bed. Ingunn lay in a feverish stupor, and before she could offer any resistance, Tora placed Eirik in her arms. Then she left.

She took her time over in the cookhouse. But all of a sudden she grew deathly afraid and ran back to the house. In the doorway she could already hear Ingunn's loud, heart-wrenching sobs. Tora rushed over to her and tore off the coverlet.

"In God's name! You haven't harmed him, have you?"

Ingunn didn't reply. Eirik lay there, with his knees drawn up and his hands held close to his nose. As tiny and thin and brownish-red as he was, he seemed happy to be near his mother's warmth. The look in his open, dark eyes seemed to signal that he was thinking.

Tora heaved a sigh of relief. She took the pail of water that Dalla brought, then picked up the boy to finish tending to him. Afterward, she carried the swaddled infant back to the bed.

"Shall I give him to you?" she asked, keeping her voice as impassive as possible.

With a long, drawn-out wail, Ingunn raised her arms and Tora put the child on the bed. Her hands trembled a bit as she did her utmost to keep talking about this and that as she propped the pillows under her sister and then put Eirik to her breast, making sure that he began to suckle.

After that, Ingunn would dutifully take the boy whenever Tora brought him over and placed him at her breast. Yet she continued to be just as sorrowful, and she seemed deeply despondent.

She was still keeping to her bed on the evening when Arnvid arrived at Berg on horseback. Fru Magnhild had sent word to Miklebø as soon as the child was born.

Arnvid came into the room, greeting Fru Magnhild and Tora calmly and courteously, as if there was nothing out of the ordinary about his visit. But when he went over to the bed and looked into Ingunn's terrified eyes, his face took on a strangely stony expression. A fiery crimson spread over her face and throat as her thin fingers fumbled with embarrassment at her bosom. She drew her shift closed as she pulled away the nursing infant, who began crying at once, and then turned his face toward the man.

"Ah, he's the sort that women call 'lovely,' isn't he?" said Arnvid with a smile. He touched his finger to the child's cheek. "It's a shame you were in such haste to have him christened. You should have been my godson, kinsman."

Arnvid sat down on the step next to the bed and slid his hand across the coverlet so he could touch the child's head and the mother's arm. He found it distressing to see Ingunn shaking so badly. And then, as he'd been expecting, Fru Magnhild asked about Olav.

"I bring all of you greetings from him. We parted in Hamar, for he wanted to hasten home to his estate. He intends to come back here around Saint Sunniva's Feast Day. By then Ingunn should be strong enough that she can accompany him south." He pressed his hand firmly against her arm, hoping to calm her.

He answered the questions that Magnhild and Tora asked him, telling them what he knew about the plans Olav now had in mind. He and the two women pretended that all was well, even though they knew that each of them was thinking the same thing: how would things go for these two? Here lay the bride with another man's child at her breast, and the bridegroom was fully aware of this as he rode south to make his home ready to receive his wife.

Finally Arnvid said that he'd like to have a few words with Ingunn alone. The two women stood up, and Tora took the child from his mother to put him back in the cradle.

"What about the boy?" she asked. "Does Olav intend for him to come south with his mother?"

"As far as I know, that is his intention, yes."

Then Arnvid was alone with Ingunn. She lay in bed with her eyes closed. He reached out to wipe the perspiration from her hairline.

"Olav asked me to stay here until he can come to take you home."

"Why?" she whispered fearfully.

"Oh. You know . . ." He hesitated. "Folks are a little more careful about what they say if there's any risk that their gossip might reach a man's ears."

Beads of sweat appeared on Ingunn's face. Her words were scarcely audible as she said, "Arnvid. Is there no way out for Olav? That he might be free?"

"No. And he has given no sign that he wishes to be free," replied Arnvid after a moment.

"What if we appealed to . . . to the archbishop on bended knee, and promised to pay a fine?"

"His bishop could grant him permission to live apart from you, if Olav should seek such dispensation. But the fact that he now wants to bring you home and live with you . . . He is doing this of his own free will. To sever the bond between the two of you so that Olav might be a free man, able to take another woman as his wife? I don't believe that's something even the pope in Rome could do."

"Not even if I retreated to a cloister?" she asked, trembling.

"As far as I know, you would have to have Olav's permission to do that. And he would still not be free to marry again. But you are surely the worst suited of all women to become a pious nun, my poor Ingunn. And you need to remember what Olav himself said to me. He said that back then he was the one who put all his efforts into petitioning the Holy Church to judge whether the two of you were husband and wife or not. He personally sought Bishop Torfinn's pronouncement that your coupling was a binding marriage in accordance with God's law, and not merely loose conduct. And Lord Torfinn said it was so. As stern as this bishop was toward criminals and those who tarnished a woman's honor, he was willing to demand that Olav should be allowed to pay a fine and become reconciled with Einar's heirs. Don't you see that Olav can't go back on his word? Nor, by his own account, does he have any desire to do so.

"Oh, here I sit, forgetting that you're still weak. Don't worry, Ingunn. Keep in mind what sort of man Olav is. Stubborn and determined. What he wants is what he wants. And I suppose you've heard the saying: as faithful as a troll."

There was nothing about Ingunn's appearance that revealed she was feeling more hopeful. Yet the other women were greatly relieved now that they'd been assured that Olav Audunssøn was not going to raise any objections but would instead take as his wife this woman he had once demanded in such an arrogant and obstinate way—and show forbearance regarding the misdeed she had committed in the meantime. When Ingunn's kinsmen—Ivar, her brothers, and Haakon—heard all the details of the matter, they said that Olav had already offended them grievously: first when he made his bride his own, second when he raised a case against her guardians before the bishop's court, and finally when he killed Einar, who had rebuked him. So it seemed only right that Olav should now remain silent, cover up Ingunn's shame, and do his utmost to bring this calamitous matter to a reputable end. And Hestviken was far away. Even if folks in the south found out that his wife had given birth to another man's child before Olav Audunssøn wed her, this marriage of his would be considered no worse than that of many other respected and heralded men. There was nothing more anyone in his home district needed to know, unless Olav and Ingunn foolishly allowed word to slip out that before she had the child, she had already been bound to Olav, and in a manner that would cause at least some priests to say that the boy had been conceived in whoredom.

Ivar and Magnhild explained all this to Ingunn. Her face was pale and her eyes dark as she listened to them. Arnvid could see that she was greatly distressed by what they told her.

"What do you say about all of this, Arnvid?" she asked one day after Ivar and Haakon had come to see her, wanting to discuss further their view of the matter. She was now able to get out of bed in the daytime.

"What I say is this," replied Arnvid quietly. "God knows things are bad enough, but surely you must realize there is some truth to what they've said."

"How can you say that and call yourself Olav's friend!" She leaped to her feet in anger.

"I *am* his friend, as I think I've shown on several occasions," replied Arnvid. "And I won't deny that I share the blame that things have taken such a bad turn. Perhaps the advice I gave Olav was unwise. I was too young and naive. And I should not have remained in the cloister guest quarters on that night when Einar took it upon himself to challenge us. But it will do my friend no good if I, or you, choose to hide our heads under our wings and refuse to see that the Steinfinnssøns are at least partially in the right."

Ingunn burst into tears.

"So even you begrudge Olav any better consideration? None of you seems to deem his honor of any worth. I'm the only one who does."

"That may be," said Arnvid. "And now he'll have to lie in the bed that you've made for him."

Ingunn abruptly stopped crying. She raised her head to look at him.

"Oh, Ingunn. I should not have said that. But I've been sorely vexed by everything they've been saying for so long," he added wearily.

"But what you said just now is true."

The child lay on the bed, wailing loudly. Ingunn went over to pick him up. Arnvid noticed what he'd also seen before. Even though she handled the infant gently and appeared to be fond of him, Ingunn seemed nevertheless to touch her child with some reluctance, and she was quite clumsy when she had to tend to him. Eirik was also a plaintive and restless child, constantly whimpering whenever his mother held him; he was willing to suckle for only brief moments at a time. Tora said this was because Ingunn was so despondent and anxious that she was unable to give him much milk. Eirik was always hungry.

The infant was again quickly done nursing, and then he lay there whining as he struggled with his mother's empty breast. Ingunn sighed. Then she fastened her clothing and stood up to cradle the child in her arms as she walked back and forth in the room. Arnvid sat and watched.

"Would you accept my offer, Ingunn, if I told you I would take the child as my foster son?" he now asked. "I would raise your son in my home and treat him as I have my own sons."

Ingunn paused before answering. Then she said, "I know you would be a most loyal kinsman to the boy. You might have expected that I'd be more grateful for all the kindness you've shown me all these years. If I die, I'd like you to . . . I'd like you to take care of Eirik. That would ease my final hour."

"Now is not the time to speak of such things," said Arnvid, trying to smile. "Not when you've only just regained your health and escaped mortal danger."

When Eirik was six weeks old, the woman whom Fru Magnhild had made arrangements with early in the spring arrived at Berg. She had agreed to accept and raise a child who had been born in secret, yet rumors about Ingunn had already spread widely. Various suggestions had been made as to who the father might be, but most people thought it had to be that Icelander who had visited Berg so often the previous summer. He had disappeared. No doubt he'd fled, fearing the woman's wealthy kinsmen. Now the foster mother—her name was Hallveig—came to Berg one evening to find out what had happened to the child. She'd heard no more about the matter.

Before Fru Magnhild could decide what to say, Ingunn went over to the woman. She said she was the child's mother, and Hallveig should take the boy home with her when she left in the morning. Hallveig looked at Eirik and said he was a lovely child. While she waited for food to be brought to her, she picked up the child and put him to her breast.

Ingunn stood close and watched as Eirik suckled hungrily. This was undoubtedly the first time in his young life that he drank until he was sated. Then Ingunn took the child and carried him over to her bed, while the woman was shown to a different house to sleep. It had been decided that she should ride up over the mountain early the next day, before folks were awake on the neighboring farms.

The two sisters were then alone in Aasa's house, and Tora lit the holy candle that they still burned every night. Ingunn sat on the edge of the bed with her back to the child. Eirik lay next to the wall, making little sounds of contentment.

"Ingunn, don't do this," said Tora solemnly. "Don't send your child away like this. It's a sin to make such a decision when it's not necessary or required."

Ingunn didn't reply.

"He's smiling," said Tora, moving the candlelight toward the boy. "Look at your son, Ingunn. He can smile now. How sweet, how very sweet he is."

"Yes, I've seen it," said Ingunn. "He has smiled several times during the last few days."

"I can't understand why you want to do this. How can you bear to do it?"

"Don't you see that I refuse to have this child of mine under Olav's roof, asking him to foster this boy that a runaway postulant left behind?"

"Shame on you for speaking that way about your own child!" said Tora, distraught.

"I *am* ashamed."

"Ingunn, if you do this, I know you'll regret it for as long as you live. You mustn't willingly abandon your own child."

"After what I've done, I will never be without regret."

Tora replied vehemently, "True enough. And in that regard no one on earth can help you. You have betrayed Olav badly. All of us agree about that. And no doubt your shame is a much heavier burden for him than for the rest of us. But are you now going to betray your child as well? This innocent young life that you've carried under your heart for nearly forty long weeks? Let me tell you, my sister, I can't believe that even Mary, the mother of God, would ask for mercy for a mother who forsakes her own son.

"Take heed, Ingunn," Tora went on. "You have caused great harm to all of us, and worst to Olav. This child is the only one you haven't yet betrayed!"

The sisters said no more to each other before going to bed. Ingunn held the boy close, with her lips pressed to his damp, silky-soft forehead, hearing over and over again her sister's last words ringing in her ears. Eirik's tiny head rested against her throat the same way the church statue of Jesus Christ showed him pressing his face to his mother's neck. How would he judge those mothers who cast aside such a little boy? "And Jesus called a little child unto him, and set him in the midst of them." In the church in Hamar there was a painting of Christ nailed to the cross between two thieves, but his mother stood close by. Faint with sorrow and fatigue, she stayed with her son during his final struggle, just as she had kept vigil over his first night's sleep here on earth. No, Ingunn knew full well that she didn't dare ask Mary's son to forgive her sins unless she gave up what she now intended to do. And she didn't dare ask the Mother of God to plead with her son on her behalf, not if she chose to abandon her own son.

"Ingunn," whispered Tora as she wept. "I did not mean to hurt you when I spoke so harshly. But it will be worse than anything else if you betray your child."

Ingunn's voice broke when she replied.

"I know that. I've seen that you are fond of Eirik. You must try . . . when I'm gone, you must . . . You must see to Eirik as best you can."

"I will. I'll do as much as I dare, without drawing Haakon's ire."

Neither the two sisters nor the child slept much that night. Toward morning, just as they'd finally fallen sound asleep, Fru Magnhild came to wake them. The woman was ready to leave.

Tora watched her sister swaddle the child, hoping Ingunn wouldn't dare give him up. Then Fru Magnhild again said that Olav himself had greatly wronged all of them, and it wouldn't be unreasonable if he had to accept that Ingunn brought her child along when she went south to join him. They wouldn't have to keep Eirik at Hestviken. Olav could send him away to a foster family.

Then, with a stern and composed expression, Ingunn carried the child outside and gave him to Hallveig. She stood and watched as the woman rode away, holding the tiny boy who was her companion.

About the time of the midmorning meal, it turned out that Ingunn had run off. Arnvid and Tora raced out to look for her. They found her wandering about in the field behind the barn, and no matter how much they begged and pleaded, they couldn't persuade her to go back inside. Tora and Magnhild were beside themselves. It was considered dangerous for a married woman to ramble about in that manner before she had gone to church for the first time after giving birth. So what would folks say about a mother in Ingunn's situation? Arnvid thought they should send word to Brother Vegard. Ingunn also needed to be granted absolution for her sin and become reconciled with God and the church before Olav returned. Then they could accompany each other to mass after he'd been granted the consent of her kinsmen. Arnvid promised to stay with Ingunn and follow her until he was able to get her back inside.

They ended up far north of the estate in a grove of birch trees. Arnvid kept close on her heels, unable to find a single consoling word to say to Ingunn. He was as worn out as a thrall, and hungry. By now it was late afternoon, but when he implored Ingunn to be sensible and go back with him, she didn't utter a word in reply. He might as well have been talking to a rock.

For a moment she paused to lean against a tree, with one arm around the trunk and her forehead pressed to the bark, as she panted like an animal. Arnvid loudly beseeched God for help. He thought she had gone half-mad.

Finally they came to a small knoll where they sat down side by side in the afternoon sun, neither of them speaking. Suddenly Ingunn ripped open her gown and squeezed one breast, sending a thin spurt of milk onto the blazing hot stone. It quickly dried, leaving little shiny spots.

Arnvid jumped up, grabbed her around the waist, and pulled her to her feet. He began shaking her back and forth.

"It's time for you to behave decently, Ingunn."

The moment he let her go, she fell full-length to the ground. Again he lifted her up.

"It's time for you to go back inside with me. Otherwise I will have to beat you!"

Then the tears came. Ingunn sagged in the man's arms, wailing her heart out. Arnvid held her, pressing her face against his shoulder and rocking her this way and that. She sobbed until she had no strength left. Then she wept quietly, tears pouring down her face. Arnvid fastened the bodice of her gown. She allowed him to half-lead and half-carry her back home, where he could hand her over to the care of the women.

Late that evening Arnvid was sitting outside in the courtyard, talking to Grim and Dalla, when Ingunn appeared in the doorway to her house. The moment she saw the old servants, she stopped in fright. Arnvid stood up and went over to her. Dalla left, but Grim stayed standing where he was, and when Ingunn walked past him, accompanied by Arnvid, the old man raised his worn old face and spat at her so the spittle slid down into his beard. When Arnvid seized hold of the man and shoved him aside, Grim made several ugly gestures and muttered the most vulgar and coarse epithets that thralls used to hurl at loose women. Then he turned on his heel to follow his sister and walked away.

Arnvid took Ingunn's arm and hurried her toward the main house.

"You can't very well expect anything else," he said angrily though at the same time trying to comfort her. "You'll have to tolerate such behavior while you're here. Things will be easier for you when you live in a place where folks don't know as much about you. But go inside now. You've tempted fate more than enough by running around outdoors today, and now the sun is about to set."

"Wait just a few moments," Ingunn pleaded. "My head is burning terribly, and it's so nice and cool out here."

It was quite dark for the time of year. Clouds were piled up across the entire sky, and the sunset was gilding them to the north. The air had turned crimson beneath the vaulted clouds, with their gleam reflected in the bay.

Ingunn whispered, "Talk to me, Arnvid. Can't you tell me something about Olav?"

Arnvid shrugged, as if impatient.

"I just want to hear you say his name," she quietly implored.

"It seems to me you must have heard it often enough these past weeks," said Arnvid with a sigh. "For my part, I've long since grown weary of this whole matter."

"That's not what I meant," she said gently. "Not about how he can be so useful a man for us now, or anything of the sort. But Arnvid, can't you simply talk to me about Olav? You who are so fond of him? You're his friend, after all."

But Arnvid stubbornly remained silent. It suddenly occurred to him that year after year he had allowed himself to be tormented by these two. He had done so much for them, that it felt as if he'd cut into his own flesh and twisted the knife in the wound. He wanted no more of this. "Come inside now."

Tora met them and said that she and her sister could sleep in Magnhild's house that night. It would be too distressing to stay in the other house, now that the child was gone.

When they were about to go to bed, Ingunn asked her sister to share Fru Magnhild's bed in the alcove. "I fear I won't sleep much tonight, and I know how sleeplessness can keep someone else awake."

There were two beds in the main hall. Arnvid was to sleep in one of them, and Ingunn in the other.

She lay there for a long time, waiting for Arnvid to fall asleep. Time passed, and she could tell that he was still awake, though they didn't speak to each other.

Now and then she tried to say her prayers, the *Paternoster* and *Ave*, but her thoughts kept whirling this way and that, and she rarely managed to say the prayer to the end. She said them for Olav and for Eirik. She couldn't very well say any prayers for herself, now that she'd decided to cast herself into damnation, with full knowledge and of her own volition. But since this was something she *had* to do, perhaps she wouldn't receive the harshest of punishment in Hell. Even there she thought it would be a relief to think about the fact that when she severed the bond between them and sank to the very depths, she would be leaving Olav behind as a free and redeemed man.

She didn't even feel any fear. It was as if she was finally worn out and hardened. She had no desire to see Olav again, or the child. Tomorrow Brother Vegard would arrive. That's what they'd told her, but she wouldn't see him. She didn't want to look *upward*, nor did she want to look *forward*, and she felt it was right that she should be damned—for she refused to accept anything that would be necessary if her soul was to be saved. Remorse, prayer, working and continuing on, seeing and speaking to those people whose company she would have share if she was to attempt to keep on living—she couldn't bear thinking of all that. She couldn't bear even the thought of God. To look *down*, to be alone and surrounded by darkness—that's what she wanted instead. And she saw her own soul, as bare and dark as the mountain ravaged by fire, and she was the one who had lit the blaze and allowed everything inside her to be consumed by the flames. There was nothing left for her.

Yet there was one *Paternoster* she said for Olav: please let him forget me. And an *Ave Maria* for Eirik: now I am no longer his mother.

Finally Arnvid began to snore. Ingunn waited a while longer, until convinced he was sound asleep. Then she slipped out of bed, put on her clothes, and crept out.

It was the darkest hour. Beyond the estate a wing of clouds hovered above the ridge and seemed to cast a shadow over the countryside. The forest surrounding the village was sated with a nighttime gloom that seemed like a thin, gray haze over the fields, settling around the curled-leaf shrubs on the ground so that they looked shaggy with darkness. But higher up the sky was clear and white, casting a pale reflection in the bay. On the heights on the opposite side of the water a sheen of the approaching dawn was already visible above the forest.

At the gate to the pasture Ingunn paused to replace the guardrail behind her. There was not a sound in the summer night except for the corncrake calling in the grain. Dew dripped from the alder thickets on the path along the stream, and the leaves and grass gave off a bitter scent in the darkness of the grove.

The thickets grew all the way down to the estate's boat landing. And now Ingunn saw that the lake had risen a great deal during her confinement. The water now reached as high as the turf and had flowed over the end of the dock connected to shore.

She stopped in confusion. With a jolt, terror suddenly overwhelmed her, splintering her hardened sense of composure. No, she couldn't do it. She couldn't wade through the water and then out onto the dock. She whimpered helplessly with fright. Then she lifted her skirts and set one foot in the water.

Her heart felt as if it were forcing its way into her throat when the icy water ran into her shoes. She gasped and swallowed hard. But then she set off, wading straight through her own fear, teetering unsteadily on the sharp stones that covered the shoreline under the water. There was a deafening sound of splashing and gurgling all around her as she moved forward. Then she put her foot on the dock.

It was submerged under water for a good distance out. The planks dipped slightly between the posts and gave a bit under her feet. The water reached high up her calves. Farther out the planks seemed to float upward but sank down when she stepped on them. Each time she held her breath, afraid that a misstep would land her in the lake. Finally she came to the very end of the dock, which rose above the surface of the water.

Not a trace of her hardened composure now remained. Panic had robbed her of all thought. Yet her trembling hands blindly set about doing what she had planned. She took off the long woven belt that was wrapped three times around her waist, then pulled out her knife and cut it in half. She used one piece to bind her skirts around her legs beneath her knees; she wanted to be decently clad when she was found, if she should happen to drift ashore. She tied the other piece of cloth crosswise around her chest and then slipped her hands underneath. She had decided it might go faster if she couldn't struggle as she sank. Then she took one last, long breath and threw herself into the water.

Arnvid awoke and lay in a groggy state, about to sink back to sleep. Then, with a dull thudding of his heart, he came wide awake, aware that what had startled him out of his slumber was the sound of someone going outdoors.

Swiftly he jumped up and went over to her bed, fumbling his way in the dark. The bed was still warm, but empty. As if not trusting his own senses, he kept on fumbling and searching, running his hands along the wall timbers, the headboard, and the foot of the bed.

Then he stuck his bare feet into his shoes, pulled the cotehardie over his head, groaning all the while. He had no idea how long she'd been gone. He ran through the grain fields and out to the meadow facing the lake. He caught a glimpse of someone out on the dock. He ran north, crossing the meadow, listening to his own footsteps thump, thump, thumping on the dry turf. When he reached the water's edge, he kept on running, wading far enough out until he was able to swim.

Ingunn awoke in her old bed in Aasa's house. At first she was aware only of the terrible ache in her head, which felt as if it might burst, and the painful sensation of her skin all over her body, as if it had been scorched.

Sunlight was flowing in through the open hearth vent, and she could see a scrap of clear sky. The blue smoke drifting up under the rafters turned brown against the bright sky when it slipped outside. There it began swirling quickly through the grass of the sod roof.

Then she remembered. And nearly fainted. The relief, the feeling that she'd been saved, was so overwhelming.

Arnvid suddenly appeared from somewhere in the room. He put his arm under her back to support her and held a wooden cup to her lips. It held a watery, lukewarm porridge, slimy and restorative, tasting of herbs and honey.

Ingunn drank every drop as she peered at him over the rim of the cup. He took away the empty cup and set it on the floor. Then he sat down on the step next to the bed with his head bowed and his hands hanging between his knees. A painful shame seemed to have over-powered both of them.

At long last Ingunn said quietly, "I don't understand . . . I don't remember . . . being saved."

"I got there at the last possible moment," said Arnvid curtly.

"I don't understand," she repeated. "I'm sore all over."

"Today is the third day. You've been lying here in a fever. No doubt it was the milk that affected your mind. And you grew so cold in the water that we had to ply you with hot ale and wine. You've been awake a few times before, but you probably don't remember."

The bad taste in her mouth seemed stronger, and she asked for water. Arnvid went out to get some.

While she drank the water, he stood and looked at her. There was so much weighing on his heart that he wanted to say, but he hardly knew where to begin. Then he blurted it out.

"Olav is here. He arrived yesterday around midafternoon prayer."

Ingunn sank back, feeling ill and dizzy. It felt as if she were sinking and sinking. Yet deep inside a tiny spark seemed to stir, wanting to flare up and burst into flame—joy, hope, a will to live, as meaningless as that might seem.

"He was here for a while last night. And he asked us to tell him the moment you were awake. Shall I bring Olav now? The others are over in the main house. It's time for the midmorning meal."

Ingunn paused before asking, her voice quavering, "Did Olav say anything? Have you told him . . . about what happened?"

Arnvid's face abruptly crumpled. For a moment he bit his lower lip. Then he couldn't keep from saying, "Ingunn, didn't you think about where you'd be today if you'd succeeded with what you intended?"

"Yes, I did," she whispered. She turned her face to the wall and asked quietly, "Is that what Olav said? What did he say, Arnvid?"

"He hasn't said a word about this."

After a moment Arnvid asked again, "Shall I bring Olav here now?"

"No, no. Wait a little while. I don't want to be lying in bed. I want to sit up."

"Then I'll send one of the women to help you. You don't have the strength to get dressed on your own, do you?" said Arnvid doubtfully.

"Not Tora or Magnhild," Ingunn begged him.

She sat on the bench next to the wall at the gable end of the room and waited. She'd put on her black cloak without fully knowing why, but she had wrapped it tightly around her body and pulled the hood over her head. Her face was white and cold with fear. When the door opened, and she caught a glimpse of the man who ducked to step inside, she closed her eyes again and dropped her head forward. She pressed her feet hard on the floor and gripped the edge of the bench with both hands because she was shaking so badly.

He stopped when he came close to the hearth. Ingunn didn't dare lift her gaze; she merely stared at the man's feet. He was not wearing any shoes, only tight-fitting hose with a slit at the ankles and laces above. She fixed her eyes on the laces, as if they could provide some respite from her swirling thoughts. She'd never seen that sort of style of hose for a man before, but the design was cleverly done, making them fit the narrow calf as snugly as if they'd been molded.

"Good day, Ingunn."

His voice seemed to stab right through her. She slumped forward even more. Olav came closer until he was standing in front of her. She could see the hem of his tunic, which was light blue, knee-length, and heavily draped. Her eyes crept up as high as his belt. It was adorned with the same silver rosettes and the buckle with the image of Saint Olav. He wore a dagger with an elk-horn haft embellished with silver.

Then she saw that he was holding out his hand toward her. She placed her thin, clammy hand in his, and he closed his fingers around hers. His hand felt rough and dry and warm. Quickly she pulled away.

"Won't you look at me, Ingunn?"

She sensed that she ought to stand up.

"No, stay where you are," he said quickly.

Then she looked up. Their eyes met, and then they kept on staring at each other.

Olav felt all his blood being drawn home to his heart. He froze, and the skin on his face went rigid. He had to clamp his lips tightly together. His eyelids fell nearly closed, and he had no strength to open them again. Never had he known that a man could feel so robbed of all power.

The unfathomable suffering and agony in her poor eyes—that was what drew his own naked soul up into the light. Gone was everything he had thought and intended and decided. He sensed that great and weighty things had now all but vanished from his mind; he was incapable of holding on to them. What remained was only the latest and deepest cruel certainty that she was flesh of his flesh and life of his life, and no matter how mistreated and despoiled and broken she might be, it could never be otherwise. Their life's roots had been entwined from the first moment he could remember. And now that he saw how death had seized hold of her with both hands, he felt as if he too had barely managed to escape from being torn apart. Then a longing came over him so forcefully that it shook him to his very core—a longing to pull her desperately close, to hide both her and himself.

"Perhaps you'll allow me to sit down?" He felt so strange, so weak in the knees. Then he sat down on the bench, a short distance from her.

Ingunn was shaking even harder. His face had looked as hard as stone—gray around the bloodless streak of his lips, and those oddly gleaming blue-green eyes of his had stared unseeing from beneath his drooping lids. Oh God, God, please have mercy on me. She thought that as yet she had only partially realized what terrible misfortune she had caused. But now she would soon find out. That's what she'd read in Olav's stony face. Now, when she thought she could bear no more, now she would hear the worst.

Olav glanced at her from under his half-closed eyelids.

"You needn't be afraid of me, Ingunn." He spoke calmly and quietly, but there was a certain hoarseness to his voice, as if something might be caught in his throat.

"Think no more about what I said when I was last here—that I might treat you harshly. Back then I was still . . . enraged about what happened. But now I've come to my senses, and you mustn't be frightened. You will be treated well at Hestviken, as much as that's within my power."

Ingunn replied with quiet despair, "Olav, you mustn't . . . Could we live together at Hestviken after this? Could you truly live there with me and remember every day that—"

"If I must, then I can," he said tersely. "There's no way out of it, Ingunn. Yet never with a single word will I remind you of all this. That I promise you."

Ingunn said, "But you are not the sort of person to forget easily, Olav. Do you truly think you could avoid remembering every evening, when you lay down by my side, that someone else had—"

"Yes," he said, cutting off her words.

"And keep in mind," he went on, his voice as calm as before, "that Hestviken is far away from here—farther than you know. Things may be easier for both of us than we think, Ingunn, when we're living far away from these districts where everything happened to the two of us. From me you will never see a single sign that I'm thinking about any of this," he added fiercely.

Ingunn said, "Olav, I am beaten and broken. Is it true that there is no way for you to be free of me, now that I have brought such shame upon myself? I don't see how that can be, when they said they could separate us back then, even though we had been betrothed from the time we were children, and we had slept in each other's arms."

"I have never asked whether I might win release from my marriage. During all these years I have considered myself bound, and I've been content with that, just as I'm content with it now. This was what my father wished for me. You say that I'm not the sort to forget easily. No, but neither can I forget that our fathers promised us to each other when we were so young; or all the years we grew up together, sleeping in the same bed and eating from the same plate, and sharing nearly everything we owned. And when we were full-grown, then it was between us as you said. There are undoubtedly many things for which I must answer before God's judgment," he said in a low voice, "so I can certainly forgive you."

"That's kind of you, Olav, and good to know. But I want to ask you to wait a year and not do anything about this matter during that time. I am tired and ill. Perhaps I won't live very long. Then you'll be glad that you can take a wife who is free of shame, so that a woman without honor may never be mistress of your estate, to besmirch either your table or your bed."

"Enough," he whispered, his voice breaking. "Don't talk of such things. When they told me what you had tried to do . . ." Overwhelmed, he fell silent.

"I doubt very much that I'd have the strength to try such a deed again," she said. A spasm, almost like a smile, passed over her face. "I will be a pious woman from now on, Olav, and repent for my sins during all the time that God may grant me to live. But I don't think that will be for long. I think I'm already carrying death inside me."

"That's only because you haven't yet recovered from your illness," Olav protested.

"Ruined," she lamented. "That's what I am. And faded. Everyone says that I've lost all color. My whole life I've shown little wisdom, and now I've lost both courage and strength. What use or joy would you have from a wife such as me? You've been sitting here and haven't once even glanced at me," she whispered warily. "I know that I'm not much to look at. And it's reasonable that you would be reluctant to come near me. Consider this matter well, Olav. You would soon find it unbearable if you should have such a wretched woman at your side, both day and night, forever after."

Olav's expression grew even more stern. He shook his head.

"I noticed it the moment you came in," she whispered, her words nearly inaudible. "And you did not greet me with a kiss when you said hello."

Finally Olav turned his head to look at her. He smiled sadly.

"I kissed you last night—more than once—but you didn't notice."

He rubbed both hands over his face. Then he leaned forward, propped his elbows on his thighs, and rested his chin on his hands.

"I had a dream in the spring. It was the night of Good Friday, and I've thought a good deal about it ever since. I remembered the dream so clearly when I awoke, and I haven't been able to forget it. Let me tell you my dream.

"I dreamed that I was in the forest, standing on a hill where the trees had been cleared so there was no shade. The hillside was hot from the sun, and you lay in the middle of the blazing heat, in the heather. The ground was covered with heather and the tree stumps were surrounded by thick lingonberry bushes. You were lying very still. I'm not sure whether I thought you were asleep.

"It's strange, but in all the years I was traveling out in the world, I often wished you would appear to me in my dreams. There are measures that can be tried to enable a person to dream of his dearest friend. I tried them many times, even though you know I've never put much faith in such practices. Nevertheless, I tried them many times while I was in Denmark, and also later on. Yet I never saw you.

"But then I had this dream on the night of Good Friday, and I saw you as clearly as I see you sitting here. And you looked like you did as a child. It seemed to me that we were both children, the way we were growing up together at Frettastein. Your braids had come undone, and you were wearing your old red wadmal dress, but it had slid up so I could see your bare legs up to your knees. You were barefoot.

"Then a snake came slithering out of the heather."

Olav took a couple of deep breaths before going on.

"I was so frightened that I couldn't move. And I thought that was so strange, for I venture to say that when I can see the danger before my eyes, then I'm never frightened. Yet in my dream I felt such fear that it was unbearable. When I think of it now, it seems to me that I've never truly known what fear is, either before or afterward. The snake slid through the heather, and I saw that it was going to bite you.

"Yet it didn't move like a snake the whole time; sometimes it wriggled like a maggot, and sometimes it was a huge, furry grub. Then it turned into a snake again, wending its way through the grass. I seemed to be holding a knife in my hand. I thought I should hit the snake with a stick and chop its head off. That would be easy enough to do. But I didn't dare, for it had again turned into a grub. Do you remember how I was as a boy? It was an agony for me to see snakes and grubs and little worms. Those were the worst things for me. I did my best to hide how I felt, but I know you could see it."

Again he rubbed his face and took a deep breath.

"I stood there as if frozen. And then the snake twined around your foot. It was a snake now, and it wound around your calf, but you lay still, sleeping so soundly. Then the snake rose up and lifted its head, swinging it this way and that in the air, with its tongue flicking. I don't know how to explain this, but I felt both horror and a sense of delight—as if I were eagerly waiting for the snake to strike. I saw that now I could easily grab the snake by the neck, but I didn't dare. And . . . and . . . I saw that it was looking for that spot on your ankle where it could sink its teeth. But I felt . . . pleasure . . . at the sight. And then it struck."

He stopped abruptly, sitting with his eyes closed and biting his lip.

"Then I awoke." Olav struggled to speak calmly, but he sounded dazed. "And I lay in bed, angry with myself, the way a person often is after dreaming of behaving in a way he never would when awake. For you know full well that I would have killed that snake. And I wouldn't have calmly stood by, to watch even my worst enemy sleeping while a snake slid over him—nor would I have thought it pleasant to see the snake strike. There weren't many things I wouldn't have done for you, back when we were children.

"So I've thought and thought about that dream, and—"

Again Olav stopped abruptly. He leaped to his feet and staggered a few steps away from her. Then he turned toward the wall and threw himself forward with his arms stretched out along the timbers and his head bowed in between.

Ingunn stood up, looking as if she'd been struck by lightning. What she saw was something that she never dreamed would happen: Olav was weeping. She hadn't thought he was capable of such a thing.

Olav sobbed loudly—a strangely raw and rough sound issuing from his chest. With the utmost effort he pulled himself together and fell quiet, but his back still moved, his whole body shook. Then the sobs overtook him again: first as little, plaintive gasps, and then a storm of wailing. He stood there with one knee resting on the bench and his forehead pressed to the wall, and he wept as if he'd never be able to stop.

Beside herself with horror, Ingunn crept nearer to stand behind him. Finally she touched his shoulder. Then he turned toward her and threw his arms around her, pulling her close. They sank against each other, as if both were seeking support, and their lips, wrung open from weeping, met in a kiss.

Holy Days and Canonical Hours

Religious Holidays in Medieval Norway

Eighth Christmas Day.............................. January 3
Epiphany Eve...................................... January 5
Feast of the Annunciation......................... March 25
Saint Hallvard's Day .... May 15
Saint Jon's Day........................ June 23, Midsummer
Saint Sunniva's Feast Day ....July 8
Saint Olav's Day....................................July 29
Saint Bartholomew's Day .... August 24
Virgin Mary's birthday ....September 8
Saint Catherine's Day .... November 25

Canonical Hours Celebrated in the Catholic Church

Matins..2 a.m.
Lauds...5 a.m.
Prime...6 a.m.
Terce ....9 a.m.
Sext .... 12 noon
None ....3 p.m.
Vespers ....6 p.m.
Compline ....7 p.m.
Times are approximate.

Notes

1 Birch Legs: A political group formed in 1174 in southeastern Norway around a pretender to the Norwegian throne when the rightful successor was disputed. The name derived from their practice of tying birchbark to their feet because they were too poor to have shoes. They continued to use the name after they came to power in 1184.

2 Bjørgvin: The medieval name for Bergen. Located on the west coast of Norway, it was the largest and most important Norwegian town at the time, becoming an international commercial center in the thirteenth century.

3 Saint Jon's Day: The midsummer celebration, beginning at sundown on June 23, celebrating the birth of Saint John the Baptist.

4 enclosed bed: an elevated bed built against the wall and constructed of wood, usually with a door; also called a box bed or alcove bed.

5 Eidsiva ting: A law province (one of four) established during the eleventh century, known by its assembly (or ting) name and covering the inland area of eastern Norway. A ting was a meeting of freeborn, adult men that took place at regular intervals to discuss matters of concern to the community on the local or regional level. The regional ting also served as a court of law presided over by chieftains, who settled disputes and ruled on cases of manslaughter and other crimes. By 1276 the four law provinces had agreed on a secular law code for the entire country ("Landslog"), instigated and formulated by King Magnus, who was subsequently nicknamed Law-Mender.

6 Ring Abbey: A twelfth-century convent founded by Benedictine nuns in Skanderborg, Denmark. Education for girls was rare in the Middle Ages, but some daughters of nobility were sent to cloisters to receive instruction, both secular and religious.

7 Hovedø (Hovedøya): A small island off the coast of Oslo, in the Oslo Fjord. The Cistercian monastery, Hovedøya Abbey, was built on this island in 1147.

8 A daughter's inheritance (or søsterlut) was half of what a brother would inherit.

9   *courtyard*: A rural Norwegian farming estate consisted of multiple buildings, each intended for a specific purpose. These buildings were usually arranged around two courtyards: an "inner" courtyard enclosed by the living quarters, storehouses, and cookhouse; and the "outer" courtyard (or farmyard) enclosed by the stables, cowshed, barn, and other outbuildings. The buildings were generally one-story timbered structures, although some storehouses had lofts that often served as bedchambers for family and guests on the estate.

10   A horned axe (*snaghyrning*) or Dane axe was a battle axe with a long shaft and a wide, thin blade with pronounced "horns" or points at both the toe and heel of the bit.

11   *allodial estate*: Land that was originally defined as owned by a family from the times when there were burial mounds, meaning heathen times. According to Norwegian law, the family had to have possessed the land continuously for four or even six generations. The property right was passed to male kinsmen, but a woman could be the heir if there were no male offspring.

12   *stave church*: A uniquely designed type of wooden church built in Norway (and to some extent in Sweden), starting around 1150. The word *stave* (*stafr* in Old Norse) comes from the load-bearing posts in the post-and-lintel construction. Smaller churches had a separate chancel but no aisles; larger types had a raised central section surrounded by lower aisles on all four sides. Between 1150 and 1350 approximately one thousand stave churches may have been in use in Norway.

13   According to Snorre Sturlason's *Heimskingla*, Øystein Glumra (788–870) was a Norwegian king of Oppland County and Hedmark, and father of the first earl of the Orkney Islands.

14   *Ambrosian hymn*: translated from the Latin in 1852 by John Mason Neale.

To Thee before the close of day,
Creator of the world, we pray
That, with Thy wonted favour, Thou
Wouldst be our guard and keeper now.

From all ill dreams defend our sight,
From fears and terrors of the night;
Withhold from us our ghostly foe,
That spot of sin we may not know.

O Father, that we ask be done
Through Jesus Christ, Thine only Son,
Who, with the Holy Ghost and Thee,
Doth live and reign eternally.

Amen.

15   In 1280, at the age of twelve, Eirik II was crowned king of Norway after the death of his father, King Magnus Law-Mender. Until he came of age in 1282, the country was ruled by a council of barons, along with Magnus's widow, Queen Ingebjørg. Eirik's brother, Haakon, had earlier been named Duke of Norway, and as of 1280 he ruled a large area around Oslo and Stavanger, though he still had to answer to the king.

16   *high seat*: The place of honor reserved for the master and mistress of the estate. The seats were usually set on a raised dais against the wall, in the middle of the long table in the main hall of the property.

17   *gallery*: An external, covered balcony, often on the second floor of a building and reached by an outdoor staircase. Some loft rooms with galleries could be reached only by means of a ladder leading through a hatch opening inside the structure.

18   Men who were declared outlaws and sentenced to exile because of misdeeds such as manslaughter could petition the king for dispensation. This would allow the man to remain in (or return to) Norway without risk of reprisal— either to himself, his family, or his property. Any property that had been confiscated by the crown would also be returned.

19   The "Lay of Kraka" is a twelfth-century Old Norse poem probably composed in Iceland. Written in the form of a monologue delivered by the Viking king Ragnar Lodbrok at the end of his life, the poem touts the king's heroic battles and his welcome into the afterlife of Valhalla, along with the hope that his gruesome death will be violently avenged.

20   Lanterns were often made with thin, translucent membranes, usually from a cow or calf stomach, instead of glass.

21   *corrody*: It was common for wealthy individuals without family to ensure that they would have shelter and food in old age (as well as a proper burial) by donating all their possessions to a cloister or other religious institution, which then granted them a "corrody," a pension or allowance. Some of the corrodians lived at the cloister; some did not.

22   For accounting purposes, marks could be carved into a special wooden stick that was divided into two equal parts, one for credits and one for debits.

23   *spital*: A shelter for the poor and sick, often provided by a church or cloister in medieval Norwegian towns.

24   *Nidaros*: One of five episcopal seats in Norway during the Middle Ages; now the city of Trondheim.

25   *ørtug*: A Nordic medieval coin, equal to one-third of an øre (ten *penninger*).

26   *Mjøskastellet*: The Mjøsa citadel was built sometime before 1234, supposedly on orders from King Haakon Haakonssøn, who was waging a heated economic battle with the church. The location was presumably chosen because it provided an excellent way to control traffic in both directions along Lake Mjøsa. In the late Middle Ages, the fortress was used as a state prison.

27 *Saint Olav's Day*: Celebrated on July 29, in honor of Olav Haraldssøn (995–1030), a Norwegian king and martyr who was canonized one year after he fell at the Battle of Stiklestad and various miracles were reported relating to his resting place and body. He was buried in Saint Clement's Church in Nidaros and became known as "Norway's king of all eternity."

28 *Bagler*: Member of the group founded in 1196 by Bishop Nikolas Arnessøn that fought in the Norwegian civil war against King Sverre and the Birch Legs. *Ribbung*: Supporter of the rebel group organized in 1219 by the *Baglers* in the eastern part of Norway. The group was defeated by King Haakon Haakonssøn in 1227.

29 *son of a priest*: Celibacy was initially not common in Scandinavia for Catholic priests during the Middle Ages.

30 The *Saga of Án Bow-Bender* (*Áns saga Bogsveigis*), composed in the style of earlier Icelandic family sagas and set in Trøndelag, is the story of Án and his brother Thorir and their conflict with King Ingjald.

31 Women gave birth by kneeling on the floor, supported by women family members and skilled helpers summoned from the surrounding village.

32 The right ski was often shorter than the left to make it easier for the skier to climb a slope.

Sigrid Undset (1882–1949) was awarded the Nobel Prize in Literature in 1928, primarily for her epic novels set in Norway during the Middle Ages. The first of these classic works, the trilogy *Kristin Lavransdatter*, was published in Norway in 1920–22, and the tetralogy *Olav Audunssøn* followed in 1925–27. She was a prolific writer and published many novels, essays, newspaper articles, autobiographical works, and children's stories. During World War II she lived in Brooklyn, New York, and wrote passionately about Norway's plight and the grim situation in Europe. After the war she returned to her home, Bjerkebæk, in Lillehammer, Norway. In 1947 she received Norway's highest honor, the Grand Cross of the Order of Saint Olav, for her "distinguished literary work and for her service to her country." Her first novel, *Marta Oulie*, and *Inside the Gate: Sigrid Undset's Life at Bjerkebæk*, by Nan Bentzen Skille, are also published by the University of Minnesota Press.

Tiina Nunnally has translated many works of Scandinavian literature, including Sigrid Undset's *Kristin Lavransdatter*, which was awarded the PEN/Book-of-the-Month Club translation prize. Among her other works are translations of fairy tales by Hans Christian Andersen and *The Complete and Original Norwegian Folktales of Asbjørnsen and Moe* (Minnesota, 2019). She was appointed Knight of the Royal Norwegian Order of Merit in 2013 for her efforts on behalf of Norwegian literature abroad.